A *New York Times* bestseller many times over, **Eloisa James** lives in New York City, where she is a Shakespeare professor (with an M.Phil. from Oxford). She is also the mother of two children and, in a particularly delicious irony for a romance writer, is married to a genuine Italian knight.

Visit Eloisa James online:
www.eloisajames.com
www.facebook.com/EloisaJamesFans
www.twitter.com/EloisaJames

Praise for Eloisa James:
'Sexual tension, upper-class etiquette and a dollop of wit make this another hit from *New York Times* bestseller Eloisa James'
Image Magazine Ireland

'Romance writing does not get better than this'
People Magazine

'[This] delightful tale is as smart, sassy and sexy as any of her other novels, but here James displays her deliciously wicked sense of humour'
Romantic Times BookClub

'An enchanting fairy-tale plot provides the perfect setting for James' latest elegantly written romance, and readers will quickly find themselves falling under the spell of the book's deliciously original characters and delectably witty writing'
Chicago Tribune

Eloisa James

Enchanting
PLEASURES

piatkus

PIATKUS

First published in the US in 2001 by Dell Publishing
a division of Random House, Inc.
New York, New York
First published in Great Britain in 2014 by Piatkus

A CIP catalogue record for this book
is available from the British Library.

ISBN 978-0-349-40442-4

Printed and bound in Great Britain by Clays Ltd, St Ives plc

Papers used by Piatkus are from well-managed forests
and other responsible sources.

MIX
Paper from
responsible sources
FSC® C104740

Piatkus
An imprint of
Little, Brown Book Group
100 Victoria Embankment
London EC4Y 0DY

An Hachette UK Company
www.hachette.co.uk

www.piatkus.co.uk

Enchanting
PLEASURES

Chapter 1

St. James's Square, London
1806

FATE HAD JUST DEALT Viscount Dewland a blow that would have felled a weaker—or more sympathetic—man. He gaped silently at his eldest son for a moment, ignoring his wife's twittering commentary. But a happy thought revived him. That same wife had, after all, provided him with *two* male offspring.

Without further ado he spun on his heel and barked at his younger son, "If your brother can't do his duty in bed, then you'll do it. You can act like a man for once in your life."

Peter Dewland was caught unawares by his father's sudden attack. He had risen to adjust his neckcloth in the drawing-room mirror, thereby avoiding his brother's eyes. Really, what does a man say to that sort of confession? But like his father, Peter recovered quickly from unpredictable assaults.

He walked around the end of the divan and sat down. "I gather you are suggesting that I marry Jerningham's daughter?"

"Of course I am!" the viscount snapped. "Someone has

to marry her, and your brother has just declared himself ineligible."

"I beg to differ," Peter remarked with a look of cool distaste. "I have no plans to marry at your whim."

"What in the bloody hell do you mean? Of course you'll marry the girl if I instruct you to do so!"

"I do not plan to marry, Father. Not at your instigation nor at anyone else's."

"Rubbish! Every man marries."

Peter sighed. "Not true."

"You've squired about every beautiful gal that came on the market in the last six years. If you had formed a true attachment, I would not stand in your way. But since you haven't made a move to attach yourself, you *will* marry Jerningham's girl."

"You shall do as I say, boy," the viscount bellowed. "Your brother can't take on the job, and so you have to do it. I've been lenient with you. You might be in the Seventh Foot at this very moment. Have you thought of that?"

"I'd rather take a pair of colors than a wife," Peter retorted.

"Absolutely not," his father said, reversing himself. "Your brother's been at the point of death for years."

Inside the drawing room, the silence swelled ominously. Peter grimaced at his elder brother, whose muscled body proclaimed his general fitness to the world at large.

Erskine Dewland, who had been staring meditatively at the polished surface of his Hessians, raised his heavy-lidded eyes from his boots to his father's face. "If Peter is determined not to marry, I could take her on." His deep voice fell into the silent room.

"And what's the point of that? You can't do the job properly, and I'm not wedding Jerningham's daughter to . . .

to . . . in that case. I've got principles. The girl's got a right to expect a sound husband, for God's sake."

Quill, as Erskine was known to his intimates, opened his mouth again. And then thought better of it. He could certainly consummate the marriage, but it wouldn't be a very pleasant experience. Any woman deserved more from marriage than he could offer. While he had come to terms with his injuries, especially now that they had ceased to bother his movement, the three-day migraines that followed repetitive motion made his likelihood for marital bliss very slight.

"Can't argue with that, can you?" The viscount looked triumphantly at his eldest son. "I'm not some sort of a caper merchant, passing you off as whole goods when you're not. Mind you, we could. The girl wouldn't know a thing, of course, until it was too late. And her father's turned into such a loose screw that he's not even accompanying her out here.

"Point is," Dewland went on, turning back to his youngest son, "the girl's expecting to marry someone. And if it can't be Quill, it's got to be you. I'll send your picture over on the next boat."

Peter replied through his teeth, each word spaced. "I do not wish to marry, Father."

The viscount's cheeks reddened again. "It's time you stopped gadding about. By God, you will do as I say!"

Peter avoided his father's gaze, seemingly absorbed in flicking the smallest piece of lint from the black velvet collar of his morning coat. Satisfied, he returned to the subject at hand. "You seem to have misunderstood me. I *refuse* to marry Jerningham's daughter." Only the smallest tremor in his voice betrayed his agitation.

The viscountess broke in before her husband could bellow

whatever response he had in mind. "Thurlow, I don't like your color. Perhaps we might continue this conversation at a later time? You know what the doctor said about getting overtaxed!"

"Balderdash!" the viscount protested, although he allowed his wife to pull him back onto a couch. "By George, you had better obey me, Mister Peter Dewland, or you will find yourself out the door." The veins of his forehead were alarmingly swollen.

His wife sent a beseeching glance to her youngest son. His jaw was set in a manner that his father would have recognized, had there been a mirror in the near vicinity.

But before Peter could say a word, his father erupted out of his seat once again. "And just what am I supposed to say to this young girl who's coming all the way over from India? Tell her that you 'prefer not to marry her'? You planning on telling my old friend Jerningham that you decline to marry his gal?"

"That is precisely what I suggest," Peter replied.

"And what about the money Jerningham's lent me over the years, eh? Given it to me without a word of advice— just sent me over the blunt to do with as I like! If your brother Quill hadn't pulled down a fortune speculating on the East India Company, Jerningham might still be lending me money. As it is, we agreed to consider it a dowry. You *will* marry the gal, or I'll . . . I'll . . . ."

The viscount's face was purple all over now, and he was unconsciously rubbing his chest.

"Quill could pay back the money," Peter suggested.

"Bloody hell! I've already allowed your brother to turn himself into a merchant, playing around on the Exchange— I'll be damned if I'll allow him to pay off my debts!"

"I don't see why not," Peter retorted. "He's paid for everything else."

"That's enough! The only reason your brother—the only reason I allowed Erskine to take on the smell of the market was because—well, because he's a cripple. But at least he acts his age. You're naught but a fribble, a sprig of fashion!"

As the viscount drew a breath, Quill raised his head and met his younger brother's eyes. In the depths of Quill's silent apology, Peter saw the manacles of marriage looming.

His father was glaring at him with all the frustration of a ruddy, boisterous Englishman whose younger son has proved to be nothing like himself. Peter cast a desperate look at his mother, but there was no help to be found.

He quailed. His stomach churned. He opened his mouth to protest, but could think of nothing to say. And finally, the habits of a lifetime's submission took hold.

"Very well." His voice was hollow.

Kitty Dewland rose and came to give him a grateful kiss on the cheek. "Dear Peter," she said. "You were always my comforting one, my good child. And in truth, darling, you have escorted so many women without making an offer. I'm certain that Jerningham's daughter will be a perfect match for you. His wife was French, you know."

In her son's eyes there was a bleak desolation that Kitty hated to see. "Is there someone else? Is there a woman whom you were hoping to marry, darling?"

Peter shook his head.

"Well, then," Kitty said gaily. "We will be right and tight when this girl—what's her name, Thurlow? Thurlow!"

When Kitty turned around she found her husband leaning back and looking rather white. "M'chest doesn't feel so good, Kitty," he mumbled.

And when Kitty flew out of the drawing room, she was far too discomposed to note how odd it was that her beloved butler, Codswallop, was hovering just on the other side of the door.

"Send for Doctor Priscian," she shrieked, and trotted back into the room.

The plump and precise Codswallop couldn't resist taking a curious look at the elder Dewland son before he rang for a footman. It was that hard to believe. Erskine had a physique Codswallop had secretly admired: a body remarkably suited to tight pantaloons and fitted coats, the kind of body housemaids giggled about behind stairs. Must be some sort of injury to his private parts. Codswallop shuddered sympathetically.

Just then Quill turned about and looked Codswallop in the face. Quill's eyes were a curious green-gray, set in a face stamped with lines of pain and deeply tanned. Without moving a muscle, he cast Codswallop a look that scathed him to his bones.

Codswallop scuttled back into the hall and rang for a footman. The viscount was supported off to his bedchamber, followed by his clucking wife. Young Peter bounded out the door looking like murder, followed rather more slowly by Quill, and Codswallop pulled the drawing-room doors closed with a snap.

SOME THREE MONTHS LATER, the whole affair was tied up. Miss Jerningham was due to arrive on the *Plassey,* a frigate sailing from Calcutta, within the week. There was one last explosion of rage on the part of the viscount when Peter announced, on the day before Miss Jerningham was due to arrive, that he was taking a long sojourn in the country. But by supper on the fifth of September, the sullen bridegroom had taken himself off to his club rather than to Herefordshire, and Viscount Dewland repeated over stewed pigeon that the marriage would be an excellent solution to all their problems. There was an unspoken acknowledgment between Thurlow and his wife that Peter, if left to his own devices, might indeed never marry.

"He'll settle down once the girl arrives," Thurlow declared.

"They will have beautiful children," added Kitty.

Only Quill seemed to have a growing sense of unease about the forthcoming marriage. After his parents left the salon, he walked restlessly to the windows overlooking the gardens. He leaned forward, resting his forehead against the hard curve of his forearm, shifting his weight slightly from his protesting right leg. He was accustomed to the blustery explosion of his father's rage. He had tolerated it for years by listening in silence and then following his own inclination. Peter had ever bent with the wind, and so it was no surprise that ultimately he gave in to the viscount's plans. Surely Peter could not have really thought to escape marriage, once it became clear that he or his son would inherit the title someday.

But an uneasy chill sat on Quill's heart. He remembered the girl's name, even if no one else did: Gabrielle Jerningham. And what would Gabrielle's life be like with Peter as her husband? It would be an urbane life, a sophisticated life. Likely the young couple would share the kind of marriage Quill saw frequently in the *ton*: cool and friendly.

He straightened, moving into a great arching stretch. His body was outlined by light thrown against the dark glass, every muscle caressed by his clothing. It was a body honed by denial, exercise, and pain: a body whose master knew its every strength and its every weakness. It was not the body of an average gentleman of the London *ton* in 1806.

Quill shrugged back his hair. Damned if it wasn't getting unfashionably long again. For a moment he froze, struck by a memory of the wind screaming past his face, wrenching his hair back from his scalp as he rode a galloping stallion.

But horses, like sex, had become a delight whose payment was greater than the offered pleasure. The rhythmic motion of horseback riding invariably instigated three days of agony in a darkened room, his body covered in sweat and gripped by nausea, his head clenched in a steel band of pain. And the only advice doctors had offered was that his head injury of six years ago had led to an inability to endure rhythm. Any kind of rhythm.

Quill's jaw hardened and he mentally shrugged off the image of a galloping horse. To his mind there was nothing worse than lamenting what could not be. Women and horses were simply part of his past, and no part of his future.

Then he grinned. The very sports he was mourning—a hard riding session and a woman's nightly companionship—were delights that held absolutely no interest for Peter. Lord, but he and his brother were as alike as chalk and cheese.

At any rate, he was probably worrying about Gabrielle and Peter for naught. Peter might not like the idea of marriage, but he did love female companionship. A decorous French miss, with whom Peter could gossip, discuss fashion, and attend balls, might well become his closest friend. And Gabrielle was an elegant name, one that brought to mind a woman versed in the ways of the world. Peter had a great admiration—nay, a passion—for beauty. Surely an exquisite young Frenchwoman would be able to coax him into compliance with an unwanted marriage.

UNFORTUNATELY, QUILL WOULD HAVE ABANDONED that hope could he have seen the aforementioned exquisite Frenchwoman.

Peter's fiancée was kneeling on the floor of her cabin,

looking into the eager face of a young girl who sat before her on a small tuffet. Gabrielle's hair was tumbling about her ears, and her old-fashioned dress was crumpled. The last thing she resembled was a sophisticated French miss from *La Belle Assemblée*.

"The tiger crept through the tangled jungle." Gabby's voice was a thrilling whisper. "He put one paw softly before the next, barely disturbing the song of the magpies far above. His long tongue licked his chops at the thought of the delicious meal that trotted before him."

Phoebe Pensington, a five-year-old orphan being sent to live with English relatives, shivered as Gabby, whose soft brown eyes had taken on a tigerish glare, continued.

"But when the tiger reached the edge of the forest, he stopped short. The goat was walking along the shore, his white hooves prancing at the very edge of the tumbling azure waves of the Indian Ocean. And the tiger was afraid of water. His stomach urged him to follow, but his heart pounded with fear. He stopped in the speckled shade of a bongo-bongo tree—"

"But, Miss Gabby," Phoebe broke in anxiously, "what did the tiger have for supper that night if he didn't eat the goat? Wouldn't he be hungry?"

Gabby's brown eyes lit with amusement. "Perhaps the tiger was so mortified by his own lack of courage that he went to a far-off mountaintop and lived on nothing but fruits and vegetables."

"I don't think so." Phoebe was a very practical little girl. "I think it's more likely that the tiger would have gone after that goat and eaten him up."

"The tiger had a cat's natural abhorrence for water," Gabby said. "He didn't see the beauty of the waves as they danced into shore. To him the curling waves looked like the claws of tiny crabs, reaching out to nibble his bones!"

Phoebe gave a thrilled little shriek just as the door to the cabin swung open, breaking the spell of Gabby's voice.

The black-gowned figure of Eudora Sibbald stared at the scene before her. Miss Gabrielle Jerningham was unaccountably positioned on the floor. As always, her hair was tumbling out of its knot and her dress was rumpled. It wasn't for Mrs. Sibbald to recognize the beauty of Gabby's shining golden-brown hair as it worked loose from pins and combs and assumed its normal position: halfway up and halfway down. No—what Phoebe's governess saw was a proper hoyden, a young lady whose hair echoed her general demeanor.

"Phoebe." Her voice rasped like a rusty gate.

Phoebe scrambled to her feet and bobbed a curtsy.

"Miss Jerningham," Mrs. Sibbald continued, rather as if she were addressing a recalcitrant scullery maid.

Gabby was already on her feet and greeting Mrs. Sibbald with a charming smile. "Do forgive us—" she began.

But Mrs. Sibbald interrupted. "Miss Jerningham, I might have misunderstood you." Her bearing indicated that she never misunderstood anything. "I trust that I did not hear you mention *nibbled bones?*"

Really, Gabby thought to herself, Sibbald couldn't have entered at a worse moment.

"Oh, no," Gabby said, her voice soothing. "I was merely telling Phoebe an improving tale from the Bible."

Mrs. Sibbald's jaw lengthened. She'd heard what she'd heard, and it didn't sound like any Bible tale to her.

"The story of Jonah and the whale," Gabby added hastily. "You know, Mrs. Sibbald, since my father is a missionary, I find it quite natural to relate stories from the Bible wherever I go."

Mrs. Sibbald's mouth relaxed slightly. "Well, in that case, Miss Jerningham," she allowed. "However, I must beg you not to overexcite the child. Excitement is injurious to the digestion. And where is Master Kasi Rao Holkar?"

"I believe Kasi is taking a nap at the present, Mrs. Sibbald. He mentioned a wish to retire."

"If you'll forgive me for saying so, Miss Jerningham, you coddle that boy. Prince or not, a deserving tale from the Bible would do him some good. After all, he's a native. Lord only knows what sort of influences he had as a child."

"Kasi grew up in my house," Gabby said. "I assure you that he is as Christian as little Phoebe."

"An unfeasible comparison," Mrs. Sibbald announced. "No Indian could be as Christian as an English child.

"It is teatime," she announced. "Miss Jerningham, your hair has fallen again. I advise that your coiffure receive immediate attention." And on that lowering note, Mrs. Sibbald left the cabin.

Gabby sighed and sank into a chair, realizing that there did seem to be a large number of wispy curls hanging about her face. Then she felt a tug on her gown.

"Miss Gabby, she forgot me. Do you think I ought to remind her?" Round blue eyes stared worshipfully at Gabby.

Gabby pulled Phoebe's leggy little body up onto her lap. "I swear you have grown half a head on this trip," she said.

"I know," Phoebe replied, looking with disapproval at the hem of her gown. She stuck out a booted leg. "My dress has become so short that my pantaloons are beginning to show!" Her eyes were round with horror at that idea.

"When you reach England, I'm sure that you will have a new dress."

"Do you think she'll like me?" Phoebe whispered into Gabby's shoulder.

"Will who like you?"

"My new mother."

"How could she not like you? You are the sweetest five-year-old girl aboard this whole ship," Gabby said, rubbing her cheek against Phoebe's soft hair. "In fact, you may well be the sweetest five-year-old who ever sailed from India."

Phoebe pressed closer. "Because when I had to say good-bye to my ayah"—a farewell that seemed to have traumatized her far more than the untimely deaths of two parents she scarcely recognized—"my ayah said that I must be very, very good or my new mama will not like me, since I don't have any money to bring her."

Gabby silently cursed Phoebe's ayah—and not for the first time. "Phoebe," she said as firmly as she could, "money has nothing to do with whether a mother loves her babies or not. Your new mother would love you even if you arrived in your nightdress!"

And she devoutly hoped it was true. From what the captain had told her, there had been no answer to the letter sent to Phoebe's only living relative, her maternal aunt.

"Miss Gabby," Phoebe said, her tone hesitant. "Why did you tell Mrs. Sibbald that your story was of Jonah and the whale? My ayah told me never to tell an untruth—and especially never to a hired person. And Mrs. Sibbald is a hired person, isn't she? She was hired to accompany me to England."

Gabby gave Phoebe another little hug. "Your ayah was right in the main. But sometimes a fib is permissible if you can make someone feel happy. Mrs. Sibbald would very much like to think that you are learning stories from the Bible. And when I told her you were, she felt happy."

"I don't think Mrs. Sibbald ever feels happy," Phoebe observed, after thinking about it for a time.

"You could be right," Gabby replied. "But in that case, Phoebe, it is even more important not to overset her."

"Do you think that if I told my new mama that I had some money it would make her happy? Would it make her like me?"

Gabby swallowed. "Oh, sweet pea, I am only talking about little fibs. You couldn't say such a thing to your new mother! That's a *big* untruth, as opposed to a small one. And it is very important not to tell even small untruths to important people like your new mother."

There was an unconvinced silence.

Gabby thought desperately. Really, for all her eagerness to have children, she was beginning to see that it was far more difficult than she had imagined.

"Are you bringing any money to your new husband?" Phoebe's voice was muffled because she had her face pressed to Gabby's shoulder.

"Yes," Gabby said reluctantly. "But that money will not make Peter love me."

Phoebe's face popped up like an inquisitive robin from its nest. "Why not?"

"Peter will love me for myself," Gabby said with quiet conviction. "Just as your mother will love you for yourself."

The little girl hopped onto her feet. "Well, then, why did you tell Mrs. Sibbald that Kasi was in his chamber having a nap? That wasn't true, and it didn't make her happy."

"A different kind of rule," Gabby explained. "My sweet Kasi is frightened to death of Mrs. Sibbald."

"What kind of rule?" Phoebe inquired.

"You have to protect the weak from the strong," Gabby said, and then amended herself. "That's not exactly right, Phoebe. You know what Kasi is like. Handing him to Mrs. Sibbald would be like feeding the goat to the tiger."

There was a slight noise behind the screen protecting the tub from plain sight. The little girl peered around the screen. "Kasi Rao, it's time to get out of there." She put her small hands on her hips. "What would Mrs. Sibbald say if she could see you in the tub with all your clothes on?"

"Let him stay there if he prefers," Gabby called across the room.

But Phoebe shook her head firmly and stated, with a force that Mrs. Sibbald would have admired, "It is time to have tea, Kasi. You needn't worry. I won't let Gabby talk about the tiger again."

A very slender boy with innocent eyes that took up half his face peeked around the corner of the screen and then checked, unwilling to emerge from the safety of the corner.

Phoebe took his hand and tugged. "There is no one here but us, Kasi."

Soft brown eyes darted back and forth between Gabby's smiling face and the hand she held out to him. Kasi wanted to come out, obviously, but it was so far across the room, and the room was so very open.

Phoebe pulled at him impatiently. "Mrs. Sibbald thinks you're napping, so you're quite safe."

"We'll have tea together," Gabby said reassuringly, as Kasi gathered his courage and hurtled himself to her chair, sheltering under her arm like a chick that had strayed from its nest. "Are you hungry, little brother?"

"Kasi isn't your little brother," Phoebe said. "He's a prince!"

"Well, that's true. But his mother was related to my father's first wife. And he grew up with me, so I feel as if he is my brother." Kasi had stopped trembling and was playing with the locket Gabby wore around her neck, humming a tuneless, happy song as he tried to open the catch.

Phoebe came around to the other side of the chair and leaned against Gabby's leg. "May I see the picture of your husband again?"

"Of course you may." Just before they set sail for

England, a miniature of her future bridegroom had arrived. Gabby gently took the locket from Kasi's fumbling hands and opened it.

"Is he waiting for you in London, Miss Gabby?"

"Yes," Gabby said firmly. "We shall all be met at the dock, Phoebe love. Your new mother will meet you, and Mrs. Malabright will meet Kasi, won't she, sweetheart?" She looked down into Kasi's pointed little face.

To her satisfaction, he nodded. She had been reminding Kasi every day that Mrs. Malabright was coming to see him when the vessel landed.

"And then what will happen, Kasi?" she prompted.

"Live with Mrs. Malabright," he replied with approval. "I *like* Mrs. Malabright." A shadow crossed his eyes and he added, "I don't like Mrs. Sibbald."

"Mrs. Malabright will take you to her house, and you needn't ever see Mrs. Sibbald again," Phoebe said, rather bossily. "I will come visit you though. I will visit you secretly, and I won't tell anyone where you are."

"Yes," Kasi said with a contented lilt in his voice. And he returned to playing with Gabby's locket.

"Do you like your new husband, Miss Gabby?" Phoebe asked.

Even looking at the miniature portrait of Peter, of his soft brown eyes and wavy hair, made Gabby's heart beat faster.

"Yes, I do," she said softly.

Phoebe, who was a true romantic, even at age five, sighed. "I'm sure he already loves you, Miss Gabby. Did you send him a picture of yourself?"

"There wasn't time," Gabby replied. And if there had been, she would not have sent one. The only portrait her father had ever commissioned made her look horribly round in the face.

She tucked the locket away again.

But even as she, Phoebe, and Kasi munched on dry toast, which was the only treat offered now that they had been at sea for weeks and weeks, Gabby couldn't help daydreaming about her betrothed and his gentle eyes. Somehow, by the grace of God, she had been given a fiancé who was everything she had dreamed of: a man who looked perfectly capable of carrying on a quiet conversation. He seemed as unlike her cold, ranting father as possible.

Gabby's heart glowed. Peter would obviously be a devoted and loving father. Already she could picture four or five small babes, all with her husband's eyes.

Every day the ship drew farther and farther from India and thus farther and farther from her father's frenzied reproaches: *Gabrielle, why can't you put a bridle on your tongue! Once again, Gabrielle, you have embarrassed me with your graceless behavior!* And the worst of all: *Oh, God above, why have you cursed me with this disgraceful chit, this prattling excuse for a daughter!*

Her happiness grew with each ocean league that passed.

Her sense of confidence grew as well. Peter would love *her*, as her father never did. She felt as if Peter's sweet eyes were already looking into her soul and seeing the Gabby inside: the Gabby who was worth loving, the Gabby who was not merely impetuous and clumsy. The real Gabby.

YES, A GLIMPSE OF Gabrielle Jerningham, along with insight into her dreams, would have shaken Quill to the backbone.

But since Quill was not overly given to the imagination, nor had he ever demonstrated the gift of precognition, he convinced himself that Miss Gabrielle Jerningham would make his younger brother a very good wife indeed. And when he encountered Peter at his club later that evening, he told him so.

Peter was in a tetchy mood, and well on the way to being drunk as a lord. "I don't follow your reasoning."

"Money," his brother replied shortly.

"Money? What money?"

"Her money." Quill had a flash of guilt, talking about Gabrielle as if she were a commodity, although in a sense she was. "With Jerningham's money, you can afford those clothes you love so much."

"I wear the very best clothes now," Peter said loftily, with the smug understanding that he stood at the very pinnacle of London fashion.

"You wear clothes that I pay for," Quill replied.

Peter chewed on his lip. It went against the grain—and against his fundamentally kindly nature—to point out that his elder brother's money would all be his someday, unless a miracle cured Quill's migraines.

Yet it would be pleasant to have his own money, no doubt about that.

Quill saw the telltale interest in Peter's eyes and laughed, his heart lighter. He slapped his brother on the back and left the club.

Chapter 2

VISCOUNT DEWLAND, not unversed in the vagaries of seabound vessels and their schedules, had sent young George, an undergroomsman, to the East India docks on the morning the *Plassey* was due. But after two weeks of sending George to the docks, the master and mistress left for Bath in the hopes that a course of waters would aid the viscount's health. Kitty left anxious instructions with Codswallop that they should be summoned the very moment there was news of the *Plassey*. And every evening for another three weeks, young George returned to the house somewhat the worse for wear, having spent his day in the pubs that lined the dock.

It wasn't until the second of November that the *Plassey* finally glided into her berth and the coxswain dropped anchor with a ceremonious splash. Young George headed back to St. James's Square on the spot.

But he entered a quiet house. The future bridegroom, Peter, was rarely seen these days. His valet said he was sulking, a source of great amusement downstairs. Sulking because he didn't want to marry an heiress!

In fact, the only family member in residence was Quill, who was seated in the back garden, reading through reports compiled by his secretary. Since his accident some six years before, Quill had been denied the normal pursuits of an English gentleman. So he had turned his considerable intelligence to investment. Not one of his teachers at Eton—where he was widely considered the most brilliant lad to pass through the school in years—would have been surprised to learn that those investments had paid off in spades. Although he had made his first fortune by speculating on the East India Company, Quill now owned a wool factory in Yorkshire and a buttery in Lancashire.

But he preferred speculation to ownership. He employed some fifteen men who scurried hither and yon all over the British Isles, investigating copper mines and coal companies. He had recently begun to send out his investigators secretly, given that a rumor of Erskine Dewland's interest in a certain firm was sure to drive up its value on the London Exchange.

At any rate, Quill's mind was wandering from the assessment of Maugnall and Bulton, dimity manufacturers, that he held in his hands. The garden path was drifted with fallen leaves. During the first year of Quill's convalescence, he had spent hours planning the gardens visible from his bedroom. Now the young plum trees had gamely put forth fruit, and late apples occasionally fell with a gentle plop at his feet.

But for some reason, in the last weeks he was restless even here. He failed to concentrate on the many reports that awaited his opinion. He walked up and down the paths, but could think of no significant improvement to the garden. The delights of the last five years seemed stifling, the garden a walled prison, his study a dusty cage.

Young George stood politely until Quill raised his eyes.

He didn't wait for a question; the young master never spoke unless he had to. "The *Plassey* has docked, sir, and Mr. Codswallop does not know Mr. Peter Dewland's where-abouts—"

Quill stood up. "Inform Codswallop that I shall fetch Miss Jerningham myself."

That was just what he needed: a trip down to the bustling docks. Even if it was to fetch his brother's bride.

Thirty minutes later, his elegantly hung cabriolet rounded Commercial Road. He threw the reins to his tiger and strode down the dock road himself rather than trying to weave the carriage down the crowded street.

Suddenly a voice bellowed, "Hi! Dewland! Hello, sir! Are you here to see a shipment come in?" Mr. Timothy Waddell couldn't suppress his curiosity. Everyone knew that whatever Dewland touched turned to gold. He would love to know the man's opinion of the Domiago cotton he'd just bought on speculation.

"Not today," Quill responded.

He turned away, his face so unwelcoming of further communication that Waddell quailed and didn't ask for an opinion of the cotton.

"Damned cold bastard," he muttered, watching Quill disappear into the crowd.

Quill didn't notice the man's affront. It hadn't occurred to him that Waddell expected more than a simple answer.

When he reached number fourteen, Quill's eyes fell on a woman, obviously a passenger recently disembarked from the *Plassey*. As he approached, Quill realized that she was holding a child by the hand. In all likelihood, Peter's bride, being a delicate Frenchwoman, had waited for an escort be-fore she left the vessel.

He strode to the end of the dock, unerringly picking out the *Plassey*'s purser. "Where shall I find Miss Jerningham?"

The purser smirked. "Right behind ye, int she?"

Slowly Quill turned around. The woman was looking at him inquiringly. *Damn!* Quill thought. And *damn, damn, damn!* Miss Jerningham was beautiful. No doubt about that. She had the most luscious, ripe mouth he'd ever seen, and her eyes . . . her eyes were brandy-colored, a warm, sweet hue. But it was her hair that caught Quill's attention. It was golden-brown, the color of burnished brass—and it was falling, loops and curls of it, falling into rumpled curls that made Gabrielle Jerningham look as if she had just risen from bed. A happy bed. In fact, she was quite the opposite of a poised, elegant Frenchwoman. *Damn.*

Then he realized that he was standing stock-still, staring at the woman without even introducing himself.

"I beg your pardon," he said, walking over and sweeping a deep bow. "I am Erskine Dewland, and I shall soon have the pleasure of becoming your brother-in-law."

"Oh," Gabby said faintly. There had been an awful moment when she thought that he was Peter, her future bridegroom. Now she realized that although Erskine had a faint resemblance to his brother, he was nothing like the Peter of her picture. No, Erskine was rather terrifyingly masculine. Too large, for one thing. And his eyes were so . . . so commanding.

She dropped a curtsy. But before she could speak, there was a tug on her cloak.

"Miss Gabby, is that your husband?" Phoebe's eyes were shining with deep excitement.

Gabby blushed slightly as she met Erskine's eyes. "May I introduce Miss Phoebe Pensington? Phoebe and I spent a good deal of time together on the voyage," she explained. "Phoebe, this is Mr. Erskine Dewland, Peter's brother."

Mr. Dewland looked at her so measuringly that Gabby felt short of breath. He seemed to be an exceedingly formal man. Perhaps he disliked her referring to his brother by his first name.

But then, rather surprisingly, he turned and made Phoebe an elegant bow. "Miss Phoebe."

When he smiled, Gabby realized, his whole face warmed. Perhaps he wasn't so terrifying—and at any rate, he would now be part of her family, so she had to like him.

"Do you know where my new mama is?" Phoebe asked.

Mr. Dewland shook his head, seemingly taking this question in stride. "I am afraid that I do not." He looked inquiringly at Gabby.

"I thought it would be raining," Phoebe said chattily. "My ayah told me that English skies are always as black as the devil's soup pot! Why isn't it raining? Do you think it will rain later in the afternoon?"

He met Gabby's eyes over her head and repeated, "New mama?"

"Phoebe is referring to a Mrs. Emily Ewing," Gabby explained. "Mrs. Ewing is the sister of Phoebe's late mother. You see, Phoebe's parents were killed in a most unfortunate accident in Madras, and Phoebe had to be sent to England. But the captain told me that the letter informing Mrs. Ewing of Phoebe's situation may have gone astray. There was no acknowledgment from Mrs. Ewing before the *Plassey* set sail."

"Why the devil did they put her on board?"

Gabby was very aware of Phoebe listening alertly to their conversation. "I am sure that Mrs. Ewing's letter crossed our path," she said cheerfully.

"Not likely, given her absence today," Mr. Dewland remarked.

Gabby gave him a quelling look. "It is also quite possible that she is not aware that we have arrived, Mr. Dewland.

Unfortunately, the *Plassey* was blown off course a month ago. We were around the Canaries, and we had tempestuous weather through the Bay of Biscay, with a prodigious sea."

"Has Miss Phoebe no governess?"

"Not at the moment. The local governor hired a woman called Mrs. Sibbald to look after Phoebe during the voyage," Gabby continued. "But Mrs. Sibbald felt that her obligation was over once we docked. She consigned Phoebe to the care of the purser and departed."

"Where is the captain? Miss Phoebe is his responsibility. We shall hand the child over to him and then I will escort you to Dewland House, Miss Jerningham."

"I don't like Captain Rumbold," came a small voice. "I don't wish to be handed over to him. I do not wish to ever see him again."

"I'm afraid that is not possible," Gabby said. "You see, Captain Rumbold is really quite happy to have reached the shore—I do believe he thought to lose the ship at one point in our voyage. And he has speculated on a number of hats that he had made up in India. They are preposterously ugly. He calls them *Chapeau Nivernois*, and he is going to try to pass them off as French——"

Gabby caught sight of Erskine Dewland's tightening mouth and hurried to a conclusion. "At any rate, Captain Rumbold has already taken his leave of us and gone to supervise the unloading of his hats.

"And he doesn't like children," she added.

Quill took a deep breath. He prided himself on his absolute calm. In the face of extreme pain, he remained collected. But this woman was likely to drive him around the bend in a way that a concussion and injured limbs had not. He stared down at Peter's future wife in silence. She was looking up at him with a sweet, earnest expression, but he hadn't even marked her words. For some reason, Quill's only coherent thought was to kiss her into silence. Miss Jerningham had the deepest cherry-red lips he'd seen in his life. She had asked him a question, he realized, belatedly.

"Forgive me," Quill said. "I am afraid that I didn't understand your request."

"I asked you to call me Gabby," she faltered in reply. Mr. Dewland's face had grown so forbidding that she knew he had to be thinking she was a rattle-pate. She must remember to hold her tongue when she was around her brother-in-law. Thank goodness she was marrying Peter rather than his brother! The very thought cheered her up.

"Gabby," Quill said meditatively. "That suits you." He gave a sudden, unexpected grin.

Gabby shyly smiled back. "I try not to be too much of a chatterbox."

"I like the way Miss Gabby talks," Phoebe said.

Both adults looked down, startled.

My goodness, Gabby thought, I clean forgot about the child. She looked back at her future brother-in-law. "May I bring Phoebe home with me? We could leave a message for Mrs. Ewing with the purser."

Quill looked about the wharf. "We don't seem to have a choice, do we?"

Try as she might, Gabby couldn't read his face. In fact, Erskine Dewland had the most unexpressive face she'd ever seen in her life. It was only when he smiled that his eyes came alive. Green eyes. A dark, green-gray that reminded her of the ocean when it was smooth as glass.

Without another word, Mr. Dewland walked over to the purser and began to query him about Miss Jerningham's and Phoebe's luggage.

Gabby crouched down next to the child. "Will you come with me to Peter's home, Phoebe? I'm afraid your new mother didn't get the message that our ship has docked. But I would very much like you to accompany me."

The little girl nodded. Gabby could see that Phoebe was close to tears, and so she gave her a warm hug. "You will stay with me until we find your mama, sugarplum. I won't leave you alone."

Buttercup-yellow ringlets rubbed against Gabby's shoulder. Then Phoebe straightened up. "My ayah said that English gentlewomen never show emotion," she said, gulping.

"I don't know about that," Gabby said. "I'm a bit afraid to meet Peter. And I already miss Kasi Rao terribly. So I would feel much better if I had an old friend, like yourself, with me."

Phoebe squared her shoulders and took Gabby's hand again. "Don't worry," she said. "I won't leave you alone. But perhaps you should fix your hair. It's all falling down again."

Gabby put a tentative hand up to her hair. "Drat!" She had deliberately tried not to touch it ever since putting it up that morning, in hopes of meeting Peter while looking her best. Gabby snatched off her bonnet and handed it to Phoebe.

Long experience had taught her that the only way to make an acceptable arrangement out of her long, messy curls was to start from the beginning.

Quill turned around from his conversation with the purser and paused, riveted to the spot. Gabrielle Jerningham was pulling pins from her hair. It was falling down her back, long bronze locks rushing in a tangled glory down to her bottom. Quill swallowed. He'd never seen a lady's hair down in a public place, and here was Miss Jerningham—Gabby—blithely shaking her curls, as if the crowd of steve-dores, sailors, and boatmen around her were naught.

Those men were staring, mouths agape, at the delectable young woman who appeared to be undressing in their midst.

Quill was at her side in a moment, his face like thunder. "Where the devil is your lady's maid?"

Gabby blinked. "I don't have one," she replied. "My father never believed in them; he said that any lady worth her salt could climb into her own garments."

"A *lady* does not groom herself in public!"

For the first time Gabby looked around them, catching a glimpse of the men just as they hastily turned away.

"I'm afraid I'm used to being on display," she said brightly. "In the village, my father and I were the only Europeans. My hair was considered to be a good-luck charm—"

She broke off as Mr. Dewland grabbed her arm. "Come along, Miss Jerningham." He looked down at Phoebe, who still clutched Gabby's bonnet. "Here, give me that." He took the bonnet and plopped it on top of Gabby's head. It looked absurd.

"Miss Jerningham." His voice was a command.

Gabby gave a little shrug and took Phoebe's hand. She could put up her hair in the carriage.

She climbed into Mr. Dewland's vehicle, tucked Phoebe next to her, and then briskly wound her hair into a knot on the back of her head.

"That looks much nicer," Phoebe said as Gabby stuck in a few extra pins for good luck.

Quill looked at her and couldn't think of anything to say. He'd never seen a woman more in need of a lady's maid in his life. She had taken all that mass of gorgeous hair and stuck it up on her head somehow, but even he could see that it was tilting to the right, and in a matter of two minutes it would start falling out of its coil.

And now that he looked at Gabby more closely, he could see that the overall impression of inelegance he caught on the wharf was due to her clothing as well as her hair. She wasn't very tall, and she seemed to have a rather—well, plumpish figure.

Quill's heart sank and he drove home in silence. His mood didn't appear to bother Gabby. She and Phoebe chattered about every bit of London they could see from the carriage. Gabby's voice matched her face. It was slightly husky, a beautiful, dark, deep voice that spoke of bedtime pleasures to Quill's mind.

But Peter—what was Peter going to say? There was no way to wrap it up in white linen: Peter was engaged to marry a plump, untidy girl who seemed to have no ladylike graces at all. The women Peter appreciated were tall, graceful sylphs. They were cool and sophisticated, women whose personal taste made them a match for Peter's exquisitely groomed person. They did not have sensuous mouths and voices that sounded provocative even when talking about the most innocent things.

Quill snuck another look at Gabby. Perhaps if they hired a maid—well, they had to hire a maid! But, no, it was impossible to imagine Gabby metamorphosing into a woman of distinction. Her hastily bundled hair had already drooped and fallen to the right side.

As soon as they reached the house he would send Gabby up to her room and instruct his mother's maid to wait on her. Something had to be done about that hair before Peter returned.

As Gabby walked up the steps to the portico of her future home, it was an even toss as to whether Phoebe held on tighter to her hand or she to Phoebe's. Her brother-in-law had almost wrenched her out of the carriage. Suddenly he seemed to be in a terrible hurry, and even now she sensed that he was practically poking her from behind in his urgency to enter the house.

The door swung open as she reached the top step. A plump man stood in the entryway, murmuring a greeting. He bowed so low that Gabby was afraid that his powdered wig might fall to the ground. And he was so meticulously dressed that for a moment she took him for the viscount. But he said hello without meeting her eyes. Mr. Dewland seemed to feel no inclination to make an introduction, simply instructing the man to fetch their belongings from the wharf.

As he took her cloak, Gabby paused and put her hand on his arm.

"Thank you," she said smiling. "Did Mr. Dewland call you Codswallop?"

The butler's eyes widened. "He did, my lady. That is, Miss Jerningham. My name is Codswallop."

Thank goodness, Gabby thought. Codswallop is not nearly as pompous as he first appeared, all starched up and fussy in his livery. She twinkled at him. "I am very pleased to meet you, Mr. Codswallop. May I introduce Miss Phoebe Pensington? She will be staying with us for a brief time."

Codswallop bowed as if he were meeting the queen. "Miss Phoebe." Then he added, "The household is most pleased to know that you have safely arrived in England, Miss Jerningham." He smiled before he could stop himself. "I am generally addressed as Codswallop, not Mr. Codswallop."

"Do forgive me," Gabby replied. "I am afraid there are many English customs that I have to learn. I have already thrown Mr. Dewland out of countenance by taking down my hair on the wharf."

Quill broke in before Gabby could detail the hundreds of social blunders she was likely to make or had already made. "Miss Jerningham would undoubtedly like to refresh herself, Codswallop. Please direct her to her chamber, and ask Stimple to aid her."

"I regret to say that Stimple has accompanied Lady Dewland to Bath, sir."

Quill frowned. Of course his mother wouldn't stir out of the house without her maid. What the devil was he to do now?

Codswallop opened the doors to the Indian Drawing Room. "I shall ring for tea," he announced. "And I shall inform Mrs. Farsalter that Miss Jerningham is without a lady's maid for the nonce. Mrs. Farsalter will solve this dilemma."

"Oh, thank you, Codswallop!" Gabby smiled at the butler. "I had no idea that lady's maids were so important in England. I'm afraid I shall have to rely on you and Mrs. Farsalter. Is she your housekeeper?"

Gabby turned expectantly to Quill, but a small voice broke in.

"I did not travel with a lady's maid either."

Gabby smiled down at Phoebe. "I feel quite certain that between them Mrs. Farsalter and Codswallop will find us two lady's maids in the twitch of an eyelash!"

Codswallop surprised himself by nearly chuckling. "I believe that Mrs. Farsalter will wish to hire a governess for Miss Phoebe, if she is making a prolonged visit," he observed.

"After you, Miss Jerningham," Quill said in a tone ripe with suppressed irritation. He cast a lowering glance at Codswallop, who hastily backed away and disappeared into the servants' quarters with their outer garments.

"Oh, goodness," Gabby said faintly, as she walked into the room. "What—what a lovely chamber."

Quill looked around. "My mother's idea."

Gabby walked rather tentatively over to a particularly monstrous table featuring a seated tiger as its pedestal.

Phoebe trotted after her and patted the animal's head.

"Where did this piece of furniture come from?" Gabby asked, with some curiosity.

"My mother calls this the Indian Drawing Room, Miss Jerningham. Her fond hope was to establish herself as a leader of London fashion. Her designer assured her that Indian furnishings were going to be the next rage."

He shrugged. "Unfortunately, it didn't happen. But having spent so much money to become Indian, my father is unwilling to return to being merely English."

Gabby looked at him sharply. Erskine Dewland's face might not express much, but she could hear just the faintest hint of laughter in his tone.

She took it as an invitation and smiled back hugely. "How odd it is," she remarked, her eyes dancing, "that we had no tiger tables in our household, given that I have lived in India my whole life. In fact, I do not remember ever seeing such . . . such lavishly tigerish furniture before."

Quill did not smile, but his eyes laughed.

"I must beg you not to reveal such an unpleasant truth to my mama," he said, leaning against the mantelpiece. "You see, having spent some twenty thousand pounds to achieve this Indian extravaganza, she would be devastated to find that most of her Indian treasures were produced in Southampton by a cabinetmaker named Fred Pinkle."

"Fred Pinkle? You had the furniture investigated!" Gabby accused.

"I should hardly call it an investigation," Quill remarked, moving over to lean against the back of a high-backed chair. "I used to own shares in the East India Company, so I have a reasonable familiarity with products one might actually buy in that country."

Gabby's mouth tightened. "You own part of the East India Company?"

Quill looked up, startled. It was the first time since he met her that Gabby had spoken sharply.

"Does that dismay you for some reason, Miss Jerningham?"

Gabby raised her chin and met his eyes calmly. "No, of course not. It is not my concern. But will you please call me Gabby, Mr. Dewland? We are to be family, after all."

Quill pushed himself upright. He must have imagined the rebuke in Gabby's tone. His leg was sending him brutal messages about the long carriage rides to and from Depford.

"Gabby," he said. "Then you must address me as Quill."

"Quill? Quill—what a lovely name!"

"Is that a *truly* lovely name, or something akin to the loveliness of this room?"

Gabby giggled, an enchanting low chuckle. "You have caught me out, Mr. Dewl—Quill." She paused. "May I ask you a question?"

"Naturally."

"Is your leg causing you pain?" She asked it rather hesitatingly, uncertain whether this question would be considered an outrageous impertinence.

Quill could have answered that. No well-bred young lady would ever ask such a personal question of a man, let alone of a relative stranger. His mouth quirked into an unwilling grin. Gabby was certainly going to wake up the staid Dewland household.

"I was in a riding accident some six years ago," he explained. "And while I have been lucky enough to recover my ability to walk, I have difficulty standing for long periods of time."

Gabby's brown eyes were glowing with sympathy. "Well, then, why haven't you sat down, you poor man?"

"Miss Gabby!" Phoebe, who had been wandering about inspecting the many groveling tigers and lions that adorned the viscountess's furniture, was back at her side. "Mr. Dewland cannot sit until you do. My ayah told me that English gentlemen never, ever sit down in the presence of a lady. I mean, if the lady is standing up."

Gabby's face turned rosy. "I am so sorry, Quill!" She whisked around the side of a couch and plumped herself down. "I'm afraid I shall make many mistakes of this nature. My father did not believe in what he called aristocratic flummeries, and so I know almost nothing of English customs."

"Please think nothing of it," Quill replied, sinking into a chair, with a silent breath of relief.

Phoebe sat primly on a small footstool at Gabby's feet. To Quill's amusement, Phoebe and Gabby presented an image of precise opposites. Phoebe's hair fell into meticulous curls that looked as if she had just brushed them. As she sat down, the little girl instinctively twitched the folds of her dress so that they spread evenly on either side. Her hands were clasped on her lap, and her ankles were neatly crossed.

But Gabby! It wasn't that there was anything precisely unladylike in her posture—but she simply didn't look groomed. For one thing, most of her hair had fallen down again. When she handed her bonnet to Codswallop, her hair tumbled with it. Her gown had a very odd look to it as well. Clearly it had been designed to hang from just below her breasts, the way women's clothing did these days. But instead it was rather stiff, and it puffed out around her hips almost as if she were wearing starched undergarments.

Codswallop entered the drawing room and said, "Tea will be served directly." He held forth a silver salver, graced with one card. "Mr. Lucien Boch has called. Are you receiving, sir?"

"No."

Gabby looked at Quill sweetly. "Please do not deny your friend simply because of my presence. Surely Mr. Boch could join us for tea?"

Quill frowned. "I think it would be best if we do not receive guests." His tone sounded pompous even to himself, but how in the world could he politely mention the state of her hair?

Gabby wrinkled her nose at him. "I may not know English customs, but I do know how irksome it is to travel all the way to a friend's house and then find that he is out!"

When Quill nodded reluctantly at Codswallop, Gabby continued sunnily. "After all, we are family and need not stand on ceremony. I would be very happy to make my first London acquaintance." She hesitated. "Will Peter be joining us for tea, do you think?"

Quill's stomach tensed. "I doubt it. Peter rarely returns home before late in the evening."

"Oh."

Quill felt as if he had told a baby chick that his favorite dish was roast fowl. His future sister-in-law looked suddenly disconsolate, biting her lip.

"Is he in London at the moment? Does he know that I have arrived?"

A delicate question, Quill thought to himself. Undoubtedly, Peter had been chased to the ground by a footman and informed of the *Plassey*'s arrival. But that particular piece of news was likely to make him stay out all night.

"No," he replied brusquely. "If he had known of your

arrival, he would have met the *Plassey* himself. When the message arrived, I was alone in the house. In fact, I should have informed you that my parents will be most sorry to have missed your arrival. They are in Bath at the moment."

Gabby instantly glowed again. "Well, of course, I should have guessed that Peter didn't know that I have arrived! Do you think a footman could send him a message?" For a moment she looked adorably confused. "If it's not pre-sumptuous?"

"Impossible," Quill barked. "I don't know where he is." Something about this whole conversation was making him irritable as a wet cat. The girl didn't sound as if she was talking about a man she'd never met, nor was she acting as if this was a marriage of convenience. A marriage between *strangers.*

Codswallop reopened the doors and announced, "Mr. Lucien Boch." An elegant man dressed in black strolled into the room.

Quill felt a wave of relief. Damned if she wasn't right. This was hard business, talking amongst the family. It would be easier having Lucien with them. He was such a charming devil.

"Lucien, may I introduce you to my future sister-in-law? This is Miss Gabrielle Jerningham, the daughter of Lord Richard Jerningham. And Miss Phoebe Pensington, who is paying us a short visit."

Lucien walked over and prepared to sweep into a graceful bow—when suddenly Miss Jerningham hopped up from the couch and stood before him. Lucien just caught himself as he stumbled back. If he bowed now, he would strike his head on her knee. He stepped back once more and produced a regrettably inelegant bow.

Gabby bobbed a curtsy.

"Miss Jerningham. I am enchanted to meet you. And you, Miss Phoebe." Lucien turned to the little girl, who had risen with Gabby.

In response, *she* dropped an exquisite curtsy.

"My word!" Lucien said. And he swept her a court bow. "It is rare to meet a young lady of such refinement."

Phoebe smiled gamely, but there was something wrong. Lucien could see that the little girl was exhausted and near tears. What an odd setup this was! This ungainly girl, Gabrielle, was to be the impeccable Peter's wife? Where was Peter? And what was little Phoebe doing in the midst of it all?

He sat down and there was an awkward pause until Gabby realized that Quill apparently felt no responsibilities as a host to make conversation. "Are you French, Mr. Boch?" she asked, smiling at their guest.

Lucien nodded. "I lived in France for most of my life, although I have been in this country for some twelve, thirteen years."

"I wonder if you might have known my mother when you lived in France? Her maiden name was du Lac, Marie du Lac."

"I fear not," Lucien said. "My wife and I lived a rather secluded life. We rarely went to Paris. Was your mother attached to the court?"

Gabby blushed. "I am afraid that I do not know. My father refuses to speak of her."

Lucien gave a sympathetic nod. "It is the way sometimes, after a beloved person has died."

Just then Codswallop bustled in, followed by three footmen bearing a huge silver teapot and various dainties. Tea was set up at a small table at the far end of the room, and it wasn't until Gabby sat in the chair Codswallop pulled out for her that she realized the teapot was placed squarely in front of her.

"Shall I . . . ?" she asked, looking at Quill.

"Please."

"I've never had proper Chinese tea before," Gabby confided to Lucien. "Those of us who grow up in India are taught that Chinese tea is akin to nectar."

Lucien chuckled. "We in England think of it as liquid gold," he observed. "It's only people like Quill, who are hand and glove with the East India bravos, who can afford to drink tea at all hours."

Gabby was carefully pouring pale golden tea into four delicate cups. "My goodness, what is an East India bravo? Am I such a person?"

"Happily not." Lucien laughed. "East India bravos are the men who run the East India trade company. They control the importation of tea from China, you know."

Gabby looked up and straight at Quill. "And you are a bravo?"

For some reason, Quill felt a chill of disapproval in the air. "Nonsense," he said with a shrug. "Lucien has a French manner of exaggeration."

"Gabby! Gabby!" Phoebe was squealing.

Gabby looked down with a start. To her horror, she found that she had forgotten to raise the spout of the teapot when she looked at Quill. Tea had spilled all over the polished surface of the table and was quietly pouring down onto the Axminster carpet below.

Hot red color rose into her cheeks. She jerked up the teapot far too quickly, and the stream of tea arched backward through the air and splashed all over the front of her white gown. Gabby instantly forgot the few rules she did know about a lady's behavior.

"Blast!" she shrieked, slamming down the teapot. Instinctively, she tried to stem the flow of tea off the table with her gloved hand—but that merely diverted the stream so that it swung left and splashed down onto Phoebe's gown.

Phoebe took one look at the stain on her gown and burst into sobs.

"Oh, Phoebe," Gabby said, taken by surprise again. "I'm so sorry." She leapt up to give the child a hug, but as she did so her tiger-adorned chair toppled backward on its spindly legs.

Gabby tried to catch her chair. But she missed when her foot caught in the hem of her gown. There was a loud ripping noise as she fell facedown across Quill's lap.

At that moment, Codswallop dove for the chair. He managed to grab the back, but when the chair fell, he fell. Butler and chair both crashed to the ground amidst much impressive splintering and grunting.

Lucien smothered a laugh, stood up, and plucked Phoebe into his arms as if he had known the little girl for years.

"Now, my little chicken," he said, his voice deep and soothing. "Tell me why you are crying over a mere tea stain." He strolled over toward the other side of the room, instinctively rubbing his cheek against Phoebe's ringlets, as she choked out a list of tragedies in which her new mama's disappearance interwove confusingly with the length of her dress, and now its tea stain, and her ayah, and what her ayah thought of messy little girls.

Gabby, who had been thrown across Quill's legs as if she were a lap rug, wiggled desperately, trying to get her feet solidly on the ground so she could scramble off his lap. Tears pricked her eyes. She was like to die from pure mortification.

In one smooth motion, Quill's hands closed around her shoulders and he put her back on her feet, rising as he did so.

Gabby didn't dare look at him. She had spilled the tea, and her best gloves had horrid-looking yellow stains on them. The same stains adorned the bodice of her best gown, and its hem was ripped clear off. The gown had been fashioned with an extra panel at the bottom in a Greek key pattern, and that panel was trailing on the ground. Quill must think she showed a complete lack of refinement.

Strong fingers closed around her elbow.

"Shall we adjourn? Our presence at the table is now superfluous." To her surprise, Quill's eyes were dancing with merriment.

Gabby looked back at the table. It was empty; the footmen were clustered around Codswallop, attempting to hoist him to his feet. She paled. "Codswallop is injured."

"I believe he is merely winded by his dash across the room," Quill observed.

Gabby still looked worried, so he added, "Don't you think the footmen resemble amateur tooth-drawers clustering around a resistant patient?"

She wrinkled her nose at him. "You are laughing at me, sir!"

"Not a bit of it," Quill said, his face almost earnest enough to convince her. "I would never be such a rudesby. Alike accidents have happened to those of the highest decorum. I believe that Codswallop's dignity is perhaps offended, but his person is intact."

"Well," Gabby said, looking down at herself. "I don't suppose there's any way I can convince you that *I* am a lady of the highest decorum, is there?"

She met Quill's eyes, and the merriment there so warmed her backbone that she giggled.

Quill, who was still rather intoxicated by the melting

bundle of soft curves that had fallen so providentially into his lap, chuckled in response. Finally Gabby burst into laughter.

And that was how Peter found them when he pushed open the door to the drawing room.

Chapter 3

GABBY HEARD THE SOUND of the door opening and swung about quickly. For a moment she didn't register who was standing a mere ten feet before her. Quill's laughing eyes had made her feel prickly all over.

But she forgot that sensation in an instant as she took in the new arrival.

It was Peter. Her husband-to-be. She took a quick step toward him and then stopped. Peter was—Surely it was he. His eyes were a rather sweet brown.

But it was impossible to tell whether his hair was brown or not, since it was heavily powdered.

He was wearing a dark coat that was embroidered along the collar, the cuffs, and all down the front. And his waistcoat! It seemed to be made of poppy-colored silk, and it was embroidered all over with wildflowers. There was a perfect froth of silver lace edged with gold thread falling from his neck. His silk stockings were perfectly white. And his shoes had large silver buckles.

Gabby's mouth fell open, and then she snapped it shut.

Her heart started beating so fast that she could feel it in her throat. The man—her future husband—didn't say a word. He simply stood in the door of the drawing room, with a black hat in his hand, and stared at her. There was a liquid pool of silence in the room.

Gabby bit her lip and then forced her mouth into a smile. Just as she was about to speak, she heard Quill's deep voice behind her.

"I gather you've been at court, Peter."

Peter—for it was he—cast a glance at his elder brother. "It's the second of November, Quill." He seemed to consider that comment a sufficient explanation.

He tucked his hat under his arm and made a leg toward Gabby. "Your servant." He turned toward Lucien, who was still holding Phoebe, and made another leg. "You needn't respond, my dear Boch," he said. "I can see that you are otherwise occupied."

Gabby cleared her throat. "November the second?"

The man turned his eyes back to her. He looked her up and down, from the very tip of her stained boots to her tumbled hair. She could read censure in the sharpness of his gaze. "November the second is the duke of Kent's birthday," he remarked.

By now Gabby's stomach had clenched into a little knot. Peter walked a few steps into the room. "I trust Codswallop has not had an attack of some kind?"

Quill shook his head. "He appears to be uninjured." Sure enough, Codswallop was back on his feet, adjusting his black frock coat to its usual perfection.

"He tripped on the chair," Gabby said breathlessly, "and he spilled the tea, and now my dress is quite ruined." She avoided Quill's glance.

Peter's eyes warmed just a trifle. "I believe you are Miss

Jerningham? I have been waiting for my brother to introduce me, but he is quite neglecting his responsibilities as a host. I am Mr. Peter Dew——"

Gabby hurried over, tripping a little on the trailing hem of her gown. She grasped Peter's left hand, the one that was not holding his hat. "Please, call me Gabby. Since I am——since we are——"

Peter choked. He gently withdrew his hand and resisted the impulse to check his gloves for tea stains. After all, it wasn't Miss Jerningham's fault that their infernal butler had dropped a teapot on her. She must feel appallingly embarrassed to be standing about in this condition.

"I believe that Miss Jerningham would like to retire to her room," he said, looking at Quill and deliberately avoiding Gabby's eyes. "Given that our butler has quite destroyed her ensemble." Although to call that horror of a gown she was wearing an "ensemble" was gilding the kitchen kettle, to be sure.

He moved to the side to allow Codswallop to leave the room.

"I can't think what you are about, Quill," Peter continued, all his animosity about this absurd situation brewing in his tone. "By all rights, you should have been at court this morning. *Everyone* was there to celebrate the birthday. Believe me, Prinny may not be hand and glove with his brother, but he always notes if Prince Edward is slighted. Now that you are walking, you no longer have an excuse for such flimsy manners!"

"I forgot," Quill drawled, moving forward so that he was standing just behind Gabby.

"You forgot!" The acid brewing in Peter's stomach leaked into his tone, making it a trifle shrill. "*No* gentleman could forget the happy occasion of doing honor to one of our princes. Just as no gentleman would force a lady to remain in public in such a state." His eyes skittered over his future wife's ruined clothing once again.

"I can't *think* what Codswallop was about," Peter went on, finally meeting Gabby's eyes. "He is not, in general, a butterfingered fool." His tone warmed as he thought about the agony Gabby must be suffering. Indeed, her face looked pinched and rather white. "One of Mother's chairs is quite ruined. Although the chair's demise is nothing compared to the affront offered Miss Jerningham."

Quill turned toward Gabby, but she looked away. She couldn't admit to being the butterfingered fool she actually was, not in front of her elegant betrothed. Even though Quill's horrid grin implied that she was acting like a naughty five-year-old by remaining silent.

Peter rang the bell cord. "I shall summon your lady's maid to escort you to your chamber. If you feel too discomposed to join us for dinner, please know that my feelings are with you. Should this insufferable accident have happened to me on my first visit to England—nay, at *any* time!—I should take at least a day to regain my spirits."

He made another elegant leg to Gabby.

Gabby gasped and bobbed a curtsy. She felt incapable of responding to anything Peter was saying. This couldn't be Peter. Well, it was Peter. Now that the shock was over, she could see that the lines of his face approximately followed those of the portrait. But this restless, elegant, shrill . . . popinjay! He was scented. She smelled it when she grasped his hand.

Gabby swallowed. She was very close to tears. She had never felt like such a loutish gawky girl in her life, and her life had been generously adorned with such moments.

Then someone took her hand. Gabby gulped and looked up. Through her slightly blurred eyes, she suddenly saw the Peter of her portrait. He smiled down at her kindly.

"I am so sorry that your arrival in our house was dampened by Codswallop's unfortunate accident, Miss Jerningham."

She smiled a bit shyly at the handsome young man before her. "Will you call me Gabby, please? Since we are to be married?" She had to say it out loud. Peter appeared to be viewing her as a mere visitor.

Peter seemed to stiffen all over, but he nodded.

For the first time, Gabby considered the possibility that Peter was not entirely happy with their proposed marriage. She herself had been so pleased to escape from her father's household, and so delighted with the portrait of Peter, that she had not given a second's thought to her betrothed's feelings on the matter.

"Shall I escort Gabby to her chambers? I believe that Mother had the Blue Room prepared." Quill looked down at his wilted future sister-in-law. She had a strained expression in her eyes that made him want to give his brother a facer.

"Absolutely not," Peter broke in sharply. "May I remind you, Quill, that Miss Jerningham is a gently bred young lady? Under no account will you escort her to the upper reaches of the house. We shall summon her maid immediately. I must say it seems remarkably odd that your father allowed you to travel without a lady's companion, Miss Jerningham!"

"My father didn't believe in lady's maids or companions. He said that—"

But Quill interrupted what he sensed was a flood of information about Gabby's unconventional father. He didn't think that Peter would be able to take any more revelations.

"I am soon to be a member of Gabby's family, Peter.

There can be no hint of impropriety if I escort my sister-in-law to her chamber."

"She's not yet your sister-in-law!" Peter snapped.

Gabby's heart sank. Peter didn't want to marry her. That was clear. She shook off the hand Quill had slipped under her arm.

"Do you not wish to marry me, sir?" Her voice was huskier than normal, due to the tears that were backing up her throat.

Peter gaped.

Lucien put Phoebe on her feet and they soundlessly retreated together to the other side of the chamber. Phoebe might be a mere five years, but she had an instinctive sense of propriety.

"Because we could—we could make some other arrangement," Gabby said miserably. "I certainly never thought to force you to do anything that you didn't wish to do."

Quill was horrified at Gabby's insight. "Of course Peter wishes to marry you," he injected, his tone rough. He grabbed her elbow. "Peter is right. You should be in your chamber, changing your attire!"

Gabby ignored him, looking up at her fiancé. "Why didn't you tell my father that you were not happy with this arrangement before I traveled all the way from India?" Her voice was choking now. "Your father's letter said that you were . . . that you were . . ."

Quill gave Peter a look over Gabby's bowed head that shook his younger brother to his toes.

Peter reached out and took Gabby's hand again. "You quite misunderstood me, Miss Jerningham—Gabby. I *am* looking forward to marrying you." And when he met Gabby's drenched eyes, Peter almost felt he could do it. She was so pitiful, standing there in her ragged, stained clothing. His eyes softened. After all, her lack of distinction likely had more to do with the lack of mantua-makers in India than with her own sense of dress.

"My tone was sharp because I was—am—mortified by the deplorable conduct of our butler. I felt all your anguish when I realized the accident that had befallen you. In fact, I believe that I shall speak to my father about having Codswallop dismissed. We cannot tolerate a servant in this household who would act in such a reprehensible fashion. Please believe that my feelings about you are quite firm.

"I can hardly wait for our nuptials," he added, rather more uncertainly.

Gabby took a deep, shuddering breath. The sight of Peter's slender white hand, adorned with one tasteful signet ring, mesmerized her.

The hand vanished as Peter realized that his future wife was likely nonplussed by his indelicacy, given that he had held her hand beyond the permissible six seconds.

"*I* shall escort you to your chamber," he said, and took Gabby's arm, drawing her toward the door.

She cast a rather desperate glance back at Quill.

He smiled reassuringly. "I will arrange for Phoebe to be housed near your chamber, Gabby."

Gabby bit her lip and nodded. It seemed ungracious to plead that Quill accompany them. A mere hour or two ago she had considered Quill a formidable and terrifying presence; now Peter's querulous, modish accents were terrifying her in quite a different manner. Helplessly, she allowed Peter to draw her into the hallway and up the stairs, listening numbly as he deposited her in a light, airy chamber papered in blue.

"Will Phoebe be in the chamber next to mine?" she asked, as Peter was bowing his way out of the room.

"Phoebe? Phoebe?"

"Phoebe is the child with Mr. Boch," Gabby explained, only just realizing that Phoebe had not been introduced. "You see, Phoebe was traveling on the *Plassey* as well, and when her relatives did not appear at the wharf after the ship docked, your brother arranged to bring her here."

Peter pursed his lips. "It seems most unusual," he observed. "I cannot fathom why you did not leave her with the ship's captain. Surely her relatives will suffer unnecessary anxiety if they are unable to locate her."

"Perhaps you are right. But the problem is that we were not entirely sure whether Phoebe's living relative—a Mrs. Emily Ewing—ever received the letter recounting the death of her sister and brother-in-law. When Mrs. Ewing did not appear at the wharf, I thought it best to keep Phoebe with me, because what if it takes some time for Mrs. Ewing to be located? Most of the crew of the *Plassey* disembarked immediately. We were blown far off course, and they were eager to return to their families. I was not at all sure who would be in charge of Phoebe."

She paused. "I'm rattling on. Please forgive me."

Peter glanced at the stained glove resting on his arm, and she snatched her hand back. "Not at all," he said politely, and bowed again. "I can see that you had no alternative other than to bring the child with you. I will arrange to have Mrs. Ewing located." He bowed yet again and backed out of Gabby's chamber.

Gabby sank onto the bed and stripped off her gloves. Tears rose to her eyes. Peter may not be set against the idea of marriage, as she had thought for a mad moment, but he was so cool, so self-contained. Obviously, propriety meant everything to him. The tears snaked down her cheeks. It was as if she were tailormade to put him out of countenance.

He was on a first-name basis with the future king of England—calling him Prinny!—and she was just as butterfingered as she always was.

Why, but why, did she tell that lie about Codswallop? Peter seemed so horrified by her disarray that the fib just flew out of her lips. What must Quill think of her? She should have confessed. Except that if Peter knew it was her blunder . . . He would never marry her if he knew what a cowhanded mess she'd made of a simple thing like pouring tea. And she *couldn't* go back to her father. Not to her father and his sharp-tongued admonishments as he outlined her many *faux pas*.

She took a shuddering breath. She simply had to become more graceful, that was all. More like the kind of woman Peter would wish to marry.

There was a scratch at her door. Gabby hastily scrubbed at the tearstains on her cheeks and stood up.

"Enter!"

Quill's deep voice answered her. "I have brought Phoebe to see you. She seems to have the fixed notion that you might have fled back to India without her."

Gabby promptly knelt on the floor and stretched out her arms to the little girl. "Sweet, Phoebe, I would never, never have left you here alone."

The child flew into her arms like a carrier pigeon, Quill thought, watching Gabby rock Phoebe back and forth and whisper into her hair. *Lucky Phoebe.* He wrenched his thoughts away and strolled across the room to look out the window at his gardens.

"Peter doesn't mean to be critical," he said suddenly. "He has a high opinion of his own consequence, but he's a very good sort, for all that."

Gabby answered at cross-purposes. "Is there any chance that your father might let Codswallop go?"

Quill turned around, even though the sight of Gabby cuddling Phoebe gave him a queer feeling about his heart. "Feeling guilty, are you?" He grinned at her.

Gabby felt too ashamed to respond to his teasing. "I cannot conceive why I fibbed, Quill," she said earnestly. "It was just that Peter looked so horrified——"

"I think it was quite a useful lie, as these things go," Quill pointed out.

"He is right, Miss Gabby," Phoebe piped up. "Don't you remember that you told me that a lie was acceptable if it made the person feel better? And Mr. Dewland felt much better once he thought that the butler ruined your gown."

"From the mouths of babes," Quill murmured.

Gabby gave him a sharp glance. "It's all very well for you to make fun," she pointed out. "I have told a terrible fib about poor Codswallop, and his injuries are actually my fault!"

She looked so dejected that Quill felt a qualm of sympathy. "Don't worry about Codswallop. My father would cut off his right hand before he dismissed the fellow—he's been in the household for years. I'll go down and bring him your sincerest apologies, how would that be?"

"I shall do it myself," Gabby said with resolution.

"You most certainly will not!" Quill retorted. "Ladies do not descend into the servants' quarters with impunity, Gabby!"

"When it comes to one's own culpability, propriety should stand aside," Gabby responded. "I'm quite sure that Papa would say so."

"Your father sounds most peculiar," Quill observed. "At any rate, Phoebe is right. Peter is now feeling quite happy about the whole episode. It wouldn't be fair if you leapt into another indelicacy before he's even recovered from glimpsing your ankles."

Gabby colored and looked down at her dress. The ripped section of her gown exposed her ankles above her half boots. She met Quill's eyes as he, too, looked up from her hem. Something in the depth of his eyes gave her a simmering sensation deep in her stomach. She glanced down again. They were perfectly unremarkable ankles, trimly clad in white cotton. And she didn't believe for a moment that the sight of them stirred Peter in any way.

Quill was discovering that, in fact, his punctilious brother might have been right when he forbade him to accompany Gabby to her bedchamber. Perhaps it was the intimacy of the nearby bed that was making his blood throb. The mere glimpse of Gabby's slender ankles had thrown him a heady vision of her legs under that drab—and now indecent—gown.

"I forbid you to visit the servants' quarters," he said abruptly. "There is no call to throw my brother into more of a frenzy than he is likely to suffer in the natural course of things."

Gabby's eyes narrowed. "What do you mean by that cryptic phrase, *in the natural course of things*? I gather you are implying that my espoused husband is going to suffer by marrying me?" she asked. "That he will suffer because . . . because I am such a bad bargain?"

"He won't suffer any more than every man does in his marriage," Quill said. "Loss of bachelor freedom and all that. That's why they call it 'leg-shackling.' "

But Gabby, of course, was not done talking. "You *forbid* me? What right have you to forbid me to do anything that I wish?"

The corner of Quill's mouth twitched. "In the absence of my father, I am the master of the household, you know."

A little frown crooked Gabby's brow. Now that she

thought about it, it was obvious Quill was considerably older than Peter.

"But I thought—" She broke off. She could inquire later why her father thought she was marrying the viscount's heir, when in fact she was marrying a younger son. Instead, she changed the subject. "Phoebe needs to be taken to bed." Her young friend had succumbed to the anxieties of the day and fallen fast asleep in her lap.

"Mrs. Farsalter has appointed a housemaid to look after the child," Quill said, observing despite himself the way in which Phoebe's head nestled against Gabby's breast. "Shall I carry her into the next room?"

Gabby looked at him and pursed her lips. "Will your leg pain you? Perhaps we might carry Phoebe together. She's not very large, and if you could carry her head and shoulders, I could carry her legs."

Quill scowled. "I exercise with dumbbells every day, Miss Jerningham. I can certainly hoist a small child into the next room."

"Dumbbells? What are dumbbells?"

"Short bars weighted at each end with a knob. After my accident I had a good deal of difficulty moving my limbs. We found a German doctor, Trankelstein, who believes that one must force injured limbs back into service by exercising with dumbbells that he devised for the purpose."

Gabby's sympathetic brown eyes rested on him for a moment like a caress. Quill shivered. Why was it that it didn't really bother him when Gabby referred to his disabled limb, whereas he was thrown into a bitter rage when anyone else did so? He scooped up the little girl and carried her into the bedchamber next door.

As Gabby was introducing herself to the housemaid and arranging to have Phoebe's clothing removed for cleaning and mending, Quill lingered in the doorway, unable to tear himself away.

She was an annoying, clumsy, plump, untidy woman.

She was a seductive jade whose sooty eyelashes and luxurious hair were begging for kisses.

She was an untidy baggage who had fibbed her way out of an unpleasant spot.

She was the first woman in years who spoke to him as if his lame leg was merely an inconvenience.

Obviously he should avoid her at all costs.

He straightened up and left the room without saying good-bye. An incivility, he thought to himself on the way down the staircase.

Incivility is sometimes warranted by a man's instinct for self-preservation.

Quill headed for his study with the blind determination of an exhausted plow horse that smells his barn up ahead. He threw himself into his neglected reports, poring over the table of figures that summed up the reasons Quill might be desirous to hold shares in Mortlake & Mudland, Victuallers to the Crown.

And yet, when a footman opened the door and announced that Quill had a visitor, he didn't hesitate. He couldn't bring himself to give a hang about Mortlake & Mudland. A bitter loneliness was twining around his heart and making it impossible to concentrate. It was even threatening to cast him into self-pity. Quill had learned years before, in the face of the world's unrelenting sympathy, that to pity oneself was the way to a morbid hell.

But he was surprised when he read the card. Lord Breksby was the Secretary for Foreign Affairs, on the verge of retirement, or so they said. They had only the slimmest of acquaintances with each other.

Breksby bustled in, rubbing his hands and looking not

at all like a man on the edge of retirement. "Good day, sir! I trust you are not overly inconvenienced by my importunate visit?"

Quill ushered him to a chair, wondering not a little what had brought Breksby out of his elegant office in the Ministry for Foreign Affairs, Downing Street.

"I called to speak to your father, not realizing he was out of the city."

Quill nodded. "I would be pleased to send him a message. Or, if your visit is a delicate one, I would be more than happy to give you my father's direction in Bath, Lord Breksby."

"There's nothing secret about my visit," Breksby said jovially. "As a matter of fact, I was calling to congratulate your father on young Mr. Peter's upcoming nuptials. Heard you will soon be welcoming the presence of Jerningham's daughter in London. By Jerningham I mean the younger one, of course. Richard Jerningham, brother of the late duke." Almand, duke of Jerningham, had died recently, leaving the dukedom to his fourteen-year-old son.

"Miss Jerningham arrived today," Quill observed cautiously. Every nerve was alert. Breksby could not possibly have journeyed over here just to exchange chitchat.

"I won't beat about the bush," Breksby said. "We need your father to help us, Dewland. Or perhaps I should say, we need Miss Jerningham's help."

Quill frowned.

"Quite right," Breksby said in response to his unspoken criticism. "Why on earth would the English government need aught from a gently bred young lady? But the fact is that Gabrielle Jerningham's father is queer in the stirrups. And I'm afraid that no one realized quite how queer until recently." Breksby's tone was grim.

"What has he done?"

"It's less what he's done than what he's supporting. He's put himself up against the East India Company over a matter of internal politics and one of the Indian rulers."

Quill thought it over. Given that he had been at one time a major proprietor of East India stock, he tended to hear about many of the wrangles in which the company engaged its army. In the previous year, the army had attacked the fortress of Bharatpur, leaving some three thousand persons killed or wounded—and failed to gain Bharatpur, naturally.

"Is the problem to do with the Holkar region?"

Breksby looked unsurprised at Quill's knowledge of internal Indian politics. "Precisely. Holkar is in the Marathas—the central region of India, you know."

"The Marathas are not owned or governed by the company," Quill observed.

"Just so. And that is why I am speaking to you, rather than to anyone at India House or any of the representatives of the governor-general. It is the opinion of quite a few of us in the government that the Board of Control is not sufficiently curbing the, uh, warlike nature of the company's army. We have been working in a quiet sort of way to make our opinion known."

Quill did not reveal by so much as a flick of an eyelash what he thought of their "quiet" methods.

But Breksby did not achieve his current eminence for nothing. "I know, I know," he said with a sigh. "Our efforts are undoubtedly insufficient. Be that as it may, Lord Richard Jerningham has apparently taken matters into his own hands—and in a way that threatens the entire Marathas region."

"What's he done?"

"Were you aware that the current ruler of Holkar had gone around the bend?"

"Tukoji Holkar? I heard some rumors," Quill said cautiously. Actually he had heard that Holkar was addicted to the cherry brandy supplied to him by East India men.

"Utterly cracked," Breksby confirmed. "Sat around all day swilling brandy until he went 'round the bend. Apparently his relatives have him tied up with rope and are feeding him only milk. I gather there are a couple of illegitimate heirs waiting around like jackals in the wings. But Tukoji does have a legitimate heir."

"The problem is that Jerningham has secreted that heir away somewhere."

Quill blinked. "Why on earth would he do that?"

"Supposedly the heir is cracked, too. Jerningham believes that if we put a half-wit on the throne of Holkar it will give the East India Company an inside track to the Marathas. He wants an illegitimate son on the throne and the company out of the region."

"And you believe that Miss Jerningham knows something of this situation?"

"Possibly," Breksby said promptly. "Very strange household, Jerningham's. You know he went over to India to be a missionary?"

"I heard that he originally traveled to India with that idea, but he discarded it," Quill replied.

"That's right. He set himself up as a huge nabob over there, deep in the Marathas country—because that's where he fancied himself saving souls. Except that rather than save souls, he has made a fortune exporting goods to China. Some say he was part of the early opium trade to that country. I don't credit it, myself."

"Why is he now involved in Holkar politics?"

"Tukoji Rao's heir is Jerningham's nephew, on his first wife's side. The boy was actually raised in Jerningham's household, side by side with his daughter."

"The relationship doesn't explain why Jerningham would

secrete the boy away when it looked as if he might become an heir to the throne."

"Word has it that Jerningham is so bitter against the East India Company that he'd do anything to cast a spoke in their wheel." Breksby took a quick look at the gold watch suspended from his waistcoat. "I shall look forward to discussing the situation at length with your father. And as I said, I do also wish to congratulate him on your brother's upcoming nuptials."

Quill stared at the closed door to the study for some time after Breksby's departure. Suddenly he gave a short laugh. Quill may not have known Gabby very long, but he was quite sure that she would loyally support her father—*and* that she could fib her way out of a tight spot without turning a hair. Perhaps Breksby, that wily old fox, was about to meet his match.

Chapter 4

THE NEXT MORNING Gabby stirred and stretched luxuriously. For the first time in months she didn't wake in a cramped bunk. There was no pitch and swell of waves under her. She had left the curtains open the previous night, and pale sunlight was spilling through the windows. Outside she could hear larks singing. At least, she assumed they were larks. Her father's poetry books had talked of larks singing in English gardens.

Having gone to bed rather worried about her future marriage, she felt renewed hope in the morning light. True, dinner had been a starched and stiff affair, during which Peter instructed her at length about members of the royal family. And he was absolutely right to point out that her education had been sadly neglected in this respect. Clearly, Prinny—as Peter called the Prince of Wales—was important to her future husband, and so she fully planned to cultivate an interest in royal doings. If she found the exploits of this Prinny a trifle . . . well, a trifle wearisome, that was beside the point.

The important thing was that Peter was so lovely. Gabby had watched him surreptitiously as he explicated the royal family's connections to German aristocracy, and she found him fascinating. His skin was as white as ivory. She had never seen another man like him. Even the Englishmen who frequented her father's palace were invariably tanned dark by the Indian sun. Peter's hair was a soft nut-brown, and it fell in perfectly ordered curls over his brow.

Gabby hopped out of bed and went over to the window. It was the beginning of November, and the garden should, by all accounts, be withered and brown. She had heard of English winters, how the wind whistled down the steely plains, and how icy rain sliced across one's face for months at a time. How people fell asleep in heaps of snow and never woke again, and how ice balls as big as mango fruit crushed the roofs of houses, without a moment's warning. Indian servants were full of tales of the English winter, stories that accounted for the bloodthirsty, formal, and rapacious nature of Englishmen. It was the cold, they told her.

But here—the garden was lovely, thick with great golden- and ruby-colored leaves and ginger-cheeked apple trees. It didn't look cold outside. Gabby pushed the heavy weight of her hair back over her shoulders and leaned close to the window. Dawn had only just come, and the house was absolutely still. It couldn't be much later than five in the morning. She listened for a moment. There was no sound at all, no distant tinkle of voices, no rumble of footsteps.

She could run outside for a moment or two and no one would be the wiser.

Quickly Gabby pulled on her night-robe and tied her hair back with a ribbon. She hesitated for a moment and then splashed water on her face and brushed her teeth. The garden was calling to her, but she abhorred the feeling of a sleepy mouth.

Finally she pulled on her half boots, which looked even more shabby and stained as they peeped out from her white nightdress. Then she tiptoed out of the room, down the wide stairs—and hesitated. How was she to find the garden? If she went out the front door, she would be on the street, and there was undoubtedly no access to the garden from the street.

At the bottom of the hallway was a braise door—the door where Codswallop had disappeared with their outer garments the night before. So that was likely to lead to the servants' quarters. And she knew that the drawing room filled with tiger tables didn't lead to the garden. Gabby silently turned the knob to the last door. A moment later, she pushed one of the tall garden doors ajar and slipped through, shivering a bit at the rush of cool air that greeted her.

The sky was a pale, pale blue, as unlike the hotly oiled blue of an Indian sky as possible. And the air smelled different. It was rich and watery, as if it breathed rain. Gabby drifted into the garden like a ghost, glancing down at her small boots, watching the toes become spotted and then drenched dark with dew.

Before her the garden curled off in three directions. She wandered down a path that was lined in flowers gamely hanging on to their last petals—brilliant cherry-red roses and seashell-pink, delicate ones that grew in clusters. The air smelled different here too, spicy, like the applesauce she had tried for the first time the night before. Gabby reached out to pluck a blossom, but they were so beautiful and, admittedly, so wet that she drew back her hand.

In the distance Gabby could just hear the sounds of London waking up. The rumbling of carts drifted over the high stone walls, mingled with the sleepy waking calls of birds. She walked farther, remembering the full-throated brilliance of the orchids that grew around her father's house and the shrieking birds that hid among those blossoms. Here the hedges hid twitters and small songs, introductory trills that sounded like songbooks for baby birds.

Her boots made whispering noises against the stone walk. She turned another slow curve—and stopped.

Her future brother-in-law was seated on a stone bench. His legs were stretched out full length before him, and his head was leaning back, eyes closed. Perhaps Quill was asleep? Gabby hesitated to wake him. He must spend a good deal of time in the garden, she thought. The sun had gilded his face a deep honey brown. One thing that she had noticed immediately was how white everyone in England was. Their faces shone like chalk or like pearl—well, like her face. Her father had never allowed her to be outdoors without a bonnet. He said he'd never be able to sell her on the marriage mart if the sun colored her skin.

Her future husband—Peter—had skin that was even whiter than hers. Peter was perfection, Gabby thought with a rather delicious shiver, from the top of his precisely cut brown locks to his white skin.

Quill was a darker hue altogether. Even in the dawn light his hair took on wine-colored glints, a mahogany that glowed in the rosy light and matched the toasty warm color of his skin. He needed a haircut, Gabby thought. She smiled. Quill needed someone to take care of him. She would make sure that he found a wife, just as soon as she made some London acquaintances.

Silently, Gabby tiptoed forward and seated herself trimly next to Quill on the bench.

To Gabby's dismay, he woke with a choked gasp. "I'm so sorry," Gabby said. "I thought you were daydreaming."

Quill looked at her without a word. His eyes were heavy-lidded, so dark that she couldn't see any color.

"I didn't expect to find anyone in the garden," Gabby

explained cheerfully. She was used to people who woke in an irritable state. "And I certainly wouldn't have woken you if I'd known you were asleep. You haven't been out here all night, have you?"

Quill just stared at her as if she were a ghost. Gabby felt a prickle of annoyance. She had already ascertained that he felt that talking was an occupation below him.

Then she grinned at him. She really liked her big, silent brother-in-law. "You might say, 'Good morning, Gabby. How did you sleep on your first night in England?'

"I may not know much about English manners," Gabby added, "but I am quite certain that greeting your future family members is customary."

His response was rather less friendly. "What the devil!"

Gabby's smile dimmed a bit. "I trust this is not *your* garden? No one told me that I should not come into the garden. And I do apologize for interrupting your sleep, but I was so pleased to see someone here, because I would dearly love to ask—"

Quill interrupted her. "Gabby."

"Yes?"

"Gabby, you are not dressed."

That seemed self-evident to Gabby. "Well, I am dressed," she explained. "I am wearing my night-robe, and my boots, as you can see." She stuck out her small boot from below the hem of her robe, and they both stared at it for a moment.

"You needn't worry about proprieties," Gabby said brightly. "After all, it's just us out here. The servants aren't even awake yet. And we won't tell anyone." By which she meant, *we won't tell Peter.* It was clear to her, after less than twenty-four hours in Peter's presence, that he had a fearful sense of propriety.

She twinkled at Quill, who was still affecting his air of

silence and looking at her in that disapproving way. But whereas the idea of Peter's disapproval made her feel rather breathless and anxious, the idea of infuriating Quill quite pleased her. It must be the difference between being with a lover and a brother, Gabby thought with a delightful sense of discovery.

She scooted over on the bench and tucked her arm under Quill's. "Now, sir, unless you are quite wedded to being mute, would you tell me the names of these plants?"

Quill looked at her as mutely as any rock. He still couldn't take it in. He'd been unable to sleep because of pain in his leg and had come outside, to find mouse-gray trees brooding over the grass in an early-morning fog. He'd walked out the kink in his leg and finally sat down—and had the oddest dream.

A dream, God forbid, about Gabby. He refused to even think about the images his treacherous mind had woven. And when he awoke, there she was. Looking like the aftermath of his dream, with her hair falling freely back over her shoulders, escaping from a loosely tied ribbon even as he watched.

"Gabby," he said in a rough voice, trying vainly to get a grasp on his imagination. "You should not be out in the garden in your night clothing. You should *never, ever* be seen outside your room in a state of undress."

Gabby ignored him and jumped to her feet, tugging him up as well. "I think we are safe for another five minutes, Quill. Just five minutes—and then I'll run back in the house."

Quill was no match for Gabby when she wanted something, and he knew it. Especially not when her lips were flushed red, swollen from sleep, and her eyes looked at him so . . . so invitingly. Her skin glowed with rosy lights that made his blood throb and his fingers twitch to touch her, to push aside the thick night-robe, to—oh, God, to fall on his knees before her and bury his face in her creamy skin—

Quill started down the garden path with a choked curse, dragging Gabby behind him. "That's a pudding-pipe tree," he said, nodding to a small tree. "Those are pears growing by the summer house. And these are apple trees."

"Oh, wait, Quill, wait," Gabby cried. "I want to look at the pudding-pipe tree. The one with flowers."

Quill reached out and snapped off a spray of golden blossoms. He shook it briskly, and a tiny shower of gleaming dewdrops flew from the plant. "Normally, it would be finished blooming, but it's been a warm autumn." He held it out to Gabby.

"It's lovely." Gabby's face glowed with happiness as she buried her nose in the flowers. When she raised her face, the tip of her nose was incongruously dusted with buttercup yellow.

Quill reached out and brushed off her nose with his thumb. She had a small, straight, patrician nose that spoke of generations of Jerninghams, all breeding noble and true, at least in the nose category.

"How did your father meet your mother?" He didn't know much about Richard Jerningham, although he was getting more and more curious.

"She was a French émigré," Gabby explained, not seeming to find his abrupt question impolite. "My father married her within two weeks of meeting her. They were married less than a year, as she died giving birth to me."

Quill was increasingly aware of the dappled sunlight that was now warming his back. Gabby seemed to have no idea what would happen if they were found together in the garden. He tugged her around and began to walk briskly back toward the house. Then he stopped. "You must enter alone," he told her.

"Quill!" Gabby said, her husky voice annoyed. "We were speaking of something important. You are most impolite to ignore me. I said my mother died at my birth, and you should at least offer your sympathies."

Quill looked down at her and once again stifled the impulse to kiss her into silence. "I would like to hear more about your father and mother," he said, after a moment. "But I am worried that we will be discovered by the servants. They must be up and around the house by now."

"Well," Gabby said, "would that be such a tragedy? We are family, after all." And she smiled up at him, her eyes as innocent and friendly as a babe's.

"You are not married to Peter yet," Quill pointed out. "If we were found in the garden together, people would undoubtedly think the worst. You would be ruined."

"That reminds me," Gabby said with a frown. "Why am I marrying Peter? Not," she added quickly, "that I have any reluctance to do so."

And Quill could tell by her sunny smile that she didn't.

"But I am quite certain that my papa thinks I am marrying you," Gabby said confusedly. "Or rather, he thinks that Peter *is* you. I am afraid that he believes that I will be a viscountess someday. But that won't happen, will it, Quill? Your wife will be the viscountess."

"You may never be a viscountess. But your son will surely be a viscount. I shall never marry."

"But——"

He cut her off. "Gabby, you *must* return to your chambers now. Go!" And he pushed her toward the Yellow Drawing Room.

Gabby had no recourse but to do as he told her. So she

trotted up the steps and slipped through the door to the house, thinking intently about what Quill had said. Of course he would marry! She didn't care a bit about being a viscountess, and what her father didn't know wouldn't hurt him. But Quill was lonely. She could see it in the bleak look in his eyes. He needed someone to coax him into speech and make him laugh—even if he did laugh only with his eyes.

Back in her room, Gabby took off her half boots and neatly stowed them under her bed, hiding the wet toes under her counterpane. Then she climbed back into bed and rang for a maid.

She forgot about the spray of blooms that she brought from the garden until a young girl named Margaret appeared. The first thing she said, after a proper curtsy, was "What lovely flowers, miss!"

"Yes, aren't they beautiful?" Gabby said cheerfully. "Did you say your name was Margaret? That's such an English name. We don't have flowers like this in India. This came from a pudding-pipe tree, which sounds so English as well, doesn't it?"

Enchanted by Gabby's friendly eyes, Margaret bustled about straightening up the room and building up a fire. She didn't even notice Gabby's wet boots, although she tucked them under her arm to be cleaned and polished. And she didn't think twice about the newly picked flowers now residing in a glass by the young mistress's bed. She'd never met a gentry lady who was so friendly and all. Why, she treated her exactly as if she, Margaret, were a friend of hers.

By the time Gabby appeared in the breakfast room holding Phoebe by the hand, Margaret had coaxed Gabby's hair into smooth curls and confined them away from her face with a bandeau.

To Quill's intense irritation, Gabby's face lit up when she saw that Peter was in the breakfast chamber.

"Good morning, Peter!" she said happily. And then, "Hello, Quill."

"Good morning, Miss Jerningham, Miss Phoebe," Peter responded, rather more coolly. Mornings were never Peter's favorite time of day. But he felt it behooved him to wrench himself out of bed at this untimely hour in order to escort his betrothed to a mantua-maker. He'd slay himself if any of his friends glimpsed his future wife in those appalling garments she affected.

Peter waited until Gabby and Phoebe had been given breakfast by the footman. "After you break your fast, I shall escort you to the establishment of Madame Carême," he announced.

"How lovely," Gabby said, helping herself lavishly to more jelly. "Do you know, this is the most delicious toast I have ever eaten in my life. What kind of jelly is this, Phillip?"

To Peter's horror, he realized that Gabby was addressing the footman. And the said footman was smiling back at her as if they were equals. "It is blackberry jelly, miss."

Phillip snapped back to attention against the wall, instinctively sensing Peter's infuriated eyes on him.

"Mmmm," Gabby said dreamily. "I *love* blackberry jelly. What do you think, Phoebe?"

Phoebe looked doubtfully at the jelly. "My ayah never let me have sugared things on my toast because they may make me fat. And then I could not get married."

"Your ayah was a tyrant! Try this, sweetheart."

Peter frowned. To his mind Gabby was the one who should be avoiding sugared things. It could just be the dress, of course, but she looked a wee bit plumper than was advisable, given the French style of clothing that was popular in London. Still, that was a topic he could bring up in private.

Gabby turned back to him, delicately licking her lower lip. Peter's frown darkened.

And Quill took one look at Gabby and got up abruptly, leaving the room without making a proper farewell. If even his brother noticed Gabby's uncivilized manners, it demonstrated that she truly was in need of correction.

"Is Madame Carême a friend of yours?"

"What?" For a moment Peter didn't follow Gabby's question.

"Madame Carême. You said we would visit her after breakfast."

"No. Madame Carême is a mantua-maker, a *modiste*, as they call them in France. She is considered the best in London. We must obtain a wardrobe for you at the earliest possible moment, so I have requested an appointment for a fitting."

"Oh, that's not a problem," Gabby replied comfortably. "We had twenty of these white gowns made up in India. I had them copied from a brand-new issue of *Le Beau Monde*. That's a magazine that discusses fashion," she explained.

"I am more than aware of *Le Beau Monde*," Peter said. He himself had been featured in its pages more than once. "However, that design does not suit you."

"It doesn't?" Gabby felt a tugging at her sleeve and looked down into Phoebe's imploring eyes. Suddenly she remembered how much misery Phoebe's short skirts were causing her.

"All right," she agreed. "May Phoebe accompany us to Madame Carême's establishment? Perhaps we shall both order some new garments."

Peter agreed. He rather liked Phoebe. She was a child who seemed to know her place, and although she should, by all rights, be in the schoolroom, she was handling the unexpected pleasure of eating with adults with composure. He noted with approval that she had had several bites of blackberry jelly and then put her toast to the side. A lady is never too young to pay attention to her figure. Gabby, on the other hand, seemed to be eating her third or fourth piece of toast.

He couldn't resist. "Do you think it advisable to eat quite so much jellied toast?" He himself had had a spare breakfast, merely a cup of tea and a slice or two of a late apple. Quill, of course, ate like a peasant. He always had. Peter delicately added a trifle more sugar to his tea, taking care not to tinkle the spoon against the bone china of his cup.

Gabby looked at the toast in her hand with surprise and then put it to the side. "Thank you for the advice," she said, smiling at him.

Well, at least she's amenable, Peter thought. Perhaps he would be able to transform her. Like a work of art.

"I should never have known that blackberry jelly makes one ill if one eats too much," Gabby continued. "Does it give you a stomachache or"—she paused—"a different sort of problem?"

Peter choked on his tea. He cast a quick look at the footman, but Phillip's face was carefully schooled to utter calm. Peter decided not to answer that particular question.

"If you are quite finished, I shall order the carriage," he said, as his gaze deliberately slid over her head.

Gabby chewed on her lip. Was it just her imagination, or did both Dewland brothers have conversational impediments? Then her brow cleared. It was likely that blackberry jelly caused a digestive problem. One could not imagine Peter uttering an indelicacy.

She carefully folded her napkin and placed it on the table.

GABBY'S INTRODUCTION TO the establishment of Madame Carême was a shock to everyone concerned. As a stiff-rumped butler ushered them into a pale golden-colored audience chamber, Madame Carême herself appeared from an inner door and effusively greeted Peter. In fact, they seemed to be close friends, and within seconds Peter was lavishly complimenting her on the ravishing ensemble that someone named Lady Holland had worn to the duke's birthday the previous day. Madame Carême appeared not to have noticed Gabby's presence beyond a nod of greeting. And Phoebe might have been invisible.

Gabby sighed and looked about. One side of the room was bedecked with mirrors. Phoebe was sitting primly in a chair next to the maid who had accompanied them, so Gabby wandered over to the mirrors. To her amusement, she found that they were arranged in a kind of three-way style so that a person standing before them could see her front and both sides at the same time.

As she looked into the mirrors, Madame Carême and Peter came up behind her. Madame Carême gave her a much nicer smile than she had at first and took her hand. "I must apologize," she said. "I had no idea that you were Monsieur Dewland's affianced bride."

Gabby smiled back. It was nice to know that Peter was so esteemed.

"Your future husband has the taste of an angel," Madame Carême was saying. "His dress is always tasteful, and yet it has that touch of fantasy, of the pleasant creation, that turns a toilette from merely customary to brilliant."

Gabby blinked and looked at Peter, who was also reflected three ways in the mirrors. His clothing seemed to be neat and dark. In fact, she much preferred his dress today to the rather gaudy embroidery and gold lace that he had worn to court. Madame Carême seemed to be waiting for her to say something, so she said, rather weakly, "Indeed, Peter is very elegant."

"Elegant!" Madame Carême's accent thickened. "You can have no conception, Miss Jerningham! Monsieur Dewland has explained to me that you have just arrived in England— but you are marrying the man who *establishes* male fashion in London. If your betrothed chooses a single-breasted white waistcoat in the evening, you can be sure that most gentlemen will wear precisely the same garment the following evening."

"You exaggerate, my dear Madame Carême," Peter broke in. "You do me too much grace."

"I am French," Madame Carême replied loftily. "I have no need to exaggerate. I speak the truth, always. There was a time when you were younger, my dear monsieur, when it was not clear who would dominate gentlemen's fashions. As I said, you were young. But now that you have come into your full powers—well, I would defy anyone to go against your dictates."

Gabby looked round-eyed at Peter.

"Madame Carême is inflating my small influence with the *ton*," he declared with a sweeping bow, pressing his lips to the very tips of the Frenchwoman's fingers. "All I can say is that the depth of your compliment is returned by the fact that I am entrusting my future bride to you, Madame Carême, to no one but you!"

"Yes," Madame Carême said, turning back to Gabby.

Her face was not quite as happy as it had been a moment ago. She looked Gabby up and down from the top of her head to the tips of her half boots.

"It will be a challenge," Peter said persuasively. "A challenge such as only the very top *modiste* in all of London could take on."

"True." The *modiste* circled Gabby, as if she were a tiger circling a goat.

"White is out of the question," Peter said.

"I shall have to give this a good deal of thought," Madame Carême announced. "I shall take a month, or perhaps even longer."

"We hoped for no less. May I ask the smallest of favors, my dear Madame?" Peter lowered his voice. "Have you any garment that might be quickly made over to fit Miss Jerningham? I am unable even to take my betrothed into the park for a drive. In fact, I ordered a closed carriage on the way to your establishment, as I am sure you will understand."

"An excellent precaution. I doubt that I can help you in an immediate sense with much beyond a day dress or two, my dear monsieur. I am afraid that Miss Jerningham is a trifle, a trifle—"

To Gabby's great pleasure, Madame Carême was interrupted before she could reveal the trifling problem that Gabby presented. The door swung open and in walked a gentlewoman accompanied by a maid.

"The Duchess of Gisle," intoned the butler, in a satisfied sort of way.

Madame Carême turned in a flash. "Your Grace! I had no idea that you had returned to London!"

Peter also rushed to her side, exclaiming happily.

Gabby watched enviously. This duchess undoubtedly presented Madame Carême with no trifling problems. Her gown looked to be made out of handkerchief cloth, and it was abundantly clear that the duchess's figure was as flawless as the rest of her.

Peter was chattering with greater animation than Gabby had ever seen on his face. She swallowed. Perhaps this beautiful duchess was the reason that Peter was reluctant to marry. Perhaps he was terribly in love with her and was even now pining away. They looked exquisite together— the duchess was just as polished and gleaming as was Peter. They would have had beautiful children.

And they seemed so intimate. Likely they were in love before the duchess was forced to marry another. Gabby had to blink away a sudden tear. How painful it must have been for Peter to watch his beloved marry someone else, probably an old, even a hunchbacked, duke!

Just as Gabby swallowed hard, imagining Peter's agonized face during the wedding, the duchess walked up to greet her. Gabby's romantic side had painted her in the last stages of grief, but common sense told her that the woman seemed to be glowing with happiness.

"How do you do?"

The duchess reached out her gloved hand, so Gabby took it, wondering whether she was supposed to shake it— or kiss it. She literally had no idea how one behaved toward duchesses. Perhaps she was supposed to curtsy? Finally she gave the duchess's hand a brief shake and dropped it.

"This is my betrothed," Peter was saying. "Miss Jerningham arrived from India only yesterday."

Gabby could tell that it was hard for him to introduce her, presumably because of her gown.

But Her Grace seemed to notice nothing wrong.

"I, too, just got off a ship! My husband and I are returning from Turkey. We have been traveling for almost a year, and I returned without a garment to my back." The duchess turned to Madame Carême with a smile. "That is why, dear Madame, I ventured to visit you without an appointment. I was desperate!"

She turned back to Gabby. "Please forgive me for interrupting your engagement with Madame, Miss Jerningham. Tell me, how are you finding London?"

Gabby responded despite herself to the duchess's merry blue eyes. "I like it very much," she said. "Although I have seen little of the city so far."

"Why don't we take a brief walk down Bond Street after your appointment is concluded? That is, if you do not have other plans."

Peter was stricken by the suggestion. Gabby could see that. He didn't want her to be seen around London until Madame Carême supplied her with better clothing.

"It seems I am to be Madame Carême's latest creation," Gabby said lightly. "I would not wish to ruin her reputation by being seen in this gown before she has had a chance to transform me."

Peter groaned silently, and Madame's eyebrows flew up. "There is little chance that anyone would mistake your gown for one of mine," she pointed out.

But the duchess looked understanding. "Surely it would not be amiss to take a brief drive in the park? If only because I have always had a foolish desire to see Calcutta, and I would love to hear your description of it."

For Her Grace, it seemed, anything was possible—except the appearance of Gabby's white dress in public. Within seconds Gabby had been whisked off to the inner recesses of Madame Carême's establishment and stripped of her clothing by Madame's assistants. They appeared to be somewhat surprised by Gabby's lack of a corset.

"My father doesn't believe in corsets," Gabby explained. "He thinks that women ought be able to dress themselves."

Madame shuddered at the thought. She stared at Gabby in the mirror. "We will try whalebones. I shall do my best," she said rather despondently.

"I am certain that you will turn me into a pink of the *ton*," Gabby said reassuringly.

"Nonsense—only gentlemen are pinks," Madame responded. But she seemed to cheer up, and then she cocked her head and said, "Of course!" With a snap of her fingers she sent away a girl, who returned with a flimsy dress in a dusky-orange color.

"I made it for the countess of Redingale," she confided. "But the silly girl is over a month late in requesting it. I believe that she overspent her allowance again. Giving the gown to you will teach her that she cannot trifle with the top *modiste* in London."

"Absolutely," Gabby said rather faintly. One of Madame's helpers was lacing her tightly into a corset. Her breasts were pushed up and out, and her waist became impossibly small. Gabby had a glimmer of hope. Perhaps Madame Carême's magic would remake her into a vision of sophisticated beauty.

Someone threw the walking dress over her head. It settled in a puff of muslin.

"Not terrible," Madame commented.

The gown had a high neck with an insert of brown velvet and faint brown stripes down the skirt. It was as unlike Gabby's starched white gown as possible, given that it moved in the faintest breath of air. The only thing keeping the skirt from floating up was the line of fur at the hem.

To Gabby's eyes, it positively screamed sophistication. "I—" Gabby took a small breath, all that was allowed given her tight corset. "I have always thought that orange was a pretty color, Madame."

"Orange! That is orange blossom, *not* orange! I do not compose in such a color," Madame Carême responded scornfully. "And the very best chinchilla fur around the hem," she added.

But Gabby was getting used to her sharp tongue. "My only fear is that there's a bit too much of me for this lovely gown." Gabby felt as if the whalebone corset was pushing her breasts up around her collarbone. The gown seemed to strain in the front section.

In a split second Madame had the girls snipping away under Gabby's arm and the dress was eased over her head again.

"Not right, not right," the *modiste* murmured to herself. She had taken to circling Gabby again. "I shall have to give it more thought. This color does not set off your hair to its best advantage, for example."

Gabby looked in the mirror. One of the girls was rapidly pinning her fallen hair back up on her head.

"And," Madame continued, "the skirt of the gown is too narrow for you."

Gabby couldn't see anything wrong with the gown, barring the fact that she could hardly breathe.

"We shall have to start a new fashion," Madame said. "For you, these French designs are not the best. And in order to be a match for Monsieur Dewland, you understand, you must be at the very pinnacle of fashion."

She seemed to be distressed, so Gabby tried to console her, although she herself couldn't see anything wrong with the gown. "Great achievements never come easily, Madame. Think of the person who first invented this infernal corset. It cannot have happened overnight, all the weaving and winding of whalebones, tapes, and cloth."

For the first time since she walked into the establishment,

Gabby had the sense that Madame Carême looked at *her*—Gabby—not at her clothing. Madame looked struck for a moment.

Gabby twinkled at her. She was starting to rather like the irascible Frenchwoman. "I can see it," she continued. "You shall transform me from a . . . a mouse into a queen, and when I enter the ballroom on Peter's arm, all the London folk will fall to the side and gasp. They will have one question, and one question only, on their minds: *Who* made Miss Jerningham's gown?"

Gabby was getting quite caught up in her own story. She lowered her voice. "I won't tell them immediately," she promised. "I shall keep them poised in anticipation, longing to know the name of the *modiste* who effected my transformation."

The corner of Madame's mouth twitched. "You don't give a bean about clothing, do you, Miss Jerningham?"

"No," Gabby admitted. "But I am willing to try to care, given that it seems important to Peter."

"There is one great truth to fashion," Madame said frankly. "If a woman has no sense of presence, the most beautiful clothing in the world will do nothing for her. I have clothed a debutante in an exquisite creation and known—*known*—that men would pay no attention to her that evening. But you—well, men do pay attention to you, do they not?"

"I have no idea," Gabby replied. "My father rarely allowed me to encounter members of the male gender. And it's really of no consequence, given that I am to marry Peter."

"Yes," Madame said. Her face seemed troubled for a second. "Be that as it may," she said, "I shall make a new fashion for you. And I guarantee, Miss Jerningham, that I will make the men of London beg to kiss the tips of your slippers."

"That sounds very pleasant," Gabby observed, grinning.

Madame gave one of her rare snorts of laughter. "You are an Original, Miss Jerningham. I am feeling very, very different about this commission than I did earlier."

"Thank you," Gabby said.

WHEN PETER SAW his future bride walking before him out of Madame Carême's establishment, her arm tucked into that of the Duchess of Gisle, he felt as if his life were passing before his eyes.

Gabby looked like a pumpkin: a round, round pumpkin. The cloth of her gown was ready to split around her chest. In fact, Peter was mortified to find out just how much of a chest the girl had. Women shouldn't be so well-endowed. He shuddered to think what his future wife would look like in an evening gown, without fabric to cover up all that flesh. As Gabby walked before him, her skirts bunched at the hips, and the fur at the bottom of her gown swung back and forth. Her stride is too long, Peter thought. She does not walk like a lady.

What's more, rather than asking the duchess polite questions or showing any recognition that she was speaking to one of the most important ladies in the *ton*, Gabby was chatting about India. India! Peter's skin crawled. There was nothing more tedious than people who talked about India. Plenty of men around London were available to do just that. The last thing one wanted from a woman was more wearisome details.

His future wife clearly had no sense of nuance. She had no grasp of the consequence and hierarchy that structured London society. He shuddered to think what his friends would make of her and how they would laugh at him behind his back.

Gabby was still chattering away. Oh, God, she seemed to be *lecturing* Her Grace on the grammatical structure of the Hindi language. Peter ground his teeth silently. His throat felt bitter.

He couldn't do it.

He could not marry this talkative, frumpy, plump woman who had no social graces and no instinct. It didn't matter how much money she had. By God, he could more easily transform a merchant's daughter into a lady.

Cold fingers crept up Peter's spine. This awkward girl would effortlessly pull down the delicate social structure on which his happiness depended, and she would have no idea what she was doing. It wasn't fair. It wasn't fair and it wasn't right.

He'd spent six years building his position in London society, befriending the high and the low. Peter thought little of those who hoped to reach the upper echelons by trodding on those below or by making cruel remarks. He was unfailingly kind, and he had accepted defeats with grace. For example, there was the intimate gathering that Bladdington gave for Prinny's forty-third birthday last year, to which he was not invited. And even though Peter's chest burned, he was perfectly amiable with Bladdington the next time he saw him, because everyone told him that Prinny had loudly demanded to know where Dewland was and said the party was no fun without him.

Bile rose up his throat again, and Peter clenched his teeth. Father had no right to demand such a thing.

His parents were due to arrive from Bath in the afternoon to greet their future daughter-in-law. He had always found it difficult to stand up to his father, but this time he would simply have to do so.

He could not go through with this marriage.

Chapter 5

GABBY, PETER, AND PHOEBE returned to Dewland House to find that an elegantly slung traveling carriage had just drawn up.

"It's my new mama come to fetch me!" Phoebe cried.

Peter looked at the little girl sympathetically. He had to remember to locate that woman—Mrs. Ewing, wasn't it? "I'm afraid not, Phoebe. That is my parents' traveling coach. They will have returned from Bath to welcome Miss Jerningham."

Gabby drew Phoebe up against her side in a hug. "We will find your mama," she said. "And meanwhile, Phoebe, just think about all those lovely clothes that Madame Carême is making for you!" For Phoebe, too, had ordered a complete wardrobe.

Phoebe's eyes brightened. "Mademoiselle Lucile said that I would have a gown with pin tucks and puff sleeves."

"Absolutely," Gabby replied. "Why, it's just as well that Peter has not located your mama yet. Because I would like the pleasure of your company, and your new garments will not be delivered for some weeks."

In Phoebe's eyes shone the passion of a young woman who already understood—even at the tender age of five—the importance of a first impression. She had had a lovely time looking at pictures of children's clothing in *La Belle Assemblée* with Mademoiselle Lucile, one of Madame Carême's assistants. "I shall wear the gown with puff sleeves," she said. "And then my mama will love me more."

Gabby frowned and was about to say something, but the footman opened the coach door. She was just a bit nervous to meet the viscount and viscountess. What if they were as disappointed with her as Peter seemed to be?

But there was no viscount. And within a few minutes of entering the sitting room, it became clear that she might never meet the viscount at all.

"He slept and slept," the viscountess was saying, weeping and wringing her hands. "When I finally woke him, Thurlow looked at me, but I could tell that he didn't know who I was."

Quill was standing in the middle of the room, saying nothing. Peter turned white and sank into a chair.

"Last night he did recognize me," the viscountess continued. "But the doctors say he is unlikely to recover the use of his limbs. And worst of all, he doesn't seem to be able to speak! Although this morning, when I explained that I had to go to London for a day and tell you what had happened, I'm sure that he heard me. Because I asked him to close his eyes if he understood, and he did. He blinked his eyes."

She started weeping harder, and Quill moved over and gave her an awkward hug. Kitty held out her free arm, and as Peter moved toward her, Gabby turned and fled from the room. There was something about seeing Kitty Dewland cling to her two sons that made tears come to her eyes. She had tried her entire life to please her father, but he would no more think of hugging her than of complimenting her.

Gabby swallowed hard and climbed the stairs to her bedchamber. The truth was that if her father had an attack and couldn't speak, she would probably be grateful. That was a terrible, terrible thought.

I would have taken care of him, Gabby thought defensively. But even as she pictured the tender care she would have given her father, she knew it would have been just another attempt to gain love. And it would have failed. If there was one lesson Gabby had learned from her childhood, it was that no amount of wooing could make someone love you.

Gabby rang the bell, and Margaret appeared after a moment. "I'm to be your lady's maid," Margaret said happily. "Mrs. Farsalter confirmed it."

"How lovely," Gabby said. "Then for goodness sake, Margaret, help me loosen this infernal corset."

Margaret looked surprised, but she began to undo the small buttons that ran up the back of the orange walking dress.

The problem was that when Margaret had unlaced the corset enough so that Gabby could take a deep breath, the gown pulled even tighter in the front.

Margaret looked at it dubiously. "Mrs. Farsalter is a dab hand with a needle. Perhaps we should see if the seams can be taken out."

"Madame Carême already did that. I'll just wear this shawl, Margaret. See? If I keep it draped over my front, no one can see that the bodice is a little tight."

"Are you quite sure, miss? Because we could tighten your corset just a trifle."

"Absolutely not. I'm quite certain that we will be taking

luncheon at home." Gabby reckoned that Peter was the only one in the household who might notice the inconvenient tautness across her breasts.

Margaret nodded. "Given the master's condition, I expect you'll be marrying right away. Perhaps Mr. Peter will obtain a special license."

Gabby looked at her curiously.

"I didn't mean to be presumptuous, miss. Mr. Codswallop had an uncle who had such an attack, and he didn't linger. The family will go into mourning."

"Oh, of course," Gabby murmured. Presumably Margaret was saying that one couldn't marry when in mourning. Yet more English rules that she had never learned. For some reason the idea of marrying Peter by special license wasn't quite as exciting as she would have thought a week ago.

She shook off the feeling. It was time for luncheon, and she was absolutely ravenous.

The meal was a strained affair. "I must return to Bath," Kitty Dewland explained to her young guest, "but I have sent a note asking my dear cousin, Lady Sylvia, to act as a chaperone in my absence."

Kitty gained a spark of animation when Quill murmured something under his breath about her choice of chaperone. "Lady Sylvia is of the highest character," Kitty snapped. She added, "Besides, it is very difficult to obtain a chaperone now, when the Little Season is upon us!"

And then she burst into tears. "Oh, if Thurlow is not able to take his seat in Parliament, it will positively break his heart!"

Gabby was very pleased to find that Peter was endlessly kind to his mother, rubbing her hand and murmuring in her ear. Quill sat silently across from them, and after the third or fourth eruption of tears, Gabby could tell that he was becoming irritated. And yet . . . poor Lady Dewland. It was clear that she had never contemplated the idea of her husband being incapacitated, and the pain was almost too much for her.

Halfway through luncheon, Kitty clutched Peter's wrist. "I cannot sit here for another moment," she declared, her voice breaking. "All I can see is my Thurlow's face, waiting for me to return." She stood up. "I am delighted to have met you, Gabrielle. I trust we can have a long coze the moment Thurlow is back on his feet. Why, I shall likely be gone only a few days."

Gabby murmured agreement, although it was abundantly clear to her that the viscount would be very lucky to speak again, let alone walk.

"You cannot return to Bath alone, Mama," Peter said. Both men had leapt to their feet when Kitty stood up. "I shall accompany you and stay as long as you need me."

"Oh, no, I could never allow that," Kitty said in a distressed tone. "Why, dear Gabrielle would be most inconvenienced if you left at this moment!"

Peter and Gabby spoke at the same moment. "He must accompany you," Gabby said earnestly. It was clear that Kitty and Peter shared a special relationship.

"I could not think of being away from you during this terrible ordeal," Peter said.

"But your friends," Kitty protested feebly. "They must think it very odd if your betrothed is in London and you are in Bath."

"They certainly will not," Peter said, with the utmost confidence of someone who knew that his sense of social protocol could never be questioned. "My place is by your side." He pressed her hand.

Kitty smiled at him tremulously. "I shouldn't. Oh, I shouldn't."

Only Quill frowned. "I am persuaded that Peter should

be here with Gabby. After all, they are to be married, and she only just arrived from India. It does not sound as if Father is in immediate danger, and I can easily accompany you to Bath for a few days."

Gabby shot him a look. "Lady Dewland, Peter must accompany you and stay as long as you need him," she said warmly. "I insist. I will not allow Peter to stay here when he could be of so much comfort to you." Obviously Peter would be much more of a consolation to his mother than Quill would be.

"At any rate," Peter said, "Gabby is not prepared to enter society. We ordered a new wardrobe for her this morning, but Madame Carême estimates it will be over a month until she is able to deliver it. Given Lady Sylvia's presence, no one can question the propriety of Gabby staying here in London."

"In that case," Kitty said with obvious relief, "perhaps I will accept your escort, Peter. Are you quite sure that you won't be disappointed, Gabrielle dear? I am certain that Thurlow will be better in a matter of a week or so, and I should hate to injure our relationship in any way. I am *so* looking forward to having you as my daughter-in-law!"

Gabby leaned forward and gave her a kiss on the cheek. "Peter is yours for as long as you need him, Lady Dewland."

Kitty laid her hand against Gabby's cheek for a moment. "We are lucky to have you, my dear. I can see that you will be a great comfort to me." And that was the closest that the viscountess ever came to acknowledging that perhaps Thurlow would not be out of his bed in a week.

Gabby watched Lady Dewland and Peter set off in the traveling coach—after some eleven bags of Peter's had been piled precariously on top—with just a touch of envy. It wasn't that she resented Lady Dewland's delight in Peter's company, but she did slightly resent Peter's delight in his mother's company. In the past two days, he had never looked at her with such glowing attention.

Because you haven't earned it, Gabby told herself. He loves his mother, and he will grow to love you.

Quill was standing sturdily on the pavement beside her. He took in the slight droop to Gabby's lower lip in an instant.

"What would you like to do this afternoon?" he asked, amazing himself. He never took excursions in the middle of the day. He had far too much work to do. Even now he could feel a rising tension due to the stacks of reports awaiting him. But he disliked seeing Gabby look dimmed by his brother's absence. At least she showed no sign of tears. Quill couldn't abide women who cried all the time.

"I should like to take a little trip around London," Gabby replied. "But you needn't accompany me, Quill. I shall hire a hack. I believe that is the proper term?" Gabby had questioned Margaret about London conveyances earlier in the day.

"Out of the question," Quill said. "I will take you wherever you wish to go."

"In fact, I would prefer to take this particular trip by myself."

"No."

Gabby waited, but nothing more seemed to be forthcoming.

"As I said," she repeated politely, "I would prefer to take a trip by myself. May I borrow your carriage?"

Quill sighed. "Gabby, a lady does not travel anywhere— ever—on her own. When you know your way around London, you may take the carriage on a brief shopping excursion or to make a call. But that is the extent of an English lady's solitary travel."

"Thank goodness I am not fully English," Gabby replied amiably. "Perhaps it is my French side that makes me so certain that I shall safely spend an afternoon on my own. I would not wish to keep you from your work."

Quill, who had just been remembering the papers awaiting his signature, instantly changed his mind. "I have no work scheduled for this afternoon. I will accompany you."

Gabby had the sudden thought that perhaps Quill didn't want to be alone, given the saddening news about his father. It was unfortunate that his mother showed such a clear preference for one son over the other! Likely Quill was feeling neglected.

She turned and walked back into the house, absent-mindedly handing her cashmere shawl to Codswallop.

Quill swallowed. What kind of gown had Gabby obtained from Madame Carême? He had never seen such an enticing garment in his life. It looked like something a courtesan might wear. From the back it perfectly outlined the rounded curve of her bottom. A curve that was longing, begging, to be cupped in Quill's hand.

And the bodice of the gown was even worse. The flimsy muslin seemed to have been molded to her chest.

"I have located Mrs. Emily Ewing," he said abruptly.

"How splendid! Does she live in London?"

"Yes."

"She must not have received the letter sent from India. I shall write her a note directly," Gabby exclaimed. "We can't simply appear at her doorstep with a child and such unwelcome news about her sister."

Quill just nodded. "I should like to know where you plan to go this afternoon."

Gabby was stubbornly silent.

Quill moved over and tipped up her chin. Standing this

close to her, he could smell an enticing, drifting smell of jasmine flowers.

"Gabby."

In his quiet voice was a command. Gabby realized that. And it was no use asking something as foolish as *Can I trust you?* Obviously she could trust Quill. Her large, silent, future brother-in-law was the very essence of trustworthiness.

"It's a trifling errand only," she said desperately.

"Gabby."

"All right. I would like to visit Hoare's Bank. My father gave me a letter——"

"Ladies do not enter Hoare's Bank," Quill explained. "The letter will be delivered, and a representative of the bank will visit our house."

"My father told me to never trust minor associates," Gabby insisted. "I should like to speak to Sir Richard Hoare myself. And I can hardly request that the director of the bank journey to our house."

"Then I shall accompany you," Quill said. "You must understand, Gabby, that a woman's reputation is her most important asset——" He broke off. Gabby had clearly stopped listening.

"Gabby, are you attending me?"

Quill was standing just in front of her, delivering his little lecture. Gabby had the oddest wish that he would put his arms around her. She must be demented. Hoping for an embrace from her future brother-in-law? It was just that— Gabby's common sense came to the rescue. Quill was an uncommonly handsome man. His eyes made her feel weak in the knees and warm in the belly.

The problem, Gabby rationalized, is that Father never allowed me to have anything to do with men. So now I am overcome by the species in general. And for the first time, she wished that Peter hadn't traveled to Bath. Because she had never been kissed by a man.

Quill had paused and was waiting for her to reply.

Gabby nervously chewed on her lower lip. The look in his eyes couldn't be described as amusement, precisely.

"Gabby," Quill said, his voice dark with—with something.

She swayed a bit and his large hands steadied her shoulders. In a second she could be in his arms, Gabby realized.

"I . . . I . . ." She fell silent, struck by a fiery wave of rebellion. She *wanted* a kiss. She didn't want to be an unkissed person for one more second.

"My mother died at my birth, and my father is not a demonstrative man," she said, looking at Quill's lips.

"Yes?" Quill's thumbs had begun a small massage just at the base of Gabby's collarbone.

Gabby shivered.

Quill was well-aware that Gabby had not told him the truth about her afternoon's errand. Hoare's Bank indeed. There was something about Gabby's eyes that gave her away when she was fibbing. Just now those beautiful eyes were looking at him in a way that made his blood rage in his veins. She couldn't mean that look. It was not an innocent look.

And then she swayed toward him, and he smelled jasmine again. Without a second's thought, Quill's mouth came down on Gabby's lips as softly as a dandelion clock floats to the ground, as sweetly as a mother's lips brush the head of her babe.

Gabby closed her eyes and stood stock-still, arms at her sides.

She tasted better than she smelled. Quill pulled her closer. His hands slid down toward the magnificent curve of her bottom.

"Put your arms around my neck, Gabby," he whispered.

"All right," Gabby said, sounding surprised. "This is very enjoyable," she whispered back.

"Be quiet, Gabby." Quill's deep voice sent a tremor down her spine. And when she opened her mouth to respond to him, he took advantage of her open lips. Tenderness was replaced by a fierce demand, by a craving, hungry request.

Gabby lost her impulse to speak. Her mind went utterly blank, replaced for the first time in her life by her body's demands. A sigh passed between them. She wound her arms around Quill's neck and held on, allowing his ravaging mouth to send flames up her back. She melted against his chest, pressing herself feverishly into the kiss, shamelessly reveling in the feeling of his hard body against hers.

Tenderness was a thing of the past. He crushed her mouth under his. Hips, hands, tongue made demands that sent liquid fire between her legs and stole the breath from her chest.

"Gabby, shall we——" The sounds of his own hoarse voice, strained with longing, woke Quill as if from a deep sleep. "Oh, my God." He snatched his hands away from Gabby's body. He lurched backward and then turned around, taking a deep breath. "I'll summon a carriage."

Gabby swayed a bit as Quill's big, warm hands fell away. Her whole body raced with a fiery liquor.

"Need we leave . . . immediately?"

Gabby's husky voice was more seductive than that of a practiced coquette. Quill turned around slowly, almost afraid to look at her again. "I should shoot myself."

"Why? Don't you enjoy kissing?"

Quill closed his eyes for a moment. Gabby was the only woman he'd ever met whose every emotion spoke in her eyes. Pleasure shot through his groin at what he read there: pure, unadulterated longing. Longing for him, for Quill.

She walked over and stood just before him again. Then she wound her arms around his neck and put her lips against his. She breathed against his lower lip, and Quill felt as if he must—*must*—bend her backward, sweep her forward, carry her outside. Anything to press that luscious body against his again.

God forgive him, the promise of her cherry-dark lips was too much. Quill pulled Gabby sharply against his body and took her mouth. It was different this time. Gabby knew something of kissing now. She opened those beautiful lips, strained toward him, uttered a little strangled moan in the back of her throat, met his tongue with her own.

And so they danced, a kissing dance. Until Quill realized that he had shaken all the pins out of Gabby's coiffure, and that he was sliding his hands through the indescribable silk of her hair. Realized that his kisses had become a fierce possession, a sexual dance, and—rather more slowly—that Gabby's hands were also tangled in his hair and that her body was matching the sinuous movement of his hips.

Worse.

The door handle leading to the hallway moved against his back.

He broke the kiss, pulled her arms from his neck, and barked, "Go away," at the closed door.

Gabby looked up at him in wonder and smiled a glimmering, shining smile of discovery and pleasure.

"Thank you."

"For what?"

"I had no idea that kisses were so . . . so much fun," Gabby said, her voice still husky. "Fun is not the right word. Fun is pale compared to this. To kissing." She moved toward him again and Quill held out his hand, stopping her. She smiled without resentment.

"Now I see why my father never let me spend any time with gentlemen. And I am truly sorry that Peter went to Bath with your mother!"

The world stilled for a moment.

"Oh, yes, of course," Quill managed. How had Gabby managed to grow up with such ignorance of men and women?

"Gabby, you must *not* request kisses from men other than—than your future husband," Quill said hoarsely. He couldn't seem to mention Peter's name.

Her eyes cleared and then danced. "I should never, never have guessed, Quill. About kissing, I mean."

"Ah," he said, rather faintly. He needed a brandy, although it was only early afternoon. "You'd best go upstairs and reorder your hair." He wrenched open the door. "I will accompany you to Hoare's Bank later this afternoon."

Gabby watched him leave as if the Furies were after him, with a pang of regret. Obviously he was sorry he'd kissed her. With a sigh, she dismissed Quill from her mind.

She went upstairs, her eyes dreamy. Perhaps by the time Peter returned, she would have her new wardrobe from Madame Carême, and Peter would look at her with the same sort of fiery appreciation that she glimpsed in Quill. Sternly, she brought to mind the many sermons she had heard regarding the evils of lust.

But they had never conveyed to her how . . . how indescribably lovely kissing was. For some reason it was difficult to imagine Peter jerking her into his arms and almost devouring her as Quill had. No doubt kissing Peter would be a gentler business, Gabby thought.

Up in her chamber, she took out the miniature of Peter

that his father had sent her. The sight of his smiling, sweet eyes and soft brown curls steadied her.

Gabby smiled. Marriage was going to be very enjoyable at this rate. She couldn't wait for Peter to return!

LADY SYLVIA ARRIVED an hour or so later. Gabby had just concluded a satisfactory interview with Codswallop. Not finding him in the front hallway, she had descended into the servants' quarters to make absolutely certain that he was not injured by his tumble onto the parlor floor. And she had even swallowed her pride and apologized for fibbing about it.

"Quill knows everything," she told Codswallop earnestly, "and he assures me that Viscount Dewland will never let you go."

Codswallop gave a little half bow and an utterly understanding smile. There wasn't a servant in the house who wasn't aware of Peter's finicky ways; he couldn't blame the young lady for being taken aback. "Now, Miss Jerningham," Codswallop said comfortingly. "We'll think no more about it. As far as I'm concerned, 'twas an angel that tripped me up and made me drop the teapot."

"No, it wasn't," Gabby said penitently. "I'm a butter-fingers, and I always have been."

"An angel's foot got in your way," Codswallop said. "That's what my mother used to tell us when we returned to the house with scrapes on our knees."

Gabby smiled. "Your mother sounds very kind."

By the time Codswallop ushered her back through the braise door into the main hallway, they were the best of friends.

As Gabby walked through the servants' door, she realized

immediately that her chaperone, Lady Sylvia, had arrived. And what a chaperone she was! Gabby's mouth almost fell open and she paused with her back to the door.

Kitty's cousin, Lady Sylvia, was as unlike Quill's mournful, emotional mother as possible. At the moment she was guffawing in response to something Quill had said to her. She was wearing a bright pink, beribboned gown with a startlingly low bodice. And she was surrounded by three yapping dogs, all of whom had matching pink bows adorning their waving topknots.

Yet for all the femininity of her attire, Lady Sylvia's face looked more like a man's than a woman's, to Gabby's mind. And she was smoking a cheroot.

Then Quill looked over his shoulder at Gabby. "Here is Miss Jerningham now," he announced. "Lady Sylvia, may I introduce my brother's betrothed, Miss Gabrielle Jerningham? Miss Jerningham, this is Lady Sylvia Breaknettle."

Lady Sylvia glanced at Gabby and then back at Quill. "What was the gel doin' in the servants' quarters, Dewland? You aren't trying to make a purse out of a sow's ear, are you? I don't approve of associating with the help." Her voice was a squawking, nasal bellow, although it had a shrewd note to it.

"Well? Cat got yer tongue, gel?"

Gabby suddenly got her bearings and bobbed a curtsy. "I was consulting with Mrs. Farsalter regarding the menus, my lady."

"Got the air of a servant," Lady Sylvia proclaimed.

Gabby felt pink creeping up the back of her neck.

"That the best curtsy you can do, gel?"

"My name is Gabrielle Jerningham," Gabby said. "I was also taught *la révérence en arrière.*" She swept into a low curtsy. Then she straightened. "However, I was instructed to do so only in the presence of royalty."

Lady Sylvia smirked at the slight edge in Gabby's tone. "Well, at least you've got some backbone, gel."

Gabby gave up on the idea of Lady Sylvia using her proper name. Clearly she considered her "gel," and nothing else.

"These are my Three Graces," Lady Sylvia said, gesturing at the dogs with her burning cheroot so that little wisps of blue smoke flew around her head.

"Charming," Gabby murmured.

"Hope, Truth, and—" Lady Sylvia peered around. "Oh, yes, that one is Beauty."

Everyone looked where she pointed. Beauty had just squatted under one of the chairs lining the entryway. A small trickle was creeping across the marble floor.

"She's too intelligent to pay mind to me," Lady Sylvia said blandly. "All three dogs are French, and they behave just like Frenchmen. Decorative but peevish."

Codswallop coughed politely. "Will the Three Graces be housed in your chamber, my lady?"

"Naturally, Codswallop. And you don't have to take up the carpet. Beauty is only letting us know that she is disgruntled about the carriage ride. She'll settle down soon enough."

Codswallop gestured to a footman, who bent down and tried to pick up Beauty. She promptly bit him on the hand.

"Burn my breeches!" Lady Sylvia exclaimed. "Never had ought to do with dogs, Codswallop? They won't let a stranger pick them up. Too intelligent for that."

Given the expression on the footman's face, it was clear that he would have liked to boot the intelligent dog out the door. But Lady Sylvia had swiveled about and was hallooing through the open door.

"Dessie? Dessie, get in here, gel! That's my companion,"

she explained to Gabby. "Desdemona, she's called. She'll take charge of the little dears."

A cheerful-looking woman entered the door. "I've sent your trunks around to the back, my lady. I don't believe they'll fit in the front door."

"Look what's happened, Dessie. Naughty little Beauty has made a statement on the floor."

Dessie bent down and picked up the dog in question and briskly swatted it on the bottom. "You know better than that."

Gabby watched, fascinated, as Beauty's topknot wilted and her small face drooped.

"Those dogs won't give me the time of day," Lady Sylvia said with approval, "but they positively adore Dessie. Good thing too. I don't mind if Beauty makes a water closet out of Dewland's front hall, but she'd be mincemeat if she tried that in my house."

Gabby choked back a giggle. Dessie had gathered all three dogs in her arms and was heading up the stairs behind Codswallop, whose rigid back indicated strong disapproval.

Quill cleared his throat. "May I escort you to your chamber, Lady Sylvia?" He held out his arm.

"Course you may," she answered. "Reckon I'll never be old enough to turn down a gentleman's escort to my chambers." Lady Sylvia looked around for somewhere to put her cheroot. When she didn't glimpse an appropriate receptacle, she tossed it straight out the open door.

Gabby watched as the smoking cheroot arced out the door and landed on the white marble steps. This time she couldn't stop herself, and a little chortle of laughter escaped her.

Lady Sylvia looked at her sharply. "Not as missish as

you look, are you, gel? I can't stand a milk-and-water miss. I haven't done any of this chaperoning business, since Lionel and I never had progeny. Only said I'd do it as a promise to Kitty. Poor thing's liable to cry up an ocean over Thurlow's latest attack.

"You, gel!" Lady Sylvia said suddenly, turning her head just as she began climbing the stairs.

"Yes, Lady Sylvia?" Gabby replied.

"I shall retire to my chamber for a rest. But I will join you for supper, and I do not wish to see that appalling gown at the table. You're too big for it; any fool could see that. If you want to dress like a light woman, I'm not going to stop you. I fancy a lady should exhibit her assets." She gave her own magnificent chest a proud glance. "But you might as well get yerself some clothes that fit. Don't see that my job as a chaperone extends to dressing you."

Gabby colored and looked down at her front. She'd completely forgotten that she meant to keep a shawl clutched around her shoulders.

Lady Sylvia cackled. "Quill has probably been enjoying it, gel. No harm in that. But I'd hate to see that bodice give out over the first course. Might put me off my feed." She elbowed Quill. "Expect you don't share my feelings, eh?"

Quill gave Gabby a long-suffering look. Lady Sylvia had always been a liability to the family, and if she hadn't had one of the longest lineages in England, likely no one would have anything to do with her.

Gabby curtsied again and Quill accompanied Lady Sylvia up the stairs.

"Nice to see you on your feet, Erskine," Lady Sylvia said jovially, as they walked down the corridor toward her chamber. "It's a pity, a real pity, what happened to you on that horse. Mind you, it could have been worse. You'll have to tell me why your father has the heiress marrying young

Peter, though. Yer the eldest. I don't mind telling you, it's causing a bit of a stir amongst the gabsters. Wondering if you survived that accident unscathed."

Quill shuddered inwardly. He had no wish to air his incapacities with the forthright Lady Sylvia.

"I take it your silence means they're right," Lady Sylvia said after a moment.

"No," Quill corrected her. "I could consummate a marriage, but it is unclear whether there would be children."

"Ah. Well, I'm sorry about that, Erskine. Always thought you were the best of the litter. Mind you, Lionel and I never regretted marrying, even when children didn't appear. But I don't suppose we would have done it if we'd known.

"I won't tell a soul," Lady Sylvia went on, patting Quill's arm not unkindly.

He pushed open the door to her chamber to find the Three Graces sitting in a docile line, watching as Desdemona directed a maid to unpack a trunk. Quill bowed and murmured something about seeing Lady Sylvia at supper. She smiled farewell, obviously unaware that he was stiff with anger.

Quill walked down one flight of stairs and closed his study door behind him, belatedly realizing that he was deep in furious plans to marry simply to spite the gossips. What good would that do? He'd have to be remarkably lucky to father a child. And meanwhile, those same scandalmongers would rattle on about his marital failings, likely making his wife more miserable than she already would be, given that she had married a cripple who couldn't dance, or ride to the horses—or bed her on a regular basis.

Quill bit back a curse and headed toward the garden. Sometimes there was nothing to do but exhaust himself, pacing the brick paths until the pain in his leg was enough to stifle his bitterness.

FROM HER BEDCHAMBER WINDOW, Gabby watched her future brother-in-law as he walked down a garden path. She almost turned to join him—but something about his savage stride cautioned her. She waited for him at supper, but at length Codswallop appeared with a message that Mr. Dewland asked to be excused, as his leg was troubling him.

Chapter 6

THE FOLLOWING MORNING Quill strode into the breakfast room to find Gabby and Phoebe eating alone.

"Lady Sylvia has not yet risen," Gabby said in answer to Quill's questioning look. Then she added, "Goodness! It's happening to me!"

Quill frowned. "What is happening to you?"

"I'm starting to let you get away without speaking. Don't think I haven't noticed how everyone caters to your silence, Quill," she said. "I am determined not to be a party to your family's indulgence."

Quill snorted and pointedly bowed to Phoebe. "I have some excellent news."

"There you are again! Whatever happened to 'How are you, Gabby?' or 'How did you sleep, Phoebe?' " Gabby broke in.

Quill took a deep breath. "How are you, Gabby? And what's put you in such a churlish mood?"

"There's nothing churlish about a little courtesy!"

Quill smiled at her, even though he didn't mean to. She was such a delicious little spitfire. Gabby's cheeks had turned pink, and her hair was rapidly toppling down from the neat arrangement Margaret had fashioned a mere half hour ago.

"Mrs. Ewing has sent a note. She should be here within the hour."

To his surprise, Phoebe looked stricken rather than joyful. "Oh, no," she cried. "My clothing isn't ready."

"Your clothing," Quill repeated.

Big tears spilled down Phoebe's cheeks. "My new mama will think that I'm dowdy!"

"I doubt it," Quill said dryly. "She's more likely to think that you're a nursling."

Phoebe turned her face into Gabby's shoulder. "I'm not a nursling," she said around her sobs. "I don't want my mama to see me like this! I want to wear my new gown with—with the pin—pin—pin tucks!"

Just then Lady Sylvia bustled into the room, followed by three scurrying dogs. "Well, well, what have we here?" She paused.

The fierce training Phoebe's ayah had ladled out held her in good stead. As Gabby put her on her feet, Phoebe dropped a beautiful curtsy, despite the little sob that escaped her on the way down.

"Lady Sylvia, may I present Miss Phoebe Pensington?" Quill said. "Miss Phoebe has been staying with us. At the moment she is feeling some concern about her apparel."

"Don't know about that," Lady Sylvia barked. "As I told you yesterday, I can't take on the business of dressing others. I've enough trouble dressing myself."

Gabby barely suppressed a grin. Lady Sylvia was magnificently attired in a pale-green morning dress with sprigs of lace let in the bosom. Her gloves, shoes, and dogs' bows all matched.

Lady Sylvia sank into a chair and idly waved a green handkerchief at Codswallop. "I shall have naught but a cup of hot chocolate and perhaps one or two pieces of toast. I'm considering a reducing diet."

Phoebe was leaning against Gabby's shoulder, still mourning the pin-tucked dress.

"Yer a pretty little gel," Lady Sylvia told her. "What are you blubbering about?"

Phoebe flushed. "I was being unladylike," she whispered. "Please forgive me."

"Nonsense! Nothing more ladylike than crying. And if you don't believe me, you can ask Erskine's mother!" Lady Sylvia gave a bark of laughter.

"Phoebe," Gabby said firmly, "your new mother will not care a pin about the length of your dress. A new dress could never make anyone love you more than they would naturally."

"Well, I don't know about that," Lady Sylvia observed with a wicked little smirk. Then she caught Gabby's eye. "Very true as pertains to parents, however. She's right, Phoebe my gel. Yer mother won't blink an eye at your garment."

Ten minutes later, Codswallop announced that Mrs. Ewing had arrived. Phoebe turned even paler and clung to Gabby's hand.

"Where'd you put her, Codswallop?" Quill inquired.

"The Indian Drawing Room, sir."

Lady Sylvia was starting on her fifth piece of toast and had accepted a plate of coddled eggs from the footman. "You go right on ahead," she remarked. "Erskine, I'll allow you to escort Gabrielle. Just don't lose control of yourself,"

Gabby looked at her curiously.

"The whole idea of chaperoning is that a gentleman may go wild with lust at any given moment," Lady Sylvia explained to Gabby around a mouthful of eggs. "Steal a kiss or something equally godforsaken, right in front of Codswallop. But we might as well begin as we mean to go on. And I'm not planning to dog your steps every time you wish to use the water closet." She smirked at Quill's furious look.

The moment Quill, Gabby, and Phoebe walked into the parlor, it was eminently clear that Lady Sylvia was correct when she said that Phoebe's new mother wouldn't blink an eye at the child's overly short hem. Not that Mrs. Ewing's own skirt was a fraction of an inch too short or too long. In fact, Mrs. Ewing looked as close to an illustration from *La Belle Assemblée* as it was possible for a living woman to be. She was wearing the most elegant morning dress Gabby had ever seen, ornamented with lace knots all the way down the sleeves. And she wore a rakish little cap, tied down with colored silk that matched her shoes.

Yet for all her elegance, she didn't appear to notice Phoebe's shabby clothing. She whirled around from the windows as they entered, and hesitated. Then she ran forward and fell on her knees before the little girl. "Oh, Lord," she whispered, cupping Phoebe's face in her hands. "You are the very image of Carolyn, aren't you?"

Phoebe looked back at her steadily, ignoring the awkward question. "Are you my new mama?"

Gabby saw with an odd twinge to her heart that Mrs. Ewing's eyes had filled with tears.

"I gather I am," she said. "I . . . I would be proud to be your new mama, Phoebe." And she reached out her slender hands and gathered the child up, holding her tightly in her arms. "I'm so sorry that I didn't know," she said into Phoebe's hair. "I would never have left you alone. I would have come to India and fetched you myself. But we had no idea that Carolyn and her husband had suffered an accident."

She stood, still holding Phoebe.

"Please, Mrs. Ewing!" Gabby said quickly. "Won't you and Phoebe sit down?" She gestured toward a settee.

"Well, yes," the young woman replied, staggering a bit as she walked toward the seat. "My goodness, Phoebe, you must be all of four years old!"

At that Phoebe raised her head. "I'm not four years old! I'm *five*!"

"Five." Mrs. Ewing's eyes flickered. Then she added lightly, "How very remiss of Carolyn not to inform me of your birthday."

Phoebe had folded her hands primly, even though she was now perched on Mrs. Ewing's knees. "My birthday is in May. I will be six."

"Oh," Mrs. Ewing said.

Gabby sat down and surveyed her guest. She was a very beautiful woman, if far too thin and tired-looking. "Mrs. Ewing, do I understand that you are related to Phoebe's mother?"

"I am." Mrs. Ewing's eyes were a lovely blue-gray, although they were positively ringed with fatigue. "I am one of Phoebe's aunts. Phoebe's mother, Carolyn, apparently chose me to be Phoebe's guardian, but she neglected to inform me."

Phoebe shook her head. "Mama and Papa didn't inform anyone," she reported. "Mr. Stokes, the English consul, had to go through their papers. And then he said that you are my guardian and likely my only living relative." She looked alertly into Mrs. Ewing's face.

"Well, I'm not your only relative," Mrs. Ewing replied. She gave Phoebe a little squeeze. "Your aunt Louise is at home, longing to meet you. And . . . you have other family as well."

Definitely there was something odd about Mrs. Ewing's lame mention of "other family," to Gabby's mind.

"Mrs. Ewing," Gabby said. "I am so sorry that I haven't introduced myself." She cast a dark look at Quill, who was leaning against the wall in a relaxed fashion, utterly neglecting his host duties. "You probably guessed from my letter that I am Miss Gabrielle Jerningham, and this is Mr. Erskine Dewland."

Quill straightened and bowed. "It's a pleasure to meet you."

Gabby was a bit annoyed to notice how appreciatively Quill was looking at Mrs. Ewing. He had no right to look at a married woman with such enthusiasm.

"I'm afraid my family had not kept in touch with Carolyn as much as we ought, and so this has been rather a shock." Mrs. Ewing's smile faded. "I can't imagine what would have happened to Phoebe if you hadn't rescued her, Miss Jerningham. What luck you were on that particular vessel!"

"It was lucky for both of us," Gabby remarked. "Phoebe was very pleasant company on the journey." The way Quill was leaning forward and hanging on Mrs. Ewing's every word was really quite annoying.

"We rarely heard from my sister," Mrs. Ewing was saying. "Carolyn had an explorer's soul, and her husband was as intrepid as she was. I'm afraid I received only one letter from her in the last seven years."

"Sometimes she and Papa were gone for months," Phoebe put in. "They had very important work to do."

Mrs. Ewing brushed a kiss over Phoebe's curls. "Did they never take you with them, poppet?"

"No, indeed," Phoebe exclaimed. "Mama and Papa had important work. Mama always wished I could come with them, but they visited unsafe places. I stayed with my ayah, and Mama and Papa came to see me when they were able."

"Was your father Roderick Pensington?"

Quill's sudden question startled Phoebe, but she nodded. "My papa was a famous explorer," she said proudly.

"He certainly was," Quill affirmed. "He was the first westerner to trace the length of the Ganges River."

Mrs. Ewing rose. "It is time that we were on our way. Your aunt Louise will be on tenterhooks until we arrive. And I imagine that Miss Jerningham and Mr. Dewland have plans of their own."

"Oh, no," Gabby exclaimed. "Please don't go so quickly, Mrs. Ewing! I have grown very fond of Phoebe, and I hate to see her leave. I was hoping you might stay for luncheon."

"Perhaps Phoebe can make a visit in the future," Mrs. Ewing replied. "I am grateful to you for your invitation. But unfortunately, I have an appointment that cannot be altered."

Gabby hesitated. There was nothing she could do about it, after all. She knelt down in front of Phoebe, who was clutching Mrs. Ewing's hand. "Will you be quite all right, sweetheart?"

Phoebe nodded, her eyes solemn.

Gabby's heart contracted, and she gave her a swift kiss. "Will you visit me?"

"Yes, but won't you visit *us*?" Phoebe replied, with a hint of desperation in her tone. "Codswallop said your calling cards have been ordered. You could call on me. You haven't met my aunt Louise."

"I would love to call on you," Gabby replied. She straightened and met Mrs. Ewing's eyes. "I know it is an imposition, Mrs. Ewing, but may I visit Phoebe tomorrow? We were together every day during the voyage, and it is quite wrenching to part with her."

Mrs. Ewing bit her lip. "Perhaps Phoebe may call on you tomorrow morning," she said, after a brief hesitation.

Gabby rushed in before she could change her mind. "I will send the carriage for Phoebe if I may, Mrs. Ewing."

"We would be grateful," she replied with a dignified nod. "My sister and I do not maintain our own cattle."

Gabby waited until they left the room and then she burst out, "Quill, I am quite sure that there is something unusual about Mrs. Ewing's household. Perhaps I should not have allowed Phoebe to leave with her. Did you notice that she does not wish me to visit?"

"I suspect she considers her house below your notice," Quill remarked. "I do not believe that Phoebe's aunts are very plump in the pocket."

"But Mrs. Ewing's dress displayed the greatest *éclat*. And I wouldn't care what sort of house she owned!" Gabby paused and her eyes grew horrified. "She is a . . . a proper sort of person, isn't she?"

Quill grinned. "I can certainly tell you've had a lot of experience with Cyprians, Gabby. Mrs. Ewing is perfectly respectable. The Thorpes, Phoebe's maternal family, are held in the highest estimation by the *ton*, for what that's worth. I believe their family seat is in Herefordshire. But, perhaps due to her marriage, Mrs. Ewing seems to have come down in the world."

"That is absurd," Gabby replied sharply. "If she were poor, she wouldn't be so elegant."

"Her gown may have been elegantly fashioned, but it was made of plain cambric," Quill observed. "Her shoes had been overdyed, and she was exhausted. I think it's quite likely that Mrs. Ewing is engaging in some sort of work. It reflects badly on the Thorpe family that she is so pressed. Perhaps they are estranged."

"Oh, dear." Gabby swallowed hard.

Then she felt a soft touch on her cheek. "Nothing you can do about it, Gabby," Quill said. His large hand tipped up her chin and he brushed his fingers over her lips.

Gabby looked up at him without moving.

It was irresistible: her drifting jasmine perfume, her speaking eyes. Quill bent his head and their lips met. She tasted faintly like blackberry jelly. But that pedestrian flavor had nothing to do with the fire that raced up his loins when Gabby's tongue met his—shyly, sweetly, something less than innocently.

Quill's frail self-control crumbled, and a large hand stroked the middle of Gabby's back, a delicious persuasion that made her press closer.

"Well, well," a strident voice sounded in the room. "Don't say I didn't warn you, Gabrielle. Leave a man alone for a moment and he is overcome by lust."

Gabby sprang back so fast that she almost overbalanced. "Forgive me, Lady Sylvia," she gasped.

"For what?" Lady Sylvia strolled into the room to the sounds of yips and yaps. "I'm not the one being kissed. The Dewlands always were a lusty lot," she added meditatively. "Now, if I think back to the details of Kitty's first season . . ."

Quill shuddered. The last thing he wanted to hear about was his parents' youthful indiscretions. "I can assure you, Lady Sylvia, that my reprehensible behavior will not recur."

Lady Sylvia waved her hand imperiously. "Go on, why don't you? Go do something intelligent, Erskine. I'm sure that I ought to deliver a lecture on propriety now, and I don't need you around to hear it."

Quill frowned.

"Leave," Lady Sylvia growled.

"Lady Sylvia, Miss Jerningham." He bowed and left the room.

"Prickly, isn't he?" Lady Sylvia wandered over to the

tiger table. "Good gracious, this table is a monstrosity. I can see that Kitty's taste has gone from being somewhat indiscriminate to appalling.

"It's none of my business, of course," she went on, blithely ignoring her role as chaperone, "but you're kissing the wrong one, aren't you, gel?"

Gabby nodded, hot crimson in her cheeks.

"Do you want to marry Erskine, then? Mind you, it's a better match, on the surface at least."

"Oh, no," Gabby exclaimed. "I'm very pleased to be marrying Peter, Lady Sylvia."

"Then mind yourself, gel. No point in kissing a man you don't want to marry. At least, not until you *are* married! And there's my lecture for you." Lady Sylvia gave her characteristic bark of laughter and strolled toward the door. "You have a caller, gel. Codswallop tells me that he's put Lady Sophie, Duchess of Gisle, into the Yellow Drawing Room." Her voice was a question.

"I met the duchess yesterday, in Madame Carême's establishment," Gabby said. She had her palms pressed against her hot cheeks.

"Well, stop looking so much like a guilty housemaid and let's go meet the woman," Lady Sylvia said. "I don't know her myself, but I've admired her style. Now, there's one that never minded a few kisses!"

QUILL STALKED INTO HIS CHAMBER, conscious of a shaming sense of embarrassment. What was it about Gabrielle Jerningham that led him to behave like such an utter ass? Kissing his brother's fiancée! You'd think he was jealous. Whereas in truth, he told himself, he felt relief rather than jealousy.

He pulled off his clothes and moved toward his dressing room, clad only in smalls. He'd had the room stripped to the walls a few years ago, and now it housed only Dr. Trankelstein's equipment. With an irritated jerk, Quill grabbed one of the German doctor's oddly shaped dumbbells and began raising it in the air. After a while he slowed into a comforting and familiar rhythm.

By an hour later, his skin glowed and his right leg was aching from exertion. Quill cast a look of dislike at the machine in the corner. It was a horselike contraption, also designed by Dr. Trankelstein. But whereas Quill quite enjoyed working with Trankelstein's dumbbells, he loathed the time he spent on the chamber horse. The doctor's idea that its rocking motion would inure Quill to the motion of a true horse had borne little fruit. But Quill's punctilious nature would not allow him to ignore the machine completely.

With a sigh, he rubbed his hands with a towel and climbed onto the horse. No two ways about it: He felt like a child riding a toy. Large leg muscles bunched on his thighs as Quill forced the horse into a rocking clip that sent searing pain through his hip and then gave him a queasy feeling in his stomach. He'd found by painful trial and error that he could go no longer than five minutes on the horse without inducing a migraine.

Today he endured his five minutes with gritted teeth, stopping the moment he saw faint purple flashes at the corner of one eye. It wasn't a day for experimentation, not while he was acting as Gabby's host.

Chapter 7

THE NEXT MORNING Phoebe arrived on the doorstep at precisely the same moment as Lucien Boch. Gabby hurried into the drawing room to find them seated together as Lady Sylvia lazily watched from a nearby armchair.

"My new mama," Phoebe was saying, "is a very important person. She decides what everyone in London wears."

Lucien rose as Gabby entered the room. "I trust you are well, Miss Jerningham? You see that I have had the pleasure of renewing my acquaintance with Miss Phoebe."

Gabby quickly bobbed a curtsy at the handsome Frenchman. "It's splendid to meet you again, sir." Then she turned to Phoebe. "How are you, dearest?"

"I am very well, thank you," Phoebe replied, in her most grown-up fashion. Then she threw formality to the wind. "My new mama is very, very important! And Aunt Louise owns a teapot that might have a genie in it, and she swears—a lot! She said, 'Zooks,' and my mama told her that she had to hold her tongue in front of me. And then Aunt Louise said, 'Zooks to that!' And Mama got really mad."

Gabby laughed. "Aren't you a lucky girl?"

Phoebe nodded. She seemed to be shedding the unnatural formality her ayah had fostered. "Mama lowered my hem, you see?" She stuck out her little boot.

"Your mama lowered the hem by herself?"

"Oh, yes," Phoebe said. "Our house isn't full of servants, as yours is, Miss Gabby. There's only Cook, and Sally, who does the cleaning, and Sherman. Sherman helps with the door, but he's very, very old and often sleeps during the day. Mama says it's more cozy with no strangers about, but we must all do our part, and this morning I carried my own dish into the kitchen after breakfast." She paused to take a breath.

Lucien was listening with a great deal of amusement. "Mrs. Ewing sounds like a most intrepid woman," he said. He twinkled at Gabby. "I only wonder how she became so very, very important—and how she determines what everyone in London wears!"

"She writes it down," Phoebe said. "Mama writes and writes, and then people read what she wrote, and they daren't wear anything that Mama didn't say they might. She knows all about clothing," she added. "I told her about the pin tucks, and she thought my new dress sounded lovely."

Gabby looked a puzzled question over Phoebe's head.

"Perhaps Mrs. Ewing writes for a fashion magazine," Lady Sylvia put in. "There are several, you know. The most influential one is *La Belle Assemblée*."

"Mama's writing is read by everyone in London," Phoebe reported. "She tells them how they should behave, as well as what they should wear."

"Quite likely *La Belle Assemblée*," Lady Sylvia commented. "Does yer mother attend many social events?"

"I don't think she does," Phoebe replied.

Just then Codswallop pushed open the parlor doors. "Miss

Jerningham, you have a caller. Colonel Warren Hastings, English Secretary to the Governor-General of India." Codswallop's voice almost shook with excitement. "I have ushered him into the library."

"Oh, fudge," Gabby said, somewhat to Lucien's surprise. "Codswallop, is Mr. Dewland in?"

"I regret to say that Mr. Dewland is not at home."

"You could put this Hastings off," Lady Sylvia drawled. "No reason why you should see an army fellow without the head of the household present."

Quill hadn't come to breakfast, even though Gabby had lingered. She sighed. "Mr. Boch, I do apologize, but I suspect that I should not keep Colonel Hastings waiting."

But Lucien was already standing. "Please do not give it a second thought. I have several calls to make this morning. But I wonder if I might have the pleasure of accompanying Miss Phoebe to her house?"

"Would you? That would be absolutely splendid," Gabby exclaimed.

Lucien gave his twinkling, intimate smile. "I admit . . . I am curious about the important Mrs. Ewing and shall look forward to meeting her."

Lady Sylvia looked at Phoebe, who had skipped over to say good-bye to her favorite tiger table. "No mystery there," she said in a lowered voice. "Phoebe's new mama is Emily Thorpe, as was. From the Herefordshire Thorpes. There was a disgrace, some sort of rumpus, and Thorpe threw both his daughters out. Now I think of it, it wasn't the eldest gel that got in trouble, it was the younger, Louise. Never seen them myself, but I know the elder turned into a Mrs. Ewing, some five or six years back. Didn't know she was writing for fashion rags though."

There was something odd about Lady Sylvia's comment that Emily Thorpe had "turned into a Mrs. Ewing," but

Gabby didn't have time to question her. At any rate, it wasn't a proper conversation with Phoebe in the room.

Lucien apparently agreed with her, as he bowed before Lady Sylvia with a great deal of elegant flare and said nothing to her account of Thorpe family history.

While saying good-bye, Phoebe leaned close to Gabby's ear and whispered shrilly, "You haven't forgotten about the secret visit that we are going to make, have you, Miss Gabby?"

"It's not polite to whisper among company," Gabby said, squeezing her hand. "But no, of course, I haven't forgotten. I shall send a note to Mrs. Ewing and ask to borrow you for an afternoon next week, shall I?"

When they were alone, Gabby turned to Lady Sylvia. "Will you accompany me to the library, Lady Sylvia?"

"First you'd better tell me what this is all about."

"Quite likely Colonel Hastings has come to pay his respects," Gabby suggested. "My father is quite influential."

"Fiddlesticks! None of the India men would bother to pay respects to a mere female, particularly over here in England. What does he want from you?" Lady Sylvia looked as stubborn as one of her hairy little terriers.

Gabby gave in. "I suspect that he will ask me the whereabouts of Tukoji Holkar's heir. Holkar is one of the chiefs in the Marathas region."

"Marathas? Marathas? Where in God's name is that?" But she didn't give Gabby time to answer. "What you're saying is that some sort of heathen prince has gone missing," Lady Sylvia said. "An Indian prince."

Gabby nodded. "The boy's name is Kasi Rao."

"Why on earth would Hastings suspect that you might know his whereabouts?"

"Kasi was raised as my brother," Gabby said. "He is my father's nephew by his first marriage. And he grew up in our household. Since he is now almost eleven, and given that his father is ill, he would probably assume the throne of the Holkars, except—"

"Except that he's disappeared," Lady Sylvia finished. "And your father had something to do with it, no doubt. God knows, from what I remember of your father, he's eccentric enough to be kidnapping princes right and left."

"I know nothing about it," Gabby said, praying for an even tone to her voice.

Lady Sylvia snorted. "Save yer rhetoric for the colonel." She lapsed into silence and raised her hand when Gabby started to speak. "Just a minute, gel. It's foolish for us to talk to this colonel alone. He's likely to bully you. We should wait until Dewland returns and let him deal with it."

"But if I refused to say anything, the colonel would have to give up and leave."

"Absurd!" Lady Sylvia snapped. "We can't just walk in there, two unaccompanied females. He'll try to intimidate you into telling the truth. Not that any male could do better than a female when it comes to deception. Just ask my husband, Lionel, about that. Of course, given that he's dead, you can't ask him, God rest his soul."

Gabby couldn't think what in the world she could say in response, so she remained silent.

"We'd better act caper-witted," Lady Sylvia announced. "I'll have the dogs brought in; they'll help. I'll play a dithering old maid." She wheeled around and barked, "You, Codswallop!"

Codswallop visibly jumped. "Yes, my lady?"

"Have my dogs brought in, and then you may escort us to the library."

Codswallop opened his mouth—and thought better of it. "I'll summon the animals immediately."

Lady Sylvia snorted as he left. "There's something a little shifty about that fellow. He didn't like the idea of fetching my little sweeties. Probably worrying about the library rug.

"All right, gel, do you think you can pretend to be a regular goose? Men, especially those as have a military title, think women are jinglebrained anyhow. It should go over well."

Gabby nodded. "Colonel Hastings isn't exactly in the army," she noted. "The East India Company maintains its own militia."

Lady Sylvia shrugged. "He's got some sort of rank. They have to have a shrunken head to fit into those tunics, you know. It goes with the uniform."

The dogs danced into the room, hysterically yelping their pleasure at being released from Dessie's stern care. Lady Sylvia grabbed two and Gabby bent to pick up the third, but recoiled when it snapped at her finger.

"Ignore the little demon," Lady Sylvia advised. "She'll follow us. Now—on with it, Codswallop!"

Colonel Hastings turned out not to be wearing a uniform. He was a barrel-shaped man, going rather bald. To Gabby's mind, his face resembled a black-and-white etching without enough detail: his nose seemed bulbous and undefined, his chin wobbled into two or three chins and then melted into his high collar, and his hair didn't appear until his forehead had sloped backward for a more than generous time.

Even as Colonel Hastings bustled toward the two ladies, it was abundantly clear that he considered himself to be engaging in child care. Lady Sylvia threw Gabby a quick, triumphant look.

"Miss Jerningham, it is indeed a pleasure to meet you." He bowed rather creakily.

Lady Sylvia fluttered toward Colonel Hastings, simpering. "Oh, la, sir. I can hardly bring myself to say so, but I must admit, in the absence of a male family member, I could never allow sweet Miss Jerningham to be unchaperoned, not that it would be of concern in the presence of such a majestic military gentleman as yourself. . . ." Her voice trailed away and she swept into a low curtsy, so low that Gabby was momentarily afraid she might not be able to straighten up.

Colonel Hastings bowed self-importantly. "I am enchanted—enchanted!—to meet you, Miss . . . Miss . . ."

Lady Sylvia shook her fan so quickly that a minor gale disturbed Hastings' remaining few hairs. "My name is Lady Sylvia Breaknettle. Forgive me, Colonel Hastings, but the shock of finding myself in the presence of one of England's bravest, finest men!" Her fan trembled with emotion. "I merely look at you and I see our brave, brave men, penetrating the wilds of the wildest continents, bravely living without the comforts of civilization!"

"Now, that is true," Colonel Hastings said, grunting a trifle as he straightened from another deep bow. "You wouldn't credit how hard it is to obtain a decent cup of tea over there. They grow the stuff, and yet it is impossible to teach the natives how to brew it." He turned toward Gabby. "Miss Jerningham, you must be very happy to have arrived in the land of civilization. India is no place for gentle ladies such as yourself."

Lady Sylvia took one look at Gabby's stiff back and fluttered forward again. "I vow she has told me that a hundred times! The land of savages, that's what we call it in this house! Lawks, sir, we must be seated. And I shall send our indefatigable Codswallop for a cup of tea, shall I?"

Gabby felt it was her turn to contribute. "I feel certain

that we can provide you with properly brewed tea, sir. For such an intrepid soldier as yourself, *nothing* is too much!"

Colonel Hastings turned a bit red under the impact of Gabby's worshipful gaze and allowed as how he wouldn't mind a cup of tea.

Once they were seated, he leaned forward. "Miss Jerningham, I know already that I am on a fool's errand, but I serve a higher master." He paused.

Gabby barely restrained a smile. Hastings sounded just like her father when he fell into what she thought of as missionary rhetoric. Her father always talked of a higher master when he was driving a particularly hard bargain.

"My master is the governor-general of India himself, Richard Colley Wellesley, earl of Mornington."

"Oh, my," Gabby gasped admiringly. "I have never had the pleasure of meeting the governor-general, but . . . but . . ." She faltered. Her father would have thrown himself across the portal before allowing the militaristic Wellesley to enter his house.

Lady Sylvia jumped in. "My young charge is so overcome at the idea of being face-to-face with the great man that she cannot find the words!"

"Wellesley is a brilliant man," Hastings confirmed. "A br-r-r-illiant man! However, I am quite certain that he miscalculated when requesting my presence at your abode, my dear ladies."

Gabby gave him an encouraging smile.

"The idea that such a lovely young lady as yourself would know aught of Indian politics is absurd," Hastings said.

Gabby was saved from answering by Quill's arrival. She looked up to find him standing in the doorway. He had an extraordinarily silent way of entering rooms, Gabby thought. It was as if he brought a little pool of quiet with him.

Lady Sylvia gave a loud trill of laughter. "Isn't this the most splendid thing, Colonel Hastings? Here is my dear, dear nephew, Mr. Dewland, and he will be able to reply to all those questions that we woolly-headed females simply are not constituted to answer!"

Colonel Hastings was beaming and climbing to his feet, clearly enchanted at the idea of having a proper male to help him question these fluttery and flustering females.

To this point, Gabby had not been enjoying the charade much, but now that Quill had entered, a sudden wave of giddy pleasure swept up her back. Since she had no fan, she fluttered her eyelashes instead. "Goodness, Mr. Dewland, I am so pleased to see you! Just imagine! The governor-general of India has sent Colonel Hastings just to question *me* about Indian politics. And you know how hopeless I am about names and things! Why, I vow I hardly remember my own maid's name from one day to the next." She cast Quill a deliciously dizzy smile.

Quill shot Gabby a quick glance and then bowed to his guest.

Colonel Hastings launched into speech. "My questions are not quite as foolish as the lovely Miss Jerningham makes out, Mr. Dewland. Although—as I was just telling the ladies—I am quite certain that I've undertaken a fool's errand. But I serve a higher master, Mr. Dewland. A higher master who will not be denied! The governor-general of India himself sent me to make inquiries."

"Goodness me," Quill said, strolling forward and seating himself. "It is quite difficult to imagine what Wellesley could possibly think our Miss Jerningham might know of Indian politics."

Gabby cooed at Quill. "Now, now, Mr. Dewland, you

mustn't underestimate a lady's intelligence. Why, I am sure that I can answer many questions for Colonel Hastings." She cocked her head to the side. "Let's see. The East India men practically run the country, I know that."

"Well, that's just it, Miss Jerningham," the colonel responded, with the air of someone instructing a five-year-old. "The company does *not* run the large part of India called the Marathas, which is where you grew up."

Gabby laughed sweetly. "Well, I know that! My father was most insistent that I learn something about the Indian continent. I grew up in Indore, which is part of the Marathas. The Marathas is a large section of central India." She spoke as if reciting the multiplication tables. "But I don't doubt that you, Colonel Hastings, know much more about India than I do."

Colonel Hastings was growing pink again under the warmth of Gabby's admiring gaze. "Are you aware of the Holkar family, Miss Jerningham?"

Gabby paused, her eyes puzzled. Then she burst out: "Indore is run by the Holkars!" She clapped her hands. "Am I doing well, sir?"

"Marvelously," Colonel Hastings affirmed. "We are curious about the whereabouts of a boy who grew up in your father's household, Miss Jerningham. We have been informed that he was brought up like a brother to you. His name is Kasi Rao Holkar, and he is the heir to the Holkar throne."

Quill was watching Gabby closely, his eyes narrowed. What the devil was she up to? If she smiled at the colonel one more time in that melting fashion, the old man was liable to have a heart attack.

"Well, I know *of* Kasi Rao." Gabby gave another little trill of laughter. "But, my goodness! My father would never allow an Indian native to be *like a brother* to me, sir! After all, I am an English lady, and my father is the son of a duke!"

"Yes, quite," Colonel Hastings assured her. "But do you have any idea of Kasi Rao Holkar's whereabouts at the moment?"

"Certainly not." For a moment Gabby's frivolous exterior faltered and her tone sounded intelligent.

Lady Sylvia leapt in, quick as a cat. "I trust you are not suggesting that my dear charge would remain in contact with an Indian man, a savage, Colonel Hastings! My dear Gabrielle left India many weeks ago, on a vessel bound for England, and she intends never to return to that godforsaken country. She is betrothed to my nephew, a proper English gentleman. And *he* has not even traveled to the Continent!"

"I knew this was a fool's errand," Colonel Hastings said, a trifle wearily.

Gabby rose gracefully and then sat down next to the colonel. "I only wish that I could help you, sir. I would be so honored to be of aid. But I am afraid that Lady Sylvia is correct. I haven't seen Kasi Rao for years. I was never allowed to mingle with the natives, you know. When we were children we may have played together, but that was long ago." She patted the colonel's hand. "But do let me know if you find the prince. I would be charmed to see him again, naturally."

Quill remembered Gabby's wish to borrow the carriage for an afternoon, and he sighed. Kasi Rao Holkar was undoubtedly in London. Hell, he probably traveled on the same vessel as Gabby.

"How long has the Holkar heir been missing?" he asked.

"We don't know," Colonel Hastings replied, in some frustration. "It's deuced impossible to get straight answers over there, you know. And, if you'll forgive me for saying so, Miss Jerningham, your father is an extraordinarily stubborn man. He refuses to direct us to the boy. If someone doesn't find the Holkar heir soon, one of his two brothers will have to take his place."

"And the East India Company is not pleased with that notion?" Quill asked.

"It's an ethical question," the colonel said, his gaze shifting uneasily to the ladies. "Kasi Rao Holkar is the only child of the chieftain and his *wife*."

To Quill's mind, the fact that Kasi was Holkar's only legitimate heir had nothing to do with why the company wanted him on the throne rather than one of his illegitimate brothers. He shrugged mentally. Quill had sold all his company shares a few years ago, having discovered that India men were deliberately flaunting government orders not to increase their holdings. In fact, he would agree with Gabby's father: Kasi Rao was better off hidden in London.

Colonel Hastings was on his feet, genially kissing Lady Sylvia's hand in farewell. She simpered her good-byes in such a harebrained fashion that it would have shocked him to the bone to see her a moment later.

"Well, gel," she barked, the moment the colonel left the library. "If Hastings wasn't one of the greatest fools in England, he would have had the truth out of you in a moment. You don't lie worth a damn."

"I don't know," Quill said meditatively. "I think Gabby shows remarkable innovation, given that she knows precisely where that princeling is to be found."

Gabby blushed, but Lady Sylvia saved her from having to speak. "Of course she knows where the boy is to be found! I expect yer father has him tucked away somewhere, doesn't he? India is a large place. They'll never find him," Lady Sylvia said with some satisfaction. "I don't like those East India fellows. Mind you, Richard Jerningham always was a proper Jack Pudding, talking of becoming a missionary, and he the son of a duke! But I expect Richard kidnapped the boy for a good reason. *Not* that I am the least bit interested in knowing what his reason was. Come along, darling girls!" She scooped up two dogs, but the third seemed to have temporarily disappeared.

"Drat!" Lady Sylvia said as Gabby wandered about the library, peeking behind leather chairs. "She's a little weasel, Beauty is. I'll have to send Dessie down to find her." And beckoning majestically, she ushered Gabby out of the room.

Quill didn't have a chance to question Gabby until after supper, when he joined the ladies in the parlor. She was wearing the orange gown again, the one that fit her like a glove and made Quill feel like a libertine. An ungentlemanly, lecherous blackguard—the type of man who seduces his brother's fiancée. Swearing at himself didn't help.

"How old is Kasi Rao?" Quill asked. He would have asked anything to prevent himself from looking too closely at Gabby. He'd tossed off two brandies, but the only effect was to fire his blood with an intolerable wish to touch her again.

"Kasi will be eleven on January the fifth. Unfortunately, he is not quite that old in his abilities. He is only just learning his letters . . ."

Quill thought as Gabby chattered on. What in the hell should he do now? Take a trip? Go to investigate a firm located a long way away—say, Jamaica? Persia? What does one do when consumed by lust for a future sister-in-law? Stay away, his conscience said. Look what happened to Claudius. He ended up killing his brother—Hamlet's father—then . . . But thinking about Shakespeare didn't really help. Everyone was so melodramatic in the old days.

For one thing, he couldn't leave. It was unthinkable,

given his father's condition. It would be a breach of good manners, given that he was Gabby's host. As long as I don't kiss her again, Quill thought, I can be her host. I am a civilized man. He ignored the treacherous pattern that Shakespeare had set. After all, everyone knew that after Claudius married his brother's wife, things didn't go well for him. It would be better to leave the country.

Gabby was still talking. "Given how difficult it is for Kasi to remember even simple things, you would not credit how well he is doing! Some letters do come out backward. I certainly hope that Mrs. Malabright has been able to keep up his studies."

Quill pulled himself together. "Who is Mrs. Malabright?"

"Father thought at first to place Kasi in an establishment. But it was very difficult to arrange that from India, and it seemed fairly certain that representatives of the East India Company would trace the arrangement. So Kasi is under the care of a Mrs. Malabright, here in London. She is an Englishwoman who lived in India for twenty years. Since he knew her well, it was less of a shock for him to leave home."

"Has Kasi lived with you for his whole life?"

"Oh, yes," Gabby said sunnily. "Kasi came to live with us when he was only a few months old."

"Couldn't he take his place on the Holkar throne?"

"Certainly not," Gabby said without hesitating for a second. "My father is convinced that the East India Company would turn him into a figurehead and then take over the Holkar region. Kasi, poor sweetheart, is not entirely all that he could be. My father says that his mother drank too much cherry brandy while *enceinte*."

"What did Kasi's father think of his wife's brandy consumption?" Quill asked.

"They both enjoy cherry brandy," Gabby said, turning

her limpid eyes to Quill. "The last time I visited the palace, the Holkar was drinking his third bottle of the day, and his wife was thoroughly incapacitated as well. The kingdom is run by the Holkar's favorite concubine, Tulasi Bai."

Quill scowled at her. "You shouldn't be talking about concubines, Gabby. Lord, you shouldn't ever have visited a palace full of drunkards."

Gabby twinkled at him. "It isn't as if I have a preference myself for cherry brandy," she observed. "And I do think that Tulasi's son will make an excellent ruler of the Holkar region someday."

"I suppose you wished to visit Kasi when you asked for a carriage."

"Yes. Father instructed me not to reveal Kasi's presence in London to anyone, not even to you or your father." Gabby hesitated. "But now that you know about Kasi, will you accompany me to Mrs. Malabright's house, Quill? I would be most glad of your company. I haven't seen Kasi for several days now, and I miss him dreadfully. Father said I should ascertain whether Kasi is happy and then find another arrangement if necessary."

"Of course," Quill said. "Lady Sylvia, would tomorrow morning be convenient for you?"

"I believe I'll let you escort the gel on her own," Lady Sylvia replied. "Yer practically going on an errand of mercy, after all. I'm sure no one could quibble with that."

"I want to thank you for your performance before Colonel Hastings," Gabby said. "It would have been a terrible thing if the East India Company found out where Kasi was living."

"I enjoyed it." Lady Sylvia's voice was a bit gruff. "You're a good gel, Gabrielle. Like the way you're looking out for the boy, even if he's an Indian lad. Mind you, I won't call you that heathen name, *Gabby,* although you are a bit of a prattlebox."

Gabby smiled at her. "I am a very grateful prattlebox," she said. "I don't think I could have managed Colonel Hastings half so well."

"Well! Time for bed!" And Lady Sylvia shooed Gabby and the dogs out the door.

But Gabby had no wish for sleep. Colonel Hastings' visit had given her a sick feeling in her stomach.

She had to protect Kasi Rao. Clearly, the East India Company was far more interested in Kasi than her father had realized. And that meant that her father's plan to conceal Kasi in London would ultimately fail. Either the company would search until they located him, or else they would set up a figurehead in his place and insist that they had found the prince.

Months ago, back in India, she had thought up a scheme to stop the East India Company. Her father had curled his lip and dismissed it as nothing more than one of her impulsive, idiotic ideas. Gabby swallowed, thinking of Kasi's trusting eyes. She could not allow him to be taken from Mrs. Malabright. It was horrible to imagine Kasi forced into a public role.

She had nothing to lose by trying. The hounds were on Kasi's trail, and her father was not here to say nay.

With a decisive movement, Gabby stood up and walked over to the writing desk in the corner of her room. She drew forth a clean piece of foolscap, sharpened her quill, and began to write. By her calculation, the plan would entail four letters, all of which needed to reach India as soon as possible.

THE ADDRESS THAT GABBY GAVE the Dewland coachman the next morning was in Sackville Street. After a brief drive from St. James's Square, they reached an area of small houses, neatly painted and kept up, but very modest.

"My goodness," Gabby said uncertainly to Quill, "this is very different from what Kasi is used to."

"Do you live in a great mansion, then?"

"Oh, yes, in a palace," Gabby explained with an utter lack of self-consciousness. "Father has a distinct love of luxury, you see. It's one of the things that made his missionary endeavors so trying for him."

"I can imagine," Quill replied dryly.

Mrs. Malabright turned out to be a bustling, kindly Englishwoman who weighed at least nine stone more than Kasi.

Quill saw immediately why Gabby and her father were determined to protect the prince from taking his place on the Holkar throne. He was a very small, sweet-eyed Indian lad, who looked more like seven than ten. He drifted into the room sideways, like a wary deer entering an open pasture, and his eyes lit uncertainly on each face, darting off to the corners of the room.

Until he saw Gabby. Then he rushed to her side and clutched a bit of her gown. "Tell me a story, Gabby!" He spoke as if he had last seen her that very morning.

Gabby cupped his face in her hands. "Of course I'll tell you a story, sweetheart. But manners first."

Kasi grinned, a shy, heartbreaking grin. "*Namasthe,* Gabby." He brought his palms together and bowed slightly.

"No, no," Mrs. Malabright broke in. "We are in England now."

Kasi started again. "How do you do, Gabby? I am pleased to meet you."

"That's for strangers, dear. You know Miss Jerningham," Mrs. Malabright prompted.

He looked confused. Then he backed up and bowed yet again.

"How do you do, Miss Stranger? I am—I am—I am . . ." He trailed off.

Gabby nodded gravely in response and curtsied. "Thank you very much, Mr. Kasi Rao. It is a pleasure to meet you."

Kasi's face brightened. The formula had been played through. "Now tell me a story, Gabby. Please, *please*."

Gabby looked apologetically at Mrs. Malabright and Quill. "Would you mind terribly if I told Kasi a brief story?"

Mrs. Malabright beamed. "He's told me all about your stories, miss. He does powerfully love them."

Gabby and Kasi snuggled onto the couch, and Quill heard Gabby begin: "Once upon a time, there was a very small mouse. His name was Joosi, and he lived in the time of the ancient emperors of China, so long ago that neither you, nor your grandfather, nor your great-great-great-grandfather, could have shared a piece of cheese with him."

Quill's mouth quirked and he relaxed for the first time all day. But Mrs. Malabright could not allow her visitor to merely listen to a child's story.

"Kasi adores, absolutely adores, stewed prunes," she said importantly. "I've been making them every day. And he has very much enjoyed apples from my back garden as well."

"Have you taken him around London?" Quill asked idly. If the truth be told, he was straining his ears to hear fragments of the tale of Joosi, who was wandering into dangerous territory as he climbed the leg of the emperor's great throne.

"Goodness, no," Mrs. Malabright said firmly. "Kasi does

not enjoy being around strangers. Why, I have to push him into the backyard once a day, even though we have high walls. He's that nervous."

"Perhaps he would like to visit a pantomime?"

"No, he would not, and that's a fact." Mrs. Malabright looked like a great bear protecting her spindly cub. "Kasi is happy here in the house, and there's no call to make him terrified by taking him outside. There is no life outside for Kasi."

Joosi the mouse was performing incredible feats of daring, such as swinging from the feathers adorning the empress's best hat.

"Is he learning to write?"

"His letters are improving," Mrs. Malabright said. "Only the *J*'s are backward now." And she trotted off to fetch a sample of Kasi's handwriting, returning just as Joosi's story came to a triumphant conclusion.

"And from that day forward," Gabby said, "Joosi the mouse was the emperor's very best friend. The emperor had a special bed made for Joosi, wrought from gold and adorned with pearls. During the day Joosi always stayed on the emperor's shoulder, ready to advise him should yet another foolish counselor suggest that China go to war. And since Joosi knew that war was a terrible thing, the reign of the emperor was long remembered in China as the happiest and most peaceful of all."

Kasi sighed happily. "I wish Joosi was my best friend, Gabby." He looked around the room. "Do you know where my friend went? She doesn't live in this house."

Gabby looked blank for a moment. "Do you mean Phoebe?"

Kasi nodded. "Phoebe." There was a world of satisfaction in his voice.

"Phoebe asked about you as well," Gabby said. "I am

going to bring her for a visit in a few days, if it would be quite all right with Mrs. Malabright."

"Could Phoebe bring Joosi the mouse with her?" Kasi asked.

Gabby was clearly used to Kasi's leaps in logic. "Perhaps Mrs. Malabright will allow you to have a pet mouse," she suggested.

Just then Mrs. Malabright bustled up with samples of Kasi's handwriting. So they stayed another half hour, and ate some of Mrs. Malabright's best spicy gingerbread, and finally left.

Quill had spent quite a bit of time considering why Lady Sylvia did not accompany them to Mrs. Malabright's house. If Lady Sylvia had intended that Quill indulge himself by kissing Gabby, Quill was not willing to satisfy her. Gabby was Peter's betrothed, and Peter's betrothed she would remain.

Not that Gabby showed any inclination to kiss him anyway. She chattered all the way home about Kasi and Mrs. Malabright, and she obviously had no idea that Quill could only think about how soft she felt in his arms, the way she trembled against him, the way her lips opened with a little gasp, the way . . . the way she made something inside him ache to hold her again.

Chapter 8

IT HAD TAKEN Lucien Boch two weeks of concerted effort to achieve his current success: luncheon with Phoebe Pensington, her adoptive mother, Mrs. Ewing, and her aunt, Louise. He was seated at a small table, Phoebe to his right and Emily to his left. And he was well aware that the ladies didn't want him there and that, in fact, he was a thoroughly unwelcome guest. And yet, gentleman though he was, Lucien had ignored all the obvious signals and stayed for the meal anyway.

At the first, Lucien had accompanied Phoebe to her house with no thought other than to satisfy a mild curiosity he had about the child's *important* new mama. But when he found himself in front of a slender, exhausted-looking Mrs. Ewing, his feelings had undergone a rapid and inexplicable change.

He had bowed his most charming bow and kissed her hand. And then he had embarrassed himself by mentioning the fact that he was a marquis before he left France. Why did he do that? He had terrible scorn for the émigrés who traveled to England and clung to their dead titles.

It wasn't that she was so beautiful. Well, she was beautiful. Moreover, she was exquisitely dressed and wearing one of the most modish little caps that Lucien had ever seen. But it was something about her blue-gray eyes that had made him visit the house the next day, and the day after. And finally, when he had deliberately appeared on their doorstep at an unforgivably unfashionable time of day, Mrs. Ewing had extended a reluctant invitation to join them for luncheon. She was wary, the beautiful Mrs. Ewing. She didn't like him very much, he could tell, and her fingers invariably had ink stains on them. She was entirely too thin. And she fascinated him.

So there he was, eating a vegetable pie dished out by an incompetent maid.

"Miss Phoebe informs me that you are a writer, Mrs. Ewing," Lucien said. She had washed the ink off her fingers before eating. They were beautiful hands—slender, with very, very long fingers.

Emily looked at her uninvited guest. What on earth was the man doing here? He was far too handsome to be a bachelor. Not that a bachelor would have any reason to visit the scandalous Thorpe sisters. She shrugged mentally. Well, if he was too much of a snob to associate with them, he wouldn't be eating with them. "I write for a fashion magazine for ladies," she said.

"*La Belle Assemblée?*" Lucien asked.

So there was the reason for Mr. Lucien Boch's appearance at her table, Emily thought. He must be the owner of a rival magazine. She'd heard a rumor of a new magazine in the press. And the owner of a German fashion magazine had tried to lure her to his journal last year. Well, that explained it. There could be no other reason for a member of the French aristocracy to be seated at her table. She was aware of an odd twinge in her heart. It would have been nice if Mr. Boch's admiring gaze was meant for her, not for her writing.

"I do write for *La Belle Assemblée*," she said brusquely. "And I do not intend to write for anyone else in the near future."

"Oh . . . of course," Lucien murmured.

She would almost think that he was innocent. Except . . .

Except Lucien couldn't think what to say next, so he queried further. "And what would cause you to write for someone else, madame? I mean, for some other magazine?"

"Absolutely nothing," Emily rejoined sharply.

That seemed to end that train of conversation. Lucien sought about desperately for another topic. "Miss Thorpe, do you write for *La Belle Assemblée* as well?"

"No," Phoebe's aunt replied, cheerfully biting into a large apple. "I'm the reprobate in the family. I write for *Etherege's Portents,* the men's literary magazine, so called. I write all the fashion copy. If you don't mind my saying so, Monsieur Boch, I am very partial to olive-green frock coats. And you are wearing a beautiful example."

Lucien stared down at his coat in some bewilderment. "Thank you. *You* write for *Etherege's Portents?*"

Louise chuckled. "Do you read my column? It is entitled 'General Observations on Fashion.' I sign it Edward Etherege," she added kindly when Lucien looked blank.

"I'm afraid that I have not had the pleasure."

Louise rolled her eyes. "Well, you may be overestimating my writing skills by referring to pleasure. Emily has a true eye for fashion, but I simply make up rubbish and print it up for any chuckleheads who care to read it."

"You are severe," Emily observed, crumbling a roll in her hands. Lucien noticed that she had hardly tasted her vegetable pie. "Louise writes extremely humorous prose," she said, turning to Lucien.

"It's just that everyone thinks I'm serious!" said the obviously irrepressible Louise.

"I'm quite certain that your prose are . . . are impeccable," Lucien said lamely. He didn't dare look at Emily again. Every time he did so he found her frowning at him as if he were a thief, come to steal their silver. Or her virtue. Lucien shifted uneasily in his seat. He hadn't felt so attracted to a woman in years. In fact, since his wife's death. And why was that? This skinny, fierce Emily was nothing like his sweetly plump wife. He pulled himself together with a start.

Louise had pulled a stack of foolscap off the sideboard and was regaling Emily and Phoebe with her newest column, bound for Mr. Etherege's magazine.

"Fashion, tasteful yet fantastic, merciless yet idolized, seats herself in the weathercock throne on the dome of elevated Pleasure," she announced in a stately, imposing tone, waving her right hand in the air.

"She dictates her unappealable injunctions to the votaries of the enchantress within, the goddess who governs our lives and our waistcoats, the divinity who dictates the drape of our neckcloths, the idol who—"

"Oh, for goodness sake, Louise!"

"Don't stop me now, Emily," Louise implored. "I'm just getting started. I have some lovely bits coming up, about how the Spirit of Fashion distinguishes the design of one neckcloth from another. Wait!" She shuffled her papers.

Emily sighed. "I'm afraid you will have to excuse me, Mr. Boch, Phoebe. I have quite a lot of work to complete this afternoon."

"Oh, no, Mama, you shall miss the custard. I beat the eggs, five of them, all by myself!" Phoebe exclaimed.

"I am not very hungry, child." Emily bent and gave Phoebe a kiss. "I will hear your lessons later, shall I?"

Then, with a final brief smile, she left.

Lucien gave himself yet another silent lecture. It was not up to him to run after Emily Ewing and kiss her until the strain disappeared from those beautiful blue-gray eyes.

The maid brought in a plate with a sagging custard.

"Drat," Louise said gloomily. "There's Emily gone off without eating a thing, and the custard has not been cooked long enough."

Phoebe was already eating the portion slopped on her plate. "I think the custard is lovely," she said.

"Well, the eggs were perfectly beaten, I can tell that with a glance," Louise said, ruffling Phoebe's hair.

"If I may," Lucien asked, "is your sister under a time constraint? She appears to be very pressed."

"We're toward the end of the month, and her copy will be due soon," Louise replied. "Her prose are greatly in demand, you know. She writes most of the copy in *La Belle Assemblée* each month, which is difficult because Emily doesn't go into society herself. She has to read long reports of what such-and-such person wore the night before and then distill them. We have subscriptions to around fourteen newspapers, I think. And every time a really pivotal engagement approaches, Emily gets more and more nervous. At the moment I believe she's fretting over Lady Fester's ball. The ball is important as it is generally the first of the Little Season. And Lady Fester maintains a very select list."

"I don't understand," Lucien said. "Why is Mrs. Ewing fretting?"

"She has to proclaim who was the best-dressed woman at any given ball," Louise explained. "But it is not easy to obtain accurate information. She always worries that one of her regulars won't get invited to a particularly select occasion."

"She has *spies*?"

"They aren't spies," Louise said indignantly. "They are older women who love fashion and are grateful for a small payment. They tell her how everyone is dressed, so that she can report it. You know—" Louise waved her hand in the air again. " 'A most noble lady wore a petticoat with festooned draperies, blah, blah, blah.' Everyone knows who the 'noble lady' is."

"Why doesn't Mrs. Ewing simply attend the ball herself?"

Louise gave him a look that was the mirror of the suspicious ones Emily had thrown him. "How on earth would she do that? We are not invited to balls."

Lucien threw caution to the winds. "And why is that, Miss Thorpe? You must forgive the impertinence of a stranger, but it is obvious that you are from a distinguished family."

"My father is an irascible man," Louise said, with a quick glance at little Phoebe. "He threw me out of the house when I was fifteen years old. Emily, bless her heart, defended me and got herself thrown out as well. And that, as they say, was that."

Lucien almost persisted in his inquiries, but held his tongue. Then, "I have an invitation to Lady Fester's ball," he said. "Do you think your sister would do me the honor of accompanying me?"

Louise had Emily's blue-gray eyes, but for some reason they didn't move Lucien at all, not even when she looked him over as minutely as a man selecting a new horse. "I have no idea how Emily would feel," she finally murmured.

"I think she should go with you, Mr. Boch," Phoebe piped up unexpectedly. "It would be much nicer than listening to Mr. Hislop."

"What do you know about Mr. Hislop?" Louise asked, clearly startled.

"I heard Mama telling Sally to stay within earshot, in case Mr. Hislop tried to kiss her," Phoebe said. "Sally said he was a hateful man, and Mama agreed, but she said that she couldn't insult him."

Lucien's stomach was undergoing a slow burn. "You led me to believe that Mrs. Ewing had female spies," he said, turning to Louise.

She flushed. "Most of them are women. But Mr. Hislop seems to be invited everywhere. And we don't have to pay him for his fashion accounts. It's just that he—he—"

"He's a bounder," Lucien said. He was startled by the icy tone of his own voice. "Is Emily meeting with him now?" He didn't notice that he'd called Mrs. Ewing by her first name.

Louise was still looking at their guest measuringly. It seemed to Lucien that her eyes had softened a trifle.

"Mr. Hislop generally arrives around eleven o'clock each Tuesday morning, doesn't he, Phoebe?" She stood up. "I trust that you will find a time to proffer your invitation to my sister, Mr. Boch?"

Lucien immediately rose. "I believe I am free on Tuesday morning," he responded. Their eyes met in perfect accord.

"Then I wish you well in your endeavors." Louise curtsied, a regally beautiful curtsy—the curtsy of a young woman who had been groomed for the highest society rather than for the shabby room in which they stood.

A few minutes later Lucien frowned at the silk lining of his carriage. They were an odd pair, the thin, intelligent Thorpe sisters. Where was Mr. Ewing, if indeed he ever existed? It seemed to him entirely possible that the said Mr. Ewing was a phantom. Emily had a startled, naive look, not a widowed look.

He should know; *he* had that widowed look. Suddenly

he felt too old even to contemplate an evening with the lovely Mrs. Ewing. He was old—almost forty now—and weary and . . . very widowed. And yet his marriage to the kindly Felice seemed so long ago. He could remember Michel much more clearly. Michel's plump little cheeks and rosebud mouth were lodged in his heart, and the memory still jumped to his throat at odd moments.

Lucien swore under his breath and thumped on the roof of his carriage. He instructed his coachman to change direction and take him to his club. He had learned not to go home to an empty house when memories caught him unawares.

Of course he couldn't ask Emily Ewing to the Fester ball. For one thing, she was apparently a social outcast and would likely feel uncomfortable. And for another, she was entirely too young. She deserved someone with a young soul, not someone burdened by painful memories and endless regret.

BY THE TIME that Madame Carême arrived in person to supervise a fitting of her new wardrobe, Gabby was like to go out of her mind with boredom. She took the carriage every morning to visit Kasi but, even so, it had been a supremely tedious month. Lady Sylvia spent her days making calls to her friends, but when Gabby wistfully asked to accompany her, she shuddered and said, "Not in those clothes, gel." And that was that.

Quill was remarkable only for his absences. He had posted to Bath twice, but he stayed only one night on each visit. Even so, he was rarely seen around the house and certainly didn't offer to show her about London. Gabby couldn't help but think that Quill had succumbed to the horror of her white dresses. Perhaps he didn't want to be seen with her, even at the Tower of London.

Gabby read *The Morning Post* every day, and she knew that small parties were being given, even though it wasn't the Season, so-called. Yet Quill never offered to accompany her to a musical evening or other gathering.

He conveyed the daily message from Bath concerning his father's health. He occasionally joined her and Lady Sylvia for supper and punctiliously inquired about Kasi Rao. But he never asked her to meet his friends or go to a play.

Thus the arrival of Madame Carême and her chattering group of assistants was a relief. On the other hand, Madame's dresses were not.

"I cannot wear this garment. I cannot!" Gabby cried, growing more distressed by the moment.

"This is the mode." Madame was unimpressed. She had shocked many a client in her day.

"Miss Jerningham, you are to marry Monsieur Dewland. You *must* exhibit a strong sense of personal style, because you will be judged harshly due to your husband's exquisite taste. Since you do not have that sense of style, Monsieur Dewland was wise to put you in my hands."

Gabby heard this without resentment. "But it is still I who must be seen in this gown," she insisted.

"You will not be seen. You will be *adored*," Madame Carême snapped back. "Men will slaver at your feet."

It was not an unattractive proposition. But, oh, if her father had seen the dress! Gabby shuddered to think of it.

"I have composed your wardrobe in slightly heavier fabrics than we are using these days," Madame continued briskly. "They will disguise the curve of your hip."

Gabby blinked. She quite liked the curve of her hip.

Quill seemed to like it too, she thought, remembering how his fingers had lingered and caressed.

"Your breasts are great assets." Madame was still ticking off her thoughts. "We display them. And your derriere is also an asset. Therefore, each gown—day and evening—has a small train. I am seeking that dip and sway," Madame said.

Her breasts certainly were on display, Gabby thought. In fact, they were only precariously confined by the evening gown she was trying on.

"Now you may emerge into the public spaces," Madame said with satisfaction. "Monsieur Dewland will be happy, no?"

"Absolutely," Gabby hastened to say. "But, Madame, what if this bodice"—she touched it anxiously—"what if it drops below?"

"Drops below? Drops below?"

With an alarmingly easy wiggle of her shoulders, Gabby demonstrated.

Madame stared with affront at the pale pink nipple that appeared in response to Gabby's motion. "You must not move in that manner," she pronounced. "All of my clients wear low bodices in the evenings, even those who have nothing to display. You should be very grateful for your bosom, Miss Jerningham. Undergarments would destroy the drape of my bodice. *Never* wiggle your shoulders. My clients do not wiggle."

Well, of course not, Gabby thought. They're terrified.

But she was tired of being in the house. If Madame Carême took the gowns away to be remade, Gabby would be unable to demand that Quill take her somewhere, introduce her to someone—anyone!

So she said farewell to Madame Carême. Margaret

helped her put on a morning dress ornamented with a knot of ranunculuses. Over it she wore a mantle of a very pale blush color with a large hood, lined in pink silk. Margaret was beside herself with excitement.

"This is the most beautiful mantle I've ever seen," she said reverently, adjusting the hood one last time. "What color did Madame call it?"

"Peach blossom," Gabby said. "But that's just a fancy way of saying pink, Margaret, no matter what Madame said."

"Oh, no, Miss Gabby, I have to have the words right," Margaret said earnestly. "They'll want to hear everything downstairs." She handed her mistress a silk handkerchief bordered in the very same peach blossom.

Gabby had her first idea of the effectiveness of Madame Carême's designs when she was ushered into Mrs. Ewing's tiny front parlor. She had been coming once or twice a week to take Phoebe to visit Kasi Rao, and she had formed a rather stilted but friendly relationship with Phoebe's adopted mother.

But this morning Mrs. Ewing visibly checked her pace when she saw what Gabby was wearing. Gabby smiled to herself. Phoebe's mother always looked so well-dressed that Gabby felt like a positive dowdy beside her.

"If you will forgive me for the comment, Miss Jerningham, you look quite elegant this morning. Your gown is truly beautiful."

Gabby smiled. "I am the recipient of a wardrobe from Madame Carême."

"She's given you a small train," Mrs. Ewing said, walking forward. "What an interesting choice! And your mantle is of merino cloth, is it not?"

"I couldn't say," Gabby replied cheerfully. "I do know

that Madame Carême has declared my hood to be peach-blossom colored, rather than plain pink. Which"—she leaned toward Mrs. Ewing and whispered confidentially—"I was naturally most pleased to learn, as I should hate to be caught wearing a color worn only by *low persons*."

At that Emily Ewing laughed, for the first time in Gabby's memory. "Madame is a terrible snob, is she not? She quite terrified me the first time I met her."

Just then Phoebe entered the room, already wearing her pelisse and carrying a small basket. "Miss Gabby," she said breathlessly, dropping a curtsy. "I am sorry to have kept you waiting, but I was helping Cook in the kitchen."

"Come here, you silly goose," Gabby said affectionately, and Phoebe darted into her arms.

"I've made Kasi Rao a little pie," the little girl said, turning back the napkin covering her basket. "I made it myself—well, almost by myself. Do you think he'll like it?"

"He will adore it," Gabby said. "Shall we be off, then?" She smiled at Emily Ewing. "I shall return Phoebe in a few hours, if that is quite convenient with you."

"Thank you very much for your kindness," Mrs. Ewing replied, giving Phoebe a squeeze and a kiss.

They arrived in Sackville Street to find that Kasi was having a particularly difficult day. It took Phoebe over a half hour to coax him out of the broom closet, where he was huddled in the darkest corner.

"It was the Watch, miss," Mrs. Malabright said unhappily. "They came to the door, collecting donations, they were. And before I realized what was happening, they walked right into the parlor. Well, I thought Kasi was safely upstairs, but he wasn't. The poor mite found himself surrounded by four men, and one of them greeted him—in a nice way, mind. But it was too much for the poor thing, and he's been in the broom closet ever since."

"I completely understand, Mrs. Malabright," Gabby said. "I've spent many an hour trying to fetch Kasi out of a dark corner. It's just the way that he is. Goodness knows, my father tried hard enough to break him of the habit."

Mrs. Malabright twisted her hands in her apron, her eyes anxious. "I know that your father instructed me to do just that, Miss Jerningham. So I did take him out of the closet once, but he became so agitated, he—well, he—"

"I know exactly what happened," Gabby said, with a comforting smile. "And I absolutely agree with you, Mrs. Malabright. There is no point to tormenting Kasi. But just look at him now!"

Kasi was sitting on the corner of the settee, blissfully eating Phoebe's pie and watching her as she chattered.

"He doesn't take it to heart," Gabby said. "If he's allowed to emerge when he wishes to, Kasi is perfectly happy."

"Oh, he's a downright cheerful little soul," Mrs. Malabright confirmed. "As long as he doesn't get overset by being outside or by being around strangers. I've never been one for the outdoors, at any rate."

That evening Gabby thoughtfully put on one of Madame Carême's evening gowns. Her train swept the floor behind her and made her wiggle as she walked. She tried to remember that while it was desirable to dip and sway *below* the waist, one must not wiggle *above* the waist. In truth, dip and sway was not an unpleasant sensation. Gabby let herself dip a bit more. She dipped and swayed her way right down to Quill's study and knocked lightly on the door.

He looked up as she entered. In the twilight of the library, his face was hard and dark, unwelcoming. It was a pity that Gabby kept forgetting the set of Quill's mouth when she was away from him. It brooded, that mouth. It was shocking how different Quill was from Peter's slim perfection. His body, even the leg that caused him such grief, was large and muscled.

"This room needs light," Gabby remarked. For a moment she walked into the room at her normal pace, and then she remembered to dip and sway.

So she made an unnecessary little turn about the library, turning the wicks of the wall sconces. Quill's eyes had darkened perceptibly by the time she returned, Gabby noted with satisfaction.

"I should like to go out this evening, Quill."

"Go out?" He was all but gaping. Not slavering at her feet, but close enough.

"Go out," Gabby said, pacing her words slowly. "I should like to go to the theater, or to a party. A Lady Stokes is having a card party with dancing this evening. And we have an invitation!" She held out one of the embossed cards that arrived every day for Peter and were ceremoniously placed on a mantelpiece by Codswallop.

"To a party," Quill repeated stupidly. "We can't do that. I never go to that sort of thing."

"Why on earth not?"

Quill forbore to answer. If Gabby couldn't guess why he avoided occasions designed for dancing and prolonged periods of standing, he saw no reason to enlighten her.

"I suppose we could go to the theater," he said reluctantly.

Gabby favored him with a smile and then drifted over to perch on the edge of his desk. She wanted to make sure that Quill had taken in the effect of Madame Carême's bodice.

After a second, she was quite certain that he had. His

eyes were simmering with a dusky, dangerous light. Gabby felt powerful—a heady sensation. She leaned toward him slightly.

"I should be very pleased to visit the Dorset Gardens. One of my favorite Shakespeare plays is being performed: *The Taming of the Shrew*."

Every damned thing sounds like a proposition, Quill thought numbly. His brother was marrying a woman whose very voice made feverish promises.

His brother. Peter. Quill reined in his melting control.

"I'm afraid that I forgot an important engagement this evening," he said stiffly, shifting his chair backward from the table. "I must ask you to forgive me."

Gabby's face fell ludicrously. Suddenly the alluring enchantress was replaced by a disappointed child. "But, Quill, I am so tired of staying in the house all day!"

"Peter will be back soon," Quill promised.

"There is no sign of it in his daily notes," Gabby pointed out. "I know that Peter is a great comfort to your mother."

"She doesn't need any more comfort," Quill snapped. "Father is doing as well as may be expected. I shall write Peter and tell him to return at once."

Indeed, Viscount Dewland was resting comfortably, ensconced in the finest of Bath's inns. Undoubtedly he would never be able to walk, and doctors held out little hope that he would speak again, but he was fully himself, scrawling irascible notes right and left. "From what Peter's letters have said, Father could go on this way for years," Quill added.

"Please don't write to Peter," Gabby beseeched. "I would not want him to leave your mother at a time when she needs him."

Quill looked unconvinced.

"You see, Peter and I are going to be married for a long time," Gabby said earnestly, reaching out to touch Quill's knee. "It would be fatal if I came between him and his mother. I have seen these situations at home, in India, and it invariably strains the love between a man and his wife."

Quill's throat tightened. It was becoming increasingly difficult even to be around Gabby. Especially when her eyes shone so sweetly and she talked about love between man and wife.

He pushed his chair even farther from the desk where she was perched. "I shall inform my brother that you wish an escort to the theater." Then he couldn't help adding, "I am sure that when Peter realizes that you are dressed like this"—he gestured at her gown—"he will rush back to town in order to prance you before his cronies."

Gabby ignored the icy drip of sarcasm in Quill's voice. His expression had chilled; something she said had infuriated him. Quill was remarkably moody, for a man. But she had always found that it was best to ignore people's little moods. "Do you think so, Quill? Madame's gowns are beautiful, are they not?" She was blatantly fishing for a compliment.

Quill couldn't bring himself to lash back at her, to say something dismissive about her gowns. Gabby knew damned well that her evening gown was unconcealed provocation. Madame Carême—clever fiend of a Frenchwoman—had seen that Gabby would never succeed at playing a frail English miss, and so she had played to Gabby's husky voice, to her lush figure, to her unspoken sensuality. Gabby, dressed in one of Madame Carême's creations, was a danger to all mankind.

"I will write Peter tonight and send it by messenger," Quill said. He was horrified to hear the rasp in his tone. He'd better start researching firms in Jamaica. Or perhaps in Zanzibar. Jamaica was too close; he would still be able to imagine Gabby dancing at that ball she wanted to attend so much. Would imagine her melting into a man's arms. At the ball, and then . . . after the ball.

Quill swallowed and stood up so abruptly that his chair almost fell. He bowed regally. "Please forgive me, Gabby. I find that I am already late for my engagement this evening."

"Oh, Quill, mightn't I go with you?"

"Absolutely not. Ladies never accompany men to private engagements," Quill snapped.

"Why not?"

Gabby's eyelashes were dark, dark brown, and then, just at the curling ends, they turned a dusky gold that matched her hair. "A lady," Quill said exactingly, "does not query a gentleman about his engagements."

"Oh." Gabby's face lightened and she smiled. "I suppose you are going to visit your *chère amie*. How nice that you have one! Is she someone I would like?"

"God," Quill muttered. Gabby was beyond unconventional. She wasn't misguided either. She was simply a force of nature. Were there any businesses located in the nether reaches of the Antarctic? Perhaps he could start a trade in polar-bear skins. "I do not have a *chère amie*," he snapped. "And it is most improper of you to mention such a thing to me."

"All right," Gabby said amiably, filing away yet another rule in her growing and seemingly endless list of English improprieties. "But why not, Quill?"

Quill had lost track of the conversation again. "Why not what?"

"Why don't you have a woman friend? In India, all the English gentlemen had female friends, or so I had heard. Not that I am discussing it," she added hastily. "I am only asking you, Quill, and you are practically my family, so it's of no account."

It was amazing how many things Gabby assumed were of no account because he was family, Quill thought sourly.

"I will not discuss the subject with you, Gabby." And this time his face was so menacing that she could not dismiss his comment as moodiness.

"It was simply a friendly question!"

Quill gave a bark of laughter. "Just don't ask that sort of question around Peter."

Gabby had a splendid wounded look, when she chose to employ it. "I view you as my personal friend, Quill. My only friend in England," she added. "If you are not to tell me how to behave, who will?"

"Peter," Quill replied decisively. "Peter is extremely good at this sort of thing." And for the first time, he felt quite happy at the image of Peter returning from Bath.

Gabby had risen from his desk and was wandering about his library, so Quill drew up a sheet of parchment and scrawled a note to Peter on the spot.

> *Future wife is now adequately attired in Carême. She demands to be entertained in society. Please return at once, or I shall be forced to introduce her myself.*

The note had precisely the effect that Quill expected. The idea of someone other than himself undertaking the delicate task of introducing Gabby to the London *ton* sent a shiver down Peter's backbone. Moreover, the idea of his elder brother—so careless and indelicate in his ways—performing that task was like to make his hair stand on end.

Viscountess Dewland fully participated in her son's feelings. "My darling, you must return to London at once," she urged him. "Quill is the best of sons, but he has no finesse. Your father is in good fettle."

Peter nodded. Within a week, he was posting back to London. It was just as well, he thought to himself in the corner of the coach. His knee-high boots had gained an appalling scratch on the inner left sole. New ones were a necessity, and only Hoby made boots with a proper sense of fashion. Nothing, but nothing, in Bath had been worth purchasing.

Chapter 9

LUCIEN COULD NOT BRING himself to make impertinent inquiries about the lovely Thorpe sisters, but he had no such hesitation about Emily's male spy, Mr. Hislop. And everything he heard confirmed his worst suspicions. Mr. Hislop was a lecherous young sprig, known to be in the petticoat line.

So, against his better judgment, Lucien presented himself at the door of Mrs. Ewing's small house on Tuesday morning at eleven o'clock precisely. He intended to deal with Mr. Hislop while making it perfectly clear that his only interest in Mrs. Ewing was avuncular. He had spent a good deal of time brooding over the concept of becoming a paterfamilias to both Emily and Phoebe. It was all he was good for, with his widowed heart and old body.

When Sally answered the door, she curtsied and said that Mrs. Ewing was not receiving callers. But Sally was no match for the lure of a shilling.

She pointed out Emily's study door. "The mistress is not accepting calls, because she's expecting a visitor," Sally whispered. Then she took herself off to the nether regions of the house, hugging her coin and comforting herself for her indiscretion with the thought that the French gentleman was that handsome. It would be good for the missus to marry him, even if he was a frog. Sally didn't think much of foreigners in general. But, then, Mr. Boch was . . . was, well, it was sinful that a man looked like that.

Emily glanced up in some annoyance when the door to her study swung open. She preferred to have Hislop introduced with as much ceremony as possible; she felt it kept him from feeling as if he were part of the household.

But it was Lucien Boch standing in the doorway, not Hislop. Something started to pound in her chest. She had found herself thinking about Lucien Boch far too much in the past few weeks.

"May I help you, Mr. Boch? I must apologize; I have been working, and I am not prepared for visitors." Emily rose from her desk and gracefully untied the apron that covered her muslin dress from accidental ink splatters. She had a terribly untidy hand. "I'm afraid I cannot converse at length, as I am expecting a visitor."

Lucien wasn't quite sure what to do. He'd come prepared to slay the dragon, and there was no dragon, yet. "I came to inquire whether you would accompany me to Lady Fester's ball," he said.

Emily drew in a slow breath. Apparently Mr. Boch was not trying to lure her to another fashion magazine. "I do not go into society," she murmured noncommittally.

Lucien raised an eyebrow. "I am offering you the opportunity to do so."

"I'm afraid that I must decline your gracious invitation," she replied.

"May I ask why?" Lucien asked, unforgivably. A gentleman never, never asked for the reasons behind a lady's refusal.

But he told himself that he had to make conversation, because he wanted to be in the room when Hislop arrived.

"I have never been formally presented," Emily explained. "I attended a few balls before leaving my family home, but I would not feel comfortable at a large gathering. Although," she added, "I am most grateful for your invitation, Mr. Boch."

"I understood from Miss Thorpe that it would be a welcome opportunity for you to examine the clothing of fashionable women," Lucien said, trying to sound persuasive rather than desperate. "I can assure you that the entire *beau monde* will attend the Fester ball."

Emily hesitated. Perhaps Lucien wasn't cut from the same cloth as the lustful Mr. Hislop. Mr. Hislop had also offered to accompany her to various occasions, but only, she was quite sure, so that he could make unwelcome approaches to her in the privacy of his carriage. Recently he had even begun to hint that he would no longer give her information if she didn't accept one of his invitations.

Lucien was still standing in the center of the room. Now he approached her and bowed. "I would be most honored if you would join me," he said gently.

Emily could hardly breathe. Men had no right to have eyelashes that long. They had no right to look at one with liquid black eyes and be so . . . so appealing.

"You are very obliging," she said finally.

"I would be grateful for the company," Lucien said. "And I would be most happy if your sister could accompany us, as chaperone."

"My sister, a chaperone!" Emily almost snorted. Even the suggestion proved that Lucien had not inquired about their situation. He couldn't know that Louise had been besmirched across all England as a wanton light-skirt. "My sister does not venture into public," she said tightly.

"In that case, I will ask an acquaintance of mine to accompany us. I would not wish you to feel uncomfortable in my company."

Emily met Lucien's eyes and felt ashamed that she had ever wondered whether he was a degenerate like Mr. Hislop. "I would be most pleased to accompany you to the Fester ball," she said. "I have changed my mind."

"That is a woman's privilege," Lucien said, a smile lighting his eyes. He bowed again. "I am honored."

"And you needn't ask an acquaintance to come with us," Emily added hastily. "I am a widow, after all. Widows do not need chaperones."

"Yes, of course," Lucien murmured.

Was there a sardonic note in his eye? Emily nervously touched the little cap she wore.

Lucien could not think of any other reason to waste the lovely Emily's time, so he had turned about to leave when Sally pushed open the doors and said, rather sharply, "Mr. Hislop is here, missus." She was in a mood, having been pinched twice on the way down the hall. She gave Hislop a sour look and stamped off.

Bartholomew Bayley Hislop was not a handsome man. Emily noticed in an instant that it was a positive cruelty to put him in a room with Lucien Boch. Lucien stood, slim, dressed in black, his manner and clothing bespeaking his state as a marquis. Or former marquis, Emily reminded herself.

But Bartholomew Hislop was not blessed in his tailor. This morning he was dressed in what he considered the highest kick of fashion: an olive frock coat with enormous metal buttons down the front, left open to reveal a waistcoat violently striped in purple and yellow. On the personal front, he had fluffy sideburns, worn rather long (in a style that Bartholomew believed to be all the rage), and thin legs, not quite knock-kneed. Add a cheerfully lascivious glint in his eye, and you had Bartholomew Bayley Hislop, the only son and heir to a butcher who had made huge amounts of money boiling cow's bones into glue—enough to send his only son off to Cambridge and now to support him in the metropolis.

Emily greeted Hislop with rather more cheer than she generally showed him. "Mr. Hislop, what a pleasure to see you again!" She watched as he bowed, and then gave him a brief curtsy. "May I present Mr. Lucien Boch?"

Bartholomew Hislop didn't recognize Mr. Boch, but that didn't bother him. He *did* recognize his tailor. "I'm happy to meet you, sir! Very pleased to meet you! I have decided to forswear the single-breasted frock coat myself. Gave it up around, oh, thirteen weeks ago. I decided the style made me look a trifle pigeon-chested. Not that the effect is so on you, my dear sir. And that particular frock coat is made by Guthrie, is it not?"

Lucien bowed. "You have located my tailor exactly, sir."

"Well, not located," Hislop said punctiliously. "I have not *personally* employed Mr. Guthrie. I'm afraid I demand, shall we say, a trifle more of an adventurous attitude in a tailor. But I believe that Mr. Guthrie is currently situated in Leadenhall Street, number twenty-seven, is he not?"

"You are correct."

"I generally am in these matters, my dear sir. Now, I can see at a glance that you are a foreign gentleman, Mr. Boch, and so you probably have not heard of me. But I can assure you that I am building a wee reputation amongst men of mode, amongst those of the first circles. I fancy that I have an eye, a flair. And"—he leered at Emily—"one of my greatest joys is sharing my observations with Mrs. Ewing. It gives me enormous pleasure to do my small something for *La Belle Assemblée*."

Lucien looked at Emily. She read the disgust in his eyes and gave him a frown.

"I'm very much afraid that I shall have to ask you to excuse us, sir. Mr. Hislop has been kind enough to promise to share his notes regarding the fashion worn at a reception given for the Duke and Duchess of Gisle, and I am sure you would find such minutiae tedious."

"The duke and duchess just returned from Turkey," Hislop said importantly. "Lady Gisle wore Carême, of course."

Lucien allowed himself to be walked to the door. He bowed and then gave Emily a wry smile. "I came to slay a dragon," he murmured, for her ears alone. "Phoebe led me to believe that Mr. Hislop was a disagreeable companion."

Emily smiled despite herself. "I am always grateful for the presence of dragon slayers," she said, her gentle voice sounding like music to Lucien. "There are so few of them in London. But you need have no worries about Mr. Hislop, sir. He is a good friend to me."

And she closed the study door to the sound of Bartholomew Hislop droning on about the precise weight of the Egyptian velvet that the Duchess of Gisle had worn.

Lucien let himself out of the house without troubling Sally, who was nowhere to be seen. He walked down the stairs, frowning. He did not like Emily's dependence on Hislop. Unless Lucien was very much mistaken, Hislop wasn't visiting every week only for the greater glory of *La Belle Assemblée*. No, Hislop was interested in the beautiful Mrs. Ewing. And Lucien doubted very much that Hislop was considering marriage to a penniless widow.

ON THE WHOLE, Peter was able to declare himself pleased by the transformed Gabby. They met at dinner the day after he returned to London, Peter having punctiliously sent Gabby a note asking her to accompany him to a ball being held by Lady Fester that very evening.

Gabby was wearing one of Madame's gowns and shining with delight to see her betrothed. Margaret had had to use so many pearl-topped hairpins that her brown hair took on a pearly glow from afar. But her slippery locks were firmly poised in the air, and that was the important thing. And her dress, a bronze-colored ball gown with an extremely daring neckline and a slight train on the overdress, was certainly à la mode, Peter observed. He would have noted the gown immediately, even if it weren't on his bride-to-be. Thank God, those big bosoms of Gabby's suited the design.

"Is your drapery made of tiffany?" He leaned close to Gabby, who was toying with her consommé.

Gabby looked up quickly. Peter's eyes were much more friendly than they had been the first time they met. "I don't know," she admitted.

Peter said, "May I?" and at her nod, he gently pressed the fabric between two fingers for a split second. "Gauze— spotted with gold embroidery," he announced. "Most suitable."

Gabby had been unhappy with the said drapery. "If this is supposed to be a shawl, it doesn't cover anything!" she had wailed to Margaret.

"You simply *drape* it," Margaret had explained.

Thank goodness Margaret had talked her out of carrying a cashmere shawl, given Peter's interest in her drapery, Gabby thought fervently.

Quill watched the happy pair from under heavy-lidded eyes. Perhaps he'd go out and get blind drunk tonight. It was a luxury he rarely, if ever, indulged in. But now the oblivion of too much brandy sounded enviable.

"Will you join us, Quill?"

Quill shook his head. In his present mood, it was only irritating to find Peter acting his generous self. It couldn't be easy for the pink of the *ton* to have a brother who was both lame and antisocial. But Peter never failed to urge Quill to accompany him to various events.

"Perhaps I will stop in later," Quill said, quite to his own surprise.

Gabby gave him one of her huge smiles. "That would be delightful, Quill! I shall look for you."

Peter ushered Gabby into the carriage, noting with approval the velvet pelisse that Madame had designed to accompany this particular gown. "You look quite well this evening," he pronounced in the semidarkness of the carriage.

"She's a beauty," Lady Sylvia agreed. "You're in luck, Peter. It's risky, getting a bride from abroad. One of my second cousins contracted a gel from Scotland who turned out to be a tallow-faced chit. He ran away to the Americas before the wedding."

Gabby sighed with relief. She'd done it. Peter approved of her.

Peter had an alarmed thought. "Do you know how to dance?"

"Yes," Gabby said. "Although I have never danced with a man," she admitted. "My father hired an Englishwoman to teach me."

Peter quite liked that idea. If Gabby misplaced a step, he could gently drop the fact that his betrothed had never been held in a man's arms before. There weren't many men in London who could say such a thing.

"Don't worry," he said comfortingly. "I will explain everything."

Gabby's heart expanded with happiness. Peter was acting precisely like the sweet gentleman of her daydreams: protective, thoughtful, admiring. "Oh, Peter," she exclaimed, "I'm so happy we're to be married!"

Peter was taken aback. What the devil was he supposed to say to that? And why would she say something so intimate before Lady Sylvia? "Quite appropriate," he finally managed.

Gabby was only a little disappointed. It was too early for Peter to express the same anticipation that she felt. But perhaps this evening they would kiss, the way she and Quill had kissed. She had sensed anticipation in Quill's hard body, in his darkened eyes. She meant to see that same emotion in Peter by the end of the evening.

LADY ISABEL FESTER was quite proud of the fact that her ball was always the very first event held after the opening of Parliament each year. In truth, she took great care to make sure that her ball marked the opening of the Little Season; when the Parliament inconsiderately delayed its opening in 1804, due to concern for the king's health, Lady Fester boldly canceled her ball, citing the same reason, and resent her invitations only once the danger was past. She felt, with some truth, that her ball had gained a certain notoriety, and for those, like herself, who could not bear to wither in the country until March or April, it served as a signal that *la haute société* had returned to London. Let all the matchmaking mamas huddle in the damp country houses until after Easter. The true *élégantes*—Lady Fester had had a French nurse and liked to show off her claims to high education— the true *élégantes* would never molder outside London if they were not forced to do so.

Thus the polite smile on her face actually gained a glimmer of true welcome when she saw one of the most elegant men in all of London, Lucien Boch, walking behind her butler.

"My dear marquis," Lady Fester cooed. She was well-aware that Boch had repudiated his title, but she believed in overlooking such foolish mistakes.

Lucien bowed extravagantly and kissed her fingers. "Dearest Lady Fester," he said, "may I present Mrs. Ewing?"

Lady Fester's eyes narrowed fractionally. Emily Thorpe—no matter what she chose to call herself—was not the sort of woman whom Lady Fester cared to welcome to her ball. But in the split second before she issued a glacial acknowledgment, her eye caught Mrs. Ewing's gown. It was created of amber-colored Italian gauze, worn over crepe of a slightly darker shade. The gauze was caught up in amber ribbons, and beads ornamented the bodice and the sleeves. In all truth, Mrs. Ewing's gown was easily the most original creation Lady Fester had seen all evening. And it would undoubtedly be detailed in the next issue of *La Belle Assemblée,* an honor that Lady Fester herself was longing to receive. She suffered a stab of envy that was almost blinding in its force.

"I am very pleased to meet you, Mrs. Ewing," she said respectfully. The gown had won the day.

"Well," Lucien breathed into Emily's ear as they strolled into the ballroom, "in case you didn't recognize it, my dear, there was a dragon guarding the entrance to this ball. And you just floated past her guard."

Emily looked up at him, her eyes shining. "How could it be otherwise? I have a dragon slayer with me, do I not?"

He chuckled. "I cannot take credit for that particular victory. Would you like to dance?"

Emily paused and looked over a ballroom shimmering with gowns in the neoclassical mode, gowns heavily trimmed with satin roses, gowns with collars of lace, and gowns whose bodices were so low that the waistlines mimicked a collar. "Oh, my," she breathed. "Oh, this is wonderful!" Then she clutched Lucien's arm. "Do you happen to know the young woman next to the window, Mr. Boch?"

Lucien looked in that direction. "Do you mean the lady with all the objects in her hair?"

"That is a *very* fashionable coiffure," Emily said, instinctively pulling him slightly in that direction. "She's dressed her hair with lace, and I can see at least one white ostrich feather."

"Don't forget all those tassels," Lucien said disapprovingly. "However, as it happens, I do know Cecilia Morgan, and I'd be happy to introduce you."

A moment later, he bowed before Cecilia. Within a few moments, Emily and Cecilia—or Sissy, as she insisted Emily call her—were deep in a discussion of the virtues of pink silk tassels as opposed to ostrich feathers, and Lucien and Sissy's sturdy husband, Squire Morgan, were relegated to the side.

As the evening progressed, Lucien found, to his utter astonishment, that he didn't mind the fact that Emily could hardly be persuaded to stand up with him. Instead, he watched her charm the women of the very society that had rejected her, ignoring their initial frosty greetings and winning them over by her engaging, infectious interest in fashion. Discussing the merits of slashed sleeves, Emily became alight with joy. She belongs here, Lucien thought with a pang. Not in that tiny house with its shabby furniture and few servants. Finally he dragged her away from an animated discussion of the fact that crepe conversation hats were quite, quite out of date, and drew her into a dance.

She floated in his arms. As they swept down the room, he had the fierce knowledge that they moved more gracefully than any of the other guests. It brought with it a mild intoxication, although it was not nearly as intoxicating as Emily's slender body in his arms.

SUCH A SWEET LITTLE SMILE lit the corners of Gabby's mouth as they walked into the Fester ball that Peter was startled. Gabby appeared to be looking forward to the evening as much as he did, generally speaking. Mind you, he was a bit more nervous than usual tonight. But normally he felt a racing sense of excitement as the evening hour approached, ushering in hours of pleasure and possibility. At every ball he strengthened his position in the *ton* just a trifle, he fancied. In every conversation, he strove to present himself in the best possible fashion.

At first the evening went very well indeed. Peter introduced Miss Gabrielle Jerningham to his friends, and according to their several interests they either gaped at her bosom or queried as to whether she was wearing Carême. Thank God for Madame. Every man in the room seemed to have eyes only for Gabby.

Gabby behaved very well and seemed rather subdued by the glittering extravagances of a London ball. She danced fairly well, Peter found. That was an important consideration. He himself thought that dancing ought to be a gentleperson's primary form of exercise, and he rarely sat out even a rousing country dance. He left more arcane forms of exercise to his brother, who, now that he couldn't ride a horse, spent hours stripped to the skin and performing grunting contortions.

Peter's favorite dance was the polonaise, and to his delight, Gabby danced it commendably. It was a slow, stately dance that appeared simple to the onlooker. But it depended on split-second timing and languid motion. There was nothing more distasteful than jerky movements or someone rushing the beat.

All in all, Peter was more than satisfied with his new betrothed. Acquaintances clustered about him and complimented him on his future wife's exquisite taste in clothing, her ladylike demeanor, her graceful bearing on the ballroom floor. Countess Maria Sefton had commiserated with him over his father's illness and had announced that she would send vouchers to Almack's. He didn't even have to ask. The lascivious Prince of Wales had elbowed Peter in the chest and whispered that his bride was a true dasher, with the voice of a siren. Peter didn't hear anything siren-like about Gabby's voice, but he didn't argue. That was high praise from Prinny.

Thus when Gabby returned from a speedy version of Jenny Pluck Pears and wanly pleaded exhaustion, Peter allowed that they might retire for a moment onto the balcony.

"What you need is fresh air," Peter announced, ignoring Gabby's pleas that they retire for the evening. It was only two in the morning, and no one was even thinking of departing. But obviously it took time to develop the fortitude required of an English gentlewoman. Under no circumstances were ladies allowed to flag or look anything less than perfectly attired and coiffed. He had kept a sharp eye on Gabby's hair and had already sent her away twice to have it pinned up.

"Lady Sylvia seems to be quite exhausted," Gabby said in desperation. Her chaperone had been dozing in a chair at the side of the ballroom for the last half hour.

Peter shrugged. "She always naps. She'll wake up for supper, and no one will think the less of you for it."

That hadn't been Gabby's point. If those chairs weren't so spindly and uncomfortable, she could go to sleep herself.

"We shall visit the balcony and inspect the gardens."

Gabby shivered. A Mr. Barlow had taken her out on the balcony earlier in the evening, and she had almost turned into ice. It was virtually December, after all. Why, any moment she might get struck on the head with a huge ice ball. It was not the weather to be outside, especially with her entire bosom exposed.

But Peter was towing her toward one of the three doors leading to small balconies overlooking the gardens. Gabby sighed. It had been, to her mind, a miserably dreary evening. She couldn't count the number of gentlemen who had accidentally touched her chest or rubbed her back. She felt like a plucked chicken that kept getting pinched by housewives looking for the very plumpest fowl.

The balcony was just as cold as she remembered. Peter left the door wide open. "We are engaged," he explained, "but I would not want to give anyone cause to question your reputation."

Gabby opened her mouth and almost remarked that Mr. Barlow had closed the doors. But then she thought better of it. Oddly enough, she found her future husband quite difficult to confide in. Much more so than Quill. That was probably because she was in love with Peter, Gabby reminded herself.

She was absolutely frozen, but perhaps—perhaps this was a good time for their first kiss? Gabby smiled.

She drifted closer to Peter, who looked up in surprise. "It's quite, quite cold, Peter," Gabby said. She didn't want to ask him for a kiss. Peter should kiss her the first time of his own initiative.

Peter peered at her. "Would you like to go inside, then?

Have you woken up? You mustn't look sleepy in the ballroom, Gabby. A lady should always look lively and refreshed, even when in the throes of exhaustion."

Gabby was now standing so close to Peter that she could easily touch him. She was aware, given the arctic temperature, that her nipples were readily visible through the bodice of Madame's gown. She had a clear memory of Quill's groan at discovering the same physical fact in the drawing room.

But Peter was showing no signs of looking at her chest, or of kissing her, for that matter. In fact, he was looking rather discomforted. "Peter," Gabby said in her sweetest, most docile tone. "Since we are to be married, I think it would be acceptable for you to kiss me."

Peter practically recoiled. "Absolutely not! No such action is acceptable at a ball, under any circumstances."

There was an awkward silence.

Gabby swallowed hard. "Do you really mean to say that you don't wish to kiss me?"

Peter thrust his hand through his brown curls. "Of course I want to kiss you, Gabby."

Gabby looked at him mutely, appeal in her eyes.

"Oh, for God's sake!" Peter exclaimed. He tipped up her chin and put his lips on hers.

Gabby stood still and closed her eyes. The last thing she wanted to do was embarrass herself by being too forward.

But Peter showed no inclination toward great intimacy. His lips pressed on hers slightly, and a second later withdrew. Gabby opened her eyes. Peter was smiling at her.

"Well, that's over," he said jovially. "I expect that was your first kiss, wasn't it, Gabby?"

Gabby hesitated, and then threw herself against his chest and pasted her lips to his. Luckily he was considerably shorter than Quill and she was able to reach his mouth.

Peter gasped in shock.

She thought he was opening his lips, precisely as Quill had taught her was the fashion in kissing, and so she followed suit.

But Peter's hands did not wrap around her. Instead, he grabbed her bare shoulders and furiously pushed her away.

"My God!" Peter was appalled. He was disgusted. His stomach was churning. "Are you crazed?" He looked at his betrothed. Her hair was tumbling down again, and her nipples were—by God, she was precisely what Prinny had said. When Prinny had called her a dasher, he didn't mean a person of style, but a coquette. Prinny was warning him! Prinny was his friend, and that was no compliment—it was a *warning*!

"You are, that is, you're debauched," he managed to choke out.

Gabby wrapped her arms around her shivering chest. Peter was the most punctilious person she'd ever met in her life. After all, Mr. Barlow showed every intention of kissing her on the balcony, until she ducked under his arm and returned to the ballroom; *he* wasn't overwrought about propriety.

"And your hair! You even look tawdry!"

"Peter," Gabby said in her most reasonable voice, "we are engaged. I am persuaded that no one would cry scandal if we briefly embraced."

Peter cast a haunted look at the open door. "Anyone could have seen us! And if they had, you would be an outcast in London society."

Gabby bit her lip. "I feel that you are exaggerating," she said carefully. "But I shall retire to the ladies' chamber." She walked through the door. Then she popped her head back onto the balcony. "Would you have kissed me in the carriage on the way home?"

Peter's stomach churned again. "Absolutely not! Do you think Lady Sylvia wouldn't notice?"

"Well, would you have kissed me if Lady Sylvia wasn't there?"

"Lady Sylvia or my mother will always be with us, until we are married," Peter retorted. "It would be most improper for us to be unchaperoned."

Gabby disappeared, presumably taking herself off to fix her hair. Peter took a deep breath and touched his cravat. Luckily it didn't appear to be too crushed.

A cheerful voice broke into his thoughts. "Knew it had to be you out here, Peter, my lad!" One of his friends, Lord Simon Putney, walked through the door and took out a small cigar. "Saw your betrothed leaving the balcony. Never thought you'd do so well for yourself. She's a beauty. Her breasts!" Simon kissed his fingers. "I always thought you'd marry one of those icy types, if you married at all," he continued genially. "But you've caught the best one of the Season!"

Simon lowered his voice and gave Peter a manly sort of look. "You know what I mean. She looks as if she'll liven up your bedchamber, old fellow."

Peter did. In fact, he was so gloomily aware of the truth of his friend's assessment that he stayed out on the balcony for a half hour, smoking one of Simon's cigars. Normally he would never do such a thing, given that the pungent odor of tobacco was so difficult to remove from clothing. But it was comforting, under the circumstances.

The only problem was that Simon proved to be intoxicated, and he waxed more and more enthusiastic about Gabby's prime feature—her breasts. Peter restrained himself from saying irritably that if he wanted to buy a cow he would have gone to the country. The pure unkindness of the remark was not fair. Gabby's chest was not her fault.

Gabby, meanwhile, was sitting in the ladies' chamber having her hair pinned up yet again when Sophie Foakes, the Duchess of Gisle, entered the room.

"Miss Jerningham!" Sophie exclaimed with delight.

"Do forgive me for not rising, Your Grace," Gabby said with a smile. The maid still had some twenty hairpins to apply, and if Gabby moved, the whole process would have to begin again.

"Oh, surely we needn't be so formal," Sophie exclaimed as she plumped herself into a chair next to Gabby. "Now, are you enjoying London, Miss Jerningham?"

"Please, will you call me Gabby?" The question was impetuous, but the duchess seemed very friendly.

"I would adore to," Sophie replied promptly, "as long as you call me Sophie. We shall scandalize the old biddies."

"Why would it be scandalous?" Gabby felt a bit wary about causing scandal, given Peter's admonishments.

"Oh, it isn't really, Gabby. It's just that women of my mother's generation who have known each other since the cradle are still greeting each other as Lady Such and So. Now, why haven't I seen you in Hyde Park or at my reception? I sent you a card."

Gabby looked about. They were the only ladies in the chamber at the moment. "I had to wait until Madame Carême's clothing was delivered," she confided. "Peter was most adamant about my remaining in the house until I was properly attired."

Sophie frowned. "That doesn't sound like sweet Peter." Then she thought for a moment. "Well, of course, your appearance would be most important to him. You look splendid, by the way. I wear a good deal of Carême myself. Tomorrow I intend to *demand* a small train on the gowns she is making up for me. I fully expect that you will start a rage!"

"Perhaps," Gabby said, and then chuckled. "I think it's more likely that I shall start a scandal. I am not persuaded that this bodice will stay in place."

"Oh, it will," Sophie assured her. "We have approximately the same figure and I have never had a problem in that respect. Madame has a magical touch. Goodness, I'm tired!" she added, fanning herself idly. "I always find this point in the evening simply unbearable."

Gabby looked at her curiously. "Why not go home, then?"

"Oh, it improves," Sophie replied. "They'll call for the supper dance soon. After eating, most people find a second wind. And, of course, by then the gentlemen in the card room have become quite inebriated. That always creates some interest," she said with a mischievous twinkle.

"How are drunken men of interest?"

"They garner their courage."

At Gabby's questioning look, she continued. "They approach women who are not their wives, or they begin absurd arguments and get themselves into a primitive display of male temper."

"That does sound more interesting," Gabby observed.

"Ladies, too, throw caution to the wind and wander off into the garden unchaperoned. That wakes up my mother and the rest of the more severe dowagers." She smiled impishly. "I used to count the evening quite wasted if I didn't give my mother at least one reason to scold me on the way home."

Gabby smiled back rather uncertainly. Then she asked, in a near whisper, "Were you ever kissed on a balcony? I mean, before you were married?"

Sophie grinned. "Yes, of course, I've been kissed on a balcony—many balconies, as a matter of fact."

"Did it cause a scandal?"

"Oh, certainly," Sophie said blithely. "Until I married Patrick, I was practically the most scandalous baggage in the *ton*. My mother used to lecture me all the way to a ball and then rant all the way home. I have some lovely memories."

To Gabby's mind, Sophie's memories stood in direct opposition to Peter's view of scandal.

"But Peter said—" Gabby stopped. She didn't really want to confide the sneaking suspicion she had, that Peter didn't want to kiss her anywhere, not on a balcony, nor in a carriage, nor anywhere else.

"Who tried to kiss you? Was it that dreadful Mr. Barlow? I saw you dancing with him."

"Yes," Gabby said gratefully. "He asked if I would like to see the balcony, and then . . ."

"He's a loose fish. What did you do?"

"I elbowed him and walked out."

"Well, Peter must approve of that," Sophie observed. "I expect he was jealous. It's my impression that Patrick takes great pleasure in interpreting my behavior as scandalous, and likely Peter is the same. But there's no way you could have known that Barlow is such a turnip." Sophie rose. "We should reappear in the ballroom, or my husband will search me out. He's still absurdly besotted."

And when Gabby smiled, the duchess added, "We haven't been married long. I daresay we will grow tired of each other any moment."

"I doubt it," Gabby said, looking at the exquisite woman before her. "Your husband is a very lucky man, Your Grace."

"You promised," Sophie complained. "My name is Sophie." She took Gabby's hand. "Patrick would fuss if I left the room with Barlow. The man is a gross lecher. I'll find you a perfectly unexceptionable escort so that Peter can't complain."

To Gabby's pleasure, she and Sophie were met at the bottom of the stairs by Peter and Lucien Boch, who was, rather unexpectedly, escorting Phoebe's mother, Mrs. Ewing.

"How lovely to see you!" Gabby said warmly to Emily Ewing.

"You missed the supper dance, Duchess," came a deep voice to her right. Gabby turned to find Sophie laughingly tapping a very handsome man with her fan. Gabby rather thought he must be the duke, and when he cupped a hand around her new friend's waist and dropped a kiss on her eyebrow, she was quite sure he was.

Five minutes later, there was a little flurry as the three men made certain that their respective escorts were comfortably seated in the supper room, after which they began to fight their way through the crowd toward the tables.

"This is splendid," Sophie declared. "It will take them at least a half hour to snatch even the barest chicken wing, so we can become better acquainted in the interim. I must tell you, Mrs. Ewing, that although I have been positively thirsting to own Gabby's gown all evening, I now find myself quite moonstruck over yours as well. It's lowering to be so riveted by jealousy."

Emily smiled, her blue-gray eyes uncertain. "Thank you, Your Grace."

Just then Lucien reappeared and touched Emily's shoulder. She turned to look up at him, and her rather solemn face broke into a dimpled smile. "Mr. Boch?"

Lucien appeared to have momentarily forgotten what he meant to ask. "I . . . I merely wondered if you would prefer fowl or fish, Mrs. Ewing."

"Fowl, please," she replied. Lucien paused, and then caught sight of Sophie's and Gabby's interested eyes. He turned rather blindly into the crowd and disappeared.

"Goodness me," Sophie said with a gurgle of laughter in her voice. "I have known Lucien Boch some five seasons, and I have never seen him struck dumb before this evening."

A faint blush rose into Emily's cheeks. "Mr. Boch escorted me to this ball merely as an act of charity. He is a very kind man."

Sophie twinkled at Gabby. "What do you think? Could kindness explain why the sweetest-tongued man in all London suddenly began stammering at the mere sight of Mrs. Ewing's smile?"

"Of course, I am not well-acquainted with Mr. Boch," Gabby replied mischievously, "but he struck me as eminently logical before this evening. . . . I wonder what could have turned him into such a noodlehead, if not your smile, Mrs. Ewing?"

Emily's blush deepened. "Truly, Mr. Boch is simply a good friend. There is naught more to his escort than pure kindness."

Gabby took pity on her. "How is Phoebe today, Mrs. Ewing?" She turned to Sophie. "Mrs. Ewing's niece and I traveled from India on the same vessel."

"Phoebe is most amusing," Emily replied hurriedly, obviously grateful for the change of subject. "She has developed a veritable passion for cooking—" She stopped, remembering that a properly raised child would have nothing to do with the kitchens.

But Sophie's face was alight with interest. "How old is your Phoebe? My very favorite place to be, as a child, was in the kitchens. I prided myself that Cook was unable to make jam without my skills as a tester."

Gabby laughed. "I know exactly what you mean! Our cook was kind enough to make me the primary household authority on custard tartlets. I absolutely loved to spoon in the filling."

Emily almost gaped. She herself had never been allowed anywhere near the kitchens. In fact, it was a rare day when she and Louise were allowed to leave the nursery at all. "I thought perhaps I should dissuade Phoebe," she admitted. "Cooking is not a very ladylike activity, after all."

"I suppose it is different when one actually has children," Sophie said thoughtfully, "but I often promised myself as a child that I would not encourage too many of those ladylike but useless activities."

Gabby nodded. "I had a succession of governesses as a young child, and some of them had the most arcane ideas of what a lady should do with her time!"

Just then Lady Sylvia bustled up. "Gentlemen have deserted you, have they? Thought I'd go sit with all the old biddies, Gabrielle. After all, yer escorted by two married ladies. Just look lively, gel. You don't want anyone to think you're napping."

"No, of course not, Lady Sylvia," Gabby murmured.

As Lady Sylvia trotted away, Sophie met Gabby's eyes in perfect agreement. "All very well for her to say," Sophie complained. "*She* had a nice nap at the side of the room, didn't she?"

The gentlemen returned, plates in hand. And five minutes later, Quill walked up. To Gabby's great pleasure, it was clear that he and Sophie's husband, Patrick Foakes, were the best of friends.

The supper room was filled with chattering, elegant gentlefolk, none of whom appeared the slightest bit exhausted. Peter began a rather ponderous discussion of the polonaise, and Gabby soon entered a kind of sleepwalking state. She was having a hard time keeping her eyes from drooping, although she conscientiously repeated to herself Peter's admonishments about ladies not showing signs of exhaustion.

Quill gave her a sharp look and then raised a finger, summoning one of the footmen. In a moment or two a steaming cup of tea was placed before Gabby.

"Oh, thank you," she said gratefully.

Peter looked disapproving. Clearly tea was not the appropriate drink for that hour. But Sophie was happily requesting the same, and so Gabby sipped her tea in peace and looked about the room.

At the table just behind Sophie's shoulder, one of those interesting events that Sophie had promised appeared to be brewing. Gabby had spent a good deal of her life fashioning stories and telling them to herself, and now she rapidly concocted an explanation for why the double-chinned lady with the nodding feathers on her headdress was looking so very infuriated. Clearly she must be a relative of the jowly lord wearing a silver-blue coat next to her. And *he* must be throwing out lures to the young miss across the table, whose bodice was quite as low as Gabby's. But of course the double-chinned lady wanted her jowly brother to marry someone quite different, perhaps the stern-looking maiden in the olive gown, who sat next to her.

"What are you thinking of, Gabby?" Sophie leaned toward her. "You look to be so much more amused than the rest of us."

"I was spinning stories," Gabby admitted. "Since I know almost no one in London, I was making up tales about strangers."

Sophie laughed. "You're a storyteller! How splendid. Please, tell us a tale and then we shall compare it to the truth. What a splendid game."

Gabby hesitated. But Peter and Lucien were smiling in

approval. Only Quill looked censorious. So she explained the tale she had woven for the next table.

Sophie's clear laughter rang out, and most of the London *ton* craned their necks, discovering with interest that the Duchess of Gisle seemed to find Peter Dewland's future wife most entertaining. Unfortunately, the jowly man's attention was also caught.

Sophie had her back to the jowly man's table and indeed had no idea that the entire room was looking at them, so she continued blithely, "You are not far from the truth, Gabby. But the lord and lady are married. The tension you sense—"

Her husband clapped his hand over her mouth. "You are a caution, my dear wife," Patrick breathed into Sophie's ear. Then he removed his hand, replacing it with a swift, hard kiss.

Sophie twinkled at Gabby. "You see, Gabby darling, men simply *live* to correct our follies."

Gabby laughed.

But laughter—alas, Madame Carême had forgotten to put laughing on the list with wiggling. Perhaps Madame believed that laughter was unlikely to occur in the highest society.

Whatever the reason for Madame's oversight, a room plumb full of the *haut ton* watched in fascination as Gabby's bodice lost its fragile claim to modesty and slid below the bosom it was designed to adorn. Gabby gave a little scream and pulled futilely at the strained silk.

Peter closed his eyes in horror. Emily froze, and Sophie instinctively leaned forward to shield Gabby. Patrick and Quill acted as one man. They both wrenched off their evening coats. Quill reached Gabby first. She felt his large comfort at her shoulder just as folds of black finecloth covered her shameful gown from sight.

Clutching Quill's coat, Gabby looked up, only to meet Peter's horrified gaze. Tears rose to her eyes.

"Miss Jerningham is overtired," Quill said brusquely. Then, without a second's pause, he plucked her off her chair and into his arms. In an instant they were gone from the room.

Sophie's husband, Patrick, burst out laughing. "I gather that Quill's leg is much improved. I haven't seen such a romantic sight in years."

"There's nothing romantic about it," Peter snapped. He owed Quill a thank you, certainly. The best thing was for Gabby to go home immediately and allow the gossip to die down. Not that it would, he was sure of that.

In fact, it was a night that very few people in the London *ton* ever forgot.

A moment or two later Sophie Foakes, the Duchess of Gisle, stood up. But as she did, she seemed to catch the hem of her gown in her slipper, or perhaps she misplaced her hand as she rose from her seat.

Whatever the cause, the attendees at Lady Fester's ball were treated to the unprecedented pleasure of witnessing another lady's bodice drop to her waist—within a mere five minutes of the first!

Sophie's husband had already removed his coat and so he was able to clap it around her shoulders, although some of the onlookers thought that the duke's laughing remonstrance, clearly heard by all—"For goodness sake, Sophie! There's such a thing as taking loyalty too far!"—did not properly address the issue.

It was widely agreed in many a ladies' parlor, the following morning, that the French mode of dressing had been adapted too rapidly by the young ladies of the *ton*. Madame Carême, too, came in for a share of censure.

But it was even more widely agreed in many a gentlemen's club, the following afternoon, that Peter Dewland was one of the luckiest men in London. The same truth had already been established about Patrick Foakes, the Duke of Gisle, and so his manifest good fortune was hardly mentioned.

Chapter 10

QUILL STARED into the fireplace, the taste of doom in his mouth. He had stepped over the bounds of civility. He had lost all claim to the title of gentleman. Not only did he snatch his brother's intended wife up in his arms and carry her off before the interested eyes of half of London, but later . . .

Yes, later.

He sighed and stretched his leg. Miraculously, it seemed utterly untouched by the experience of carrying Gabby through Lady Fester's house and into the carriage. Quill had deposited Gabby on the seat, with every intention of escorting her home in the most proper fashion. But then she started sobbing.

At first he couldn't understand a thing Gabby said. Then her words tumbled together into a miserable acknowledgment of a fact that, unfortunately, Quill agreed with.

"He'll never love me!" Gabby had cried, her breath caught with sobs. "Peter looked at me with just the distaste that my father—that my father—" And her speech wandered into tangled incoherencies again.

Quill felt helpless in the face of such a storm of female unhappiness. Awkwardly, he pulled her head against his shoulder and patted her back. But he found himself patting his own evening coat, since she was still wearing it, and he couldn't tell whether she even felt his touch through its thick folds.

Then Gabby raised her head and looked him straight in the eye. "Peter will never love me the way I love him, will he, Quill?"

Quill's heart skipped a beat. "It depends on how you love him," he finally said, well-aware that his pedantic tone was not at all suitable to the occasion.

"I love him," Gabby sobbed. "I love his . . . I love his picture, and I thought he would never look at me with reproach. And he does! And he wouldn't kiss me, and I so wanted him to kiss me. Probably every man would look at me that way, but I can't bear it, because I thought that Peter would be, would be—" And she broke down sobbing and collapsed against Quill's chest again.

Quill couldn't make heads or tails of her explanation. He did grasp that Gabby wanted Peter to kiss her. Well, naturally she does, he told himself. She's in love with him. She's *marrying* him.

"I am sure that Peter wants to kiss you," Quill said, taking a deliberate plunge into the shady area of possible untruths.

"He doesn't! We went on the balcony, and when I kissed him, he pushed me away! He was very fierce," she added.

"Peter has a strong sense of propriety," Quill answered, relieved. This wasn't as bad as he thought. "Peter would never kiss a woman in the middle of a ball."

"Why not? A horrid man, Mr. Barlow, tried to kiss me."

"Because propriety matters to Peter," Quill replied lamely. He was wishing desperately that someone else had joined them in the carriage. Where was Lady Sylvia? This sort of conversation needed a woman's touch.

"I don't think so," Gabby whispered. She was starting to calm down, only occasionally giving a little hiccuping sob.

Quill took out a large linen handkerchief and dried her face. Tears had turned Gabby's lips a deep crimson that did nothing for his peace of mind.

"I don't think Peter wishes to kiss me at all." The rejection in her voice caught at Quill's heart. "I'm going to be married to a man who doesn't like kissing me."

"Your conclusions are illogical," Quill pointed out. "Just because Peter has a strict sense of propriety doesn't mean that he—"

"He didn't enjoy kissing me," Gabby replied firmly. "I could tell. Do you think that he is in love with someone else?"

To Quill's relief, she seemed to be calming down. "I doubt it," he said, after a moment's thought. "Peter has squired quite a few ladies about without showing signs of being smitten. In fact, he used to escort your friend the Duchess of Gisle occasionally, when she was Lady Sophie York."

"Perhaps he was in love with Sophie, until she married the duke," Gabby said dolefully. "And now he's being forced to marry me against his will."

"I never saw any sign that he was in love with Her Grace," Quill said, feeling a distinct surge of guilt at how close she was to the truth—half of it, anyway.

"Whether Peter is or isn't in love with someone else, he doesn't care for kissing me. Why, I might die without ever being properly kissed by my true love."

At that Quill gave a bark of laughter. "Don't you think you're being rather melodramatic, Gabby?"

"I am entitled to be as melodramatic as I please. I've just been rejected by my future spouse. Ladies have thrown themselves off bridges for less!"

"What on earth are you talking about?"

"A traveling company came to our village, and the heroine threw herself off the bridge, or perhaps it was a balcony. At any rate, she did it because her betrothed fell in love with someone else," Gabby explained. "It was most affecting."

"Rubbish."

"It *was* affecting. I wept so much at the end that my father was mortified and wouldn't take me to the performance the company gave the following night."

"I would have refused to take you as well," Quill observed. "You obviously didn't enjoy the evening."

"Oh, yes, I did," Gabby cried. "It was lovely! The playwright had a very fine understanding of the pains of love, especially how much women suffer. It's not uncommon, you know. Women's hearts are much more tender than are men's."

To Quill's pleasure, Gabby's face had brightened and she was obviously feeling more cheerful.

"What about Ophelia?" she demanded. "When Hamlet rejected her, she went stark raving mad and threw herself into a river, didn't she? You know that part when he tells her to enter a nunnery? That was *just* the kind of look that Peter gave me tonight!" Gabby's face was the picture of self-conscious woe. She was clearly visualizing herself as a forlorn Shakespearean heroine.

Quill grinned. "Let me get this straight. Because Peter quite properly refused to kiss you in clear sight of most of the London *ton,* you are considering a bath in the Serpentine? I could instruct the coachman to turn in that direction," he said helpfully. "Of course, there's a bitter wind on the river tonight, but I gather that won't stop you, since you are so desperate."

"I gather you think that I am making too much of it?" Gabby gave a watery chuckle. "That's a fault of mine," she admitted candidly.

"Deuced uncomfortable habit."

But Gabby looked up at him, her beautiful eyes appealing. "Do you *honestly* think that Peter wants to kiss me, Quill? The way you do, I mean?"

Quill recoiled. "How the hell do you know what I want?"

Gabby shrugged a little. "You never say much," she observed. "But you look at me." She fell silent.

"Every man under the age of ninety was looking at you," Quill tossed off. "Your gown is designed to make men look at you."

"When you look at me," Gabby persisted, "it makes me feel—uneasy."

"That doesn't sound very pleasant." Quill could feel a black cloud descending on his chest.

"It isn't. I feel as if ants are dancing on my skin."

"Truly unpleasant," Quill growled. "I apologize. I shall endeavor not to cause you any further discomfort." His tone had grown polite and remote.

Gabby frowned. "I'm not describing it correctly. Your look is like your kisses," she whispered, mortified by her own temerity in speaking such a thing out loud. "They make me feel quivery—here." She put her hand on her stomach. Her words drifted in a cloud of embarrassment inside the carriage.

She felt a light touch on her ear and turned. Quill had dropped a kiss there and was grinning at her.

"Feel quivery yet?"

"No!" Gabby said indignantly. "Stop funning, Quill! I never should have told you."

"True," Quill agreed.

"Peter doesn't look at me in the same way."

Quill bit his tongue before he agreed again. Finally he said, "I'm sure that he wants to kiss you, Gabby. Peter is only being mindful of your reputation." He hoped to God that he was right. And he hoped the opposite as well.

And then . . . and then Gabby looked up at him with her lovely wide-set eyes, and her look said, *Kiss me.* Quill smiled.

"Will you always be the one to ask for kisses?" he asked in a casually conversational way, bending over her.

He swallowed her indignant denial with his mouth, stilling her with the fierce sweetness that overcame him every time he looked at Gabby's lips, every time he saw her eyes shining or heard her husky voice tripping on and on. . . . He took her mouth, then took her head in his rough hands, shook out those curls, came dangerously close to pulling his own jacket from around her shoulders. But he stopped himself.

What was the state of Gabby's bodice now? If her bodice was still at her waist, if he would tug off that jacket, only to find creamy flesh . . . Quill shuddered at the thought and deepened the kiss, turning it to a dangerously passionate entreaty.

Gabby uttered a little moan, a throaty sound, and twisted up against him, her arms sliding around his neck. And the jacket slipped, fell from satiny smooth shoulders, dropped to the carriage seat.

AN HOUR LATER, as he stared blindly at the crumbling ashes on the hearth, Quill could only think that madness had struck him. Yes, he thought, in an inspired sort of way, perhaps he could excuse himself by referring to a sudden fit of insanity. He pictured Peter's scandalized face. Or perhaps not. It was too late for buying tickets to Persia or the North Pole now.

One does not caress the disrobed figure of one's future sister-in-law and hope to escape scot-free. Quill just hoped he could talk to Peter about it without going into details. Even remembering that moment—all right, more than one moment—before Quill regained his sanity, made his pantaloons uncomfortably tight and his breathing quicken.

The study door opened quietly.

"Codswallop said you wished to speak to me."

Quill turned about. Peter had already walked into the study and closed the door behind him.

Before Quill could open his mouth, Peter spoke. "It's *off*, Quill." His voice was defiant. His brown eyes were glowing with anger.

Guilt rolled through Quill's stomach. He had betrayed his brother, his only brother.

"I'll admit—"

"I can't do it," Peter continued with a fierce vigor that was strange to him. "I *won't* do it."

"Won't? Won't do what?"

"I won't marry that—I won't marry Gabrielle Jerningham," Peter managed jerkily. "I thought I could. But she's—" He broke off again.

Quill saw that Peter was descending into one of his hysterical, sullen sulks, where he could stay for days.

Peter's bitterness spilled out like acid: "She's gawky, and overfleshy. And she practically—"

Quill's breath caught in his chest. "Gabby is *not* gawky or overfleshy!"

"She is, she is," Peter moaned, starting to walk restlessly about the room. "She's a dowdy, Quill, a veritable dowdy. It's worse than that: She has no instinct, no sense of delicacy. I cannot bear the notion of being tied to her for my entire life. You must not have spent any length of time with her, whereas I escorted her about all evening. God, she talks. She talks like a spigot. I've never heard anyone talk so much. I swear to you that my friends Tiddlebend and Folger were silenced, absolutely silenced. Folger made a little joke after she left, told me her manners were absolutely unaffected."

"What's wrong with that?"

"It was clearly a hint to me," Peter explained. "She's a gabbleface, and he didn't want to say it straight out. Thank God Folger wasn't in the parlor when Gabby lost her bodice." He broodingly walked over and kicked the burning log in the fireplace. Then he swore and jumped back, his voice rising. "Do you see? Do you see my boot?"

Quill didn't answer. He never answered that sort of question from Peter.

"I do not wish to marry the woman," Peter said. "I will *not* marry her. Father can't make me marry her, you know."

"Certainly not," Quill observed, "given his current condition."

Peter looked relieved. "I forgot for a moment." Then he went back to kicking the log, regardless of the built-up soot on his shining boots. "I've been thinking about it since you took her home," he said finally. "I know it shows a lack of propriety in a gentleman to break an engagement. But I am persuaded that I would not be judged too harshly under the circumstances. It's not that I don't like Gabby. She's a pleasant person. Normally I would be quite taken by her. I would even enjoy bringing her in fashion."

Quill waited.

Peter suddenly looked very young. "But I can't bear the idea of marrying her. I simply can't bear the idea of living with a woman like that forever!" His voice was rising again. "I will not marry her! And Father——" He broke off, clearly recalling the viscount's state of health again.

"When are you going to grow up, Peter?" Quill asked in some disgust. "You act as if you are being sent off to the salt mines."

"It may be amusing to you," Peter flashed back, "but it's hell for me. Fiend seize it, I don't wish to marry. And now to marry such a fleshy——"

Quill cut him off. "Why don't you wish to marry, Peter? You must have expected to wed at some point, didn't you?"

Peter had turned back to the fireplace. He was leaning against the bricks, his head propped up by his arm. He seemed to be watching his shining boot as it grew more and more encrusted with black ash.

"Even if I thought I could go along with Father's scheme to match me to an heiress," he said, "I've found that I don't give a hang about money. I'll starve! I'll——I'll start trading in stocks, the way you do."

Quill shuddered visibly at the thought of Peter speculating on the market.

"Oh, stow it!" Peter shouted. "When am I ever consulted about anything? When did you last ask my advice? *Never!* I can assess quality just as well as you can, Quill. I may have spent my time in a different way, but I am extremely successful at what I do!"

Quill walked across the room and stood next to his brother. It was true that their six years' difference in age tended to cast Peter's achievements in the shade.

"Father would be mortified if you began speculating on the market," he said. "He only allows me to do so because I am lame and so he doesn't think of me as an able Dewland. And he consults me about the estate because he doesn't want me to feel like a burden."

"Who cares if Father thinks you're lame? He consults you about the smallest thing to do with the estate. He never speaks to me about anything."

Quill opened his mouth and shut it again. "Father doesn't mean to disregard your opinion." God, what an evening. He seemed to have spent the whole night making weak excuses for the behavior of family members. "Stop kicking that log, Peter. Rinsible will go into apoplectic arrest when he sees your boots."

"Rinsible can go hang!" Peter said, consigning his dearly beloved valet to the dark depths.

But there was something that Quill still needed to know. "I don't understand, Peter. Why don't you wish to be married—to another woman, if not to Gabby?"

For a second, he thought his little brother hadn't heard him. But then Peter turned his head and looked at him, that familiar face white, his curls tossed as if he'd been in a high wind.

Then he knew that Peter *had* heard his question. And suddenly Quill understood something he had certainly known, without thinking, all along.

Peter acted as if the question had never been posed. He leaned his forehead against the arm he had draped on the mantelpiece. "I'll go to America," he said, his voice half stifled.

"I'll marry her," Quill said quietly.

But Peter was too absorbed in his own misery to hear him. "I thought perhaps—but I cannot do it, Quill. I'll kill myself first."

"I will marry Gabby," Quill repeated.

Peter dropped his examination of the undoubtedly ruined boot and swung about so quickly that he almost unbalanced. "You! That's impossible."

"Actually, it is quite possible."

"Father said—Father—you said that you were unfit for marriage," Peter stammered, "that you couldn't consummate it."

Quill could feel an errant and mysterious cheer rising in his heart. He felt like laughing aloud. Peter's mouth had actually fallen open. "I can consummate a marriage," Quill explained. "And I would enjoy doing so."

Peter gaped. "You would?"

"I like Gabby's flesh." Quill couldn't stop himself from grinning, an unfamiliar but not unpleasant sensation. "I like her, too. Of course," Quill pointed out, "if I marry and Gabby has a child, you would never become a viscount."

Peter's face grew stony. "That is the most offensive thing you have ever said to me." His body was rigid.

The smile fell from Quill's face. "I didn't mean it as it sounded, Peter. I know you are no title-hound."

Peter still looked bleak. "You told me to marry Gabby so that I would have money for clothes. I was drunk at the time, but I remembered it clear enough the next day. You and Father both think I'm nothing but a fribble. In fact, Father is incapable of distinguishing between a man of mode and a mindless fop!"

"That would imply that we ignored your First in Classics from Cambridge, Peter. I was trying to make you fall in with Father's scheme so that I wouldn't have to be married," Quill admitted. "I apologize."

"Why did you tell us that you were unfit for marriage?" Peter asked bluntly. "You know what Father assumed. Was that a lie?"

"It isn't so far from the truth," Quill admitted. "My sexual encounters of the past few years have been entirely enjoyable, but followed by a three-day bout of migraine headache."

"Oh." Peter's face was shocked into sympathy. "Your headaches are due to *that*? Can't the doctors do anything for you?"

Quill shrugged. "It seems to be a remnant of the head injury. It might go away spontaneously, but likely not."

"That's the devil. But if you marry Gabby . . ." Peter said. "Well, how are you going to marry Gabby?" He looked discomforted. "I could be wrong, but I'm fairly certain that she has a penchant for me."

"Oh, she fancies herself in love with you," Quill replied cheerfully.

"Well, then, how will you change her mind? We can't tell her that I refused to go through with the wedding."

Quill stopped himself from inquiring what Peter had been planning to tell his fiancée when he left for America. "She's a romantic," he said. "She's a storyteller. Half the time she's dreaming up some improbable tale."

"You don't have much in common," Peter remarked dubiously.

Quill shrugged again. "It's only a marriage. I'll tell her I fell in love with her at first sight. The moment I saw her on the dock. And I'll tell her that my passion is too great to ignore."

"Do you think she'll believe it?" Peter's tone indicated acute disbelief.

In Quill's estimation, Gabby was well-aware that his self-control was at the breaking point, given the recent carriage ride. "She's a romantic," he repeated.

Peter bit his lip. "I feel like a shabster, passing her off like that."

"Only because you don't want her," Quill pointed out. "I'm perfectly willing to marry Gabby. And clearly marriage between the two of you would be a disaster."

"What will we tell Father and Mother?"

"We'll give them the same story I'll tell Gabby. That I fell hopelessly in love and couldn't—"

"No one is going to believe that tarradiddle," Peter broke in. "Gabby might, since she doesn't know you, but no one else will."

"I don't see why not."

Peter smirked, a little brother's smile. "Forget it, Quill. No one in his right mind would ever picture you in love. Why, you never even get angry. Men in love are hopelessly irrational, you know. Remember how Patrick Foakes behaved when he fell in love with Lady Sophie York? He was the picture of a lovelorn mooncalf."

"Patrick seemed perfectly rational to me."

Peter snorted. "You do remember that Foakes stole his wife from his own best friend, don't you? The word was that he demanded to have the marriage a mere week after Lady Sophie broke her engagement. Of course her parents scotched that plan. But believe me, in the fortnight before they married, everywhere you turned you were sure to find Foakes stealing kisses from his betrothed. The man acted as if he were deranged. He showed no self-restraint whatsoever. Let alone respect for the rest of us!" Peter looked properly appalled.

Quill quite liked the idea of stealing kisses from Gabby. "I can certainly kiss Gabby in public, if that's what it takes to prove that I'm in love."

Peter gave a little shudder of distaste. "I could never do it myself. Why, just this evening she—" He broke off.

"She told me," Quill drawled. "Gabby wanted to kiss you and you refused."

"Well, for God's sake," Peter snapped. "The door to the balcony was wide open. She simply pitched herself into my arms. Tiddlebend was looking right at us. I was like to die from mortification."

Quill grinned. "I'll be sure to inform my intended bride that she is not allowed to kiss other men in public."

"Thank God for small favors," Peter muttered. He had gone back to kicking logs. "Are you certain, Quill? Because you'll have to keep up the farce, you know. You will have to play lovesick for at least three months, since it will destroy Gabby's reputation if you marry in haste."

"Absolutely." Quill turned and walked to the door. "I shall inform Miss Jerningham of my, er, my hopeless adoration for her at breakfast."

"At breakfast! You will do no such thing! You don't have a romantic bone in your body, Quill. She'll smell a rat in a moment."

Quill paused and gave his brother a look of polite inquiry. "Why?"

"Because no one—not even Patrick Foakes—could fix an interest at the breakfast table!"

Quill had an enlivening conviction that he himself would happily brush aside the coddled eggs and make love to Gabby on the table itself, but there was no reason to elaborate the point.

"You must wait until after supper," Peter declared. "We shall have to serve champagne, lots of champagne. Wait until she's properly muddled, Quill. That way Gabby won't be in a position to think rationally about what you're saying."

"I think Gabby should be sober when I ask her to marry me," Quill suggested mildly.

"No. If she's not drunk, she'll never fall for the idea that you're in love." Peter said it with total conviction. "Once she's half-seas over, you can launch your story, and perhaps she'll believe you."

"Hmmm," Quill said. He opened the door to the hallway.

"Quill!" Peter's voice was shrill with urgency.

"I shall take your suggestion into advisement," Quill replied gravely.

He had no intention of making Gabby dizzy with drink before asking her to marry him. As he had said, Gabby was a romantic. He had the shrewd idea that she had talked herself into falling in love with Peter, and she could just as easily talk herself into falling in love with him. Anyway, telling her barefaced lies about being in love was bad enough; he didn't want to compound his sins by drinking his future bride under the table.

It had been a long night. His leg was throbbing now, and he had a perceptible limp as he climbed the stairs.

Still, as he passed the door to the Blue Room, Quill only barely stopped himself from turning the door handle and walking in. Into Gabby's bedchamber. The bedchamber where he would be master in just a few months. Quill shook himself like a dog emerging from a puddle. He could wait.

It wasn't until six in the morning that Quill came to a realization: His assumption that he would be able to wait for three months before entering Gabby's bedchamber was dangerously shaky.

Part of the problem was that moment when his coat had fallen from Gabby's shoulders and he had swept his hands down her back. Down that beautiful, smooth, naked stretch of skin. He had brought his hands in a slow and dreamy dance around to her front. And only then had Quill allowed himself to draw back from Gabby's lips and look at what he held.

Now desire rocketed down his body, shocked him awake again and again, filled him with the conviction that he—no less than the besotted Patrick Foakes with his Lady Sophie—could not wait three months to marry Gabby. He could not wait a week to touch Gabby's satiny skin, the silk of her shoulders, let his hands drift lower, and lower still.

Quill decided to rise. Given that he obviously wasn't going to be able to sleep, he decided to do some research. Gabby was a romantic, and Gabby liked to attend plays. Fine. He would memorize a few bits of theatrical nonsense and use them to convince her that he was in love. Because as dawn coldly lit the far corner of the garden wall, Quill was painfully aware that Gabby was unlikely to find his admission of hopeless love convincing. Damn it, he'd never been in love, and he saw no possibility for the future. Peter was right. He simply wasn't the type. He hadn't the faintest notion how to act besotted.

Quill threw off the covers and pulled the bell cord. When a bewildered early-rising footman appeared, Quill requested bathwater and then collected some research materials from the library. Luckily for him, there were reams of poems that discussed the effects of love. He had always found in transactions of business that research gave him a satisfactory edge over his opponent.

And his research was eminently satisfactory. By an hour later, Quill was bathed and seated by a roaring fire, surrounded by books marked with slips of paper. It was fortunate that he had an excellent memory. The only question was whether to borrow from Shakespeare—there was a possibility that Gabby might recognize the words—or from a more obscure playwright.

Shakespeare was an enticing possibility. *I burn, I pine, I perish.* Quill liked the sound of that. Of course, it was all nonsense, except perhaps the burning part. He was burning, all right. The question was: How much of this nonsense did he have to spout in order to make his point?

There was another good bit in the same play: *With her*

breath she did perfume the air. Sacred and sweet was all I saw in her.

Under his breath, Quill tried it out. "With your breath you did perfume—no." He tried again. "When I first saw you on the dock, she—you—your breath perfumed the air. And everything I saw was sacred and sweet."

That was along the right lines. *What stars do spangle heaven with such beauty, As those two eyes become that heavenly face?*

Quill muttered it a few times. He couldn't bring himself to say it out loud. What if his valet walked into the room? It was rubbish. He had thought Shakespeare didn't write such twaddle.

Gabby's eyes weren't like stars. They were amber brown, except the very rims, which were black, dark black. And they didn't shine or sparkle or spangle—whatever spangling was. They were kind of a brandy-golden brown. They *spoke*. To meet Gabby's eyes was to be invited into her tumbled world of laughter and words, hasty emotion, and lush desire. He was quite certain he had seen her eyes grow hazy with desire. They grew more brandy-colored whenever he kissed her.

Quill rose. The time had come to put the question to the point. He silently rehearsed his little scraps of twiddle-twaddle.

It was seven o'clock in the morning.

The perfect time for a theatrical performance.

Chapter 11

WHEN MARGARET BUSTLED into the room early in the morning and announced that Mr. Erskine had requested to see Gabby immediately, she groaned. She hadn't slept well at all. Half the time was lost in the throes of humiliation, as she relived the moment when her dress fell off, and the other half was spent reliving the way she'd acted in the carriage.

She was a wanton hussy, no two ways about it. Her father would have tossed her out of the house if he had any idea what she was really like. Perhaps Quill was summoning her for that very purpose. She stared blurrily at the mirror as Margaret brushed out her hair. She'd thrown herself at him the night before. What had come over her?

Margaret stopped brushing for a moment. "You mustn't take it so hard, miss," she said earnestly.

Gabby met Margaret's eyes in the mirror with a profound sense of shock. How did Margaret *know*? Could the coachman have gotten an idea, or could the footmen who stood behind the carriage have seen something?

"The worst that will happen is that gossip columns will take note."

Gabby shivered. What an appalling idea. Perhaps returning to India wasn't such a terrible prospect.

"I'll send someone out to buy the papers," Margaret said, starting to brush Gabby's hair again. "My mum always said that you're better off facing up to the worst. After all, it must have happened to other ladies before you. Everyone knows those French bodices are just asking to fall off. Perhaps the papers won't mention what happened. It's a delicate subject, after all."

"Hmmm," Gabby replied. While she was relieved to find that Margaret was talking not about her scandalous behavior in the coach, but about her scandalous behavior at the ball, she had little hope that delicacy would stop a gossip column from elaborating on the collapse of her bodice. She had seen no avoidance of delicate subjects in *The Morning Post*. Perhaps Quill already had one of those gossip columns, and that's why he wished to speak to her.

She walked down the stairs as if she were a Frenchwoman going to execution. In fact, before she noticed it, she had woven a little story in which she was a marquise, keeping her head high as she made her way tearlessly to the guillotine.

"Oh, for goodness sake!" Gabby whispered to herself. The last thing she should be doing was making up foolish tales. That was what got her in trouble last night.

Quill must have been listening for her, because he spoke before she entered. "Come in, Gabby." His deep voice sent butterflies into her stomach. *Why* did her brother-in-law— well, her future brother-in-law—have this effect on her?

Gabby walked into the room feeling rather defiant. It wasn't her fault that Madame Carême's bodices were badly designed. In fact, that all of her gowns were ill-constructed.

It was Peter's fault. He had chosen the *modiste* who created the gown.

Quill was standing with his back to the fireplace, hands clasped behind him. He had his utterly impenetrable look on, Gabby thought to herself. He looked like a piece of granite.

Now that she thought about it, it wasn't Peter's fault—the whole thing was Quill's fault. She scowled at him rather than say good morning.

Quill opened his mouth and then saw that Gabby had left the door open. He'd be damned if he was going to voice any bibble-babble when a footman might hear him. He walked past her and shut the door firmly. After a second's thought, he turned the key as well.

Then he turned around. "Gabby," he announced, "I have something to say." This was a preface that worked to great effect in business meetings. Invariably, a whole circle of men would fall into a hushed silence and wait with bated breath for his pronouncement.

It didn't seem quite so successful this time. "So do I," Gabby responded. She scowled at him again.

Quill pressed his lips together. Better to get the difficult matter out of the way first. "I'm pining to marry you," he said.

The scowl disappeared from Gabby's face, replaced by a look of utter astonishment.

"I'm burning and pining to marry you," Quill said. Then he remembered the whole line. "Burning, pining, *and* perishing," he added.

"Perishing?" Gabby repeated blankly.

"Precisely."

There was a moment of silence while Quill prepared his next lines. This wasn't as hard as he had anticipated.

"When I saw you on the dock, your breath perfumed the hair."

Gabby looked perplexed.

"Sorry," Quill corrected himself. "Air! Air. When I first saw you on the dock, your breath perfumed the air. And then I discovered that your eyes were like spangled stars." He was taking a few liberties with Shakespeare, but he liked his version better.

Gabby still hadn't said anything, so Quill walked over and stood just before her. He looked down at her downcast head. "Everything I see about you is sacred and sweet."

He took Gabby's chin in his hand and forced her head up. It was evident in a second that his plan had gone awry. Gabby was shaking all over like a blancmange. It didn't take a lummox to realize that she was nearly killing herself trying to restrain her laughter.

"Forgive me," Gabby said in a choked tone. "I—I—" She gave up, breaking into a gloriously husky shout of laughter.

Heat rushed up Quill's legs and into his chest. He had the impulse to violently shake the woman before him. It was all her fault that he had behaved like a nodcock. Ice replaced the embarrassment, and he stepped back. He began turning over cool, mocking phrases, shaping a comment that would make it absolutely clear that he, Erskine Dewland, had never in his life compared a woman's eyes to stars.

But then he remembered. He had promised Peter that he would marry Gabby. He couldn't snub her.

Besides, this was all gibberish, nothing more than a silly fable to make a romantic woman marry him. He needn't feel embarrassed. It was all lies, after all.

Not for nothing had Quill attended Drury Lane when the great actor, John Philip Kemble, was performing. If Kemble could do it, so could he. Gabby was still giggling to herself. Quill reached out and dragged the minx into his arms.

She fit there as if she were designed to melt against him, as if every one of her curves was matched by a hollow in him.

She stopped giggling, but her voice was still husky with laughter. "Quill?"

"Gabby." He swooped, bending her over his arm with Kemble's own dramatic flair.

She tasted like laughter. She tasted like Gabby.

His lips were everything his words had not been: carnal and dangerous, sure in their approach, commanding her attention.

Gabby twisted in his hands, trying to pull away from the undertow of desire. She didn't want this again. Not the drugging feeling that turned her stomach into liquid fire, sent her up against Quill's body, trembling and making pleading noises. It was morning. It was indecent to feel this way even at night. Especially——

But he wouldn't let her go. His large hands held her against his muscled thighs. He pressed her indignant eyes shut with his lips and then kissed his way back to her mouth.

Despite herself, Gabby stopped pulling away and shuddered closer, her arms coming up around his neck, her mouth opening to his demands.

And there it was again: the burning, the loss of breath in her chest, the sweet fire in her chest, lower, in her stomach, lower . . . Gabby's tongue met Quill's, her heart speeding to a beat that sent a rhythm through her entire body.

"I *burn*," Quill said, tearing his mouth away from hers. He was unable to keep his hands steady——or to keep them in gentlemanly bounds. He ran his fingers down her neck and then ruthlessly pulled down the delicate muslin of her morning gown.

Gabby gasped but didn't protest. Her little cap sleeve

slid without resistance to her elbow, and her chemise followed.

Quill's voice was a low rumble, dark with passionate need. "I *burn*, Gabby. I *pine*, I *perish*." He kissed the sweet cream of her shoulder, his hands tracing a bold demand. His lips drifted to her neck, breathed the words against her skin. "I am burning, Gabby."

She sighed as his palm rounded her breast, sending a wave of tiny shivers down her body.

"You must . . . You must." His voice died against her skin and was replaced by silence.

Quill raised his head to find Gabby speechless, perhaps for the first time in her life. He kissed her lips gently, a butterfly kiss, and then took her face in his large hands, holding its perfect oval. His fingers trailed a caress over her curved eyebrows, down the sweep of her high cheekbones. With his hands, he marveled. With his fingers, he sang a poem, trailing over her lips. Gabby's eyes were a brandy-golden color that a star would weep to call its own. *"What stars do spangle heaven with such beauty,"* Quill said quietly, *"As those two eyes become that heavenly face?"*

Gabby's hands came up to cover his. She met his eyes. "That's not fair," she whispered. "Bianca hasn't a decent line in the whole play."

"Sod the play." Quill pulled her into his arms again and spoke against her mouth. "I want you, Gabby." His hand was on the sweet curve of her bottom, pulling her against his hard body. "Oh, God, I can't live without you. I *am* perishing."

Gabby heard the rough plea in his voice and gave a little sob, twisting up to put her mouth against his lips. "Kiss me, Quill. Kiss me again."

And he did, of course.

They fell, together, in a whirlwind of desire. In the heat

of it, Gabby swayed backward, and Quill followed, his body finding its rest naturally, his weight sinking onto Gabby's sweet lushness, hard close to soft.

His mind woke to find his body lit from head to toes with white-hot lust. Pure, shaking, shuddering lust. And he found himself poised on the brink of pulling Gabby's dress up, or down—it hardly mattered. On the brink of thrusting himself into relief, into the silky heat that he knew would mimic the welcome of her mouth. Hard shivers shook her body as he rubbed his thumb over her nipple, and she strained against him, murmuring unintelligibly.

But alas, Quill's rational mind had fallen back into place. He waited until Gabby opened her eyes.

She lay back against the Persian carpet, her hair loosed from its pins and spread around her head in waves. A smile trembled on her lips. "*I burn,*" she whispered. "*I pine, I perish.*" Her hands reached up and cupped his hard face.

"Will you kiss me again? Will you . . ." But she couldn't bring herself to the question she really wanted to ask. Of course it was Quill she wished to marry. Of course it was Quill she wished to bed.

His eyes met hers with perfect understanding. "I will kiss you every time you ask," he said. "And I will marry you, Gabby, if you'll have me."

Gabby blinked. "Do you love me?"

"I fell in love with you the moment I saw you on the dock," Quill answered. It was almost too prompt, his answer.

Gabby sat up. "I am not sure of my feelings," she said hesitantly. "I am not sure that I love you yet, Quill. But I think it will not be difficult."

A smile twitched at the corner of Quill's mouth. Thank goodness he was free of the twiddle-twaddle associated with romantic love! It was so clearly self-delusion. Gabby, who had considered Peter her true love a mere five hours before, was well on her way to being *in love* with him.

"That would be nice," he said gravely, picking up her hand and kissing the palm.

Gabby began fussing with her bodice. Her hair swung forward over her shoulders.

Quill couldn't stop himself from touching it. It was such a lovely bronze-brown color, streaked and shadowed like the pelt of a wild animal. Gabby's curls had no similarity to the pale, confined ringlets that were exhibited by most young English ladies.

"Oh, blazes!" Gabby said impatiently, hauling at her sleeve. "Madame Carême's dresses are naught but a few bits of cloth, barely sewn together. I shall have to find someone else to make my clothing if I don't want to be half dressed most of the time!" She was chattering in an effort to ignore the prickly feeling in her stomach, the embarrassing warmth between her thighs.

Quill grinned. "I like Madame's gowns," he remarked.

Gabby managed to wrench the sleeve of her morning dress back into place.

"They are well-designed," he continued. "You see, Gabby? Having been tussled to your elbow, the bodice jumps up to cover your magnificent bosom, looking none the worse for wear."

Gabby met Quill's teasing eyes a bit shyly. What on earth had she been doing, lying about on the carpet? "I hope you are not going to make a habit of this," she said rather stuffily.

Quill helped her to her feet. Then he bent over and whispered into her ear. "Wait until we are married, Gabby."

She felt pink rising up her neck. "What do you mean?"

Quill's dark green eyes were devilish. He reached out his hand and trailed one finger down her neck.

Gabby jerked away, embarrassed by her reaction to his simple caress. "I had better return upstairs," she said, raising her hands to the waves of hair at her neck. "Lord knows what Margaret will think of my appearance."

Quill shrugged. "Who cares?"

"How like a man to say so! *I* care. Otherwise, why would I say it?"

To Quill's mind, females regularly said all sorts of things they didn't mean. But the important thing was that Gabby had agreed to marry him—and she did seem to mean that.

"I will send a messenger to Bath and inform my parents of our plans."

"Oh." Gabby thought of the viscountess and her invalid husband. "Will your parents be angry?"

"Not at all," Quill replied. "They initially thought you would marry me, after all."

"Well, then, why didn't they send your picture over to India?"

The back of Quill's neck crawled. The last thing he wanted to do was explain postcoital headaches to his newly betrothed. No doubt she would rethink the engagement if she knew the whole truth. So he shrugged.

His family was well-aware that Quill rarely answered questions and could never be counted upon to keep up his side of a conversation. But to his irritation, Gabby obviously did not understand his personality yet.

"Quill? Why didn't your father send your picture to India instead of your brother's? And why does my father think I am marrying a future viscount, given that you are the eldest son?"

"He——" Inspiration struck. "My father is afraid that Peter will not be able to make a match on his own. You see, he's rather shy."

"Peter? Rather shy?"

"Oh, yes," Quill said, more confident now that he was well-embarked on his tale. "Do you remember last night, when you tried to kiss him? How is Peter going to make a marriage when he cares for etiquette above kisses?"

Gabby's brows drew together. "That is not necessarily the case. Peter is remarkably easy in conversation, and he is a leader of the *ton*. Madame Carême herself told me so. Certainly he could find a bride if he wished, and he wouldn't need to break any proprieties to do so."

To his relief, Quill heard a scratching at the door.

It was Codswallop, whose eyes widened a bit when he realized that the study held not only the master's son but also a somewhat disheveled Miss Jerningham. And he had distinctly heard the key turn in the door after he knocked.

He held out his silver tray. "Lord Breksby's card, sir. His lordship has indicated that his visit is urgent."

Quill nodded to Codswallop. "Please show Lord Breksby to the study. And ask Lady Sylvia to join us," he added.

"Oh, goodness, no," Gabby said. Patting her hair had confirmed that most of it was lying down her back. "I shall leave you to entertain your guest, Quill."

"He is calling for you," Quill remarked.

"What?" Gabby, in the middle of replacing a hairpin, looked sharply over her shoulder. She didn't seem to realize that the greater part of her hair was falling down to the right.

"Let me," Quill said. He pulled five or six hairpins out, so that a great mass of hair fell down Gabby's back. Then he swiftly twirled it into a bun and stuck it back on the top of her head.

"Oh, thank you," Gabby said, clearly taken aback. "Where did you learn to do that? No, don't tell me." She turned around. "Why does Lord Breksby wish to see me? And who is he?"

"Lord Breksby is England's Secretary for Foreign Affairs," Quill remarked. "He approached me just after you arrived from India, wishing information about the whereabouts of Kasi Rao."

"Oh, no," Gabby breathed.

"Yes," Quill said dryly. "Perhaps you should tell him, Gabby. The Foreign Office is not the same thing as the East India Company, and I believe that Breksby is a man of honor. If he believes that Kasi is unfit to rule, he will ensure that the boy is kept safe."

But Gabby shook her head. "I doubt he's to be trusted, Quill. My father's experience with representatives of the British government has been almost as unsatisfactory as his relationships with East India men. The government seems to have no ability to control company officials. Look what happened at Bharatpur. Hundreds of people died, and yet my father said the company had no authority for an assault on Holkar territory."

It was Quill's turn to look rueful. "I am very sorry to say that I agree with you for the main part. But Breksby himself is not a bad sort. And he has a great deal of power here in London. If he decides that Kasi is not an adequate ruler—and how could he decide otherwise?—then the company will have to leave Kasi alone."

"They will not do so," Gabby retorted. "I am quite familiar with the machinations of East India men, Quill. They will lie and steal and bribe to get control over territory that does not belong to them. Kasi would be naught more than a pawn to them. And I don't believe they would show any mercy if it came to putting him on the throne, not if they thought they could gain more territory as a result."

Quill watched his newly betrothed warily. She had an unexpected side to her. He hadn't anticipated such steely rationality from someone who at first glance seemed little more than a chatterbox.

"Do you agree with me, Quill?" Gabby asked impatiently. She could hear footsteps approaching in the hallway outside.

Quill bent his head. "The East India Company would do well to accept female directors." And found himself surprised again.

Lord Breksby declared himself enchanted to meet Miss Jerningham in person. "I am the Secretary for Foreign Affairs," he announced.

Gabby sat down and clasped her hands together. "Lord Breksby, I would be delighted to aid the English government in any way possible."

"We understand," Breksby said, "that your father may have had a young visitor in his household while you were growing up, the son of the ruler of Holkar. The directors of the East India Company are under the impression that Lord Jerningham may have sent Kasi Rao Holkar to England. It would have been a natural action, given that your father has many contacts in this country."

"I'm afraid that I have no information about Kasi's whereabouts," Gabby replied sweetly.

Her eyes didn't even flicker, Quill thought. His future wife was quite an accomplished fibber.

"Well," Breksby announced, "certain representatives of the East India Trading Company appear to believe that the prince has been—"

At that moment Lady Sylvia entered the room and gave a crow of pleasure at the sight of Lord Breksby. To Gabby's dismay, it transpired that Breksby and Lady Sylvia were old friends, since Lord Breksby's wife had grown up in a village next door to Lady Sylvia's country estate. It wasn't until Gabby decided that Breksby was going to describe every single one of the fourteen bedchambers in the cottage he and his wife had just bought in the same village that she lost her patience.

"Dear sir," she implored Lord Breksby. "Please, may we return to the subject of Kasi Rao?"

Breksby smiled genially. "My apologies, Miss Jerningham. I was so caught up in conversation with this charming lady"—he smirked at Lady Sylvia—"that I forgot your natural distress. As I was saying, representatives of the East India Trading Company appear confident that the Holkar heir is to be found in London."

Gabby chewed on her lower lip but said nothing.

"Now, I cannot say where or how they came by their information," Breksby commented. "Nor, of course, can I venture a guess as to its reliability. But I did wish to inform you, Miss Jerningham. Because in my view—only in my view—it would be far better for the English government to discover Mr. Kasi Rao Holkar than it would for representatives of the East India Company to do so."

Quill waited.

Gabby gave Lord Breksby a sad little smile. "I most certainly agree with you, sir. I fear that representatives of the East India Company wish to find Kasi for their own nefarious purposes."

"No question about that," Breksby replied promptly. "They love the idea of putting a half-witted ruler in the Holkars. Give them a handle into the whole Marathas region, no doubt about it."

"Couldn't you stop them?" Gabby pleaded.

A rare look of chagrin flitted across Breksby's face. "The company has been one of the few failures of my tenure," he admitted. "We managed to pass the India Bill in '84, but it has been a dismal failure in terms of curbing their territorial greed."

Gabby seemed to have made up her mind. "I certainly wish I could help you, Lord Breksby," she cooed, tilting her head to the side.

Quill watched cynically from the other side of the room as Breksby melted in front of his eyes. At least he wasn't alone in being bowled over by Miss Gabrielle Jerningham. Although he rather thought he, Quill, hadn't been lied to yet. If so, he reminded himself, it was only a matter of time.

Lady Sylvia turned about the moment the door clicked shut behind Lord Breksby and shot Quill a steely glance. "I don't know what you think you're playing at, Erskine, but I won't have you handing yer brother damaged goods. It isn't the work of a gentleman."

Hot color rushed up Gabby's neck. "Oh, Lady Sylvia, I . . . Quill . . ." She faltered.

"You may be the first to congratulate us," Quill said calmly. "This morning Miss Jerningham agreed to be my wife."

Lady Sylvia gave him another scathing look. "Well, then, I won't have you trotting damaged goods up to yer own altar either."

Quill met her eyes steadily. "You need have no fear of that, Lady Sylvia. I should prefer, however, that you do not impugn the honor of my betrothed."

"Oh?" She gave Gabby a monstrous frown. "Miss Jerningham, I clearly instructed you not to spend time alone with a man, *any* man. Yer gown is crumpled in the back, and there are hairpins all over the hearth rug. If you two haven't been tumbling about on the floor, then I'm a monkey's uncle!"

Gabby thought it wasn't possible for a person to feel so embarrassed. But Quill spoke before she could try to defend herself.

His eyes were icy with fury. "I'll tumble my fiancée any damned place I please."

Lady Sylvia drew herself up sharply. "Gabrielle is not a milkmaid, and there will be no such behavior while I'm her chaperone. We'll see what yer father has to say about this!"

Silence fell as all three people realized that Viscount Dewland would have nothing to say, given his incapacity.

"I suppose poor old Thurlow can't complain," Lady Sylvia said after a moment. "But he won't like it if you have a six-month child. *I* won't like it. I'm supposed to stop this sort of thing."

Gabby rushed forward and took her chaperone's hand. "Please, Lady Sylvia, forgive me for my behavior this morning. I will not spend any time alone with Erskine before our wedding, that I promise you. And . . . and I'm not damaged goods!" she finished in a rush.

Lady Sylvia gave a reluctant little smile. "I thought as much," she admitted. "Erskine here may be a hothead, but he isn't a debaucher."

"I should not have spoken to you in that fashion," Quill said. "Please forgive me, Lady Sylvia."

She shrugged. "The way you've been wearing your heart on your sleeve, Erskine, I should have expected a little plain talk. I suppose you're going to want the wedding set within the next week or so."

Quill had fully intended to have an engagement that lasted a good three months, just as Peter had advised the night before. But he had no illusions about the source of his current bad humor. Every inch of his body was instructing him to tumble Gabby on the hearth rug again. And he wanted a sixth-month child no more than would his father.

"Absolutely not," he replied stiffly. "Gabby and I shall have a formal announcement and wait a suitable period of time before solemnizing the wedding. Perhaps a month," he added.

Lady Sylvia laughed. "You're far gone, Erskine. Not that I dislike seeing it. My Lionel was that eager to get me into bed! He swore it was time to measure a casket when my father refused to have the ceremony for six months.

"At any rate, you've chosen your new bridegroom just in time, Gabrielle. I've a note here from Kitty. She says she's coming to London, and I expect she wants to see Peter married quickly. You'll have to inform your brother that he's lost his heiress, Erskine." Lady Sylvia gathered up her reticule and fan. "Gabrielle, come with me, please. Your hair needs immediate attention, and I suggest you spend the next hour or so composing yourself. Now that you've not only been introduced to society but created your first scandal, I warrant we shall have a flood of callers this morning."

So Gabby meekly set off, leaving behind her one frustrated fiancé and seventeen pearl-tipped hairpins.

LADY SYLVIA PAUSED at the door to her bedchamber. "I'm not such a bad chaperone as you suppose," she said suddenly. "I could see as well as any that you and Erskine were the better match."

Gabby blushed. "I'm truly sorry about this morning. I should not have visited Quill's study by myself."

"There's a time and place for chaperones too," Lady Sylvia replied. "And giving a hand to a wedding proposal isn't one of them. Looks as if Erskine did just fine on his own."

Gabby couldn't help smiling at the roguish look the older woman was giving her. "Yes, he did," she said.

"A good boy, he is. All heart, and don't let the fact he doesn't say much change your opinion. He's a good boy."

Gabby nodded.

Lady Sylvia pranced into her room, instructing Gabby to lie on her bed for at least forty minutes, so as to prepare herself for the onslaught of gabsters they could expect for morning calls.

"Mind you," she scolded, "given that your bodice gave up its moorings last night, quite a few of them will be here simply to crane their necks. I've no doubt but what that tale has spread all over town. Still, if the men of the town could have chosen a bodice to drop, I daresay that most of them would have chosen yours. That will irk the ladies. Pure and simple jealousy."

Gabby walked into her room and dutifully lay on her bed, but it was impossible to relax. Finally she sat up and took out Peter's miniature. But his gentle eyes and soft brown hair had lost their allure. She'd lost her appetite for perfectly arranged curls and a gentle manner. Quill's eyes were stormy and his hair was never perfectly arranged—if indeed his valet did more than draw a comb through it. And yet she only had to think about him to feel a rush of happiness. He talked with his eyes, and they told her that she was beautiful and desirable—yes, and intelligent too.

LUCIEN STOOD IN THE ENTRYWAY of Emily's small house feeling tongue-tied, a most unusual emotion for a man known for his eloquent compliments. "I came to ask whether you might accompany me to a small party being given by Lady Dunstreet," he said. "I much enjoyed our evening together."

"As did I," Emily murmured. But Lucien couldn't see any trace of pleasure on her face. Then she raised her eyes.

"I must speak to you, Mr. Boch. Will you spare me a moment?"

Lucien's heart sank as he followed Emily into the sitting room and sat down opposite her.

"Mr. Boch, I am afraid that I shall not be able to see you again," Emily said decisively. "While I greatly enjoyed the ball—" She broke off. "I am responsible for my small household, which now includes Phoebe. I am most grateful to you for inviting me to Lady Fester's ball. But I must not make a habit of such pleasures."

Lucien shook his head. "Can you not think of it in the way of business?" he said, hoping that there wasn't a plea in his voice. "I was under the impression that attending social events could only help your writing."

Emily twisted her gloves in her lap.

"Did you not enjoy it?" he added—and he knew that there was desperation in his voice.

At that Emily looked up quickly. "Oh, I did! It was more . . . more lovely than I would have dreamed. But I cannot do it again, Mr. Boch. I do not belong in that world. I am a working person."

"As I said, could you not—"

"Absolutely not," Emily said with quiet certitude.

Lucien opened his mouth, but she raised her hand. "Mr. Boch, I will be frank with you. I cannot afford to live as a woman of the *ton*. My sister and I sewed late every night last week to make the gown I wore."

"It was exquisite," he said promptly. "I was accompanied by the most elegant woman in the room."

Emily colored but shook her head. "I do not belong in that world, nor can I afford to masquerade in it. I have Phoebe to care for, as well as my sister. Even my evening gloves were beyond our means." She rose.

Lucien perforce rose as well. He walked behind her to the door, suppressing an angry wish to complain. But what could he say? He could hardly offer to buy her a ball gown. It would be a grossly impertinent breach of etiquette.

"May I call on you in the future?"

Emily had the most open, candid eyes he had seen in his life. "I shall not be at home if you call," she replied gently, disengaging her hand from his.

Lucien bowed once more, his heart a leaden stone in his chest. "I much regret your decision."

Only Louise knew how much Emily regretted her own decisiveness; she came down the stairs to find her sister brushing away tears.

"Did you send him away?" she asked.

Emily nodded, her chin wobbling in an undignified fashion.

Louise sighed. "Why, Emily? Why should you begrudge yourself a few evenings of pleasure? You have most certainly earned them."

"He has no serious intentions. . . . And I have no time for frivolity. I have Phoebe to care for," Emily said.

"Pooh!" Louise replied.

"I am too fond of him," Emily said.

"Is that such a problem?"

"I do not wish to become a kept woman."

"You never would," Louise said stoutly. "So why not just enjoy what is offered and refuse the *carte blanche* when he offers it?"

"Because . . . because I am afraid."

"Afraid of what?"

"I might wish to become his mistress," Emily whispered miserably.

There was a moment of silence.

"That is a problem," Louise acknowledged.

Emily's chin wobbled, but she managed a small smile. "Isn't it just?"

Louise gave her a tight squeeze. "I will say one thing, Emily."

Her sister paused, looking back from the stairs.

"If you are truly honest, you will note in your next column that a certain young woman accompanied by a former French count wore the most beautiful costume at the Fester ball."

"Lucien is a marquis, not a count," Emily corrected. But she smiled.

Chapter 12

GABBY SPENT THE REMAINDER of the morning in a stranglehold of anxiety. When should she tell Peter that their engagement was off? Or would Quill prefer to tell Peter himself? She would forget this nerve-racking problem only to find her heart beating rapidly as she imagined Kasi Rao being forcibly dragged from Mrs. Malabright's arms.

The only positive aspect of her paroxysms of worry was that her dropped bodice faded in her mind from a dire humiliation to a mere embarrassment.

Lady Sylvia's prediction about the number of callers they might expect proved to be absolutely correct. By the time Gabby returned downstairs, the Indian Drawing Room was crowded with people come to see the fashionable lady with the indecent gown——or the indecent lady with the fashionable gown, however one wished to phrase it.

Sophie, the Duchess of Gisle, arrived just after visiting hours commenced. "I thought if we were in the same chamber, we could accept commiseration together." Her eyes were dancing with laughter. "I do believe that we ought to complain to Madame Carême, don't you, Gabby?"

The assembled ladies quickly noted the duchess's familiarity with Miss Jerningham and adjusted their opinions accordingly.

"I, for one, will never patronize that particular *modiste*." A thin, waspish-looking lady shivered dramatically. "Obviously, it was her design that was at fault."

"You wouldn't have to worry," Lady Sylvia snapped. "No gown is going to fall off yer chest, Amelia. And if it did, there's nothing to expose." Lady Sylvia was proving herself a formidable opponent, taking off the head of any person brave enough to insinuate that ladylike behavior did not include disrobing in public.

Gabby nodded, and smiled, and murmured polite nothings, and blushed whenever bodices were mentioned. She tried to ignore the fact that her throat tightened every time the door opened. Quill was nowhere to be seen. It was rare for him to appear until the evening, but surely today he would join them for luncheon?

"Well, you got away with it, gel," Lady Sylvia said after the throngs of visitors had trickled to nothing and the room finally emptied. "Thanks to Her Grace. That girl is a right 'un, I'll tell you that."

The door opened once again and Gabby's heart jumped into her throat. Here she was, besieged by trouble, and she kept being distracted by memories of Quill's hungry kisses and the way he groaned in his throat when she—She took a deep breath.

But it was Peter, not Quill, who entered. Gabby could barely meet his eyes. What would Peter think of her if he knew what she had been doing with his brother? She was jilting him. She was going to humiliate him in front of the entire *ton,* given that he introduced her to all his friends as his fiancée only the night before.

She wanted to die of mortification. Even more strongly,

she wanted to burrow into the fierce warmth of Quill's arms and remember why she was doing such an unladylike and scandalous action as marrying her fiancé's brother.

The thought made her shiver again. In fact, what with one memory and another, she had spent the entire morning with a feverish pulse, and ill humor was beginning to creep over her.

Quill entered the dining room just as the rest of the family was sitting down, so Gabby assumed that he had not spoken to Peter. And yet, by halfway through the meal, the tension between the brothers was so clear that Gabby changed her mind.

The group was idly discussing a large fire that had destroyed a brew house and a public house in Argyle Street, suspected to be the work of a disgruntled patron of the public house who was refused a meat pie.

"There are two questionable items in the tale as it stands," Gabby pointed out. "The first is the unlikelihood that a public house would refuse to give anyone a meat pie, and the second is that, in such an unlikely event, a customer would care enough to actually burn the premises. Why not simply buy a pie from another establishment?"

Quill's eyes rested on her with something warmer than the appreciation one might show for a logical point. Gabby frowned at him in a warning that he ought to be more reserved with his attentions.

Peter was vigorously defending his account. "Apparently there was only one meat pie left, and the landlord had promised to save it for the Watch, or rather, for the Watch's wife." He smiled at Gabby and said, just a trifle ponderously, "We ought not to censure given that the recipient of the meat pie was a fair woman."

Quill snorted. "Troy burned for the love of a beautiful woman. Are you saying, Peter, that London would have been well lost in order to satisfy the appetite of the Watch's wife?"

"The landlord ought to be commended for placing his promise to a lady above mercantile concerns such as planks and mortar."

Quill answered Peter with such a mocking smile that Gabby had the feeling that the conversation would have disintegrated into a family quarrel had not Codswallop appeared with the next course.

After the meal Quill disappeared before she could question him, and it wasn't until five o'clock when he sauntered— yes, *sauntered*—into the parlor and asked Gabby if she would care for a ride in Hyde Park. It took all her fortitude not to scream her profound irritation to the skies.

Instead, she managed a stifled "yes" and went to change her clothing.

Quill looked after his betrothed curiously. Did she seem just a trifle disgruntled? She appeared to be a moody sort of girl. Sensitive, they called it when women were cantankerous.

Peter leapt to Quill's side and dragged him over to the windows, out of Lady Sylvia's hearing. "Well?" he asked eagerly. "When are you going to ask her?"

Quill looked down at his brother. "What in God's name did you do to your hair?" he asked. "Is that pomade?"

Peter almost stamped his foot. "As I said, when are you going to ask her? I thought you planned to do so at breakfast. I didn't dare speak a word to Gabby all day. I am quite certain that she noticed my incivility."

"I asked her this morning," Quill said, staring out the windows. It was all he could do to maintain a casual tone. He felt like shouting it. Gabby—beautiful, luscious Gabby— had agreed to marry *him*. A crippled man. A silent merchant. A man who had given up fashionable company for the inelegant world of trade.

Actually, that was the problem that had absorbed him all day. She didn't know what a bad bargain she was getting.

"Well?" It was Peter who was almost shouting.

Quill had spent the day wrestling with his conscience. "She will give me an answer this afternoon," he said negligently, as if the most important conversation of his life was naught more than a simple yes or no.

"Oh, God, it's all over," Peter groaned, raking his hand through the locks that had taken Rinsible forty-five minutes and a quantity of pomade to arrange. "If she put you off, then she was trying to think of a way to let you down easily. I *knew* Gabby would never take you."

"She seemed encouraging this morning," Quill said, wrenching his mind away from a memory of Gabby's throaty little moans.

"She's a nice woman. I am certain that she will refuse you gently. I told you, Quill, under different circumstances I would enjoy her company." Peter sat down and stared straight ahead. "I think I will just go ahead and do it, Quill. I can't move to America. They don't . . . it's full of savages. Impossible. I'll just marry the woman. At least she seems to have escaped utter ruin, thanks to the Duchess of Gisle's dropping bodice."

Peter roused himself from dejection enough to look up at his brother. "I say, Quill, do you think it was a little odd that Her Grace's bodice took the plunge just after Gabby's?"

To Quill's mind, it was not odd but obvious. Sophie had moved into the number-two spot on his secret list of treasured females, and there were only two females on it. Although he did maintain an errant affection for a milkmaid named Anne, who divested him of his virginity some fifteen years before.

He shrugged.

Peter was used to his unresponsiveness and didn't even notice. "So Gabby didn't give you an answer yet?"

Quill shrugged again. Of course, Gabby *had* said that she would marry him. But that was before he decided in all conscience that he had to detail what a bad bargain he truly was. Smelling of the shop, and dragging a gimpy leg. But most important, there were the migraines.

"Well, just give me a wink at supper," Peter said gloomily, straightening his neckcloth and heading for the door. "As I said, you needn't worry about me. I've decided to take my medicine and marry the chit."

Codswallop appeared at the door. "Miss Jerningham awaits, Mr. Dewland."

Quill stepped out of the salon and found Gabby pulling on her gloves in the entranceway. She was tightly buttoned into a pelisse of a deep rose color, and all her gorgeous hair was tucked away under a tight bonnet. She cast him an impatient look. Definitely she was in a cantankerous mood.

His curricle was pulled up before the house. Quill deftly helped Gabby up onto the seat and then followed. He waved off his groomsman and took the reins himself.

It was odd, Gabby thought to herself, how different it was in the carriage without Phoebe. Or perhaps it was because when Quill drove her from the docks, she was so much in love with Peter. She hadn't noticed the way Quill's muscled thighs took up most of the seat. But now . . .

She cleared her throat. "Have you informed your brother of our engagement?"

"No. I thought I should be certain that you wish to marry me first."

Gabby blinked. Hadn't she made that clear in the morning, rolling around on the rug like a trollop? "We agreed to marry," she said, her voice stiff.

"I thought perhaps we should discuss the issue more rationally," Quill replied smoothly, turning the curricle into Hyde Park.

Hot rage was rising in Gabby's throat. He had tumbled her around on the floor, and now he wanted to back out of the marriage? She was no idiot. He had decided to renege. Probably the tumbling had convinced him that he didn't want damaged goods, as Lady Sylvia had put it. Well, she wasn't going to make it easy for him. She managed to school her voice into calmness.

"Certainly. What in particular do you wish to discuss?"

"I feel that I should clarify what sort of a husband I will be," Quill replied.

There it was: he was going to say that she deserved a better man, and therefore he was breaking off the engagement for her own good. There was nothing she hated more than a cowardly approach.

"Do go on." After all, it wasn't as if *she* had proposed to him. She would have been perfectly happy married to Peter. Still would be happy, Gabby thought savagely.

"A gentleman does not engage in the activities with which I fill my day, Gabby," Quill was saying. "I have invested in several English firms, an activity that is anathema to my father, for example."

Gabby felt a flush of triumph. He couldn't use this as an excuse! "*My* father spends his days exporting goods to the Netherlands and China," she said, her tone cool. "I was not raised to believe that a gentleman should spend his time dawdling about the streets waiting for his next meal to be served."

Quill paused. He'd lectured himself all morning about

the necessity to be absolutely truthful with Gabby regarding the various infirmities stemming from his horse-riding accident. To be blunt about it, he had to tell her about his postcoital migraines.

"I would like to be very clear about the outcome of the accident I suffered six years ago," Quill said. Now that it had come to the point, he was remarkably reluctant to give her a real reason to back out of the engagement. "Doctor Trankelstein feels that I will always have a limp when tired, for example. I cannot dance. And there are other limitations—"

Gabby turned her beautiful eyes up to his. He felt a shock. Could they be flaming with anger? Surely not.

"Your limp does not concern me, Quill."

He opened his mouth and she cut him off. "Neither do any other bodily ailments that ensued from your accident." There! That shut him up, Gabby thought. But the persistent beast was continuing. He truly has changed his mind since the morning, Gabby thought with some pain.

"I feel obliged to warn you—"

But Gabby interrupted him again. "You needn't go on," she said, her tone airy and light. "I realize that you have decided to . . . throw me over, and I would rather not discuss it. After all, I have a positive embarrassment of riches. At the moment I have two fiancés. I shall quite happily marry Peter." She almost dusted her hands to emphasize the finality of her comment, but she clutched them together instead. Something about the way Quill's face had darkened during her little speech made her heart skip a beat.

"Do you dare to imply that *I* am trying to break off our engagement?"

Gabby nodded.

"I would never do such a thing." Quill's voice was thunderous.

Gabby suddenly realized her mistake. Once again she had insulted the English sense of propriety. She had offended Quill by implying that he wished to break off their engagement. A gentleman never spurned a lady—he forced the lady to break off the engagement instead.

She placed a gloved hand on his sleeve. "Quill, as friends, can't we speak truthfully to each other?"

Quill stared at her in some bewilderment. He didn't want her to speak truthfully if she was going to gibber on about having two fiancés and it not mattering which she married. She had *one* fiancé. And he was it. And she was going to have him as a husband too. After plaguing him all day, his conscience had gone silent. She was *his*.

He scowled at her. "Go ahead, then," he barked.

Gabby bit her lip. He looked just as angry as Peter had when she tried to kiss him in public. Truly, English gentlemen gave absurd credence to their rules of conduct.

"All I mean to say," she said, as reasonably as possible, "is that given our friendship, you needn't pretend that you still wish to marry me. You needn't try to find ways to make me jilt you. I completely understand."

There was a sick pain in her heart that belied her statement, but she'd think about that later. The important thing now was to preserve her dignity as much as possible, given that she'd just been thrown over. Luckily, the only person who knew about their brief engagement was Lady Sylvia, since they had decided not to disclose her change of fiancés to morning callers.

The horses were trotting down a lane on the north side of Hyde Park. Quill pulled on the reins, put on the brake, and tucked the reins into the curricle rail, without saying another word.

Gabby was feeling quite sick to her stomach now and would much rather return to the house than continue this unpleasant discussion. She expressed this desire in a slightly querulous tone.

Satisfied that his geldings were peacefully at a standstill, Quill turned his large body toward Gabby, which caused his thigh to press against her leg. Gabby flushed. It was embarrassing to remember how she had clung to his body that morning. No wonder he had rethought their marriage.

When Quill didn't say anything immediately, Gabby took a deep breath and repeated herself. "If you wouldn't mind, I should very much like to return to the house."

The traffic in the park was gradually increasing as the hour of six o'clock drew near and London gentlefolk turned out to admire themselves—at least those who braved a chill. The snap in the air had given Gabby's cheeks a pink glow that made her look as delectable as an apple tart, to Quill's mind.

He had registered the fact that she leapt at the chance to break off their engagement. Not that he was going to let her get away with it. Quill was used to setbacks. They happened frequently in business endeavors and only made him the more determined to gain whatever it was he wanted. However, there was no reason to further blacken Gabby's reputation by jerking her onto his lap in public and kissing her until she begged him to marry her.

That could wait for the evening.

Without bothering to say another word, he untucked the reins, loosed the brake, and deftly turned the horses back into the circular drive.

Gabby swallowed hard. For a moment she had thought that he was angry enough to kiss her. But he must have caught himself, remembering that he had got what he wanted: he was a free man once more. She stared at the flicking ears of the horses, trying hard to calm the furious misery in her heart. Luckily she still had her first fiancé. It was providential, like keeping one's money until the milk had been tasted. Now that her second fiancé had turned sour, she hadn't really lost anything.

Except that the lump in her throat told her that there had been an irrational—and quite stupid—transfer of affections. To put it in a nutshell, she wanted rather desperately to marry Quill, and she didn't give a fig whether she married Peter or not. And to make matters worse, she thought that Peter probably felt the same about her.

She pressed her lips together hard. You will *not* cry, she told herself. You thought you were in love with Peter only yesterday, for goodness sake.

Quill cast her a sideways glance. She had a queer, pinched look around her eyes, his Gabby did. And then he remembered a line of Peter's, something to the effect that Patrick Foakes had convinced everyone that he was madly in love with Lady Sophie by throwing civility to the winds.

He stopped the curricle, pulling it over to the right once again.

"Quill! I should very much like to return to Dewland House now!" His future wife spoke in a regrettably shrill voice.

When he was finished setting the brake, Quill turned to Gabby and dragged off his gloves.

Gabby's eyes darted to his bare hands and then back to his face.

Without a word he reached out and took her left hand. He bent his head and began to painstakingly unbutton the small pearl buttons at her wrist.

Gabby stared at his tousled hair. What the devil was he doing? He tossed her left glove to the floor of the curricle and began on the buttons of the right. Gabby looked up, but when she caught the eyes of a stranger passing in a carriage, she looked back at Quill's head. He tossed her right glove to the floor.

It was shockingly intimate, the touch of his bare hands on hers. Still without speaking, Quill drew her hands to his mouth and placed a kiss on each palm. His mouth lingered, velvet soft, slipping to her wrist. Gabby shivered as a flush of heat swept down her legs.

One hand rounded her shoulders, slid down her back, leaving a path of molten nerves behind it. Gabby heard Quill's breath catch in his throat as the hand swooped under her bottom, paused for a moment, and then lifted her onto his lap in one sure movement.

His mouth came down on hers with a shudder. She opened her lips to his silent command, and he plunged into her mouth. Gabby didn't notice that she was winding her fingers through his hair and holding his head in case he tried to stop kissing her. She had no idea that four separate carriages drove slowly past the curricle, their passengers eagerly assessing the boundaries of the scandal.

In fact, when Quill finally did pull back and say, his voice a hoarse whisper, "Do you still think I want to jilt you, Gabby mine?" she couldn't find words to reply.

Instead, she leaned toward him and feathered her lips across his. He stopped the torment. A large hand jerked her head against his lips, held her there while his mouth ravaged hers.

But he drew back again, leaving her with choked breathing and a racing pulse. "Do you still think that I want to jilt you?" he repeated.

"No," Gabby breathed.

"Then don't ever say it again," came a growling command. He had pushed off her bonnet, and her hair was falling around her ears.

He pushed both hands into the amazing, beautiful weight of it. "You're going to be my wife. Not Peter's wife. Not Peter's fiancé even. Mine."

"I would like that," Gabby whispered. A trace of shyness counteracted the flush high on her cheekbones. "I don't want to marry Peter, Quill. I want to marry you."

There was just a trace of conscience left in Quill's soul, and he summoned it to the forefront.

"Even given—"

"Even if you were thrown under a carriage on the way home," Gabby said.

"Let's hope it doesn't come to that," Quill said, gathering together the shards of his self-control. He picked up Gabby and placed her on the seat, his fingers only lingering for a second on the delicious curve of her bottom.

Gabby picked up her bonnet, with trembling fingers, and pulled it over her tumbled hair.

Quill shot her a glance as he maneuvered the horses back onto the drive once more. "I'm afraid that I've dented your reputation once again."

"That's all right." Gabby's heart was singing. She was in love and he was in love and they were going to be married. She was marrying Quill—great, huge, beautiful Quill.

"Will you speak to Peter this evening?"

"Yes."

"I don't believe that he will mind terribly," Gabby said meditatively, picking up her gloves from the carriage floor as it swept around the corner into Piccadilly, heading toward St. James's Square.

"You may be right," Quill returned, his face deliberately noncommittal.

Chapter 13

QUILL HELPED GABBY down from the curricle, with a secret smile that warmed her to the tips of her toes. She fled upstairs to dress for dinner, only to be thoroughly scolded by Margaret. Margaret had no belief in the benefits of fresh air and felt that winter was no time to be taking drives in an open curricle. She dismissed Gabby's rather feeble excuses with a sniff.

"You'll be sick as a stout, no doubt about that. And you coming from a warm country as well! Just mind what Mr. Peter says about this. I expect he won't want you to be tucked away in bed for the next few weeks."

"Actually, I have decided not to marry Peter," Gabby said cheerfully, helping Margaret remove what few pins remained in her hair.

Margaret's mouth fell open. "You're not marrying Mr. Peter?"

"I have decided to marry Erskine instead."

Margaret crowed. "You're going to be a viscountess! Oh, this is splendid!" Her eyes were shining with excitement. "I'm going to be a personal maid to a viscountess!"

Then her face fell. "That is, if you still want me. Perhaps you had better hire one of those French maids. Viscountess Dewland has an awfully starched maid named Stimple. She calls herself a *mademoiselle-de-service,* rather than a plain maid."

Gabby laughed. "Never fear, Margaret. You will be a lady's maid to a viscountess. But not for a long time, hmmm? I wouldn't wish the viscount any ill."

Margaret sobered immediately. "Of course I don't wish that, miss." She started to brush out Gabby's heavy locks. "None of us does, belowstairs. We're that fond of the viscount. It doesn't seem right, him dying off in some strange place rather than in his own bed."

"I don't think he's dying," Gabby said, rather startled. "I believe that his health is improving all the time, Margaret."

Margaret shook her head. "Once a person has one of those attacks, there's another right around the corner, miss. He should be home where he belongs, that's what. We all think so."

"I'm sure he'll return to London just as soon as the doctors think it advisable," Gabby murmured, rather shocked by Margaret's comment. "And I certainly hope you are wrong about the possibility of future attacks."

Margaret set her mouth obstinately and would only repeat her belief that the viscount ought to have been brought home by now.

The viscountess arrived from Bath just in time to join the family for supper. At first Gabby was very glad for the interruption, because she and Peter were avoiding each other's eyes in a tedious fashion. She could only assume that Quill had caught his brother after their ride in the park and informed him that the betrothal was at an end.

But Kitty's news was not good, and it seemed that Margaret had, in fact, been correct in her lugubrious prediction. Apparently Thurlow had slipped into a state of confusion, from which he was roused only with difficulty. He seemed to sleep most of the time, and the doctors held out very little hope for recovery.

Gabby looked at her hands, uncertain how to offer sympathy. Peter stood behind his mother's chair, gripping her shoulders. And Quill stood alone, next to the mantelpiece. What she really wanted to do was to walk over to Quill and take his hand. But she stayed next to Lady Sylvia on the settee.

This time Kitty wasn't the least hysterical, and she did not weep as she told them the news.

"How much time has he got, Kitty?" Lady Sylvia's voice was uncharacteristically gentle.

Kitty's blue eyes were bleak. "Likely only a few days." She paused and the words sank into the room's silence.

"You and the boys should leave tonight," Lady Sylvia said after a moment.

Kitty turned to Gabby. "My dear, I am terribly regretful that this unhappy event has occurred during your first weeks in England."

"Oh, no! It is of no account. I am sorry, my lady. . . . I am so sorry to hear of the viscount's health."

"You are a sweet girl, Gabrielle. I am sure you will be a great comfort to me."

Kitty had clearly accepted the fact of her husband's imminent death. Gabby's heart twisted. What if it were Quill lying there? Without thinking about it, she rose and walked over next to him.

Quill looked down at her and smiled. He put an arm around her shoulders. "Mother, Gabby has decided to marry me rather than Peter," he said.

Gabby instinctively looked at Peter, but he wasn't angry. As a matter of fact, he smiled and nodded at her most genially.

Kitty Dewland's eyes rested on Gabby and Quill in bewilderment and then lightened. "I am *so* happy, Quill! And dear Gabrielle." She rose and walked over, taking each of their hands. "I always hoped that my children would marry for love, as I did." She bent and kissed Gabby. "A double welcome to the family, dearest."

She kissed her elder son and then paused. "We shall soon be in mourning, Quill."

He nodded. "Perhaps I should marry Gabby tomorrow, by special license, Mama."

A glimmer of tears shone in Kitty's eyes, but her voice was quite steady. "Perhaps that would be for the best, dearest."

Quill leaned down and kissed his mother on the cheek.

She blinked away tears. "I'm sorry. I don't mean to be maudlin. It's just that Thurlow would have liked to see you and Gabrielle . . ."

"Shall we be married in Bath?" Quill suggested.

One tear escaped and rolled down Kitty's cheek. "That would be very amenable of you, Quill."

"Then that is what we shall do, Mama." He drew his mother over to a chair and she sank into it, clearly exhausted.

Lady Sylvia took charge. "Time we told the servants to pack," she said. "And then we must have that meal before Cook has conniptions. If we're going to be in a carriage half the night, we need some hot food first." She rang the bell and snapped at Codswallop when he appeared. "Quill, you'd better go out and rouse Beilby Porteus. He is a bishop, and he is also a friend of the family. He'll hand over a license with no fuss."

It took most of the night to reach Bath, and there was

little conversation in the coach. Gabby finally fell asleep on Quill's shoulder as they jolted their way down the Bath road.

The following morning Gabby dressed in the most demure of Madame Carême's gowns, and Margaret piled her hair into an elaborate design. Most surprisingly, Margaret then produced a wedding veil, a beautiful bit of gauze embroidered with white-on-white flowers.

"Where on earth did you find a veil?" Gabby asked, startled. She hadn't thought there would be anything weddinglike about the ceremony, under the circumstances.

"The master fetched it from Madame Carême yesterday," Margaret explained, deftly pinning it to her mistress's hair.

Gabby smiled. Quill had left the house directly after their conversation, and while the rest of them ate a glum and rather silent dinner, he was presumably obtaining a special license. But it seemed that he thought about the wedding itself as well.

A few moments later, Lady Sylvia appeared. The wedding was to be held in the viscount's bedchamber on the upper floor of the inn. Gabby stood rather awkwardly on the side of the room, trying not to peer at the bed. Given that she had never even met the viscount, it seemed very odd to be in his chambers.

Quill was standing beside a young minister as he blessed the viscount. Gabby shivered. She couldn't help thinking that the occasion was rather morbid. This wasn't how she had pictured her wedding day. She had envisioned an elaborate ceremony and had seen herself walking up the aisle of an enormous church while Peter watched, his brown eyes alight with adoration. Gabby sighed. Quill had only glanced at her this morning. Except for the fact that he pulled her onto his shoulder in the coach, they might have been nothing more than acquaintances.

Grief had pulled Quill's face and darkened his eyes; exhaustion was giving him a pronounced limp on the right side. Gabby longed to help him, but had no idea what to do. It didn't seem correct to move toward the bed.

After what felt like an interminable period, the minister walked over to her and bowed. "Miss Jerningham, my name is Mr. Moir. I am ready to conduct the ceremony." He, too, was looking pale and strained. This was a most unusual wedding for everyone.

The family moved to the side of the viscount's bed. Lady Sylvia remained seated at the side of the room, next to the viscount's doctor.

Quill's face was expressionless. Gabby stood next to him and the minister, on one side of the bed. Kitty and Peter stood on the other side. Kitty picked up her husband's limp hand.

"We might as well go ahead," Quill said. His voice was not rude, but there was no emotion in it at all.

Gabby put her hand on his arm. "Quill," she half whispered.

"What is it?"

"Will you introduce me to your father?" she asked awkwardly.

"Of course," Quill said courteously, and he moved away from the bed so that she saw the viscount for the first time. He was a tall man, with an unmistakable resemblance to his elder son. He had Quill's eyelashes, lying dark against drawn cheeks. Death spoke in the white look of his face. But he also seemed very peaceful, sleeping so quietly that the breath hardly moved in his chest.

Quill stooped over and said, "Father, I would like to introduce you to Gabrielle Jerningham. I am going to marry her."

There was no response from the sleeping man.

Kitty put her hand on his cheek and said, "I believe that Thurlow can hear us. This morning I told him all about the wedding." She leaned over and called, "Darling!"

Thurlow's eyes flickered open and sought out his wife, standing by the bed. He murmured something.

"What is it, darling?"

"Cherish," he said, quite clearly. "Lovely Kitty."

Gabby could feel tears in the back of her throat. She reached out and laid her hand briefly on top of the viscount's. "I am very pleased to meet you, sir."

"Dearly beloved," Mr. Moir said, his voice gentle. "We are gathered together here in the sight of God, and in the face of this family, to join together this man and this woman in holy matrimony. . . ."

Quill took Gabby's hands in his large, warm ones. Gabby looked up at him and clutched his hands as if they were lifelines.

"It is not by any to be enterprised, nor taken in hand," Mr. Moir was saying, "unadvisedly, lightly, or wantonly, to satisfy men's carnal lusts and appetites, like brute beasts that have no understanding, but reverently, discreetly, advisedly, soberly, and in the face of God."

Quill took a deep breath. Part of his mind still couldn't believe that he, Erskine Dewland, was marrying Gabrielle Jerningham. As a matter of fact, it was hard to believe that he was marrying at all. He was aware of his father's inert body at his right shoulder, of Mr. Moir talking of procreation and remedies for sin, of his mother holding his father's hand to her cheek.

But most of all he was aware of his almost-wife. Of Gabby's lovely brandy-colored eyes, shining with grief for a man she had never met. Her glorious hair was shaded by a veil that looked like a wisp of cloud.

And he repeated after the priest, "I, Erskine Matthew

Claudius Dewland, take thee, Gabrielle Elizabeth Jerningham, to be my wedded wife, to have and to hold from this day forward, for better, for worse, for richer, for poorer . . ."

Gabby was dimly aware that the viscountess was cradling her husband's hand against her cheek and that Peter was smiling slightly on the other side of the bed. But the room had narrowed to Quill's deep-green eyes and to his large hands, still holding hers tightly. "In sickness and in health," she said clearly, "to love, cherish, and to obey, till death do us part, according to God's holy ordinance; and thereto I give thee my troth."

Quill smiled then, and the smile flew to her heart. He took her hand and slid a ring onto the fourth finger.

"With this ring I thee wed," Quill said. "With my body I thee worship, and with all my worldly goods I thee endow."

Gabby swallowed hard. The viscountess was weeping silently on the other side of the bed.

Mr. Moir put his hand on top of their joined hands. "I pronounce that they be man and wife together."

Quill stepped forward and put one hand under Gabby's chin, tipping her face up. He bent his head and his lips met hers. There wasn't a trace of the intoxicating fever that generally assailed him when he touched Gabby. His lips lingered with a sense of sweet possession.

Gabby's arms came up around his neck and she clung to him. For a moment Quill forgot where he was in a rush of exultant triumph. He had wooed her and wed her. She was *his,* this whole enchanting bundle of woman, Gabby, wife.

Then Kitty hurried around the bed, and a second later Gabby was enveloped in a scented hug. "I am so happy, darling, and so would Thurlow be as well. He would wish you all the best. That is, he *is* wishing you all the best, because I'm quite certain that he is aware of what just happened, Gabrielle."

"Mother," Quill said quietly. He was still standing at the head of the bed.

The viscount's eyes were closed and his hands were relaxed. Gabby thought he had gone back to sleep. But then Quill tenderly laid his father's hand back on the coverlet, and Mr. Moir came forward, touched the viscount's head, and said, "Go with God." Kitty whispered, "Oh, Thurlow, no, *no*," and Peter came around the bed and drew her into his arms.

Soundlessly, Gabby retreated to a chair next to Lady Sylvia.

LIKELY, MARRIAGE VOWS always brought with them a terrifying feeling of change, Gabby thought later, back in her room.

One part of her was fascinated by the fact that Quill could—he had the right!—walk into her bedchamber at any moment, even though she was wearing nothing more than a slight chemise. A hastily summoned seamstress was measuring her for a suit of black clothing.

Another part of her was trying hard not to think of her wedding as a turn from white to black, from joy to sadness. That was the problem with an imagination like hers. It was entirely too active and too ready to leap to idiotic suppositions.

Superstition, her father had often said, was the bane of uncivilized cultures. Gabby tried to hold on to that thought.

But it wasn't until the door swung open and a large body walked through, as if there was nothing unusual about entering a lady's bedchamber, that Gabby really understood just how much her life had changed.

Quill's eyes moved down her body, his face inscrutable.

His eyes dropped to the seamstress, who was scrawling notations, and then to Margaret, waiting to dress her mistress again.

He jerked his head, and Margaret jumped to her feet and grabbed the seamstress's arm.

And then, before Gabby could have said Jack Robinson, Quill was standing alone in the middle of her bedchamber.

Chapter 14

GABBY BIT HER LIP. Was he going to consummate their marriage right now? It was two o'clock in the afternoon. Of course, Quill had kissed her on the library rug when it was only eight in the morning. She felt a prickly flush rising up the back of her neck.

Likely he was. She had heard maids talk of newly wedded husbands. Husbands who didn't let their wives out of bed for three days after the marriage. Husbands who couldn't keep their hands from their brides, even during the ceremony. . . . Gabby had always listened with fascination.

She stood still, watching as her husband sent Margaret away. Her skin woke up, all over her body, and spoke to her about Quill's fingers and where they would linger, about his lips and slow kisses.

In fact, Quill had no such intention when he entered the room.

He had in mind a sensible conversation with his wife. He would instruct her, plainly and simply, about the parameters of their marriage. He would inform Gabby that consummation would have to wait until after the funeral.

He could not risk missing the ceremony because he was reduced to a pain-ridden husk, lying in a darkened room with a wet cloth over his eyes.

It was too late for her to back out, Quill had told himself all the way down the inn corridor. She'd done it: married him. Promised to obey him. Perhaps he'd consummate the marriage in a month or so. When they were back in London. After his father was—he shied away from that thought. He had never been close to Thurlow, and they had grown quite distant in the years since the accident, given his father's inability to hide his shame at having a crippled heir, let alone an heir who dabbled in commerce and other ungentlemanly business pursuits. But Thurlow had been his father. There was a hot feeling at the back of Quill's eyes that stiffened his backbone.

The important thing was to begin the marriage as they meant to go on. He would tolerate a certain amount of nonsense on Gabby's part—talk of love and such—but only a reasonable amount. And he himself wasn't going to indulge her by telling more lies about being in love. She was his now, and there was no further reason to perjure himself. Honesty had always served him best.

And yet for all that, for all his arrogant decisions and composure, Quill felt like a drowning man when he walked into Gabby's bedchamber. Because she was wearing nothing, his wife. Naught more than a scrap of delicate cotton.

The gray sky had parted to reveal scraps of blue. A pale spill of sunlight turned Gabby's chemise into nothing more than a thin veil between himself and the rounded curves of her hips. He could see the outline of her body as if drawn in ink: the delicate way her waist curved in from her ribs and then blossomed out again, a hint of full breasts between her left arm and her side, the turn of her neck as it blended into delicate collarbone.

He inspected her from head to foot, from the sheen of her glossy hair to the tips of her silk slippers. He surveyed her as if she were a figure made of the finest china, one that he was considering for purchase.

He couldn't find any words.

"Quill?"

Gabby sounded nervous, to Quill's mind. She was clutching her hands rather tightly before her.

In the nick of time, his self-possession, gained from six years of crippling injury, abruptly reasserted itself. His body would *never* rule his mind—even in matters of erotic pleasure rather than acute pain. But he was shocked at how close he came to leaping on Gabby, and to the devil with his headaches.

Instead, he nodded casually and strolled past her to sit down in a chair by the fireplace. He stretched out his boots and stared at them meditatively, quite as if his body wasn't on fire, straining at every pore to jerk his half-naked wife into his arms. Take her there, without ceremony and without forethought. Take her on the carpet, on the bed, on the chair. Over and over until this intolerable lust was satisfied and he could return to being himself: a calm and rational person. A person whose emotions were mild and composed into neat categories labeled *marital duty* and *filial respect*.

Filial respect. He had almost forgotten about the funeral again.

Gabby's heart was beating so fast that she felt ill. The moment Quill took his eyes off her she rushed over and put on her night-robe. If she wasn't mistaken, he had seriously considered tumbling her right on the bedchamber floor.

She didn't mind that he had changed his mind, Gabby told herself. Everyone knew that men and women did those things—tumbled about—in the dark, in their beds, under the covers. *Not* in the early afternoon. At a decent time, in a decent place.

She tied the cord of her robe firmly about her waist and sat down opposite her husband. He looked dangerously magnificent, relaxed in a chair. Since he was temporarily ignoring her, Gabby let herself stare at him. Quill hadn't changed into black clothing yet. His thighs were large and muscular in his fawn-colored pantaloons. In the sunlight she could see red tints in his hair as it tumbled forward. Those large hands—they had done amazing things to her in the library, when he asked her to marry him. She felt a delicious tremor in her knees.

Gabby flushed and shifted slightly in her chair. She had a rising sense of confusion interlaced with an uncomfortable wish that Quill would look at her again.

But when he did, there was none of that wicked pleasure with which he sometimes looked at her. His eyes were flat, unspeaking.

"I feel we should discuss our marriage." He cleared his throat. "We should . . . make a beginning. Begin as we mean to go on."

Quill ground his teeth together. He sounded daft. No wonder Gabby looked so bewildered.

"I mean to say that we ought to be frank with each other."

Gabby nodded. Her stomach was curling into knots. It didn't sound good, all this talk of frankness. Her mind darted desperately in several directions at once. Perhaps he regretted the marriage. Oh, why was she wearing such a thin shift when he walked into the room! Perhaps he didn't like her hips. Perhaps . . .

"There will be times when you will say the same to me, my dear, and I will accept it with equanimity. With luck, after all, we will be married for years."

Gabby didn't understand what he was talking about. She knit her brow.

He kept talking, calmly speaking of separate chambers and marital courtesies.

By a moment later she was quite certain that Quill was regretting their marriage. She stared at him, flabbergasted, and then blurted out, "No!"

Quill lifted an eyebrow.

"I had no idea that you were looking forward to this event so eagerly, Gabby. I would prefer to sleep alone, given my father's impending funeral. But if you insist?"

Gabby felt a hot wash of humiliation. Of course she wasn't looking forward to it to *that* degree. She opened her mouth, but couldn't find words. But she was . . . she was . . . *Be frank with each other,* he'd said. But how can one be frank about things that weren't spoken out loud?

"I have no objection." Then she couldn't think of a single comment to add. Having no experience, she could hardly make a slighting remark about the expendability of the act.

He must not feel the same way she did. She, Gabby, felt as if she might suffocate if Quill didn't take her in his arms again. She knew without hesitation that she wouldn't be able to sleep tonight. The moment Quill said, "with my body, I thee worship," she had come into a strange sense of her own body. An awakening sense that arrived with a quickened pulse and hummed through her body, a sense that intensified whenever she looked at him, at the masculine perfection of his body and the sense of leashed power about him.

"But I thought—" She stopped, the words choking in her throat. This was just going to embarrass her more than ever. So he didn't want to consummate their marriage until they returned to London. Where was her sympathy? Her father was still alive. Likely she wouldn't want to . . . to do whatever it was either, if she had her father's funeral to attend.

She bit her lip. "I am so sorry, Quill." She bent her head. "I did not mean to be disrespectful to your father or to your grief. I am ashamed that I questioned your feelings."

Tears mounted to her eyes and she scrambled to make amends. "I feel so badly for you and for your family. *Please* forgive me. I'm afraid that my father and I are not close and so I forgot how very much you must be missing the viscount. It was inexcusable of me to forget your grief. That is, I didn't forget your grief, it's just that I . . ." Her voice trailed off in a near whisper.

Grief? Quill thought likely it *was* grief he was feeling, watching the pale skin of Gabby's wrist. He couldn't risk looking at her face, at her wine-red lips.

He had rarely had such a cruel sense of the world's injustices. He, Erskine Dewland—no, Viscount Dewland now—couldn't bed his new wife when and where he pleased. It was manifestly unfair. And the queer pang around his heart had nothing to do with Gabby's bewildered disappointment.

For disappointed she was, his new wife. He'd already disappointed her, and they had been married less than three hours. Quill savagely pushed the feeling away. He had disappointed his father a thousand times, starting when he could not rise from his bed just after the accident.

"Dewlands don't malinger!" the viscount had thundered. "Look to your will, man! Rise from that bed!" And he couldn't. Quill still remembered his catastrophic sense of failure. He'd tried. And tried again, after his father stamped from the room. Couldn't do it, and fell on the floor—and even more humiliating, had to remain there until his valet arrived, hours later. He'd wet himself while sprawled on the floor, because he was unable to crawl to the chamber pot and unable to reach the bell cord. Twenty-some years old, and as useless as a newborn babe.

The memory made him feel sick, and a wash of useless anger swept over him. His father was dead. And if he did what Gabby, with every embarrassed tremor of her lips, was asking, he would be unable to make arrangements for his father's funeral.

The thought stiffened his backbone. He could bed Gabby later. She was his and she could wait. But his mother would never forgive him if he succumbed to a migraine attack when she needed him most.

"Probably it is all for the best," he said coolly. "We haven't known each other for very long, after all." He shrugged. "And bedding is painful for women at first, Gabby. But I suspect you know that?"

Gabby swallowed, yet another flush following the one that had barely faded. "No, I didn't know that," she whispered.

Irritation replaced the ugly memory of his father's disappointment. By God, Gabby was his possession, and she could damned well wait until he had time to see to her. He wasn't some sort of stallion, to perform on demand from his wife. After they returned to London, they would share a bed only every few weeks. He had far too much work to suffer migraine attacks more frequently than once a month.

He got up and walked to the other side of the room, fierce indignation in the tilt of his chin, rejoicing in the restoration of his self-possession. Gabby had almost lured him into an indecent intimacy, only hours after his father's death. He took a quick turn at the end of the chamber, turning on his heel next to the bed Gabby had slept in the night before. Anger made him feel careless and cruel.

"I realize that you are a very passionate woman, Gabby." He tossed it over his shoulder, not bothering to look. "But since we are being frank, let me say that I will not tolerate it if you make sheep's eyes at anyone other than myself."

Gabby could hardly breathe. "I won't," she said. She was ready to die of mortification. He obviously thought she was a strumpet. He was treating her as if she couldn't wait until after the funeral to be bedded.

Quill didn't hear her. "What did you say?" He was inspecting the mantelpiece, running his finger along the polished mahogany slab.

"I won't," Gabby repeated.

"Right. Well, then, I think we have reached an understanding, Gabby." He turned about and rocked back on his heels. "As I said, it's best to begin as we mean to go on."

There was a moment's pause in the room. Gabby took a deep, unsteady breath. Quill looked as if he was about to leave, and she couldn't allow it. She might not have known Quill very long, as he had pointed out, but she knew that his unpleasant tone was not normal.

"Wait!" she half shouted.

Quill turned about as his hand reached for the door handle.

"What is it, Gabby? I have a number of arrangements to make."

She stood up and walked toward him, ignoring her shaky knees and stopping only when she stood a hairbreadth away. Then she put her hands on his chest, spreading her fingers against his warmth.

"I think we should talk further," she said carefully, ignoring the churning sensation in her stomach. "Not"—she shook her head when he opened his mouth to protest— "Not about when we consummate this marriage. I have no objection to your plans in that regard."

Gabby's mouth curved into a faint smile. "I am no siren, Quill, to lure you into bedding me when you are distraught by grief for your papa." She paused, but Quill said nothing, just stared at her with his shadowed eyes.

"Sometimes grief is easier if one shares it." Gabby lowered her eyes and twisted one of the silver-plated buttons on the front of Quill's coat. "I realize that my father is still alive, and so I can have no true understanding of your feelings. But I did lose a dearly beloved friend, in my childhood. His name was Johore, and I loved him very much. And after he died . . ."

Quill was hardly listening. Gabby's friend Johore had died of a fever. He heard that. But she was standing too close for rational thought. He could smell drifts of jasmine rising from her perfumed skin, like airy promises of delight.

"You see," Gabby was saying with sweet earnestness, "we are married, Quill. And I don't believe it matters when we consummate the marriage. What matters is that we speak without anger to each other."

Quill gave his head a brutal shake. How the hell did Gabby turn the conversation into a discourse on marriage? "When one is angry, one speaks with anger," he pointed out.

"It is best to keep that anger where it belongs," Gabby said. Her beautiful brown eyes were warm with sympathy. "You are not really angry with me, Quill, and yet you sounded enraged, as if I had done something wrong."

Quill felt like a five-year-old hauled in front of a nurse to admit his shortcomings. Yet common sense agreed with her. "You are likely correct," he said, breaking the silence. "I should not have spoken angrily to you, Gabby, and I apologize."

He stepped backward and her hands fell away from his

chest, leaving a momentary, and unwelcome, coolness there. He bowed. "Please accept my apologies, madam."

"Madam? Why do you call me that?" Gabby was worrying her lower lip in confusion, turning it a deep cherry red.

Quill shrugged, trying in vain to regain his self-possession. "You are a madam now. You are Viscountess Dewland."

"Yes," Gabby said. "But *you* need not address me so, Quill."

He shrugged again and backed up, his hand searching behind him for the door handle. "Have we talked sufficiently?"

Gabby faltered. It was still wrong. But she couldn't *make* him talk, could she? She swallowed. She could try again. Not for nothing had her father called her pigheaded.

"No, we have not talked sufficiently," she said, turning about and perching on the edge of the bed. She avoided her husband's eyes, guessing that courtesy would not allow Quill to leave the room without a proper farewell.

Reluctantly, Quill felt a smile tugging at his mouth. She was stubborn, his new wife. She wasn't going to let him stamp out, full of self-righteous male indignation.

He walked over, the toes of his boots rapping on the wooden floor. For a moment he stood looking down at her, and then he, too, sat on the edge of the bed. His rational self told him loud and clear that sitting on a bed—or near a bed—with Gabby was an extremely foolish action.

Her eyes were liquid with sympathy. Quill smothered a sense of irritation. He hated to be pitied. But this was his wife. Gabby would likely pity him for the rest of his life once she knew the extent of his injuries. And there was nothing he could do about it.

"I don't like to be pitied," he said, before he could stop himself.

Gabby blinked. "It's a natural feeling," she said. "You loved your father, and he's dead. How could I not feel sorry that you have lost something so precious?"

Quill didn't know what to say to that. He was silent.

After a moment, Gabby broke the silence. "Quill, you have to start speaking more frequently, or we'll spend our married life twiddling our thumbs!"

"Luckily, I like to hear you speak." His joke fell rather flat.

Gabby snorted. "There's no point in speaking to oneself. I should like to hear *you* speak. Why are you in such a foul mood?"

Quill said nothing.

"I assume," Gabby said, with a small edge to her voice, "that you didn't really mean to make me out to be a wanton seducer and you no more than an innocent lad from the country?"

He turned his head and chuckled, despite himself. "Did I?" he said, with emphatic innocence. "Surely not!"

"You did!" Gabby retorted. "I felt like some sort of a . . . *très-coquette* who had approached you on the street."

"What do you know about streetwalkers, Gabby?"

"Very little, and you know it. Since you are aware that I am not experienced in these things, why did you try to make me feel . . . like that? Indecent? It was not well done of you."

Ruefulness warred with shock in Quill's eyes. "Damn it, Gabby," he managed, "do you always speak whatever is on your mind?"

"Speak the truth and shame the devil," Gabby said. "As my father maintains."

"I apologize," Quill said, feeling his way. "I never wished to make you feel indecent, Gabby. I felt remorseful because . . . because we will not share a chamber until after my father's burial.

"Oh, hell and damnation, Gabby, I need to tell you something." Quill groaned.

Gabby put a hand on his as it lay on the counterpane between them. He stared down for a moment and then interlaced his fingers into hers, holding her hand tightly.

"I can't make love to you, Gabby," he said huskily. "I would give the world to fall backward on this bed right now, but I can't do it."

There was a pause. And then Gabby said, "Why not?"

Quill laughed shortly. "Why not indeed? I married you under false pretenses, Gabby. You could annul the marriage." The muscles in his jaw were clenched tight.

Gabby had turned very pale. "Are you unable to . . . to have relations, Quill?"

"Better that I was," he said bitterly. "Then it wouldn't be in front of me, like a carrot before a damned donkey."

"I don't understand."

His fingers were clenched so hard on hers that her hand felt bloodless. "How—*why* can't you have relations with me, Quill?" She felt hot, her mind groping stupidly for explanations, none of which were pleasant. Could it be that he didn't desire her enough to perform? She had heard of that from maids as well. Aye, men couldn't do their part if the woman didn't appeal to them.

Quill didn't answer her. Perhaps he didn't care to hurt her feelings.

She cleared her throat. "Is it something to do with me, Quill? Because you needn't tell me if—" She wanted to know and she didn't want to know. She felt as if her heart were breaking right in two, a blinding pain in her chest. It seemed her father was right when he thanked God for giving him a man who would take his daughter to wife sight unseen.

"It has nothing to do with you," Quill said heavily. "I tried to tell you before we wed, Gabby. When I was injured in that accident, I didn't completely heal."

"Oh," Gabby breathed.

"I am still functional," he said, his tone bitterly dry. "But there are consequences each time I make love."

"Consequences?" Gabby echoed. Against all odds, her heart was lightening.

"Have you ever heard of a migraine, Gabby? Some people refer to it as a megrim."

Gabby thought about it. "No."

"A migraine is a type of headache," Quill explained. "A very severe headache, accompanied by nausea and vomiting that lasts three to five days. I am incapacitated during that time."

"Is there nothing that can be done?" Gabby's tone was appalled.

"If I stay in a darkened room and eat almost nothing, it goes away more quickly."

"But is there no medical remedy?"

Quill shook his head.

"I didn't know . . ." Gabby whispered. "Were you in pain when we were in the library?" She raised agonized eyes to his. "You should have told me, Quill!"

His mouth took on a sensual, crooked curve. "Did I appear to be in pain?"

"Yes—no?"

At that a chuckle escaped. "I *was* in pain, Gabby. But not that kind of pain."

A large hand touched her cheek. Gabby pushed it from her face. "Don't do that, Quill! I can't think if you start touching me. What kind of pain are you talking about?"

Her eyes were the color of autumn leaves, Quill thought. Nut-brown. Words didn't seem available to catch the way they changed with the light. He leaned forward and kissed her, his tongue making a ravishing foray into Gabby's mouth.

She gasped, a small sound, easily silenced. He caught her lip between his teeth, caught a softness that stole his breath and drove a shiver down his body. Then he undid the tie at her waist and pushed the robe off her shoulders. She gasped again.

"Am I in pain, Gabby?" His voice was a husky murmur, low and unsteady. A hand clasped her cheek, fingers tracing the curve of a delicate ear.

"No," Gabby said. A rose flush crept up her cheekbone, but she twisted away from his hands and mouth. "You are distracting me. If you weren't in pain in the library, then what causes these headaches? I don't understand."

Quill almost reached out, but stopped himself. He was trying to avoid the truth. "I get the headaches after intercourse," he said flatly.

Gabby blinked uncertainly.

"Connubial relations. Conjugal felicity." Quill racked his mind for more euphemisms for the event. "Intercourse," he repeated. But Gabby was twisting her hands together, and Quill grasped the truth. "You don't know what I'm talking about, do you?"

"Of course I do!" Gabby rushed into speech, stung by embarrassment. "I just am not quite certain about the details, perhaps. I have a general idea. And I should like to point out that there are undoubtedly other young women who have exactly my level of knowledge. My mother died when I was born, you know. And one couldn't expect my father to explain the intimacies of marriage!"

Her father's advice had been blunt and to the point: *If he doesn't die of your insipid jabber before marriage, he'll go to drink after. Better he than I. So for my sake, keep your tongue between your teeth till he's properly leg-shackled.* That was the sum total of her father's marital advice.

The memory made her falter. "I don't know precisely what you are referring to," she admitted, weaving her fingers together in her lap. She cleared her throat. "Could you explain it to me? I would hate to cause you to have a headache without knowing." She was so embarrassed that her face had taken on a fevered look.

Quill reached out an arm and pulled her against him. Then he smoothly lifted her into his lap, stifling a groan as enchanting curves, covered only by sheer cotton, settled onto his legs.

Gabby didn't look up at him. She pressed her fingertips to her cheeks, trying to calm what she knew must be an unattractive ruddy flush.

Quill's hand wandered from her neck to her breast. Gabby startled and her back instinctively arched, pushing her breast into Quill's hand. A hoarse noise escaped his throat.

"Are you in pain now? Does that hurt?" She sounded as if she were ready to leap from his lap.

Quill almost laughed. "No." He couldn't speak for a moment because he was savoring the way her body trembled as he rubbed a thumb across her nipple. Not to mention what was happening to his body.

"Do you know, Gabby, I've never been married before."

"I do know that," Gabby choked. Perhaps she should stop him from—from what he was doing. It was hard to think clearly.

As if he heard her thought, he did stop. His fingers stilled, cupped around the weight of Gabby's breast. Her body quivered like the string of a violin waiting for the gentle sweep of the bow.

"I've never been married before, and thus I've never made love," Quill said carefully. "I've had relations with women. They say there's quite a difference." Actually, the only person with whom he had ever discussed such an intimate topic was an old school friend, Alex Foakes, the earl of Sheffield and Downes. In a fit of mild intoxication one evening, Alex had said making love to one's wife made intercourse with other women look clay-cold, like being frozen to the bone.

"Oh, quite," Gabby replied.

He could tell she had no idea what he was talking about. Gabby was leaning against his chest and he couldn't see her face, but he would bet anything that she was chewing on her lower lip.

"When you had intercourse with these women, did the migraine always follow?"

"Yes." His thumb was moving in idle circles again.

"I find it doubtful that marriage will change the situation," Gabby noted with a rather surprising use of logic. "I'm afraid that we shall have to expect the migraine, Quill. It sounds to me like a physical reaction. One of my friends in India, Leela, always vomits after eating papaya."

"Yes," Quill admitted, giving up the dream that married sex was different. "I wish it was only a question of papaya."

"Have you spoken to doctors about it?"

"I have," Quill said rather bitterly. "I have consulted with Sir Thomas Willis himself."

At Gabby's raised eyebrow, he continued. "Willis is the leading specialist on migraine headaches. He had the temerity to inform me that I must be wrong in my description, as his theory precluded migraines resulting from head injury."

"How very annoying! Did you convince him of your symptoms?"

"Yes," Quill said dryly. "The next time I suffered an attack, I had him brought to the house. Willis had to admit that it looked as if I was suffering a migraine. But since he's convinced that migraines are caused by swollen vessels in the brain, he declared my case an exception. In the end, it turned out he had no medicine other than laudanum anyway."

Gabby put her hand over his, stopping his fingers' lazy movement. But Quill refused to move his hand when she tugged, and just dropped a kiss on her hair.

"Quill, I think we should speak about this rationally. I need you to tell me about the . . . the marital act." She said the last bit quickly and then launched into her idea. "We'll have to figure out exactly what stimulates your headache and then avoid it. That is how Sudhakar discovered why Leela was vomiting and losing weight. She loved papaya and was eating more and more, trying to soothe her stomach."

"I love your breast," Quill said silkily. And then, "Who's Sudhakar?"

Gabby turned her face up to his and scowled. "I shall go sit over there, Quill, if you can't be reasonable." She pointed to a chair by the fire.

"I'll be reasonable." The arm Quill had wound around her shoulder and hips held her to him like a vise. Somehow Gabby's warmth and sensual presence made his despair seem overblown. Perhaps he could just bring her to pleasure and ignore his own—

Gabby shifted in his lap, and he gave up that idea.

"All right," Gabby said, having made herself comfortable. "Sudhakar is the *vaidya* of the village I grew up in. A *vaidya* is a kind of doctor who specializes in poisons. Sudhakar explained that Leela was being poisoned, but only because papaya didn't agree with her stomach. In fact, why don't I write to Sudhakar?"

"Absolutely not," Quill said firmly. "I'm not having my problems discussed in your village. Besides," he added ruefully, "if the best doctors in London cannot do anything, I'm afraid that it is unlikely that a poison doctor from an Indian village will do much better."

She opened her mouth and Quill put a finger on it. "I want your promise, Gabby. I do not wish my migraines to be discussed with anyone. They are a private matter."

Gabby nodded unwillingly. "But, Quill—"

"No."

"Well, all right," Gabby said with a sigh. "We'll have to work it out ourselves. Could you explain about conjugal felicity, or whatever it was you called it? I know you do it at night, and in bed. What are we going to do?"

Quill looked down at his wife in amusement. Her eyes were clear and full of curiosity. She looked like someone inquiring about the road to Bath. Or the proper way to string a bow. He didn't answer.

Instead, he swooped fiercely onto that curious little mouth, silencing her logic, her thought, her questions— making her into *his* Gabby. The Gabby who struggled for a moment and then gave in with a little pant. A second later her eyelids drifted shut and her tongue met his, chasing fire down to his groin.

With a deft twist Quill lifted Gabby to the side and placed her on the bed. From there a liquid collapse backward was inevitable. His body followed hers as naturally as wheat stalks bend together in a high wind.

He caressed her lavishly, feverishly, knowing he had to stop. Gabby twisted beneath him, uttering delightful little noises. He backed off and kissed her forehead and her eyelids and her ears.

But the moment he left her mouth, he heard a voice, breathless but insistent, inquiring whether he had a headache coming on. And so he stopped nibbling on the delicate tips of her ears, slid down the smooth planes of her flushed cheeks, allowed himself that agonizing, delirious moment of surrender when her mouth opened to his and he swallowed her words.

He was throbbing all over. Unfortunately, his head was as clear as a bell. It told him that he couldn't stay in bed all afternoon. It instructed him loudly that he should be arranging a funeral, comforting his mother (although Peter would do that better than he), posting letters hither and yon. He thrust the inner voice away with a groan and bent to Gabby's breast. He kissed her through the frail cloth of her chemise, watched her nipple rise in a small circle of damp muslin. He listened to her make a small squeak every time he pulled the nipple back into his mouth, felt a delirious tremor in his body that matched the tremor in hers.

But Gabby kept trying to pull away. "Quill! You *must stop*!"

With one swift and obstinate movement, Quill ran his hand under Gabby's chemise.

Gabby gasped in surprise as the damp spot over her breast was replaced by the strength of a large male hand. Cool air drifted over her legs and she instinctively tried to jerk her chemise back below her waist. But Quill had rolled so that his hip pinned her down, and her head became confused by his hand on her breast and the roughness of his trousers on her bare thigh. And then his hand—

"Take your hand away!" Gabby was shocked to the core of her being. She twisted her legs together as sharply as possible and rolled away.

Quill, dazed by his fingers' bold exploration into melting warmth, lost balance and let her go. Long legs flashed as she scrambled sideways.

Gabby ended up kneeling on the bed, still panting slightly, cheeks rosy. She glared at her husband. "You mustn't do that ever again. I don't like it. It's . . . it's an imposition. *Worse* than an imposition." She couldn't even think of a word strong enough.

"I wanted to," Quill said with a wicked grin. "And I want to touch you again." His hand crept toward her bare knees.

Gabby jerked her chemise down and started wiggling backward. "We will have to discuss this rationally," she said. "There are certain liberties that I will not allow. That—that are not allowed by the Church!"

To her shock, Quill burst into a snort of laughter. "You sound like a nun," he laughed. "Or a bishop!"

Gabby scooted off the opposite side of the bed, her brow lowering. "I don't think it's funny," she said, crossing her arms over her bosom. "Whatever making love is, I know it doesn't include anything as indecent as what you just did, touching me there."

Quill couldn't help it. He broke into a huge burst of laughter, letting the gathered tension and grief of the day roll out of him. "Oh, Lord, Gabby, you'll be the death of me!"

Gabby stalked furiously over to the door and pulled the bell cord. Hopefully Margaret hadn't gone out for a stroll, because she wished to be dressed immediately. Doing her best to ignore Quill, she walked over to the clothespress and opened the doors. She had nothing black. The darkest color she had was a puce walking costume. Fine. She would go for a walk.

Quill was still sprawled on her bed in an unseemly fashion. Gabby turned around, hands on her hips. "I should like you to leave my chamber now," she said sharply. She walked to the door. "Margaret will be coming to dress me." Lord, but he was a good-looking man, she thought unwillingly. He was all muscle and grace lying on her bed, propped up on one elbow.

"What if I told you that such touches were common practice?" he said winningly.

Gabby snorted in her turn. "No decent woman would allow that sort of thing," she said without a trace of hesitation in her voice. "If my father knew—" She broke off. That was an inconceivable thought. "You're a reprobate," she said. "And what is more, you, you *looked* at me!"

"You're beautiful," Quill said, his eyes dark green and narrowed. "I want to look at you again and again, Gabby. Morning and night."

She gasped. "Never! And it's no wonder you're giving yourself headaches, if this is the sort of thing you've been up to!"

Quill struggled with himself and managed to choke back his laughter. But Gabby saw the humor in his face and glowered.

Margaret scratched on the door and Gabby snatched it open. "Where have you been?" she demanded unfairly. "I can't sit around in my chemise all day long!"

Quill lazily got himself to his feet and strolled over to his wife, who still had her arms folded across her chest, presumably hiding the damp cloth from Margaret's eyes. He bent over and murmured in her ear. "You're going to love it, you know. You will *beg* me to continue."

"I would never do such a thing!" Gabby whispered back furiously.

"Care to make a wager?" said her husband.

"Gambling is the devil's pastime," she retorted. "I begin to think that you were raised with no morals!"

"I begin to think that you were raised with too many morals." Her husband sighed and dropped a kiss onto the tip of her ear.

Margaret was on the other side of the room, pulling undergarments from the press. With one swift glance over his shoulder, Quill gave his inclinations free rein. He held Gabby tightly against the front of his body. Then he ran a hand down her back and cupped her delicious bottom, pulling her even tighter, up and against him.

"Gabby," he said hoarsely, into her hair. "I am not only going to touch you all over, I'm going to kiss you in the same places."

Gabby was silenced.

After he left the room and Margaret was lacing her into a corset, the only positive inference Gabby could draw from the whole conversation was that her father would have nothing to say to Quill's sinfulness. She was absolutely certain such a wicked thought had never crossed his mind, nor that of any other man of God.

She walked numbly along the street, Margaret following behind. He wasn't going to heed her refusals. She knew that. Quill was silent, but she would never make the mistake of thinking he was pliable. No, Quill was planning to touch her all over and look at her . . . and kiss her. She felt an unwilling lick of fire.

Oh, God, she *was* the devil's child. Her father had been right all along. A chill breeze accounted for the high red in her cheeks. But nothing could justify the spreading warmth she felt in her belly, or the unsteadiness of her knees.

Still, she walked with her head high. After they returned to London, she would become one of the devil's children in truth. Because whatever her father had said, she always thought privately that the devil didn't care very much about talkativeness. But even she couldn't fool herself that behavior of this sort wasn't wicked.

And yet . . . And yet . . . somehow the prospect didn't alarm her as much as it should have. Gabby sighed. She was well-aware, and had been since age fifteen, that she had far less regard for God's commandments than she ought to. She had been brought up by Indian servants, who paid lip service to her father's beliefs, but were Hindu by inclination. And her father himself often forgot that he was chosen by God to be a missionary, particularly after starting a new exporting venture.

After a brisk forty-five-minute walk, Margaret was whimpering and Gabby had regained some calm. One thing her father had preached far more intently than he did religion was the fact that wives and daughters should be subservient to their masters.

And that meant, Gabby thought, ignoring the treacherous pulse of fire in her loins, that it was her duty to submit to whatever sinful practices Quill wished to impose on her.

She entered the inn feeling far too cheerful for such a somber occasion. After supper with the family in a private parlor, Quill escorted her to her chamber and then left. She could tell that Margaret was perplexed to find that she was sleeping alone. But Gabby didn't feel piqued by Quill's absence. He had bowed punctiliously at the door.

But then when he straightened up, he had leaned over and said just five words. They burned into Gabby's heart. His voice was hoarse and utterly belied his gentlemanly demeanor.

"I am burning, Gabby. *Perishing.*"

Chapter 15

CONTRARY TO HER OWN PREDICTION, Gabby did not lie awake that night wishing that her wedding night was less lonely. Instead, she puzzled over Quill's headaches. Clearly, something had to be done about them. She was not satisfied with the idea that doctors could do nothing. Surely there was some medicine they could try. It was most unfortunate that Quill had expressly told her not to consult Sudhakar.

Gabby chewed her lip. There are times when a person *should* be deceived, for his own good. Perhaps Sudhakar had no remedy for Quill's headaches. In that case, what Quill didn't know wouldn't hurt him. Finally she got out of bed and sat down at the delicate little writing table in the corner of her room. She was going to break a promise, but she was doing it for Quill's own good.

She penned a letter to Sudhakar, the *vaidya* of her father's village. She described Quill's problems as clearly as she could. It was up to Sudhakar to decide whether he would be able to help her husband. But the *vaidya* was of the highest Brahman caste. He was unlikely to deny a plea for help if he knew of a medicine that might cure Quill's headaches.

After a moment's thought, she also wrote a letter to her father. She informed him that she was married and that due to the unexpected death of his old friend, Thurlow Dewland, she was now Viscountess Dewland. Then, without detailing any of the circumstances, she pleaded with him to encourage the *vaidya* to help with her husband's ailments.

Finally she curled back into a small circle and went to sleep. She dreamt that she and Quill were dancing and he wasn't favoring his leg at all. But when she pointed it out, he smiled and said that was because they were in a field. And when Gabby looked around her, he was right. They were dancing in a grassy field next to a pond full of frogs. She woke up groggily to find it was sunrise and her maid was pulling back the curtains.

"Time to rise, my lady," Margaret said. "The coaches are waiting to take us to the estate in Kent." She paused, self-importantly. "They've dressed up the one coach all in black, even the roof."

At Gabby's inquiring look, she said, "That's the coach for the old viscount. Calling it a hearse, they are. Got to get to Kent, doesn't he?"

Gabby shivered, but Margaret chattered on about the black plumes that adorned the horses' heads and the fact that even the servants' coach had swags of black crepe covering the windows.

The gloomy procession reached Dewland's country seat around four the following afternoon. Very little had been said in the main coach. Gabby sat next to Quill, who held her hand, but didn't say one word during the entire journey. After around two hours, Gabby started wondering just how long Quill could remain silent at a stretch. He did answer questions when they stopped for the night at the

Queen's Cross Inn, and there was a dizzying moment when he drew her into an alcove and kissed her insensible. But he kissed her without speaking, and once back in the coach the next morning, he fell silent again.

Gabby chewed on her lip for the last hour of their journey, wondering how on earth a woman who talked too much and a man who didn't see the use of words were going to rub along together.

Kitty Dewland sat opposite her, looking utterly composed and making pleasant conversation. In Gabby's opinion, Kitty had not yet realized that her husband was dead. And Peter slept in the corner most of the afternoon. To Gabby's amazement, he reclined so stiffly that his velvet coat was not rumpled in the least when they climbed from the coach in the late afternoon.

By the time they reached the Dewland estate, the manor had already been put into mourning. The largest parlor was hung with black silk, and the servants wore black hatbands, armbands, and gloves.

During the weeks before the funeral, Gabby hardly saw Quill at all. He was out of the house most of the time, walking the estate with his father's manager. "He can't ride, you know," Kitty explained. "And walking takes a good deal more time. But one can't see the fields properly from a carriage." That was the first Gabby knew that Quill wasn't able to ride a horse.

Her husband sat next to her at meals, but their conversations were trivial and often fell away into silence. Quill's mother, Kitty, had developed a bewildering habit of switching back and forth from light fashionable conversation to hopeless sobbing. Gabby spent her time worrying about Kasi Rao's future and writing more and more letters to London and India.

On the day before the funeral itself, Gabby was sitting

alone in the breakfast room eating a scone and guiltily wishing that the ceremony were over. Sometimes it was hard not to compare the relentless swags of black cloth draping the walls of Dewland Manor to the vases of bright orchids adorning her home in India.

Just then someone walked into the breakfast room. Instantly Gabby's heart started to race. Every instinct told her that Quill had just sat down and that it was his black sleeve that lay close to hers. Finally she raised her eyes.

"Gabby."

She bowed her head in a polite greeting. "Good morning, my lord."

"Wife," he said quietly, bending closer.

Gabby swallowed. Should she reply in kind? No. "Husband" would sound idiotic on her lips. But Quill's "wife" sounded gloriously possessive.

His lips touched hers softly. "Are you sleeping well?" A trace of a wicked grin played around his mouth. Quill had decided that a light flirtation might dispel his driving lust for Gabby. It was dehumanizing, this lust. It reduced him to a tortured care-for-nobody who wanted to ravish his wife before breakfast and the devil with the consequences.

"No," Gabby replied, clear brown eyes fixed on his. "I can't sleep well at all. I miss you." Her voice trailed off. Then she whispered, "Husband."

Quill froze and barely stopped himself from lunging at Gabby and carrying her straight out of the room.

With a deep breath, he shakily reassembled his self-control and made another stab——not quite so successful—— at a flirtatious tone. "Damn it, Gabby, you're supposed to make pleasant conversation, not drive me into a frenzy of lust. Just look at the condition I'm in now." He cast a disgusted look into his lap.

Gabby looked at his pantaloons, but she didn't see anything unusual.

Her husband broke into laughter and she scowled at him. "I don't see anything funny about it," she said with dignity.

With a sudden movement Quill bent his head and took his viscountess's mouth, kissing her with a languorous thoroughness that sent scorching spikes of heat through his body.

When he pulled back, Gabby's eyes were dazed and had gone a dusky brandy color. Quill caught up her hand and kissed her palm. She shivered instinctively. He took that hand and deliberately placed it on his groin.

Gabby jumped and tried to pull her hand away.

"Remember what I said I would do to you?" Quill said, his voice a hoarse promise.

Gabby nodded.

"Will you do the same to me?"

Gabby's eyes grew round with surprise. At least Quill hoped it was surprise, rather than horror. He lifted his hand, and to his eternal delight, Gabby didn't pull away from him. In fact, she didn't move at all. It was a new kind of torture.

Finally he had to remove her warm hand himself and sweep her into another kiss, or who knew where they would end up. Probably making love on a bed of crumbled scones.

That kiss, not to mention Gabby's touch, did nothing for Quill's condition, as he'd described it to her. In fact, when Lady Sylvia walked into the room accompanied by two whining Graces (Beauty was temporarily living in the servants' quarters, as the move had proved too disturbing for her fragile bladder), Quill had to sit in his place and eat approximately five scones more than he cared for, because he was unable to walk from the room.

The viscount was laid to rest the following morning in the chancel of St. Margaret's. Gabby had met many members of the London *ton* at Lady Fester's ball; she met members of the county nobility over funeral baked meats. What was most surprising was how exhausting it all was.

Gabby curtsied, and curtsied, and curtsied again. She accepted congratulations on her marriage. She encountered delicately raised eyebrows when it was revealed that she was not, in fact, married to her fiancé but to his brother, the new viscount.

And she overheard a conversation that made it clear that a certain Lady Skiffing, for one, believed that Gabby had discarded Peter when she realized that Quill would shortly be a viscount. It was hardly a comfort that Gabby detected a note of admiration in Lady Skiffing's voice.

It wasn't until late morning that the last callers were ushered from the black-hung parlor, whispering their final condolences as they left. Only the family lawyer, Mr. Jennings of Jennings and Condell, remained.

The dowager viscountess was drooping on a settee, her face strained and white. Lady Sylvia sat across from her, the very picture of elegant mourning attire. Gabby clutched her hands together tightly, trying not to steal glances at Quill.

The butler bowed himself out of the room after informing them that a light luncheon would be served in twenty minutes.

Kitty shuddered. "I shall be in my chambers," she said faintly.

"Mama, it would be best if you ate something," Peter said.

"I couldn't, I just couldn't."

"Kitty," Lady Sylvia broke in, "it is time to discuss the future."

"I shall read Viscount Dewland's will after luncheon," Mr. Jennings stated, looking alarmed.

"Yes, yes," Lady Sylvia said, waving her hand dismissively. "I don't mean you, Jennings. I'm sure there's nothing interesting in Thurlow's will. What I mean is, Kitty, what would you like to do now?"

"Do?" The question seemed hardly to register on Kitty Dewland. "I shall . . . I shall retire to my chambers," she replied. "And then we will return to London."

"When Lionel died, I sat in the house and cried until I thought I was turning into a fountain," Lady Sylvia stated, her tone brisk. "It was a wretched time. Mind, some crying is good for you. Has to be done. But sitting around in the house where you lived with your husband is not the place to do it."

Tears welled in Kitty's eyes. "Oh, I couldn't—"

"Yes, you could," Lady Sylvia snapped. "You're prone to melancholy at the best of times, Kitty. And I'm not going to sit around while you turn yourself into a watering pot. We're leaving the country. You can cry yourself blue in the face just as easily in Switzerland as in London."

Kitty sobbed. "How can you even suggest that I leave the house where dear Thurlow was so happy? You've never been so unfeeling, Sylvia!"

"I've got feelings, all right," Lady Sylvia retorted. "I don't want you to malinger. You're going to cast a pall on the house, Kitty. Think of that. We're widows. We don't belong with a newly married couple. You think that Gabrielle and Erskine are going to feel cheerful with his mama bursting into tears at every meal?"

Gabby shot Lady Sylvia an indignant look. "Quill and I would never wish you to leave your home because of us, Lady Dewland. We aren't intending to be cheerful anyway," she added, rather confusedly.

Lady Sylvia snorted. "Whether you're planning on cheer or not, gel, you're not going to have it if Kitty is sitting around weeping all the time."

Kitty wiped her eyes with the handkerchief Quill silently handed her. "You're right, Sylvia," she said finally. "The last thing I wish to be is a burden to dearest Gabrielle and Quill."

"You wouldn't be a burden!" Gabby cried. "I would feel terrible to think that you left the house because of us. We should be the ones to move."

Kitty gave a watery little laugh. "What a comfort you would have been to your mother, Gabrielle. You shan't move, because this house belongs to Quill now. I suspect I own the dowager house?" She looked inquiringly at Mr. Jennings, who pursed his lips to indicate that the information was privileged, and then nodded. "I shall retire to the dowager house so I won't be in anyone's way."

"For goodness sake, Kitty, you're giving me palpitations from pure irritation, and it takes quite a provocation," Lady Sylvia snapped. "Thurlow wouldn't want you to retire to the country like some kind of bird-wit! If you still wish to turn into a hermit once we return from the Continent, you may. But meanwhile, I've a hankering to see Paris again before I die, and you're coming with me. And if we can't go to France because of the antics of that blown-up little puppet, Napoleon, we'll travel about the Continent for a few months until the French toss him out the door." Any rebellious Frenchman could have gained backbone from Lady Sylvia.

"Oh, I couldn't," Kitty faltered.

Quill leaned down and patted his mother's hand. "I think you should go, Mother. I believe that a change of scenery will be good for you."

"I suppose it doesn't matter where I am," Kitty replied, slipping back into the dazed state she had maintained before the funeral.

"There you are," Lady Sylvia said, nodding at Quill. "I've got to get her on the move, that's what. Otherwise she's like to simply fade away. Not the sort of thing I would do, mind. But Kitty's a delicate sort. Always has been, even when we were mere girls."

"May I accompany you, Mother?" Peter sat down next to his mother and stroked her hand.

Tears were falling silently onto her black gloves. Her eldest son drew another handkerchief from his pocket and handed it to her. Kitty struggled to speak.

"I think it would be best if Peter traveled with you," Quill observed.

That seemed to settle the matter.

"We shall sail on the *White Star*," Lady Sylvia announced. "The vessel is going to Naples, and Lady Fane told me Naples was thronged with Englishmen last year.

"Supposed to be a pretty city too," she added as something of an afterthought. "I asked Jennings to look into it."

Mr. Jennings cleared his throat. "I took the liberty of booking passage for Lady Breaknettle, Lady Dewland, and their attendants, of course." He bowed toward Peter. "I shall obtain a berth for yourself and your valet directly, Mr. Dewland. The *White Star* sails from Southampton in three days."

"Three days," Kitty moaned. "Oh, I can't do it! I can't do it." Gabby was fascinated to see that she instinctively turned toward her elder son.

"Nothing for you to do," Lady Sylvia commented. "I told Stimple to start packing up your things this morning. She's probably well near finished with your trunks by now. It's not as if there's much to bring. We can always buy blacks over there, you know. No one does clothing better than the French."

Kitty didn't answer, but just leaned against her youngest son's shoulder and burst into hopeless tears. Quill silently handed her yet another handkerchief.

PROMPTLY AFTER LUNCHEON the family moved to the library. Mr. Jennings cleared his throat importantly and began to read.

The will began with a pious declaration: *"In the name of God, amen. I, Thurlow Dewland, in perfect health and memory, God be praised . . ."* Gabby's mind wandered as Mr. Jennings droned on and on with a list of lesser bequests to the household servants in London and to those who resided on the Kent estate. The viscount left money for the poor in the Dewland parish, and fifty pounds toward the new roof needed by St. Margaret's, their parish church.

Kitty sniffed and said that Thurlow always thought of those less fortunate than himself.

Mr. Jennings recommenced with a long list of debts to be discharged from the estate. Then he looked up, briefly, and noted that the following codicil had been added the previous January: Viscount Dewland strictly instructed that no debt should be settled if presented by a Mr. Firwald, as he had sworn never to pay for the worthless merchandise provided by the said Firwald.

Quill frowned. "Pay it."

Jennings nodded briskly and made a note to himself.

"Why are you going against Father's directive?" Peter asked, sitting up in his chair.

Quill didn't stir but just looked at his brother with heavy-lidded eyes. "Firwald sold Father the crystal vase that he bought for Mother last Christmas."

"Oh." Peter leaned back into his chair. "I see."

"Thurlow's wishes should be respected," Kitty interjected.

"Mother, the vase was broken when Father was in a state of choler," Peter said delicately.

"He always said there was a crack in it," Kitty replied feebly.

"Father had a constitutional dislike for paying his debts," Quill remarked.

That seemed to close the subject, and after clearing his throat, Mr. Jennings continued with a list of bequests. A second cousin living in Buckfordshire received a carved ivory tusk, as well as a French bedstead with canopy, on account of the cousin's admiration for the said piece and the viscountess's disdain for the same.

"To my wife's cousin, Lady Sylvia, I leave the silver-gilt bowl made in Italy, now found in the Yellow Drawing Room. She can either use it for herself or share it with those animals she erroneously calls the Graces."

"Fustian!" Lady Sylvia said, looking pleased all the same.

"To my beloved wife, Katherine, I hereby double the income she would have received from her original marriage settlement, in consideration of the fact that I should wish her to live as one that were and had been my wife."

Kitty broke into sobs again, and Mr. Jennings paused before detailing the dowager house with appurtenances situated near the main Dewland manor in Kent.

"To my youngest son, Peter John Dewland, I hereby leave a tenement with the appurtenances situated in the Blackfriars, London; a messuage in Henley Street in the borough of Kingston, with barns, stables, orchards, gardens attached; and a one-fourth life interest in the income of my estate in Kent, as well as residence in the family domicile."

"Very generous," Lady Sylvia interjected at this point. "Very generous indeed."

"To my eldest son and heir, Erskine Matthew Claudius Dewland, I leave all my remaining worldly goods, to include the great house in London, Dewland Manor in Kent, and all the rest

of my goods, chattels, leases, plate, jewels, and household stuff whatsoever."

Mr. Jennings paused. "I believe that the deceased would have eliminated the following codicil, given recent events," he noted, in a particularly colorless voice.

"Under those circumstances well-known amongst my family, it is unlikely that my first son shall have a lawful male heir. Therefore, I earnestly enjoin my youngest son, Peter John, to marry with all expediency, reminding him that the lineage of the Dewlands is a long and noble one. I also request that his brother, Erskine Matthew Claudius, single out his brother for his affectionate respect, in light of the fact that Peter John will be viscount after him. As my children are aware, I have long held the fixed belief that a gentleman should not work for his living, although I have compromised my principles in the case of Erskine Matthew Claudius. In the event that his brother's income is not sufficient to support Peter John in the manner of a viscount's heir, I enjoin upon Erskine Matthew Claudius to share the profits of the said business endeavors with his brother and heir."

A moment of silence followed the reading of the will. Mr. Jennings busied himself with arranging sheaves of parchment into a neat stack.

"Father was always remarkably good at spending other people's money," Peter finally said, a note of wry apology in his voice. "He had no right to give me the Henley Street residence. Didn't you pay for that, Quill?"

Quill shrugged. "I have no need of it."

"I daresay Jennings is right and Thurlow would have crossed out that codicil had he lived," Lady Sylvia commented. "I don't like the fact that he put in that comment about you working for a living, Erskine. Smacks of hypocrisy. Everyone knows that money flowed through Thurlow's hands *and* that he was liable to find himself on queer street until you became so flush."

"He did not consult me," Kitty said, "or I would have told him that darling Erskine has always shared what he has with his brother. Even when they were little boys." She sniffed disconsolately.

"I apologize for him," Peter said with some dignity. "Father should not have slighted your endeavors, Quill. And he need not have instructed you to aid me."

At that, Quill smiled wryly. "I'm not taking it to heart. Besides, Father was right in his own way. I have a vulgar habit of making money, and I refused to reform when he asked me to. That is what really bothered him. Why shouldn't I give it to you? I don't need it."

"Thurlow gave Peter a very generous settlement," Lady Sylvia snapped. "He can live nicely on the rents of the Henley Street properties alone, regardless of his life interest in the Kent estate. You'll be handing that money to your own children, Erskine."

Quill visibly started and flashed a look at his wife. Gabby smiled at him. She hadn't said a word during the entire proceeding, so it was no wonder he forgot her existence. Let alone that of their unborn children.

"Well, we got through that pretty well," Lady Sylvia was saying, gathering up her flimsy reticule and a fluttering black handkerchief, clearly designed for show rather than for use. "Thank goodness Thurlow didn't indulge himself in too much advice. Why, I heard that the Marquess of Granby went so far as to write in his will that his nephew's escapades with his mistress were ludicrous and that's why Granby was leaving the nephew only three thousand pounds per annum. And this was read aloud in front of the nephew's wife, mind you."

Quill didn't move from where he stood. Gabby had risen and was helping his mother to do the same.

He stared at the burnished gleam of his wife's hair. His

mind was chaotic with images of Gabby holding a small child. He, Quill, had been alarmingly stupid. He had paid no mind to the future. After his accident, he had mentally excised the possibility of a wife and children. What woman would marry him, given his injuries? And yet . . . he had enticed one to do so.

Because she had no idea of your injuries, said a small, sharp voice in his mind.

Yet Gabby showed no particular concern once she knew. She didn't blink an eye. She didn't appear offended, and she didn't threaten to annul the marriage.

Moreover, she was still peeking at him. Quill had taken to cataloging every time Gabby looked at him secretly from under her eyelashes. He reckoned those glances indicated that she was smoothly transferring her affections from Peter to him. He didn't inquire why the transference was so important to him.

As he stood frozen in the library, his mind kept offering him an image of Gabby, holding a small scrap of baby in her arms and smiling at the babe the way she smiled at him—as if nothing he could do would ever shake her faith in him. The very idea gave him a strange sensation in his chest, an exultant flush of feeling, an unfamiliar, prideful joy.

Jennings cast one look at the new viscount and decided to approach him at a later date about a few of the more complex issues to do with settling his father's estate. The man looked perturbed. Likely he took that little codicil of his father's the wrong way. Not, Jennings thought to himself, that there was a right way to take it. Practically stated outright that the viscount was incapable.

The party separated at the stairs and retired to their various rooms until dinner. Gabby walked slowly toward the magnificent bedchamber designated for the viscount-ess. Kitty had gracefully relinquished it when they arrived at the manor, and when Gabby had protested, she pointed out that she had no reason to wish for a connecting door with her son. Gabby had blushed and ignored the door as best she could.

Now Gabby walked into the chamber, an airy room hung in sea-green silk, and stared at that same connecting entryway. It was just a door. But on the other side was Quill's bedchamber. How did he feel, sleeping in his fa-ther's bed? How did he feel, knowing that she was just on the other side of the wall? The door was a solid, imposing one made of mahogany. Gabby chewed her lip.

The funeral was over. The viscount was buried. But if they made love tonight and Quill succumbed to a three-day headache, how would he see his mother off to Southampton? And she had the strong sense that he wished to return to London immediately. Presumably he couldn't travel while in the grip of illness.

For the first time Gabby began to grasp the parameters of Quill's medical problems. Exactly when would Quill de-cide that he could afford to relinquish three days in a row? From what she had seen in London before their marriage, he worked every day. And he liked working. Would he ever be willing to give up three days?

She looked up when the solid mahogany door opened and Quill strolled in.

"Hello, wife," he said.

Gabby blushed. She hadn't seen him in private since the afternoon in Bath, after they were married. Does one curtsy to one's husband even in the privacy of the bedchamber?

Quill's eyes were shining with a wicked appreciation that made all of Gabby's worries fly out of her head.

He walked toward her like a tiger stalking a goat. And Gabby danced backward, just as a goat might dance on its nimble hooves in the spray of the Indian Ocean.

"The bell will ring for dinner in a few minutes," she said nervously.

Quill was grinning at her. "So it will," he replied. His voice was deep and sent tendrils of heat down Gabby's spine. "Perhaps we should have a small meal here, in your room," then he corrected himself, with a glance at the adjoining door, "or perhaps in *our* bedchamber?"

Gabby's mouth felt dry. "Quill," she said, before she lost all capacity for speech, "we need to have a rational discussion."

"Do you know, you request rational conversation quite regularly?" Quill was laughing at her.

"My father believes that women are unable to be rational," Gabby explained. "I'm afraid that I adopted the phrase out of desperation." And then she added, "My father's conversation is often incoherent."

Quill ambled toward her again. "You must tell me all about your father someday," he said, his voice as smooth and liquid as silk. "He sounds like a fool."

"He isn't," Gabby protested, nervously retreating a step. "Quill, I meant it when I said we need to speak! *Before* we . . . do anything further."

A chill touched Quill's spine, but he courteously stood still. "Have you decided that you would prefer to annul the marriage?" he asked, quite as he would ask for a cup of tea.

Gabby frowned. "Rational conversation, Quill," she said pointedly. She turned her back and walked toward the fireplace, sitting down in an upholstered rocking chair.

Quill sat down opposite her and steepled his fingers. "All right, Gabby, what have we to discuss?" He was well-aware that he had limped throughout the funeral. His leg was dog-tired from days of walking the estate. During the reception, he'd heard more than one muttered speculation about the extent of his injuries. Likely Gabby hadn't realized just what a useless cripple he was until today.

"I am worried about consummation," she said, stumbling over pronunciation of the last word.

"Are you concerned about my fitness to do the task?"

"No! That is . . ."

Quill got up and walked to the window and stood with his back to Gabby. It was evening, and fingers of yellow light fell from the house windows. Quill noted without thinking that the rosebushes had not been properly pruned. "It would be understandable if you wished to annul the marriage, Gabby, now that you've had time to consider the consequences."

To Gabby, his voice sounded indifferent.

"To be honest, I am not concerned about whether or not I produce an heir," her husband continued. "No one will blink an eye if you annul the marriage. I could instruct Jennings to start the proceedings immediately."

When there was no reply, he turned around, reluctantly.

Gabby was glowering at him.

"Well?" He kept his tone flat and polite. "This needn't be an unpleasant conversation, Gabby. We are friends, as you have said in the past."

"In that case, I would request that you return to your chair and do not stalk around the room in that melodramatic fashion." Gabby stuck her chin in the air. "We are going to have a rational conversation, Erskine Matthew Claudius!"

Quill smiled without humor. "If you were listening to the will that closely, you must have noted that my father believed my injuries would prevent the conception of children." But he walked over and sat down. His heart felt like a cold lump in his chest.

"When I said we needed a rational discussion, I simply meant that . . . before we . . ."

Quill waited politely. He wasn't going to make it any easier for her, clearly.

"Oh, I can't *say* these things aloud," Gabby cried in frustration.

Before Quill could move, she jumped up and sat down on his lap, wrapping one of her arms around his neck.

She felt the surprise throughout his body, but then he relaxed against the back of the chair. Gabby leaned against his shoulder. From here she couldn't see his face, and it was considerably easier to speak.

"First, I should like you to stop making corkbrained suggestions regarding annulment," she said. "While I may well wish to murder you at some date in the future given your tendency to jump to absurd conclusions, I have been anticipating this——" She broke off and added, crossly, "You're not stupid, Quill, so don't talk drivel."

"Second, I should like to point out that if we consummate our marriage tonight, there is a good possibility that you will not be able to accompany your mother to Southampton. Third——" She couldn't remember exactly what her third point had been. He smelled wonderful, her husband. He had an indefinable masculine scent overlaid by soap and clean-pressed linen. "Third," she said hastily, "I think that if our marriage is to be a success, we need to come to an understanding."

"An understanding," Quill echoed. He felt as if she had dealt him three or four sharp blows to the stomach. "Gabby, do you *always* say precisely what you are thinking?"

"No," Gabby replied meditatively. "In fact, although I

admit this only because you are my husband, I have quite a reputation for telling fibs back home."

"You can lie to whomever you want as long as you don't lie to me," Quill said, tightening his arms around her rather fiercely. "And this *is* home."

"Mmmm," his wife replied, rubbing her head against his shoulder like a lazy cat. "Not yet, it isn't."

"What would make it home?"

She lifted her head and looked up at him.

A delirious shot of heat went down his backbone at the look in her eyes. Quill sighed. "All right," he said, shifting her weight slightly to avoid a potential injury. "What sort of an understanding do we need? I warn you, Gabby. If you make me wait even one more day, there's no telling what the consequences might be."

"All I am suggesting is that we proceed with caution," Gabby said. She started ticking off her fingers. "We know that kissing doesn't give you a headache."

"True," Quill muttered, suiting action to word by kissing the top of her head.

"And we know that caressing my chest doesn't give you a headache. Well, what does?" She looked at him expectantly. "Because if we knew precisely what the action was, we could simply avoid it."

Quill was nonplussed. "Gabby," he said slowly, "how much do you understand about conjugal intercourse?"

"Almost nothing," Gabby said promptly. Then she blushed. "I know that you are going to look at me. Will that give you a headache?"

"Never." Quill had been seized by an odd trembling sensation, almost as if a joyous laugh was trapped in his bones and couldn't get out.

Gabby was looking at him with narrowed eyes. "What did you expect? As I've already explained, my mother died when I was born. And the servants in my father's house were most punctilious in their conversation. My father is particularly fierce about female concupiscence."

"Female concupiscence. Why not the male version, or plain old English lust?"

"Women are the devil's handiwork," Gabby remarked. "They exist primarily to drive men into sin."

Quill looked at her sharply and was relieved to see a slight smile on her face. "You're a good exemplar," he said, his hands irresistibly slipping under her arms to the front of her gown. "You can drive me into sin any day, Gabby."

"I thought so," she said happily. "My father always said that I had my mother's sinful body and, although I never told him, naturally I thought it might be a useful inheritance."

Quill broke into laughter as he began nimbly undoing the small pearl buttons at the back of her gown. Gabby tried to pull away. She clearly wasn't done with rational conversation.

"Gabby," Quill said, appalled to hear how hoarse his voice had become. "There are certain times when conversation, rational or incoherent, is not helpful." He picked her up and carried her over to a bed hung in watered silk.

"This is one of those times."

Chapter 16

EMILY EWING WAS DISMAYED to discover just how much she missed Lucien Boch's conversation. It had been over three weeks since Lady Fester's ball, during which time Mr. Boch had called four times. She had refused to see him each time, steeling her heart with the thought that she could not raise Phoebe in a house of shame. And she had completed her account of the Fester ball with no mention of an amber-colored gown fashioned of Italian gauze, or of a former marquis, for that matter.

Unfortunately, Bartholomew Hislop had taken the news that she had accompanied Mr. Boch to a ball as a sign that he should be graced with the same attention. It was hard to contemplate, she thought numbly. This morning Hislop was tricked out in primrose trousers that were so tight as to cause him obvious discomfort. Even if she hadn't ever met Lucien, even if she had no one with whom to compare Hislop, she wouldn't have wished to be seen in public with him. At any rate, it was too late, too late, too late. The words rang dully in her head. She *had* met the elegant Mr. Boch, she had met him and she had—almost—succumbed to his practiced seductions. Yet virtue was a cold comfort, faced as she was with the bumptious and lusty Mr. Hislop.

"I wish you to accompany me to the balloon ascension tomorrow afternoon," Mr. Hislop was saying, with more than a hint of petulance leaking into his tone.

"I am afraid that I must decline," Emily replied. "I write in the afternoons, and I cannot take excursions of this sort." Too late, she realized that she had played directly into his hand.

"Fine!" he chortled. "In that case, we shall spend the evening at the theater. An intimate evening will cheer you up."

When she opened her mouth to refuse, Hislop's flabby lower lip puffed out. "Or I won't be helping you any further, Mrs. Ewing." He placed one stubby finger on the stack of foolscap balanced on the table. "It took me time, it did, to gather all this information. *Quid pro quo*, as they say in the legal profession."

Emily swallowed and opened her mouth to answer, but Hislop held up his hand. "I will give you time to consider," and he leered at her again, eyes lingering on her chest. "I will leave you with this thought: You need me, Mrs. Ewing. For example, no one but the most fashionable will be invited to the Countess of Strathmore's ball. You need me and"—he giggled naughtily—"I need you."

Emily pressed her hand hard to her roiling stomach as the door closed behind Mr. Hislop. Finally she lowered herself into a chair and concentrated, hard, on not crying. She didn't even jump when the door to her study burst open and Phoebe came running in.

"Mama, Mama! Sally and I went to visit Kasi Rao, and Mrs. Malabright was packing everything!"

"Packing?" Emily tried to shape her face into lines of sympathy.

"They are leaving. Mrs. Malabright said that you must tell Miss Gabby, because she doesn't dare write a letter. She said that men want to take Kasi back to India."

"What?"

Phoebe nodded, her blue eyes round with fear. "They would make him go out in public, Mama. Around *strangers*. Kasi cannot talk to strangers!"

Emily took a deep breath. "Goodness, how surprising. Where is Mrs. Malabright taking Kasi Rao?"

"To her brother's wife, who lives in Devon," Phoebe said. "She told only me, Mama, and you are to tell Miss Gabby just as soon as she returns to London."

"Mrs. Malabright was right to put her trust in you, darling," Emily said, closing her arms around Phoebe's round little body.

She would do anything—*anything*—to save Phoebe from the scorn of polite society. And if that meant that she had to say farewell to the seductive Lucien, so be it. And good-bye to the informative Hislop as well.

Phoebe looked up at her anxiously. "No one could take me away from you, could they, Mama?"

"Never!" Emily said fiercely. "You are my very own little girl." She swallowed more tears. "Time to wash before supper! Quick as a bunny, Phoebe."

GABBY'S HEART WAS POUNDING so hard that she could hear it in her ears. She wasn't ready. It wasn't nighttime. She didn't wish to disrobe in an open room, with candles burning. But it was her duty, she told herself. Her father had made it quite clear that her husband's wishes were to be her law.

"You said we would wait until we returned to London."

"No," Quill replied. "Can't do it."

There was a pause as he made his way down the long row of pearl buttons.

"The bell is going to ring for dinner. Your mother will think it quite odd if we don't join her."

"She's eating in her room."

"Well, then, Lady Sylvia will be affronted. You are her host."

"Nonsense," Quill said. "She's more likely to applaud. She expects me to produce an heir, in case you didn't notice this afternoon."

Quill eased Gabby's dress forward and stood her up. A pool of black fabric fell to the floor. He twirled her about and started unlacing her corset.

Gabby stared numbly at the embroidered coverlet. "I believe this is a mistake. How are you going to travel to Southampton?"

"Since Peter will be accompanying Mother and Lady Sylvia to the Continent, there is no particular need for me to travel with them."

"What about your headache?"

There was no answer. Her corset fell forward and joined her gown on the floor. Under it Gabby wore only a light chemise.

Quill turned her around slowly. The chemise was laced to the waist and then fell in pleats to the floor. He let his hands glide from her shoulders, past her short sleeves, and down her bare arms.

His eyes were a decadent shade of green. Even with Gabby's inexperience, she could read desire in them. "I wish you wouldn't look at me like that," she whispered.

"I can't help it. You're mine now, and you're beautiful." His hands moved to her waist.

"I would rather not do this at the moment," Gabby said clearly. "I don't feel it is a proper time or place."

"Mmmm," Quill replied. He was rubbing his thumbs over her nipples in a manner that made Gabby feel hot and terrified at once.

"Quill, are you listening to me?" Gabby tried to ignore the sensations in her body, especially those below her waist.

Without answering, Quill maneuvered her to the bed and pushed her backward. Then his knee nudged her legs open—and the knee touched her.

"Quill!"

"I'm listening," he said lazily. He bent and licked her nipple just as he had before, in Bath, right through her chemise.

Gabby took a deep breath, trying to control a rising sense of panic. What was there to be so afraid of? *Pain,* for one thing. The thought gave her resolution and she pushed at his shoulders, trying to get him away from her breast. He had to stop doing that; he was making it hard to think rationally.

Then, without warning, Quill abandoned one breast and moved to the other, sucking it into his mouth. A large hand started roughly caressing the wet nipple. To Gabby's shame, a guttural sound burst from her throat.

The shock gave her a burst of strength. "No!" She squirmed sideways so quickly that Quill let go of her in surprise, and she lurched forward off the bed.

"I do not approve of this," Gabby said, trying hard to ignore the throbbing sense in her lower body. "We haven't discussed it—"

"Rationally," Quill chimed in. He was grinning like a devil, lying on the bed looking wicked, and delicious, and male. . . . Gabby almost sobbed with a combination of bewilderment and longing.

"It is illogical to continue. You won't be able to travel for days. What about your work in London?"

Quill stood up and unbuttoned his waistcoat. He tossed it to the floor next to her gown.

"I don't want to!" she said desperately, watching with fascination as Quill drew his linen shirt over his head. His body was lean and muscled, as different from her own as could be imagined. Heat pulsed in her veins.

He was still grinning, an audaciously wicked smirk.

"It's not dark. We should be under the covers, in the dark. You shouldn't bare yourself like this—where is your night-shirt?" Her voice rose. "And you're looking at me again!"

"You're looking at me too," Quill said mildly. He was pulling off his boots now.

Gabby's vision blurred with tears. She winked them away and crossed her arms rigidly over her breasts.

"Why so coy, love?"

A sob escaped from Gabby's throat. "I don't want—*this*," she cried.

"Why not?" To her relief, the seductive tone was gone from Quill's voice.

But how could she answer him? She stumbled into speech. "What we're doing is shameful. It should be done in the dark, under the covers. You can touch me if you wish, because you are my husband and I can't say nay, but you can't look at me like that. You can't make me do naked things—in the light!"

Quill sighed. Then he backed up and sat on the edge of the bed. "Come here, sweetheart." He held out his arms.

Gabby took one look at his chest and shook her head. "I'm almost certain that your headaches are caused by mis-conduct. Your behavior is not Christian." Her voice was strained and earnest.

"Christian?" He bent forward and grabbed one of Gabby's wrists, pulling her slowly toward him. She perched reluc-tantly on his knees, back straight so that she didn't touch his naked chest. It was mortifying, the way her fingers yearned to caress him.

"We're behaving like heathens," she whispered miserably, adding the "we" for his benefit. Frankly, *he* was the heathen. "Back home, in India . . . my father—" She stopped.

"What would he say?"

"A couple was seen making love by the river." Gabby's voice was quite sunk with mortification. "He pointed them out in church and made them stand up and said that God would strike them down."

"And did God strike them down?" Even Gabby couldn't miss the potent anger in Quill's voice.

She shivered. "No. But they had to leave the village."

"Your father is—" He broke off. He wrapped his arms around her and rested his chin on her soft hair. "Do you like your father, Gabby?"

"One doesn't have to *like* a father. One only has to obey him."

"And did you always obey him?" Quill asked, making an educated guess.

There was silence. "No," Gabby admitted. "I was a thorn in his side." She was clearly quoting.

"Why didn't you obey?"

Gabby didn't seem to notice that she had relaxed her spine and was leaning against Quill's chest. Quill was aware of every soft breath she took. Carefully, he drew on self-control learned from years of pain. "Why not, Gabby?" he repeated.

"Father is sometimes too strict," she said, so softly he could hardly hear her voice. "He can be cruel."

Quill's calm tone applauded. "It sounds that way to me. How is he cruel?"

"We live in a small village," she explained. "Father arrived as a missionary. He built a house and a church."

"And?"

"That couple," Gabby said. "He said they couldn't live in the village anymore, or Sarita might contaminate the other women. He made Sarita and her husband do penance all night, and then they had to leave the village with nothing. I don't know where they went." Her voice trailed off miserably. "It wasn't right. Sarita was a friend of mine, and she wasn't a . . . whore. He called her a whore."

"How did you disobey, then?"

"I sent a servant to gather Sarita's things—to throw them away, Father thought. But actually I sent all their belongings to her family."

"Did your father find out?"

"It happened just before I left for Calcutta to travel to England."

"I'm surprised he allowed you to be friends with village women," Quill remarked.

"Oh, he didn't. And I wasn't really a friend of Sarita's. I was allowed two servants, and they told me about the village every day. I felt as if I were friends with some women, because I heard about them my whole life. Sarita was my age, and she would smile when she saw me."

"Didn't you have any friends at all? What about the woman you told me about, the one who couldn't eat papaya?" Quill was quite proud of how steady he had kept his voice.

"Her name was Leela. And, no . . . I didn't have friends to speak to, not after Johore died."

Quill searched his mind. "Who?"

"Remember? I told you that I had a friend who died of a fever. Johore was Sudhakar's son, and since Sudhakar was from the highest Brahman class, my father let me play with him as a child. After Johore died, there was no one appropriate left in the village to play with. But my nurse would tell me what the children were doing, and I felt as if Sarita and Leela were my friends, even though we couldn't speak to one another. I wasn't lonely. I had Kasi Rao to take care of."

Quill's lust had been replaced by a healthy dose of rage. "Let me understand this correctly," he said slowly. "Your father allowed you no companions except his feeble-minded nephew. He exiled people from the village on the slightest whim, not allowing them to take their possessions with them."

"Yes," she agreed.

"I'm sorry, Gabby, but men like your father are the reason I sold my East India stock. There are too many Englishmen over in India living like little kings, answerable to no one. Bastards, all of them."

He cupped his wife's chin with his hand. "Gabby?"

Tears were glinting in her beautiful eyes. Quill kissed them shut. "We need to speak—*rationally*." There was only a hint of a smile in his voice. "Your father sounds like a small-minded scoundrel.

"Open your eyes, Gabby. I would make love to you on the banks of the Ganges River," he said, his voice a ragged whisper. "I would make love to you on the banks of the Humber River, out in the back gardens, for that matter. In fact, I probably will before our lives are over. I would do it in broad daylight, with an audience of Codswallop and the rest of the staff, if I had to."

Gabby opened her mouth and he touched it with a finger. "All right, I would rather not have Codswallop in my near vicinity. He's a dreary-looking sort and not conducive to lovemaking. But my point, Gabby, is that God would only celebrate us for making love—no matter where we were, in light or darkness, under the sheets, or on a muddy riverbank. Your father's idea of sin was narrow-minded and loutish."

Gabby smiled crookedly. "You sound like Sudhakar."

"The Brahman?"

She nodded. "He played chess with my father every Thursday night. And we used to converse if my father was late, which he often was."

"He spoke frankly," Quill said, rather stunned.

"Sudhakar is a Brahman. To him, Father is of a lower caste . . . a lower race. But he liked me." She bit her lip.

Quill let his hand run cautiously down his wife's back. "Gabby, will you make love to me now? We are not on the banks of a river. The viscountess's bedchamber has witnessed the conception of many Dewlands, and there is no place on earth more appropriate to consummate this marriage." He kissed her ear in a delicate caress that sent heat to the back of her knees.

Gabby cleared her throat. "I should like to know what you are going to do to me."

Quill chuckled and bent to kiss her again, but she pushed him away and stood up. "I'm not funning! I want to know about the pain."

"Have you been worrying?"

"Of course I have," she said crossly. "And I have to admit, I'm not sure it's worth the bother, given that I am going to be in pain and you are going to suffer a three-day headache as a result!"

"I'll ask you tomorrow whether it was worth it, shall I?"

"If you are correct, you'll be lying in a dark room tomorrow," she snapped.

"Hmmm," Quill said. He didn't want to think about that. "You know, Gabby, you're absolutely right. Let's proceed rationally."

She noticed that his wicked grin was firmly back in place. He stood up as well, and his hands went to his waist. She stilled, and her heart started pounding in her throat again.

Quill took off his pantaloons and started unbuttoning his smalls.

He pushed the white linen down his hips casually, as if he were alone. But in fact his hands were shaking and his negligent attitude was deceptive. Gabby hadn't looked at him yet. He waited, watching as her eyes slid down his body.

He heard her gasp.

He turned away and walked over to the fireplace. He lit two more candles that were standing on the mantelpiece and carried them over to the bed. Twilight was drawing in and the room was growing shadowy.

Gabby's eyes raced down the tight line of his buttocks as Quill crouched to light the fire already laid in the hearth.

"Quill," she said, despising the weakness of her own voice.

"Yes?" He stood up and turned around, and oh, he *was* just as magnificent as she had thought.

Quill walked over and said, "Time to remove your chemise, darling."

Gabby gulped and unwrapped her arms, which were tightly crossed on her chest again. Quill undid the ties at her waist, and strong masculine hands pulled up the soft pleats of her chemise. There was a moment of airy blindness and then Gabby found herself standing naked before her husband.

He didn't touch her. For a second he couldn't breathe. A dark flame surged through his body at the sight of his wife. She was so beautiful, her skin like milky cream, smooth expanses blooming into full breasts. It was torture not to touch her, not to brush her shining strands of hair behind her shoulders, not to run his hands over her generous curves.

In the fireplace, a log caught in a crackle of sparks. Fireglow leapt across the room, danced over creamy female hips and powerful male legs.

"Here we are," he said gently. "As God made us, Gabby." His throat was tight with lust, but he steadied himself. He couldn't frighten her—he had to get this right or the rest of their married life would be plagued by her idiot father and his nasty ideas.

Her eyelashes were silky against her cheeks, which were stained scarlet. She hadn't looked up since he removed her chemise. He reached out and delicately touched her face. "Gabby? After stealing glances at me whenever you thought I wasn't looking, now you won't look at me at all?"

When she didn't answer, he tried teasing her again. "After all your demands for a rational explanation?"

"There's nothing rational about this," she whispered, stung into lifting dusky eyes to his face. "I never, *ever* thought to be naked like this, so indecent—" She broke off, unable to express the shameless way they were behaving.

"There's no indecency here," Quill replied, walking a step closer so that he was just before her. "The dark is for thieves and vagabonds, Gabby. You are my wife. I would celebrate you in the light."

Gabby bit her lip. Despite herself, her body was turning to liquid fire, a slow betrayal, a bending to his ideas. To be truthful, in the firelight his body didn't seem sinful. Not the beauty of his muscled shoulders or lean hips. His body should be celebrated too, she thought, so beautiful it was, and so hard-won.

Quill picked up her hand and placed it just to the side

of his manhood. "You see, Gabby? We fit together, like a hand and a glove."

Gabby shuddered. Her fingers trembled, but didn't fall away from his curls.

And then . . . silently, without outward sign, she succumbed. The shame that was catching her in the back of the throat fell away. She gave in to the pleading in Quill's eyes, to the brave leanness of his injured body. To his delight, she tentatively touched him with a finger.

His flesh leapt at her touch and she drew back instantly. "Did that hurt?"

Quill grabbed her hand and put it squarely on him. Surges of heat raced down the backs of his legs. He was at the limits of his self-control.

"Gabby," he said hoarsely. "This will hurt, but only at first. Come here." He opened his arms.

And his wife, his brave wife, with one nervous swallow wound her arms around his neck and brought her luscious body against his.

Quill kissed her neck, little trailing kisses that sat innocently on her skin and sent messages through her body. He swept a hand down her back, brushing aside tangled curls, curving around her naked bottom.

Gabby closed her eyes, and it was like being in the dark. She concentrated on his hands, how he had picked her up and was walking, skin to skin. She kept her eyes closed as he gently lay her on the bed. In the velvety darkness behind her eyelids, there was nothing indecent about her husband's lips as they trailed down her neck, leaving a murmur of pleasure behind. His lips reached her breast, and the murmur turned to a whisper that spoke throughout her body.

Sure, strong hands cupped her breasts. Then Quill's breath swept her skin and his mouth closed on her nipple.

She arched up, inarticulate sounds falling from her lips, hands clutching his shoulders.

She kept her eyes closed. Protected by blindness, she registered a demanding hardness against her thigh, felt his hands between her legs, suffered the little shivers that followed his fingers. She felt the weight of her own breasts and the fiery warmth between her legs—and gasped as strong hands pulled her thighs open. An inarticulate plea burst from her throat. And then there was no room for shame, not with the twisting flames that raced through her veins, not with the potent demand that pooled between her thighs. Without thinking, she pressed up against his fingers.

"Gabby, open your eyes."

She kept them tightly shut, ignoring him, moving her hips and silently pleading for that delicious pressure.

"Open your eyes!" Quill was panting, his voice a growl in the back of his throat.

Finally she did. She opened her eyes to find her husband propped on his elbows over her, hair fallen over eyes black with desire. Gabby opened her mouth and swallowed. Then she instinctively pushed against him—not against fingers, but against Quill himself.

"Please." Her voice cracked and broke in a pant.

Quill smiled a devil's carnal smile, and Gabby didn't care. She wanted more of him—more pressure, touch, entry.

He came to her then, came like a thief in the daytime, like a devil in the sunlight. With light shining on his face and shoulders, and their eyes open, he came into her with a surge that made design and function rationally, logically clear.

It hurt.

It hurt a lot. It must hurt for Quill too, because his face looked tormented. She would have protested, but she was pinned by his weight, by the carnal presence of him inside her. And then, as she opened her mouth, he moved, just a trifle.

He kissed her forehead, kissed her cheeks. Only when he reached her mouth did he thrust himself forward again. Gabby gasped at the flash of pain. But an elusive tingle of pleasure answered. She reached toward his mouth, found a sweet meeting that caused a trembling rise in her body. He thrust, and this time . . . no pain. Instead, a bolt of liquid pleasure ran through her depths, and a long shiver clutched her body.

Quill stopped yet again and made himself count silently to ten. Her body was so small; she had to grow used to him. But in the pause between seven and eight, Gabby moved in an inexperienced, awkward lunge and gasped his name in a broken pant that said nothing of pain and everything of pleasure. Quill bent his head and took her mouth, a fierce and welcome intrusion. And then he pulled back and shoved toward her center, hard, fast, over and over.

Gabby, quite given over to indecent pleasure, found an exquisite, rising ache that grew as she arched toward him and met his strokes. Her breath was a sob in her chest. Her body was dancing with liquid fire.

And so the devil's daughter, as her father was like to call her, found wings of her own.

Now her eyes were closed because eyesight was not needed, not with the potency of the body connected to hers, not with every nerve crying with sharp joy. Not when she was flinging herself against him, trying with ever-increasing skill to match his rhythm.

And then Quill gripped her hips, pulled her up, and gasped, "Now, Gabby!" and without hesitation, Gabby followed her father's first commandment: Obey thy husband, above all else. Her body arched hard, and dimly she heard cries from her own lips and an answering growl from Quill.

A torrent of pleasure answered with its own lovely music the question of indecency and sinfulness.

When it was finished, Quill slumped on top of his wife. She didn't seem to mind his weight, he thought. Her skin was glowing with a thin sheen. He rubbed his lips against her forehead and tasted salt.

Gabby opened dazed, gleaming eyes. "I know what you were trying to say before." Her voice was an intimate breath against his cheek.

He twined his fingers through hers and waited.

"With my body, I thee worship," she whispered. The words rose from her heart like a prayer that washed away her father's sermons and bitter words. "It's all in the marriage ceremony, isn't it?" she asked, wonderingly.

He clutched her hand. He was still deep inside her and it was hard to shape words.

"You haven't got a headache, have you, Quill?"

"No." But he didn't want to let go of the moment. If he fell asleep, he knew, the headache would come. Already he could see faint purple flashes at the edge of his vision, a warning that pain would follow.

He rocked forward, experimentally.

Her eyes widened and her body involuntarily shivered. He moved again, a deep, lazy seduction.

"Oh," Gabby sighed.

"Indeed," Quill murmured.

Chapter 17

QUILL WOKE IN THE EARLY MORNING, opened his eyes, and shut them instantly. Light was unbearable in the grips of a migraine. Throbbing pain answered every beat of his heart and hammered at his temples. Experience told him that wrenching nausea was on its way.

He turned his head, and the pain burst down into his neck and shoulders. But there was Gabby. She was curled on her side, tangled, tousled, velvety curls shading her face. He could just see the voluptuous curve of her bottom lip.

He had to get into another room. He couldn't let her see him like this. Stifling a groan, Quill reached out an arm, felt blindly for the bell cord, and pulled it. When the door opened, he barked, "Help me out of here," without opening his eyes.

Five minutes later, he was resting as comfortably as possible, having made it halfway into his own chamber before losing the supper that he and Gabby had shared late the previous night.

He lay still as a board, a wet cloth over his eyes, enduring boiling nausea and a pounding brow. Bitterness crashed over him, leaving an acid taste in his mouth that coupled with the sour persistence of vomit. He wanted—*needed*—to be back in that bed next to Gabby.

He would have kissed her awake and taught her the sleepy pleasures of morning intimacy. He'd have helped her with her morning ablutions, washed each lush curve himself. Unless they started practicing celibacy, Quill thought, he would never be able to see Gabby wake in the morning. It was hard to take. Unfair. But grinding his teeth made hot agony surge to his temples. With the skill of long practice, he forced himself to relax and lie still. After unpleasant experimentation, he had found that indulging in any form of movement prompted a migraine to linger for a week.

With nothing to do but weather the attack, he quickly lost track of time. He moved only to lean over the side of the bed and spew into a basin. Every hour or so Willis entered the room and changed his head cloth.

So he had no idea when it was that Gabby tiptoed into the room. The moment he realized who had entered, his body stiffened. Willis had no right to allow Quill's wife in the room. He refused to vomit in her presence.

It was no use. That instinctive stiffening led to a sickening lurch in his innards, and without even speaking to his wife, Quill leaned over the side of the bed and hoped to God that he wasn't splashing bile on her gown. He didn't open his eyes. There was no need to see the disgusted revulsion on her face. He could imagine it with no difficulty.

Quill lay back, silently cursing himself. What had he been thinking when he married? Bitter experience had hewed knowledge of his inadequacies. What type of knave cursed his wife with a lame excuse for a man? Only a reprobate would take a woman to wife because he lusted after her, would take her to wife with no thought for her happiness or future.

"What the devil are you doing here?" he managed to say in a harsh whisper.

"I came to see you." Gabby sounded unmoved by his hostile greeting. A chair close to the bed scraped the wooden floor, and a corresponding stab of pain lit up the inside of Quill's skull.

She apparently noticed his intake of breath. "I'm sorry, Quill," she said. "May I remain for a few minutes, if I make no further noise?"

Quill was struggling with a sense of surprise. His sense of smell became unbearably acute when in the grips of a migraine. Smells—all smells—made him nauseated. But not Gabby's. She had just had a bath; he could tell that. Jasmine was floating on the air, jasmine and the silky, innocent scent of Gabby herself.

"Your mother, Lady Sylvia, and Peter just left for Southampton. Your mother sent her love." Gabby was almost whispering. "I could tell you a story," she added in a rush.

She was embarrassed. Quill would have bet a small fortune that his wife was twisting her hands together and that a rosy tinge was creeping up her cheek.

"I'm not much good at nursing," she was saying. "But Kasi is often sick, and I used to distract him by telling him stories."

Quill let his silence be a yes.

"I thought you might like to hear a tale of India," she said. "This is a story that my ayah told me, and then I told it to Kasi, and in the process it has changed, because that is the nature of stories.

"The story begins where it ends: in a great palace on the

outskirts of Barahampore. On one side of the palace flowed the dark and winding river called the Bohogritee, and on the other was a market for singing birds. The palace was constructed of great arched pillars of marble, decorated all over with pictures of the birds that were for sale outside its gates. Over each of the arches, bands of musicians played on their various instruments, morning and evening, imitating the sweet music of the birds."

Quill had always thought that Gabby's voice was sensual, with its husky, uneven timbre. Now he realized that it was an instrument that she used like a harp.

"The prince who lived in the palace," she continued, "was the greatest songbird of them all, the most skilled musician in all India. His name was Mamarah Daula, and there was no instrument that he could not take to hand and play so exquisitely that the very stones wept to hear him. People thronged from the corners of India to hear his music, and thus he lived in a style of unrivaled elegance and beauty. The very earth poured out her treasures to deck his household. He wore shoes of bright crimson velvet, embroidered with silver, and he never traveled without an escort of twenty or thirty servants. Mamarah Daula was a very fortunate man. He was also extraordinarily foolish."

Quill sank into a hazy silence, nothing akin to the angry, lonely torpor that usually accompanied his migraine attacks. The prince's exploits kept him fascinated for an hour or so, after which he slept deeply rather than drifting in and out of a painful waking state as was normal.

Gabby returned later in the evening and held his hand as she told him of Daula's thirtieth birthday. It seemed that Sakambhari, the tree goddess, resolved to give Daula a musical instrument that would create the most beautiful music in the world. But Sakambhari warned him that if he used it for a vain or prideful purpose, it would give him extraordinary pain in his head.

The corner of Quill's mouth twitched. Gabby waxed lyrical about the lovely music that Daula created with his new instrument.

Finally he opened his mouth. His voice was gravelly and brittle, but he ignored it. "Tell me his instrument was a *pipe,* Gabby."

If Quill's eyes hadn't been covered by a wet cloth, he would have seen his wife's dimples. "It might have been," she agreed. "Indian musicians create beautiful music with their . . . pipes."

By the next morning the pain was decreasing and Quill didn't vomit once in Gabby's presence. Unfortunately, Mamarah Daula was unable to control his pride, and his glorious pipe dealt him one brutal headache after another.

In retrospect, Quill's attack lasted precisely the same duration as those that had come before it. But its severity was lessened. Quill didn't fool himself about why. He took Gabby's comfort, her sweet fragrance and sweeter voice, the wisp of a silly story that she held out for his enjoyment— he took them and knew that he was undeserving. In the black middle of the night he stared at the wall, his stomach contracted not from nausea but from self-loathing. Gabby, lovely Gabby, deserved a man whose body had the same provocative beauty as hers, a man who would—but thinking of that man caused a harsh clenching of his muscles. He'd kill such a man before he let him near Gabby's intoxicating body. Her flesh was *his.*

By morning, Quill had achieved the Herculean task of putting his gaping, bewildering guilt to the side. He justified it thus: Ladies did not truly like sexual congress. Everyone knew that. Gabby was undoubtedly shocked by his migraine, but she would learn to relish days of freedom, without the presence of her crippled husband to question her movements. In the end it would be best for her.

He shakily rose from the bed, and he and Gabby made their way back to London. After a few hours Gabby fell asleep with her head on his shoulder. Quill knew why she was tired. Willis was not the only person who had changed his head cloths in the middle of the night. Gabby had come to him as well. He ruthlessly squashed an errant swell of guilt.

Having long ago dismissed the idea of marriage and love, he had wasted no time thinking about the condition. He did recall idly judging that a dependent wife would be quite tiresome.

But of course he was the one in danger of dependency. It was frightening, how much he craved the presence of his talkative, sweet-smelling wife. It gave him a queer twinge in the area of his heart when she whispered "I love you" against his chest, even though he knew perfectly well that the words were romantic fribbles and naught else.

In fact, he almost could have whispered something frivolous himself as he watched Gabby sleeping, as airy curls started to slip from her coronet of braids and tumble free.

Almost.

THEY ARRIVED IN LONDON in ample time for dinner. Quill climbed from the coach and turned to help Gabby. Behind him was a flurry of movement. He turned around, Gabby's hand warm on his sleeve, to find that the upper servants had formed a neat line on either side of the marble steps leading to the house, with Codswallop magisterially poised at the top.

The butler descended the steps. "Welcome to the household, Viscount Dewland," he intoned. He bowed. "Lady Dewland."

Quill gaped, startled by the unexpected display. Of course—it was his house now. They were his servants.

Beside him Gabby inclined her head in greeting. "Codswallop, how kind of you to welcome us on this sad occasion," she said in her clear voice. All the servants looked approving.

Quill shook himself and escorted her to the steps. "Good evening to all of you," he said. "This is my wife, the Viscountess Dewland."

Mrs. Farsalter approached, hands tucked under her apron. "I would be pleased to show you the household accounts whenever you would wish, my lady." She held out a large ring of keys. "The dowager viscountess always gave me these when she left the house. They rightly belong to you now, my lady."

"My goodness," Gabby said. "Mrs. Farsalter, shall we meet tomorrow morning after breakfast? I am quite convinced that your housekeeping skills are so far above mine that I shall have no suggestions to make, but I will be very pleased to help you as much as I am able."

Mrs. Farsalter beamed. "I'll serve a light repast in an hour or so, shall I, my lady?"

Quill turned to Gabby and held out his arm. Her fingers rested on his sleeve as he led her into the hallway—*my hallway*, he thought numbly. "Would you like to rest before dinner?"

"Thank you. I am not tired, but I would like to bathe."

There was a slight bustle as Codswallop dispatched a footman to fetch hot water.

Gabby began to climb the stairs, Quill just behind her. When she reached the second floor, she moved toward her old chamber, but Quill gently held her back.

"They will have moved your clothing into the viscountess's chamber, Gabby."

She bit her lip. "Your poor mama . . ."

"It's the way of things," Quill said. "She will have the very finest guest bedchamber whenever she wishes to visit. But the master chambers are ours now."

He bent his head and kissed her, a brief, sensual promise. "What is the point of having an adjoining door if one cannot watch one's wife dressing—or undressing?"

Gabby jumped backward so quickly that she knocked his hand off her arm. "It matters nothing if that door is shut," she said firmly. Gabby had given a great deal of thought to the future during the days she waited for Quill's migraine to recede. Only a bedlamite would consider engaging in behavior that caused her husband pain. And if he thought she was going to be party to instigating another such attack as racked his body for three days, he would have to think again.

But there was no point in arguing in the open hallway. Gabby mustered her dignity and moved toward the viscountess's chambers. Her husband dogged her heels. She entered, and he closed the door behind them.

Gabby sighed. "Don't you think it would be better to have this discussion after we have washed and eaten a meal?" She drifted across the room, pretending to inspect the gilt chairs positioned before the fireplace.

"I believe that we should discuss it now," Quill replied.

She turned around, her fingers trailing over the polished surface of a rosewood writing desk. "Obviously we cannot indulge in the kind of behavior that caused your migraine."

"I see nothing obvious about it." Quill's voice sounded tight, almost angry.

"I should think it is unquestionable. Something about . . ."

She paused and chose her words carefully. "Something about connubial relations gives you a migraine headache. Therefore, we shall not repeat the experience until a cure is found."

"For God's sake," Quill shot back. "Do you think that I didn't attempt to find a cure?"

"We shall have to try harder," she replied stubbornly. "I know you, Quill. You could hardly bring yourself to speak to me about it. There are likely hundreds of doctors both here and abroad with a cure for your malady."

Quill crossed his arms and leaned against the mantelpiece. "The leading expert on migraine headaches is an Austrian named Heberden. I had him brought over to England to consult with my doctors. Heberden remarked that bleeding was detrimental."

He smiled grimly. "I already knew that, having had leeches attached to every part of my head in the previous year. Heberden's prime remedy is a concoction of Peruvian bark; that, too, was inefficacious. I might add, Gabby, that Heberden seemed somewhat startled by the number of cures I had already undertaken, which included taking valerian, myrrh, musk, camphor, opium, hemlock—even sneezing powders. And there was the fraudulent doctor in Bath who covered me with fomentations made of hemlock and balsam. I smelled like a pine forest for days."

Gabby bit her lip. "Did Dr. Heberden have any ideas other than the bark?"

"He advised me to put blisters behind my ears during an attack," Quill said with a sarcastic twist of his lips. "You can judge the efficacy of that remedy from the lack of blisters around my person. He then tried to push opium on me, but I have a persistent dislike of the idea that addiction is an appropriate substitute for sexual activity. After that, I decided that I had better live with the malady as it is. In fact, the last medicine I took was a miracle drug my mother bought from a quack located in the Blackfriars. Doctors informed me two weeks later, after I recovered from a prolonged attack of delirium, that the drug almost killed me. It did not, however, cure my migraines."

Gabby thought of mentioning her letter to Sudhakar, but dismissed it. Quill had a fiercesomely stubborn look to him.

"I have vowed not to take any further medicines, Gabby." He cleared his throat. "I realize that my weakness impinges on your happiness. I probably shouldn't have married you."

"Well, that's just it," she said.

Quill's heart sank to his knees. He could feel the sarcastic smile on his face turn to stone. She was right, of course. She had every reason to scream at him, to leave him, to divorce him. All justifications were flimsy before her well-earned reproach.

"You *did* marry me," Gabby pointed out. "And now the problem is ours, not yours."

"I fail to follow your reasoning," Quill said with deadly courtesy. "I shall be quite happy not to bother you with invalidish behavior. I assure you that I will not require nor request your presence during these episodes." His heart was beating so slowly and heavily that he felt rooted to the ground.

Gabby scowled at him. "I said nothing concerning your behavior during migraines. I merely said the problem is now ours rather than yours alone. What I meant is that we should approach the question of remedies together."

"No one—and certainly not a wife—is going to dictate my decisions," Quill said between clenched teeth. "I refuse to take any more half-baked remedies. The situation stands, and you will have to live with it."

Gabby felt a slow burn up her neck, but she grappled with her temper. "Your attitude is not a gracious one. Surely you can see that this is a decision to be made between us?"

"No, it is not." Quill spaced his words with brutal precision. "When I first had my accident, my mother dictated everything in my sickroom. Had I continued to listen to her, I would be malingering in that bed to this day. She almost killed me with spurious cures, and then she fought tooth and nail against Trankelstein's ideas—and it was Trankelstein's massage and exercises that got me out of bed."

Gabby pressed her lips together. "I fail to see what your mother's error in judgment has to do with our current situation."

"I—and I alone—will make all decisions to do with medicine, Gabby. I have no wish to half kill myself by taking a cure given to me by a deranged doctor whom you have heard about over tea." He folded his arms across his chest, ignoring her frown. "My decision is final."

"Well," Gabby said after a moment of silence, "in that case, I must inform you that all decisions pertaining to my body are also my own."

"Naturally." Quill nodded.

"Good. Then you will not mind if I have this door"— Gabby pointed to the door leading to the viscount's bedchamber—"sealed. We have no further use for it."

"What are you attempting to say?"

"I attempt nothing." She shrugged. "I merely point out to you, *husband*"—she gave it a delicate emphasis—"that my body is no longer at your disposal. Thus you will suffer no more migraines and will have no need for deranged cures." She turned about briskly and began pulling pins from her coronet.

"And if I visit a concubine?" Quill's voice was dangerously steely and came from somewhere behind her left shoulder.

Gabby didn't look. "That is your choice, as it always will be. I may sympathize with the migraine you incur, but at least I won't be responsible for it."

"And as for yourself?" His voice was a sneer. "How will you achieve satisfaction, Gabby? Are you planning to make me a cuckold?"

She bit her lip hard. Her throat was closing with tears. But she had to do this right, or Quill would incur that pain again—and it would be her fault.

"Oh, no," she said, managing an airy tone. She shook out her hair and began brushing it. "While I enjoyed our night together"—she paused just enough to lend doubt to that statement—"I see no particular reason to engage in that kind of behavior again. It was pleasant, but not . . . necessary." Some part of her was amazed at how difficult it was to tell Quill this particular lie. It felt as if she were stamping on her own heart to say so.

She turned around and met his eyes. She had always found that her father was more likely to swallow a fib when she looked straight into his eyes. "It was rather messy, wasn't it, Quill?" She gave a delicate shudder. "I'm afraid I greatly disliked the fact that my sheets were untidily marked. Not to mention that I did not like being naked in the open room, nor that you looked at me so freely."

"For God's sake, Gabby! You bled because it was your first time. It will not happen again."

"Hmmm," she replied. "My point is only that I will not make you a cuckold, Quill. I am not interested, and I would never resort to other men. You are my husband, but why on earth would I allow a stranger to use my body?" Well, that was true enough, Gabby thought. She had no interest in other men. She only wanted Quill.

Quill's teeth hurt from clenching his jaw. He knew that ladies disliked sexual congress, of course. And he'd seen for himself how much Gabby feared being naked. He must have misunderstood. He thought she had put that dislike aside in the pleasure of the moment. He must have been blinded by lust.

He turned to leave, but paused with his hand on the doorknob. "And if I try various cures, will you allow me to use your body?" He hated himself for asking, loathed himself for exposing his vulnerability. He didn't turn around so that he wouldn't see pity in her eyes.

Gabby couldn't answer. The windowpane blurred before her eyes.

He waited and then repeated himself. "So, Gabby, do I get one bout of marital intercourse for every draught of Peruvian bark I drink? Or do I have to resort to the leeches in order to get access to my wife's bed?"

Somehow she wrenched her voice out. "Do we have to——"

"Well, yes, we do," Quill replied. His voice was frigid. "In order to try a cure, Gabby my wife, I must incur a migraine. So I gather we'll wait until a quack presents a concoction of stewed insects, and then I shall beg you for permission to engage in a bout of marital activity."

A sob tore its way up her throat. She pressed her hands hard over her eyes. "I"—she gasped—"I don't want to *do* that again, Quill! Can't you understand?"

"Quite," her husband said. His voice was even and, oh, so icy. "I will not intrude on your chambers again, madam. You may instruct the servants to do as you wish regarding the door leading to my room. Nail it shut, by all means."

He bowed, but Gabby didn't turn around. Tears were spilling hotly over the hands pressed to her eyes.

She heard the door open and then close. Sobs ripped from her throat. Oh, God, what a liar she had become! She had told him that—and he believed her. He believed she was indifferent.

It was so far from the truth. Every finger longed to touch him. At night, lying between cool linen sheets, she thought of nothing but the heavy pleasure of his body, of the way he pounded into her, of the hoarse moan that broke from his lips. And even . . . she even remembered how he spread her legs and touched her until she writhed before him, naked as the day she was born. Shamelessly raising her hips to his hand.

That was how absorbed by wicked desire she was, how far she was in sin. How far she was from indifferent.

When the bathwater arrived, Gabby told Margaret that she had a headache and would not join her husband for dinner. Then she lay curled in misery while the bathwater steamed and finally cooled. Only when it was stone-cold did she lower herself into it. *Punishment,* she thought dimly. For lying and for desiring—which was worse? But she knew the answer. Quill was right about desire. There could be nothing wrong about the way their bodies met and loved each other, in daylight or at night. But there was everything wrong about telling him that she disliked the act.

And so she sat in chill water and watched her nipples turn a dark cherry red, as they had for her husband. As they did when she thought of him.

And she sobbed. Because she loved him and she wanted him. And the two could not go together. Because she loved him, loved the way he laughed with his eyes but not out loud, the way he looked at her silently, the way he touched her, as if she were beautiful and worth cherishing.

She loved him more than she loved herself, and thus they could not make love.

The cold bath worked. Other memories replaced the heated memory of lovemaking. During his migraine, Quill's skin became deathly pale, as if the honey had leached from his skin. His face looked ashen, haggard, and his eyes were sunken. And the vomiting . . . No.

She was right to lie. It was horrible to deceive Quill, but it was for his own good. Instinctively she knew that he would rise from a migraine attack and come back to her bed. He would suffer that pain over and over again.

Because he loves me, Gabby said to herself. He had not said so, not since asking her to marry him, but Quill was shy with words. Since he loves me, he would always make love to me. He would not wish me to be deprived of pleasure, no matter the toll it took on his own health. But now . . . he would not think to make love to her. He wouldn't even wish to do so, coldhearted jade that she seemed.

And that was the most important thing.

LUCIEN WAS IN HIS CARRIAGE, heading with something less than enthusiasm to a champagne breakfast being given by the Duke and Duchess of Gisle, when he realized that it was a Tuesday morning. To be exact, it was Tuesday just after ten o'clock, and if he sent the carriage in the opposite direction, he might arrive on Emily's doorstep at the same time as Bartholomew Hislop, thereby making it absolutely clear to Hislop that Emily was no straw damsel for his taking.

He rapped sharply on the carriage roof. But when they drew up before the small house, there was no sign of Hislop. Perhaps he should drive on. Emily had repeatedly refused to see him. Every time he presented himself at the house, Sally told him that Mrs. Ewing was not at home.

The memory steeled his backbone and Lucien almost motioned to his waiting footman to close the carriage door again. Undoubtedly Hislop was already in Emily's study, breathing on her shoulder or committing some such other gross indelicacy.

Lucien gritted his teeth and stepped out of the carriage, drawing on his gloves. He'd be damned if Emily would deny him and be at home to Hislop.

Sure enough, when he rang the doorbell the little maid, Sally, once again stammered some nonsense about Mrs. Ewing not being at home. He gave her a look and a sovereign; she fled back down the hallway.

Lucien hesitated for a moment outside Emily's study and then pushed open the door without knocking. Immediately he knew he had made a mistake. Emily and Hislop were standing just before her desk, with their backs to him. They looked cozily intimate, and Lucien saw distaste on Emily's face when she looked around.

"Forgive me for disturbing you," he said, his French accent particularly marked due to embarrassment. Clearly Emily did not mind Hislop's company. Why, he had a hand on her wrist.

Hislop casually let go of Emily and bowed to Lucien. "Fancy seeing you again," he said, not as genially as he had when they first met. "Odd coincidence, that."

"I visit frequently," Lucien said grimly. His black eyes were narrowed.

"So do I, so do I," Hislop replied, seeming to have no sense of his personal danger.

Emily rustled forward. "Mr. Boch, how lovely to see you again." She had a delicate flush in her cheeks that Lucien could only think was due to delight at Mr. Hislop's touch.

He bowed formally. "I regret to have interrupted you," he

said mendaciously. "I am afraid that I quite forgot Mr. Hislop's weekly appointments to discuss fashion."

"Appointment is not the right word," Hislop said. "It sounds too businesslike. I prefer to think of myself as Mrs. Ewing's good *friend*. In fact, I have asked her to spend this evening at the theater with me."

Lucien's jaw tensed. Did Emily have any idea of the connotations of what Mr. Hislop had just said? He looked at her, but she seemed impervious to the insult. Moreover, he himself had asked Emily to the theater, and she had refused. "Perhaps I shall see you both there," he said politely, and bowed again. "I will ask you to excuse me, Mrs. Ewing, Mr. Hislop. I have an engagement this morning."

Hislop strolled forward, blocking Lucien's view of Emily. "Going to the Duke of Gisle's breakfast, are you? I was invited—I am sure of that, because I'm the best of friends with Gisle, you know—but my invitation must have gone astray. It happens, it happens."

"Quite." Lucien turned to go.

"Mr. Boch!" The words sounded torn from Emily's throat.

He turned. "Yes?"

"I . . ." She faltered.

He waited.

"Once when you visited," Emily said in a half whisper, "you offered me aid. I should like to take advantage of your expertise."

Lucien paused. What the devil was she talking about? Then he suddenly remembered that he had told her he came to slay dragons.

"Mr. Hislop," he said with a casual, thin-lipped smile, "since your invitation so unaccountably went astray, why don't you accompany me to Gisle's breakfast? I am certain that Patrick will be delighted to see you."

Hislop didn't hesitate for a moment. He turned to Emily and made a hasty bow. "I'm sure you will understand if I leave, Mrs. Ewing. Perhaps I can find time to return to you later."

Lucien's eyes narrowed at the offense in Hislop's farewell. But a look at Emily's embarrassed eyes reassured him. Whatever Hislop thought was happening between them, she was not partner to it. In a way it was comforting: at least she hadn't chosen Hislop over him.

The moment the carriage door closed, Lucien lunged forward and twisted Hislop's neckcloth in his hand, jerking him forward and out of his seat.

"What are you doing?" Hislop shouted, but the rest of his sentence was unintelligible. Lucien kicked his boots out from under him, and he fell heavily into the well between the seats as Lucien let go of his neckcloth.

He sat on the carriage floor, staring at Lucien in horror. "What the devil did you do that for? You've wrecked my neckcloth, damned if you haven't!" He felt the folds of cloth with trembling fingers. "Wrecked!" he half shrieked. "The arrangement cost me three cloths this morning. And what will the duke and duchess think of me now?"

Lucien noted with amusement that Hislop seemed to take irrational violence in stride. Perhaps his acquaintances were often driven to commit such outrages.

"You will stay away from Mrs. Ewing," he said in a gentle voice. "If I ever hear that you have been seen near her or her house, I will personally make certain that you are never again invited to an event given by the *haut ton*."

Hislop pushed himself up and sat down on the opposite seat, looking at Lucien as if he were a rabid dog. "I don't know what you're so excited about. It isn't as if I've done anything the woman disliked! I've been the perfect gentleman, if you want to know."

"I don't give a damn," Lucien said through his clenched teeth. "As long as you understand that your 'friendship' with Mrs. Ewing is over."

Hislop's full lips formed a pout. "I've been working on this for months," he complained. "And you only showed up the last few weeks. Wouldn't it be more of a gentlemanly thing to allow that I have a prior claim?

"All right!" he shrieked, as Lucien made a sudden violent movement. "For God's sake, I'm not that interested anyway. She's a beauty, but a bit somber for my tastes. I was thinking of trying the sister—but I won't," he exclaimed, meeting Lucien's wrath-filled eyes. "Won't go anywhere near the house, since that's what you wish."

Lucien leaned back on his seat, which seemed to give Hislop courage.

"Don't see why you'd mind if I made a play for the sister," he complained. "You can take Emily, and I'll back out like a gentleman, even though I do have the prior claim. So why not let me have the sister? I can set her up, you know," he said generously. "I've got a little house out in Chelsea that's perfect for this sort of thing, and it's been empty for all of two months now."

Lucien knocked on the roof so hard that the carriage shook. It swayed to a halt.

"What're you doing?" Hislop asked in some alarm. "You said you'd take me to Gisle's breakfast! And I want to go!"

"Get out," Lucien said as the door swung open.

"Well, I'm not going to," Hislop said indignantly. "You promised to take me. And you've gone and stolen my lady-bird from me, without so much as a by-your-leave, *and* with a good deal of unnecessary personal violence. The least you can do is keep your promise."

To his own surprise, Lucien heard himself break into a snort of laughter.

Hislop stared at him.

"You'd better straighten your neckcloth," Lucien said.

PERHAPS AN HOUR LATER, Patrick Foakes, the Duke of Gisle, poked his friend in the ribs. "Who's that little mushroom you brought to our breakfast?" he said, nodding toward Hislop, who was happily chatting with the duchess.

"Bartholomew Hislop," Lucien said lazily. "Lovely, isn't he? He's been trying to turn my future wife into his *chérie amie*."

"What!"

Lucien hadn't known until the sentence left his lips. But he liked the sound of it. "I'm planning to marry Mrs. Emily Ewing," he explained. "But I had to slay her dragon first."

Patrick blinked, looking at Hislop and his crumpled neckcloth. "That's a dragon?"

Lucien grinned. "We dragon slayers have to take our work as it comes."

Patrick rolled his eyes. "Why did you bring him here? Hoping that my cook will poison his meal? He looks perfectly healthy to me."

"Hislop and I came to terms about Mrs. Ewing," Lucien remarked. "But I had promised to bring him to your breakfast and he felt that, as a gentleman, I should keep my promise."

Patrick snorted. "Sounds more like a mouse than a dragon." But at that moment, Sophie sent him an unmistakable look of appeal over Hislop's head.

"I'll have his gizzard," the duke said between clenched teeth as he lunged across the room.

SADLY ENOUGH, Bartholomew Hislop's unexpected invitation to the Duke of Gisle's breakfast did not go as smoothly as he could have hoped. For, as he told his close friends the following evening, he did nothing more than accidentally drop an apricot tart near the duchess. "Not on her bodice," he painstakingly explained. "*Near* it." And when he bent over to make absolutely certain that her gown was not stained, why, the duke went into a frenzy.

His friends' eyes widened and they leaned closer.

"Naturally," Bartholomew reported, "this small *contretemps* will not affect our friendship, and I have no doubt but that I shall be invited to many future events at the Gisle house. But I must warn you all to avoid the duchess. Frankly, Gisle is just a trifle *bourgeois* with regard to his wife. After all, Her Grace displayed her bosom to the whole of the Fester ballroom, didn't she? So why would he mind if I happened to catch a glimpse?"

His friends entirely agreed with him, which mitigated the pain of a darkish purple bruise that had unaccountably appeared under his right eye.

Chapter 18

"GABBY! What on earth are you doing in Abchurch Lane?" Sophie exclaimed. "I've never met another soul I knew here."

Gabby smiled a bit shyly. "I came to visit an apothecary. How are you, Sophie?"

Sophie turned about and tucked Gabby's arm into hers. "Bored, dearest. I am yawning with tedium. I visited Mr. Spooner's bookstore in hopes of finding a Norwegian grammar book, for nothing more than curiosity. And he failed me. But I must apologize: I have been horribly remiss. I meant to call last week to congratulate you on your marriage."

Gabby opened her mouth, but Sophie kept right on chattering. "You married the right brother, you know. Peter is a dear, but Quill . . . well, if I hadn't already met Patrick by the time Quill emerged from his sickroom, I might have thrown my hat into the ring." Sophie gave her a twinkling smile.

"In that case, I am glad that my husband's illness lasted so long," Gabby said. "I wouldn't have stood a chance."

"Pooh! My Patrick says that Quill is besotted."

Gabby laughed, but she felt a secret gleam of delight. "That sounds like foolishness. How could your husband possibly know whether Quill is besotted or not?"

"Oh, men." Sophie gave her delicate French shrug. "Who knows how they understand each other? Sometimes I think Patrick must speak in code to his brother, Alex, because they rarely converse, yet Patrick always knows if something is wrong. They're twins, you know."

"I didn't know that," Gabby said with some curiosity. "Do they look alike?"

"People seem to think so. But I have never agreed," Sophie replied. "I would love to introduce you, but Alex and his wife, Charlotte, are still in the country because Charlotte is expecting a child."

"I see," Gabby said, not seeing at all. Since they were in mourning, she and Quill had not attended many public events. But she had seen women everywhere who were large with child.

"Charlotte had some bother giving birth to her first child," Sophie explained, "and Alex is simply rabid with worry and won't let my poor friend rise from the couch. Patrick keeps complaining that he's getting ulcers due to Alex's nervous spates."

"So each knows what the other is feeling?"

"Yes, I believe that's the way of twins. Is this your apothecary, Gabby? I must say, it looks undistinguished." They stood in front of a tiny shop with square projecting windows and small panes of filthy glass.

Gabby pulled from her reticule the advertisement she had clipped from *The Times*. "Yes, this is it."

"I think we had better leave our maids here. We won't all fit inside," Sophie said dubiously. "Lift up your skirts!" she called as Gabby pushed open the dingy door, causing a bell to ring.

The shop of Mr. J. Moore, Apothecary, was crowded with oddly shaped bottles, each adorned with a scribbled label. There was no one behind the counter.

Sophie bent over one of the bottles. "Just look at this! Worm powder. Do you think it's made of worms?"

Gabby shook her head. "I doubt it." Where was the proprietor? She clutched the advertisement in a gloved hand.

"No, it's not made of worms," Sophie was saying. "It brings away worms of all sorts of lengths and shapes and leaves the body in perfect health." She snorted. "Gabby, what *are* we doing in this place?"

Just then an old man entered through the curtained back door. Gabby almost stepped back in dismay. His eyes were covered with a milky-white film, and he felt his way along the counter to stand before them. "Hello! Hello! I'm Mr. James Moore," he said cheerfully. "Purveyor of real and effectual medicines, fit for the use of old and young. How may I help you?"

"I've come in response to your advertisement," Gabby said, wishing she'd never opened *The Times* that morning.

"Ah, my lady, so you suffer from gip in the guts? Windy belches? Or perhaps . . ." He paused. "Wind in the bowels?"

Sophie took Gabby's arm. "I don't believe we are in the right shop," she murmured.

"So there are *two* lovely ladies," Mr. Moore exclaimed. "All the better! Now, a trifling anxiety is natural in these circumstances. But is it better to be a bit mortified here or to suffer true mortification when an eruption occurs in a crowded place?"

Gabby felt purple with embarrassment. "I've come because you apparently cured a woman who had violent headaches," she said.

"Quite right! Quite right," Mr. Moore said, rubbing his

extremely filthy hands together. "That would be my lovely niece, Miss Rachel Morbury of Church Lane. She insisted—positively insisted—that I allow her to place that testimonial in the paper, my dear madam. Suffered for two years, she did. The headaches had become so bad that she was like to lose her place. She has a good place with Mrs. Huffy, who lives in Church Lane. Finally, Miss Rachel allowed me to give her a dose of my effectual medicine.

"And she hasn't suffered a bit since!" he said triumphantly, beaming at the wall just over Gabby's shoulder. "Miss Rachel placed that advertisement of her own free will, ladies. For the benefit of mankind, she said. She's a good niece to me."

Sophie's hand had been tightening on Gabby's arm during Mr. Moore's little speech. "Gabby," she hissed, "the medicine is quite likely unsafe."

Gabby cleared her throat. "How do you make your headache medicine, Mr. Moore?"

"I can hear that you are delicate ladies," he said jovially. "So I won't tell you the ingredients. Because I'd hate to turn a ladylike stomach and possibly stop you from taking one of my real and effectual medicines!"

Sophie was positively tugging on her arm, but Gabby stood firm. "I won't buy the medicine unless you tell me the ingredients."

"Very well, very well. I use rare ingredients, madam. Very rare. That's why the headache cure is a trifle more expensive than many of my other medicines, to tell the truth."

"Yes?"

"Well," Mr. Moore said reluctantly. "It's a mercurial powder, madam. The same as the noted Emperick Charles Hues ordinarily took. And by mercurial powder, I mean that it has a tincture of quicksilver in it."

"What else?"

"Tartar emetic and just a drop or two of opium—"

"There's nothing very unusual about that remedy," Gabby said bluntly.

"It's a mystery ingredient that does the trick, madam. But I can't tell you the last." Mr. Moore put on a regal air. "A doctor has to keep his mysteries, madam. Or else every ruffian in the street will be selling my real and effectual medicine."

"In that case, thank you very much for speaking to us." Gabby turned to go.

"Wait!"

"My husband will not try any medicine without a full understanding of its ingredients," Gabby replied. "I bid you good day, Mr. Moore."

"For the good of mankind," the apothecary gabbled. "For the good of mankind and, more especially, to relieve your good husband, madam, I will tell you. But I must have your solemn word that you will breathe a word to no one. My secret ingredient is a tincture of Indian hemp, madam. The medicine is to be repeated every two or three hours."

"Indian hemp? Where did you get that idea, Mr. Moore?"

Mr. Moore clearly felt that since he was in for a penny, he might as well be in for a pound. "I bought the remedy off a traveling Indian, some sort of a doctor, he called himself. It has worked miracles, madam, miracles!"

Gabby paused. "All right. I'll take one bottle."

Mr. Moore beamed. "That will be five sovereigns, madam."

"We are *leaving*," Sophie said, her voice fierce. "Don't you pay this mountebank a penny, Gabby!"

"I'll give you one sovereign." Gabby laid the shining coin on the filthy counter.

Mr. Moore grabbed it, placing a grubby brown bottle in

its place. "There you are, madam. A better bargain you never made. One large spoonful to be repeated every two or three hours while in the throes of an attack. And"——he bowed—— "may I say how very pleased I would be to serve you again, madam? As I may have said, my real and effectual medicine for wind is esteemed throughout the country."

"Thank you," Gabby replied. "Good day, Mr. Moore." She followed Sophie from the shop.

"If you weren't my friend, I would begin to worry about your wits," Sophie said. "You just gave that sovereign away."

"Very likely," Gabby said, feeling dispirited.

"And I would be very surprised to learn that Quill agreed to take that medicine."

Gabby didn't want to say that she could guarantee he *wouldn't* take it. It was too humiliating; the whole business was so humiliating. Tears pricked her eyes.

Sophie took one look, tucked her arm under Gabby's, and began walking back down the lane to where their carriages were waiting. "We shall have to discuss this, Gabby," she said firmly. "I take it that Quill's headaches are quite severe?"

"Yes, they are," Gabby mumbled.

"All the same, who knows what Indian hemp might do to him? I find it hard to believe that Quill would take such a medicine—even a *real and effectual one,*" she said, mimicking Mr. Moore's voice, "without knowing the consequences. What if it caused him further injury, Gabby?"

"I know," she said miserably. "It's just that when I saw the advertisement in the paper . . ." Her voice trailed off.

"His niece, ha! Moore placed that advertisement himself, the old quack."

"You're probably right." Gabby couldn't keep the bleak tone out of her voice.

"We need tea," Sophie said suddenly. "Here. I'll tell your carriage to follow, shall I?"

Gabby allowed herself to be handed into Sophie's carriage by a footman. They went to Madam Clara's Teashop for Ladies.

"This is my favorite place to drink tea in all London," Sophie said cozily. "All the gossips watch one another while pretending not to, and since the tables aren't close enough for eavesdropping, they suffer agonies of curiosity."

Despite herself, Gabby started to cheer up at Sophie's irreverent chatter. And then, over a cup of steaming tea— and after ascertaining that Sophie was indeed right, and no one could hear them over the chatter—Gabby blurted out the whole story.

"But you have to promise not to tell your husband," she said at the end. "Please, Sophie!"

"Of course I won't tell Patrick," Sophie replied absently. "This story is nothing for a man to hear. Make him nervous and he'd start giving himself headaches out of sympathy."

Gabby chuckled, but Sophie was still thinking out loud. "Quill's old injury obviously triggers the migraines. How?"

"He has a large scar along his hip," Gabby said dubiously.

"Too far from his head," Sophie said.

"Well, perhaps not," Gabby exclaimed, feeling a twinge of excitement. "What if the headaches are caused by using that hip?"

"Using? Oh, I see what you mean! Does it pain him to move that leg normally?"

"No, he's never said that," Gabby said. "But he does limp. And I have noticed that the limp is more pronounced when he's tired."

"Then let's assume that it hurts most of the time,"

Sophie said. "Men are positively idiotic about admitting pain."

"Well, then, what if the migraines are caused by straining his leg?" Gabby frowned. "It wouldn't be a question of the leg, in that case. More likely his hip." She could feel that her face was a rosy pink.

"It could be either," Sophie pointed out. "I mean"——she paused and then plunged ahead——"he likely supports himself on his knees and moves his hips." Her eyes took on a mischievous gleam. "So tonight you must refuse to allow him to move his hip or put weight on his leg."

Gabby's heart bounded and then thudded back to earth. "I can't, Sophie. I told him that I didn't like . . . didn't enjoy . . . so that I wouldn't be responsible for any more migraines. He's not angry. But now, it's been several weeks, and he doesn't even kiss me good night." To her shame, her eyes filled with tears again.

"Change your mind," Sophie said bracingly.

"I can't! What if it doesn't work?"

"It *will* work. And you can't go on like this, buying filthy medicines from cracked apothecaries. You're like to kill Quill one of these times."

"I've never actually given him any of them," Gabby said miserably. She had a secret little collection in her desk. "I was waiting until he had a migraine attack."

"Well, he's never going to have an attack if you don't take him back into your bed," Sophie pointed out.

"He said he would visit a concubine," Gabby whispered. One tear spilled down her cheek.

"Absurd! Quill is undoubtedly lying abed at night planning to break down your door. Patrick and I stopped having relations for a time during the first year of our marriage, and he never visited a concubine. He glowered at me for his entertainment."

"You did, really?" Gabby was fascinated.

"You'd be surprised at the foolish things we did," Sophie replied dryly. "But I'll save them for our next cup of tea, because I promised to take a young guest to see the Tower this afternoon."

Gabby bit her lip. "I don't know how to thank you enough, Sophie. It—"

"Poppycock!" She laughed. "I sounded just like my mama there. Have you met my mama yet?"

Gabby shook her head.

"Count your blessings. Now—" She leaned conspiratorially across the table. "I shall think of you tonight, Gabby. Be of strong heart."

GABBY RETURNED HOME to find that two letters had arrived from India. She snatched them from the salver, only to discover that neither was from Sudhakar.

She read the first letter with keen interest. It appeared that her plan to save Kasi Rao was well in train. She felt a little gleam of pride at the idea that one of her fantastical ideas might actually be useful.

Then she turned, reluctantly, to the letter bearing her father's handwriting. Richard Jerningham's letter was like to blister Gabby's fingers as she read it. Her father had never heard of a request so absurd as hers. Was she aware that no right-minded Englishman would take a foul brew handed to him by a *vaidya*? What was good enough for an Indian person would kill the delicate constitution of an Englishman. Did she want to kill her husband? Under no circumstances would he allow any person from his village to be involved, let alone help her, with her infernal plans.

And he suggested, rather as an afterthought, that she repent her sins and confess all to her husband.

Gabby was well-aware of her father's low opinion of her, but this was rather surprising. She wouldn't have thought he would accuse her of murder!

With a sudden jerky movement, she tore the parchment in half. And in half again. She was staring at a desk covered with small scraps of paper when her husband entered her bedchamber.

"What on earth are you doing?" Quill asked.

Gabby colored and hastily swept up the scraps of paper. "It was nothing more than—"

"Love notes from another man?" he suggested, with just a flash of seductive humor.

"No!" Gabby said, and then, "Oh, Quill—"

But he had turned away, and to her horror, he picked up the small brown bottle she had brought home from the apothecary. She had forgotten to secrete it away.

When Quill looked at her, his face was closed and tight. "Where did you buy this rubbish, Gabby?"

"Abchurch Lane," she said miserably. "I thought perhaps—"

"But I was under the impression that you had declined to sleep with me," Quill said with great politeness. "When were you planning to administer this . . . medicine?" He held it up.

"You said you would visit a concubine," Gabby said, stumbling.

"Oh? I see. Since you dislike connubial relations, I am to visit a concubine. And then when I incur a migraine due to my labors, you are planning to administer this medicine?"

Gabby felt as if she must be purple with embarrassment. "I saw an advertisement. And it looked—"

"How many medicines have you bought, Gabby?" he interrupted.

She blinked.

"You see," he continued, "I watched my mother do exactly the same thing. She bought medicine from every quack who placed a false testimonial in the papers. After she almost killed me, I swore not to take any more medicine. And I shall not break that vow."

Gabby swallowed. "He said it was a most efficacious—"

But he had turned away. "Where are the rest?"

Gabby watched in silence as he started to rummage through her clothespress. Anger was building in her chest, but she kept silent. When he began looking in her desk, she could no longer countenance his actions.

"You have no right!" she said fiercely. "Take your hands out of my things!"

"I have every right," Quill responded as he jerked open another drawer.

"That is my desk!"

"Here they are," her husband said. "I suspect that *my* medicines have somehow found their way into *your* desk."

Gabby pressed her lips together as Quill gathered three small bottles and put them on the table. He picked up the first. "My mother visited these charlatans as well." The bottle crashed into the fireplace. There was a brief scarlet blaze. "Must have had alcohol in it," he remarked.

He picked up another bottle. "Don't recognize this one." The bottle followed the first into the flames.

"Don't you wish to be cured?" Gabby said desperately, seeing her purchases disappear before her eyes.

"Not at the expense of my life," Quill responded. He was looking at the third bottle. "This is a bit more interesting. Did you know that it will cure plagues of every kind and description? Rubbish." The last bottle shattered against the bricks in the fireplace.

"Those were mine," Gabby said hotly. "You had no right to destroy my purchases."

"Were you intending to dose yourself?" Quill asked. His voice was calm, but his eyes were alive with anger. "I shall not drink another fraudulent concoction—*ever*."

"That is irrational."

"I must request that you do not buy any more headache cures," Quill said. He turned his back to her and strolled over to the fireplace.

"Don't turn away!" Gabby said in a wild fury.

He poked a few scraps of thick glass back onto the hearth and spoke over his shoulder. "I am waiting for your response, Gabby."

She saw red. She reached out blindly and caught Mr. Moore's brown bottle in her hand. "You forgot this one!" she shrieked, and threw it at her husband as hard as she could. It sailed past his shoulder and smashed against the fireplace. Brown liquid seeped down between the seams of the bricks.

Quill jumped back when the bottle exploded. There was silence as viscous liquid dripped onto the hearth. Slowly he turned around.

Gabby's hair had fallen around her shoulders, and she had her arms crossed. She was beautiful. She was wrathful. He would give anything to take her in his arms and change her mind about the virtues of connubial pleasure.

He walked toward her. "Apparently, I married a woman with a formidable temper," he said.

"My lady," Margaret called through the door. "Would you like to change from your walking dress now?"

"Promise me, Gabby."

"I promise not to buy any more concoctions for your headache, Quill." Her voice was leaden.

"Thank you."

"Although I am not the only one with a temper."

"I swear I never played the maniac until I met you."

The scratching was repeated. "My lady?"

Gabby sighed. "One moment, Margaret." She looked up at her husband. "I was only trying to help."

He dropped a kiss on her nose and turned to leave. Gabby stretched out her hand, but let it fall. After what had just happened, she couldn't follow Sophie's advice and try to seduce her own husband. In fact, she ended up pleading a headache and eating a light supper in her room, conscious of her own cowardice and unable to overcome it.

THOSE LADIES of the *ton* who specialized in gaping, gadding, and gossiping often found London sadly flat in the months before the Season truly began. But this year the prattling crowd had reached the conclusion that the household of the new Viscountess Dewland was likely to provide them some entertainment.

"After all," Lady Prestlefield gleefully reported to her crony, Lady Cucklesham, "not only has the girl created a scandal by dropping her bodice, but it must be clear to the simplest mind that she jilted her fiancé the very moment his elder brother inherited a title."

"I think we need have no doubt about her motives," Lady Cucklesham agreed, conscious of the fact that she herself had married a man old enough to be her father for precisely the same reason. "We might, however," she added, "question the graceless manner by which she traded a fiancé for his brother within moments of his father's death, if I have heard correctly!"

"Yes," Lady Prestlefield added, "and we can only hope

that she didn't make a bad bargain . . . given the rumored extent of Erskine Dewland's injuries."

There was a delicate pause.

"Perhaps we should pay a visit to the young viscountess," Lady Cucklesham remarked. "Hers must be a most interesting household. And if she is as encroaching and, to be blunt, as scandalous as she would seem, it is our *duty* to unveil her character before the Season begins."

Lady Prestlefield offered no objection to this thoughtful and fair observation.

"HER GRACE THE DUCHESS OF GISLE, Lady Prestlefield, Lady Cucklesham," Codswallop said majestically. There was nothing he preferred to welcoming a whole gaggle of aristocrats into the household.

"What a pleasure to see you," Gabby said, curtsying to Ladies Prestlefield and Cucklesham and offering a shy smile. She had clear memories of the withering advice each lady had offered regarding her lost bodice.

"We simply could not wait to offer you our congratulations," Lady Cucklesham announced.

Luckily, Sophie walked in just behind Lady Cucklesham. "How is your husband today?" she asked.

"Quite well, thank you," Gabby replied, trying not to blush. She knew what Sophie's teasing look was truly saying.

Codswallop reappeared. "Mrs. Ewing and Miss Phoebe Pensington."

Gabby looked up in surprise. "Phoebe, sweetheart. And Mrs. Ewing, how lovely to see you!" To tell the truth, she was rather surprised. She had visited Phoebe several times since returning to London, but Mrs. Ewing had never paid her a return call.

She was exquisitely dressed, of course, but Gabby thought that Mrs. Ewing looked even more tired and peaked than usual. She seemed to pale as she looked over Gabby's shoulder and saw the little cluster of ladies assembled in the parlor.

"We ought not to stay," she said. "I only came because Phoebe was so very anxious to find out whether you have had word of . . . of Kasi Rao." She lowered her voice as she said his name.

"I received a letter this very morning." Gabby beamed at the little girl. "Apparently our friend loves being in the country. He has made friends—" She bent over and whispered in Phoebe's ear.

But Phoebe's shrill little voice was not yet modulated for secrecy. "A chicken!" she squealed. "Kasi Rao has made friends with a chicken?"

"Apparently," Gabby laughed.

Phoebe plucked her sleeve. "Are you quite sure that those bad men won't be able to steal him away from Mrs. Malabright?"

"Quite sure, darling. But we oughtn't to speak of it, just in case."

"Of course," Mrs. Ewing said hurriedly. "We knew that . . . we simply . . ." She looked miserable.

"Please do join my guests, if only for a moment." Gabby looked down at the little girl. "Would you like to visit Margaret and have a jam tart?"

Phoebe smiled. So Gabby turned her over to Codswallop and escorted an obviously reluctant Mrs. Ewing into the room.

Lady Cucklesham looked up with avid interest. "I'm afraid . . . who did you say that you are?"

"My name is Mrs. Ewing," Emily said stiffly.

"And your husband must have been one of the Herefordshire Ewings?"

She shook her head. "No, he was without family."

"Indeed. But surely you are Emily Thorpe. At least, you *were* Emily Thorpe. Perhaps you can tell us how your dear, dear father is faring," Lady Prestlefield said. "I heard something to the effect that he was ailing. But I have no doubt you can tell us more exactly."

"I am afraid not."

Sophie leapt into the breach. "Was that lovely little girl yours?" She turned to Lady Prestlefield. "I met Mrs. Ewing at Lady Fester's ball and spent a good part of the evening sighing over her gown. I had no idea that she was the mother of such an exquisite child! Now I have two things to envy you for, Mrs. Ewing."

Lady Prestlefield smiled, the poisonous smile of a delicate viper. "Have you a *child,* then, Mrs. Ewing? Oddly enough, although I had heard so much about your . . . beauty, I had not heard that you and your husband had a child."

Emily's skin hadn't a trace of color in it, but she met Lady Prestlefield's eyes steadily. "Phoebe is my sister Carolyn's child, Lady Prestlefield. Surely you remember Carolyn Thorpe? I believe you made your debut in the same season."

Sophie choked back a laugh. Unless she was mistaken, Carolyn Thorpe had been a beauty, like her sister, and undoubtedly had cast Lady Prestlefield in the shade.

The door opened and Codswallop entered. "Mr. Lucien Boch."

Lucien entered the parlor, with a smile on his lips. Tomorrow was Tuesday, and he was planning to ask Emily to be his wife. "Lady Dewland," he said cheerfully, "I was just passing your house and—"

He stopped. The blood rushed to his head. His wife-to-be was sitting before him. "Mrs. Ewing." There was no disguising the expression in his eyes as he kissed Emily's hand.

"My dear Ladies Cucklesham and Prestlefield, what a great pleasure it is to meet you so unexpectedly," he added hastily.

Lady Prestlefield nodded perfunctorily and then turned back to Mrs. Ewing. "Of course I remember your sister," she commented. "Who could forget your father's distress when his eldest daughter threw herself away on a penniless explorer? And then when not a single one of his daughters found a husband—oh, dear, you must forgive me, Mrs. Ewing," she cooed. "I quite forgot that you *did* find a husband, even if briefly."

Lucien's eyes narrowed. "That reminded me, Lady Prestlefield, of a story I heard last week. It was undoubtedly a pack of nonsense, I assure you. I am certain that you are not related to the Lord Prestlefield in question. . . ."

Sophie smiled at him. "We can be quite certain that dear Lady Prestlefield is not related to anyone scandalous," she said sweetly. "Do tell us the amusing story, however."

" 'Twas a terrible tale," Lucien commented. "I am not at all certain I should repeat it before ladies—but surely you have heard the tale yourselves?"

Lady Prestlefield's lips were a thin white line. "Scurrilous gossip bears no interest for me," she said repressively.

"Oh, but it has, of course, nothing to do with you," Lucien replied. "No, for this tale involved a tame goat—"

Lady Prestlefield rose from her seat. "I am afraid that I must leave."

"—and a priest," Lucien continued. He smiled cheerfully. "I am convinced that everyone involved must have drunk a prodigious amount of alcohol. And I believe that the judge ruled accordingly," he added.

"I myself know nothing of goats," Lady Prestlefield said coldly. "I try not to think of such unappealing topics. And no one in my family drinks to excess, ever."

Lady Cucklesham was thinking quickly. If Mrs. Ewing were to marry the extremely rich former marquis, the widow's social status would change radically. She rose to stand next to her friend.

"We were just leaving," she said, taking Lady Prestlefield firmly by the arm. "Mrs. Ewing, it has been a pleasure to meet you."

Lady Prestlefield bowed her head arctically. "I am not one to beat about the bush," she pronounced. "I have no idea why you are in *this* house, Mrs. Ewing, but you are not welcome in mine!" She left, dragging Lady Cucklesham behind her.

Lucien raised an eyebrow and kissed Emily's hand. "An odd thing," he said in a husky tone. "No matter whose house you choose to visit, I am certain that I would rather you were in *my* house."

Emily stilled for a moment, and color rose into her face as she looked up at him. Then she stood. "I must take Phoebe home," she said.

"May I apologize for my tiresome guests?" Gabby asked.

Emily Ewing's slight, weary smile lit up her eyes. "Not at all. I consider myself lucky. After all"—and she curtsied to Lucien—"a dragon slayer happened to be here as well." With a hasty bow, Lucien followed her from the room.

"Her little girl is beautiful, isn't she?" Sophie asked Gabby wistfully. Tears shone in her eyes.

"Why, what is the matter?" Gabby asked, startled.

"Foolishness," Sophie admitted. She impatiently dashed away a tear. "I lost a babe last summer, and I grow stupidly melancholic at times." Her voice shook.

Gabby squeezed her friend's hand. "It must have been terrible to lose a child."

"I am hoping for better luck this time," Sophie said, smiling a bit tearily.

"Oh, Sophie, that's wonderful! When will your baby arrive?"

"Perhaps in August," she replied. "I am not quite certain, as the doctor seems to think I am farther along than I had believed. I'm beginning to show already, and I've only missed two fluxes."

Then she visibly pulled herself together and turned to Gabby. "Well? What about last night?"

Gabby shook her head. "I couldn't do it! I just couldn't."

"Why not?"

"We had an argument, and then Quill went to his study—" She ground to a halt. "I could not interrupt him for no reason. And we don't . . . we don't sleep together at night."

"You must interrupt him," Sophie said positively.

"No, you don't understand. Quill has important work. Even the servants hesitate to disrupt his schedule."

"When I interrupt Patrick, he is invariably welcoming. Your husband will be as well."

Gabby could feel heat rise up her throat and face. "You don't understand, Sophie. You're so beautiful and sophisticated. It's easy for you. But I—we've only tried this once—"

"What on earth are you talking about? You are one of the most luscious ladies in the *ton,* Gabby. Half the gentlemen in London are lusting after you. *Especially* after you exhibited your chest to most of Lady Fester's guests," Sophie added impishly.

"Well," Gabby could feel her face getting warmer and warmer. "That still doesn't—"

"Why don't you do it again?" Sparks of mischief were fairly flying from Sophie's eyes.

"Do what again?"

"Lose your bodice! Do you still have that particular gown?"

"I expect so," Gabby said, chewing on her lower lip. "You mean that I should—"

"Exactly. Put on that gown, and then when Quill retires to his study, follow him. Position yourself in front of him and take a deep breath." Sophie giggled. "If he doesn't lose his self-control, he's not the man I take him for."

Gabby shook her head, but a smile was pulling at the corners of her mouth. "You don't know Quill. He never does *anything* without thinking it out first."

"Ha!" Sophie replied. "He's a man. Men believe they have brains, but it's a known fact that if their lower regions of the body are in use, their upper regions are incapable of activity."

"I'm in mourning," Gabby pointed out.

"No one will know what you wear in the privacy of your own home. Tell Quill that you are tired of black." Sophie stood up and shook out her skirts.

"Oh, now I can see a little curve!" Gabby cried, fascinated.

It was Sophie's turn to grow pink. "I hope you have just as exciting news for me on the morrow."

Gabby gave a nervous little laugh and then followed the duchess to the door. "You're a dear, you know," she said suddenly.

"I shall do an imitation of my mother," Sophie announced. "Fiddlesticks!" And she was gone.

Chapter 19

CODSWALLOP HELD OUT his silver tray. "Lord Breksby has called, my lady. His lordship has indicated that his visit is urgent, and he would like to see his Lord Dewland and yourself. The gentlemen await you in the library."

Lord Breksby didn't waste a moment. "Lady Dewland, I am sorry to bother you, but developments have necessitated that I speak to you again about the Holkar heir."

Gabby sat down, biting her lip. Quill stood at her right shoulder, ready to support her if the news was bad. And he had a sharp sense that it would be.

"It appears that Kasi Rao Holkar's father is now dying, and he must begin his training to take over the throne," Breksby stated.

"Kasi is not capable of ruling a country," Gabby protested. "He cannot yet count to ten. He will never be able to make the sort of decisions that are required to hold together the Holkars!"

"That remains to be seen," Lord Breksby said. "Naturally, if we discover that the boy is a simpleton, the English government will not support the actions of the East India Company."

"Kasi . . . I suppose one could say that Kasi is a simpleton," Gabby replied. "He is not quick in thought."

Breksby gave her a kindly look. "If Mr. Kasi Rao is merely slow, I am afraid that he will have to take on the throne of the Holkars. After all"—and Breksby gave a little giggle—"our English rulers have not always been among the brightest in the land.

"But we shall soon have an opportunity to judge the boy's intelligence," Breksby continued. Quill noticed that he was watching Gabby extremely closely. "Certain representatives of the East India Trading Company announced last night that they have discovered the whereabouts of Kasi Rao Holkar and in fact have taken him into custody, with the intent—"

Gabby squeaked in dismay. "They have found Kasi?"

Breksby nodded. "Mr. Kasi Rao is now in the custody of the East India Company, at the house of Mr. Charles Grant, to be exact. I gather that the prince will be introduced to various members of the English government tomorrow evening. This particular set of events is clearly being orchestrated by Mr. Grant, who is known among us as being imprudently in favor of extending the company's territory into central India. We shall surely not allow a simpleton to be put on the throne merely to suit Mr. Grant's wish to control the Marathas region."

"Do you know where they located my father's nephew?" Gabby asked. To Quill's mind, there was a peculiar urgency to her tone.

Breksby looked surprised. "Where? Why, where else but in London?"

To Quill's astonishment, Gabby's whole body relaxed. It was clear to him, at least, that Gabby was pleased with Breksby's answer. His curiosity sharpened.

"Are we invited to tomorrow's fete?" Quill asked.

"Certainly not," Breksby replied. "The last thing that Mr. Grant would welcome is the presence of Lady Dewland, who may be able to persuade my colleagues that Mr. Kasi Rao is incapable of rule. However, I am invited. And who is to say whom I shall bring on my arm? As it happens, I choose to be accompanied by a beautiful viscountess." He looked properly mischievous.

"There's nothing we can do to stop tomorrow's affair," Quill told Gabby. "The best you can do is stay close to Kasi so that he feels comfortable."

"I will do all I can to make this a pleasant occasion for the young prince," she replied sweetly. Quill frowned. He would have expected Gabby to make a passionate protest at the very idea of Kasi Rao being dragged into a room full of gawking strangers.

"If it is as you say," Breksby observed, "we shall immediately ascertain his inability to rule the Holkars. Mr. Kasi Rao will have one uncomfortable evening, and then we will inform Mr. Grant that his scheme has failed. I should tell you, however, that Mr. Grant seems quite confident that the boy will be able to take on his responsibilities in a timely manner."

"I shall accompany my wife," Quill remarked to Lord Breksby.

Breksby bowed. "I will be most happy to have you with us, my dear sir."

"I know Grant," Quill said rather grimly. "He is, in fact, one of the reasons that I sold my East India shares some years ago. He's a buffoon, and whatever business he's involved in is likely to be discreditable." In the last few years Charles Grant had become the dominant figure at India House. It was a pity, since he held the fervent belief that the only way to repay the company's huge debts was to acquire more and more Indian territory. One hardly needed to add that Grant increased company holdings any way he could—by fair means or foul.

"My feelings precisely," Breksby said cheerfully, standing up. "Lady Dewland, I shall look forward to tomorrow evening with unabated pleasure." He bent and kissed Gabby's hand with a flourish, swept Quill a bow, and left the room.

Gabby didn't dare look Quill in the face.

"You must be overset by these events," Quill said. "I am very sorry that Kasi has been taken into custody, Gabby." He watched his wife with a puzzled frown.

"Yes, I am distraught," she replied, rather vaguely.

When she didn't say anything further, Quill added, "Tomorrow I will make inquiries as to how Kasi Rao is faring. I still have friends among the East India Company I can call on."

Gabby nodded, still mute.

For his part, Quill stood by the door, trying to make himself leave. But his eyes kept drifting to Gabby's body. It was too easy to imagine pulling down her little cap sleeves and running his hand down—he wrenched his eyes away. He would never, never take an unwilling woman. And that's what she was. Unwilling.

He'd given it long, hard thought during nights of unhappy celibacy. Gabby's naïveté made her unwilling to have a sexual relationship with him; he judged that it would take him perhaps a week to cure her of her distaste for messy bedsheets and naked skin. But they hadn't a week. They could have another night, but after that the migraine would make him unavailable again. Try as he might, he couldn't think of a way around her shudder of distaste.

So he stood in the library doorway, cursing the lust that tied him to a female. Cursing the burning urge in his loins to bed his wife, to take her, to make love to her.

To never let her go.

SUPPER PASSED IN AN AGONY of polite conversation. She was wearing the dress that had caused a scandal, but Quill showed no signs of recognizing it, and she had never felt less attractive in her life. When Quill requested the salt salver, she had to gesture to a footman rather than hand it to him. She was afraid that the climax of her little performance would come far too soon and enliven the servants' evening rather than her husband's.

Precisely at nine o'clock, Quill finished a last bite of lemon tart. "I am afraid that it is time for me to retire to my study, my dear," he said, with the studied politeness that passed for marital intimacy between them.

She gulped. "Perhaps I shall visit you later in the evening, Quill?"

He looked startled. "Of course," he agreed after an infinitesimal pause. "I am happy to greet you at any time, naturally." His lips pressed the back of her hand for the merest moment and he was gone.

Gabby wandered upstairs with no real location in mind. Once in her room she drifted to the dressing table. Most of her hair was still neatly plaited into a coronet. With a sudden thought, she started pulling out hairpins. Quill liked her hair. Perhaps if she took it down, it would help her act seductive.

Because she didn't feel seductive. Never mind what Sophie had said. She felt overly plump and unattractive, a woman whose husband had threatened to go to a concubine.

When she had taken all the pins out, Gabby worked her fingers through the braids and let her hair fall in great rippling golden-brown sheaves down her back.

Thankfully she encountered no servants in the hallway, nor on the stairs leading to the floor below. Gabby knocked lightly and pushed the door open.

Quill was sitting at the far end of the long room, white sleeves pushed up around his elbows to protect his cuffs from ink. An oil lamp burned on the table, casting a warm light that made his hair shine with burgundy tints.

He looked up and instantly rose. "How nice to see you," he murmured, quite as if he hadn't said good night to her a mere fifteen minutes earlier.

Gabby felt a pulse of despair. Quill sounded as uninterested as a man married for twenty years. He would likely yawn if her breasts popped free of her gown. Still . . . what else could she do? She walked toward him across the room, consciously forcing her hips to sway, dip and sway, as she walked. Her hair felt like a bushy curtain. It likely made her look five times rounder than she already was, Gabby realized with a sense of horror.

"May I offer you a glass of sherry? Or ratafia?" He gestured toward a sideboard.

Gabby swallowed. "Yes, thank you." Her voice sounded oddly breathy. She accepted a glass of sherry and took such a large swallow that her glass was virtually emptied in one gulp. The liquor burned its way comfortingly down her chest. Quill looked faintly surprised, but refilled her glass.

"I received a letter from Lady Sylvia that might interest you," he remarked.

"Oh? What does she say?"

"The travel has done Mother good and she is less lachrymose, to use Lady Sylvia's phrase. And they met one of Peter's university friends in Switzerland, Simon Baker Wollaton, who has come to Greece with them. Apparently, Wollaton is quite amusing."

"That's good," Gabby said faintly. She made herself walk away from him. It wasn't clear whether he had even noticed that her hair was unbound. If so, he hadn't flickered an eyelash. She walked at random over to a bookshelf and stared blindly at a copy of Herbert Bone's *The London Perambulator*.

"This book looks interesting," she said, her throat tight, touching the volume with one finger.

Quill loomed up at her shoulder. "Not a scintillating read," he commented.

"Lud!" she exclaimed. "I didn't even hear you coming."

"Well, here I am." He leaned his forearm against the bookshelf. His arm was bronzed against his white linen sleeve. "Here I am," he repeated softly. "The puzzlement is that . . . here *you* are."

Gabby raised an eyebrow. Now that she was face to face with Quill, her apprehension was trickling away. Nerves, she thought. Naught more than nerves. "And why shouldn't I be here?" she asked, looking at him provocatively through her lowered lashes.

He shrugged. His eyes were hard, with a questioning gleam.

Yet Gabby felt more sure of herself every moment. Even her hair had miraculously transformed from a bushy thicket to a silken, sensual screen. She reached up and pulled some of it forward so that it hung over one breast.

When his jaw tightened, Gabby mentally noted the small victory.

"The question is," Quill said meditatively, "why my chaste wife has unexpectedly left off her blacks and dressed herself like Bathsheba about to leap into the bath— although I remember quite clearly that the said wife has no interest in marital pleasures."

Gabby swallowed. His reference to Bathsheba was more apt than he realized, given her plans to disrobe. Obviously it was time for the gown—time to lose the gown, rather. She gave a little twist and a shrug of her shoulders.

Nothing happened. Silk remained firmly anchored over her nipples.

"Gabby?" Quill's voice had taken on a sardonic tone.

"It was tedious upstairs, by myself," she said quickly. She surreptitiously wriggled her shoulders again.

Quill's eyes softened. "You know we cannot have a public life yet, Gabby. But in a very few months our mourning period will be over and we can go into society."

"Yes, I know."

"Unfortunately, the funeral and my illness put me far behind in my work. I cannot entertain you this evening." He took Gabby's elbow and turned her about.

"But I haven't even finished my sherry!" she protested.

"Please forgive me," Quill said. His tone was oddly angry, Gabby thought. She drank her second glass of sherry.

"All right," she said reluctantly. She thought of wiggling again, but she was afraid he might think she was suffering from an itch. And he looked so very, very uninterested.

Quill marched her over to the door of the study, but Gabby stopped there. She felt like a naughty child being ejected from the schoolroom.

"Surely you are not too busy to escort me to my chamber?" She managed to turn the question into a delicate reference to his manners.

There was a second's pause and then he answered evenly, "Naturally, I would be most pleased to do so." They walked silently beside each other up the curving staircase. Gabby trailed her fingertips on the satiny rail, trying desperately to think of another tactic.

Her heart was sinking. It seemed that Quill truly was busy. And she was the one who had banished him from her bed. Perhaps he'd put the whole business out of his mind, and that was why he was treating her like a nuisance. She was so dispirited that she didn't even dip and sway as she walked before him down the hallway.

As they paused at her bedchamber, Gabby reached toward the door a fraction of a second after Quill leaned around from behind her. Since Quill had already pushed the door open, she lurched through the entrance and stumbled into the room. She caught her toe on the edge of the carpet and plummeted to the floor, landing on her left shoulder.

For a second the only sound in the room was Gabby's heartfelt "Bloody blistering botheration!"

Only when she rolled to her back and gripped her sore shoulder—her *bare* shoulder—did she realize that her dress had given up its fight midway to the ground.

And only when she looked up and met her husband's eyes as he stood frozen in the doorway did Gabby realize that she had inadvertently scored all the points necessary to win this particular round of marital chess.

She propped herself up on her elbows, quite enjoying the fact that she had, to quote Quill on their wedding night, truly magnificent breasts.

"Well," she said, grinning shamelessly at her husband.

He cleared his throat. His eyes had gone quite black, she noted with satisfaction.

"I believe I've changed my mind about nudity in the confines of my bedchamber," Gabby explained. Really, the man looked moonstruck. As if the very sight of her had turned him into a want-wit.

She was able to cherish that notion for all of two seconds. Then Quill walked into the room and closed the door quietly behind him.

Chapter 20

HE KNELT BESIDE HER in one swift movement. "Am I to understand that you have changed your mind?"

Gabby swallowed. "Yes," she said, rather faintly. "That is, I have an idea, Quill."

"An idea?" He reached out and caressed her sore elbow. Then he brushed her hair back over her shoulder.

"Perhaps your migraines are related to your hip injury," she said, trying to ignore the way she was sitting half-clothed on the floor.

"My doctors have concluded that they are the result of a concussion I received in the accident." Quill was definitely not listening to her.

A honey-dark hand rounded the curve of her breast. His thumb trailed across her nipple and Gabby shuddered inside, excitement and nervousness beating a double rhythm.

"Luscious Gabby," he murmured. He looked at her with his wicked smile. "I'm glad you changed your mind."

"Quill, did you hear what I said? If the migraines were connected to your hip injury rather than to your concussion, then—"

He stretched himself out on the carpet next to her and began kissing her shoulder, little nipping kisses.

She started over. "Perhaps the migraines are the result of your hip injury."

Quill shook his head and answered patiently. "I exercise my hip frequently, Gabby. I never suffer migraines as a result. And concussions are known to cause headaches."

She pushed his head away from her breast. "Please listen to me!"

"I don't want to," Quill whispered against her skin. "Gabby, I exercise daily, and don't suffer headaches as a consequence. The only activities that give me migraines are sexual intercourse and riding horses."

"Riding horses?" Gabby tried to pull her rational self together. One of Quill's hands drifted to her stomach and was making little teasing circles, pushing at the crumpled gauze of her dress, threatening to go lower.

Abruptly he suckled her. When he finally raised his head, his breath had become a flame in his chest, an erotic hymn in his throat. "There's no escape from migraines, love. My doctors have all agreed that motion exacerbates the old head injury. There's no mystery about it."

"You walk all the time," she protested. "Obviously, not all motion causes problems."

"True. But this is not a good time for conversing, Gabby," he added, lowering his mouth to her breast again.

She couldn't help it; she gasped as he roughly pulled a nipple into his mouth. Her body involuntarily turned toward his, asking for his weight, his pressure, again.

"Mmmm," Quill muttered, his hand sliding seductively down her back. He pushed it under the drape of her gown.

Gabby squirmed and her breath came harshly. He cupped her bottom and swung her toward him, picking her up in one smooth motion.

"You shouldn't!" Gabby said, panic in her voice. "If your hip is the cause of your headaches, you shouldn't pick me up."

He shook his head, teasingly running his lips across hers. "No, sweetheart. That's not a logical conclusion. Besides, I don't mind a migraine now and then."

And she could tell he *didn't* mind, that he wouldn't begrudge a moment of pain for the time in her arms.

Quill lay her on the bed and then slowly, slowly pulled the infamous gown from her body, letting it fall to the floor. She was wearing silk stockings and shoes, nothing else. "You're so beautiful." His voice was a caress.

Gabby took a deep breath and resisted the impulse to dive under the covers. "I would like to try to make love without straining your hip, please," she said, forcing her voice to sound authoritative. He may not care about the headaches, but she did.

"An experiment?" Quill's eyebrows arched. "I have a good deal more experience than you do, Gabby. I honestly feel that you will be more comfortable with old-fashioned methods."

He was trembling with the effort of standing casually before her. He was fighting off an overpowering urge to fall on her and push himself inside without grace or forethought. He let his eyes range from the delicate bend of her knee to her shining, tangled hair. Slowly he drew off her slippers, his fingers lingering on the arches of her feet.

"What happened to you, wife?" His voice was thick in his throat. Willy-nilly he leaned forward and curved a hand possessively around Gabby's creamy breast. "You're naked in the open, as if you never protested nudity."

She glanced down at her uncovered breast, at his hand on her bare skin, and didn't bother replying. If he thought she had turned into a wanton who didn't realize that her dress was on the floor, so be it. Her eyes sought his. "Do you have any ideas, Quill?"

He had no idea what she was talking about. "Ideas?" He came onto the bed and his large body loomed over hers. He pulled a rosy nipple into his mouth again.

Her hands clutched his shoulders. "A plan," she gasped. "Plan?"

Gabby bit back a moan. "For this," she insisted.

Quill raised his head. "What are you talking about, Gabby? I didn't need a plan the last time I took you to bed, I can assure you."

Her breath was catching in her chest. "How—how— you didn't listen to me!" She pushed at the knee wedged between her legs.

Quill shook his head. Then he ran a frustrated hand through his hair. "I'm listening. What are you trying to say?"

"You put weight on your hip," she said, pointing. "That's your scarred hip, isn't it?"

Quill closed his eyes for a moment. "I *told* you what the doctors said." But from the depths of his lust-driven body, a silent voice spoke. Do whatever she wants, advised the voice. Otherwise she might exile you from the bedchamber again.

"Right," he said, smiling down at his wife. "We will spare my hip." He stroked her stomach as if he were caressing a cat. Shivers followed in the wake of his fingers. Suddenly he rubbed his thumb across silky damp curls, pulling her trembling thighs apart with his other hand.

Gabby gave a funny, half-strangled gulp. Quill withdrew his hand and moved backward, swinging his legs off the bed. He left her shaking, with a fluid burning heat between her legs. "Quill?" She reached her arms out to him. Her eyes were a dusky golden color and hazy with desire.

Obviously his wife had abruptly found herself in the throes of the same lamentable lust that had plagued him for the last fortnight. Suddenly Quill started thoroughly enjoying himself. "You know," he said lazily, "I think we should outline our plan. So that we're both clear about our duties."

Gabby read the challenge in his voice and responded instinctively. "That sounds like a good idea," she said airily.

"Well?" He stood in front of her, large and imposing, his legs spread, an amused smirk in his eyes that told her of secret laughter. "Why don't you detail the first step?"

"Oh." She cleared her throat. "Will you remove your clothing, please? I would prefer not to be in this state alone." She registered the even tone of her own voice with a sense of gratitude.

At that, Quill smiled a crooked, sensual smile that didn't reveal his surprise, if he felt any. "I think not, Gabby. What if I strain my hip? You had better do it for me."

She sat up and came to her feet. Her heart was pounding unevenly. "Of course," she responded, quite as if he'd asked for a second cup of tea.

She began to untie his neckcloth.

"If we are to spare my hip," Quill remarked, "you shall have to do most of the work."

"Of course," she murmured.

He grinned. "Gabby, how much do you remember of our wedding night?"

Gabby pulled his neckcloth from around his neck and dropped it neatly over a chair. "I remember everything, of course." She avoided his eyes as she began unbuttoning his shirt.

"If I am to put no weight on my hip," Quill said, tone soft as a devil's, "you will have to be more . . . forthright than you were that night, my dear."

Gabby swallowed. "Naturally," she replied without expression. She reached the last button and eased the shirt off his shoulders. His chest was a smooth sun-brown, without a single hair. Bewitched, she drew her fingers uncertainly over his taut muscles.

"Do you understand what I just told you?" Now it was Quill who was having trouble keeping his voice even.

"Mmmm," she replied. True, Gabby didn't have the faintest idea what it meant to be forthright in the bed, but she didn't feel like fussing about it. She brought her hands up to his neck and let them slide down his chest again. Little shudders followed in her wake. Daringly, she leaned forward and kissed the heated skin her hands had just caressed.

Quill cleared his throat. He didn't know how much longer he could keep up this civil air. He was throbbing so hard that his trousers might not even be able to slide down his hips. "The rest of my clothes, Gabby?"

In fact, he'd lost his urbane tone and his voice burst with hungry violence.

But she fumbled with his trouser buttons, and in the end he shucked the remainder of his clothing himself.

In a lightning-quick lunge, he grabbed her and fell backward onto the bed, pulling Gabby on top of him. Her eyes were dreamy, cheeks flushed as she straddled him. Then her eyes widened with shock and a glimmer of understanding came into them.

"Do you think?"

Quill didn't, couldn't, answer. In reply he clasped her hips and lifted her into position.

Gabby choked and instinctively pressed forward.

"Yes!" Quill whispered fiercely. "Come to me."

Gabby trembled, caught on a wave of embarrassment so

acute she couldn't move. She was poised above him un-clothed. She quivered with mortification. Naked in the open. It was depraved! At least before she had been hidden underneath him.

But then she looked down and there was Quill—his beautiful gray-green eyes asking desperately for something only she could give. She forgot her exposed flesh and leaned forward, kissing him gently as she nudged downward against his heat and demand.

He groaned against her lips and forced them open, pos-sessing her sigh with his mouth, taking her breath into his lungs.

"You're making me forget," Gabby whispered when his lips moved from her mouth to her neck, leaving a scorching trail behind. Hands tightened on her hips as if he was about to pull her down.

"Gabby . . ." His voice was a plea.

Despite herself, a little squeak broke from her lips as she pushed down again. And pulled back. And fell downward again—deeper and sweeter. The breath was burning in her chest. She tried again, and again. Deeper each time. Quill's face was agonized.

"Gabby!" he said roughly, and she knew that in a mo-ment his self-control would break and he would pull her hard onto his body.

"Yes?" she whispered sweetly, and sank down until they were joined together like puzzle pieces made by a master.

A harsh cry broke from Quill's lips and he arched his hips off the bed, holding her hips tightly against him.

Now it was her turn to cry out. But then: "Stop that," she gasped. "You are not allowed to move your hip!"

For a moment a ravishing smile lit Quill's eyes. "You drive a hard bargain, love." His voice was husky, taut with control. A hand found its way to the front of her thighs and tried to distract her.

Gabby fell silent, intent on learning the rhythm of the rise and fall. She rocked awkwardly. She rose quickly and sank too slowly. She drove him half to distraction. . . . Quill ground his teeth and stroked his wife's back. He rediscovered the delights of having a breast temptingly near his mouth. He counseled himself in patience and tried to keep in mind the fact that awkward lovemaking with Gabby was ecstasy compared to lying in a bed without Gabby.

He learned patience and then abruptly lost that hard-won virtue. His muscular body arched roughly upward, a thumping rise that sent a bolt of lightning through his body.

Reprimanded, he regained patience and whispered loving words he never meant to speak again.

Finally . . . finally, by the grace of God, his wife found a rhythm in her beautiful hips. Began to rise and fall in a dance that made the blood pound through his body in a delicious cadence. His heartbeat meshed with hers.

And then, as Gabby's neck arched back and she cried aloud, Quill gripped her hips and thrust upward. Drove into her with every inch of strength he had and heard only dimly the wild cry that burst from Gabby's throat as her body convulsed and she fell forward onto his chest.

It was enough. It was more than enough. He clutched her against him, all of her beautiful soft curves, his own jasmine-scented wife, and gave her everything he had.

And it was enough.

In fact, Quill was glad that her face was in his shoulder so she couldn't see his own face. He felt as if his soul had jumped out of his own body, it was so . . . enough.

Instead, he said hoarsely, "That was very good for a first try, Gabby." And then, ashamed of himself, he was glad to find that she had fallen asleep, right there on top of him, without hearing his foolish comment. He kissed her ear and her hair over and over, in an excess of tenderness that was profoundly embarrassing. *It's gratitude,* he told himself. Gratitude for being saved from a fast.

It wasn't until six in the morning that Quill understood that intuitive medical diagnoses should be seen as one of Gabby's virtues, not the least of which was a masterful sense of rhythm. Rosy light crept into the corners of the room, but no ominous purple shadows flashed at the corners of his vision. His stomach didn't lurch when he carefully eased Gabby's sleeping body off his shoulder and stood up. He *was* stiff. His hip was sore, as if he'd worked too hard in the orchard. It protested when he stretched. But his head was miraculously clear. A grin of pure, unadulterated joy broke over Quill's face.

He leaned over and ran a hand up Gabby's satiny thighs. In her sleep, she sighed and her legs fell slightly open. Shuddering, Quill forced himself to back away. He had a shrewd notion that his hip had taken all the motion it could handle at the moment. But tonight . . . ah, tonight.

It was enough to make a devil holler hymns.

Chapter 21

EMILY SLOWLY ROSE from her desk and cast a regretful look at her stained fingers. Somehow she had to learn to use a quill without endless splatters.

Lucien Boch bowed before her. Emily curtsied. When she looked up, she found that he had moved to stand just before her.

"Emily," he said huskily.

She opened her mouth to say something polite, but the words died in her throat.

"I came to make certain that your dragon did not reappear," Lucien said. "But he isn't here."

"No," Emily managed. "Mr. Hislop did not visit this morning."

Lucien took her hands in his and turned them over, looking at her beautiful, dirty fingers. "Perhaps you should wear gloves."

"They cost too much to ruin with ink," Emily said, pride in her voice. She tried to tug her hands away.

He kept her right hand and raised it to his lips, pressing her palm against his mouth.

"I would like to buy you gloves," he said suddenly.

Emily tugged harder at her hand. "So would the dragon," she pointed out. "I buy my own gloves, monsieur."

"Do you speak French, Emily?"

"I prefer Mrs. Ewing. And yes, I speak some French. I had a tutor as a child."

"Forgive me the impertinence. I have thought about you as Emily, and it slipped out. I should like to know more about your childhood."

It was a very odd conversation, to Emily's mind. What they were saying seemed to have little to do with the way he was looking at her. Or, she very much feared, the way she was looking back at him.

He was beautiful, this Frenchman. He was just a half head taller than she was, which meant that she could see long eyelashes curving against his cheek as he looked down at her hands. Her heart was pounding in her throat now.

"Mr. Boch," she said. She felt like an idiot child, unable to form words.

"I would like to invite you——" Lucien began. But he stopped. Her eyes were the blue-gray of a sea mist, and they looked at him so innocently. He forgot that he was old, and widowed, and no good for her. He forgot that Emily had her whole life before her and deserved a man who was not wounded by life. He forgot it all in the blue-gray depths of her eyes.

He kissed her without touching her. He even dropped the hand he held, moved forward one step and bent his head. They were much of the same height, after all.

And she—the lovely, untouched Emily who *deserved* a better man than he—Emily kissed him back. He knew in an instant she had never been married. Her mouth trembled against his and then slipped open with a sigh.

Lucien kissed her, and stopped. He drew back and

looked down at her and somehow managed a sensible tone of voice. "I prefer Emily because Mr. Ewing never existed."

"Mr. Ewing died in a carriage accident," she said. Her knees were weak and she knew perfectly well that she ought, as a gentlewoman, to order the man from the room. He was trying to seduce her. He was undoubtedly planning to turn her into his paramour, given that he wanted to buy her gloves. And yet she couldn't work up any indignation. Her heart was pounding too hard.

Lucien bent forward again. Emily swayed, slightly, as he took her mouth and his arms pulled her hard against him. She gasped as he tasted her sweetness, tasted something that was not innocence but desire.

When he raised his head again, she didn't try to escape. She simply looked back at him. He blurted out, "I should like you to marry me."

She said nothing.

"Forgive me," Lucien said awkwardly. "I should have phrased that more . . . Mrs. Ewing, will you do me the honor of becoming my wife?"

Emily swallowed. She had thought about Lucien Boch endlessly in the last months. She had thought she knew why he called, morning after morning, why he invited himself to lunch. Either he owned a rival magazine or he was a rake planning to make her into a fallen woman. On the whole, she had preferred the second explanation. But marriage had never occurred to her.

"I do not have a dowry," she said. "My father threw me out of the house years ago. He gave us a small sum of money, and said there would be no more. And he has not wavered in his opinion."

"Your father is a blockhead."

He had taken hold of her hands again and was pressing

her palms to his lips. Emily felt a treacherous wash of heat. "I can't marry you," she said rather desperately. "I'm a social outcast. I have no family. I have responsibilities— Phoebe, and Louise . . ."

Lucien leaned forward again because he couldn't stop himself. He pressed a kiss on her mouth. "You are my Emily," he said. "I want you. I want you in my home, and in my bed. I don't need a dowry, and I don't have a family either." He stopped, remembering all the reasons he had not to get married.

When he didn't continue, Emily tremblingly raised one hand to his shoulder. "Did you have a family once?" Her soft whisper fell into the silence.

The agony in Lucien's eyes blinded her, and she almost looked away, but didn't.

"You might not want to marry me, Emily. My marquise's name was Felice. My son was Michel. I didn't . . . I couldn't protect them. When I was away, trying to secure passage to England, they, they—"

She crossed the few inches that stood between them and brought her arms around his neck. She could see the shadowed darkness in his eyes. "They died," she finished for him. "I'm so sorry, Lucien. Now they live here." She pressed her hand to his heart.

Lucien cursed himself. He hadn't cried in years—in *years*. He hadn't cried when he ran desperately through the charred remains of the chateau, when a shout told him that the men had found the bodies of his wife and child, when he buried them in each other's arms, as they were in death.

So Emily cried for him. Huge tears filled her beautiful eyes and ran down her cheeks. Her shoulders jerked and she pressed her face against his shoulder. His arms went around her reflexively.

"It was a long time ago," he said.

"I suppose there is no time long enough, is there, Lucien?"

There was a heartbeat of silence.

"Probably not. I should not have asked you to marry me, *mignonne*. I am not good for it. Although, although you are the——" He stopped again.

Emily seemed to have stopped crying. All he could see was a smooth sweep of golden hair, but she wasn't trembling anymore. Her arms were still hard around his neck.

"Hush" was all she said.

Lucien thought for a second and then brought his arms down from her back and picked her up. She weighed nothing, his Emily. He walked over to a comfortable settee and sat down, tucking her against his shoulder again. Then he started dropping kisses in her hair. Which wasn't, he realized, the right thing for him to be doing, given that he had just withdrawn his marriage proposal.

"I will marry you."

Lucien stopped kissing her hair. "I don't want to be married for pity," he said, his brusque tone at odds with his heart. His heart didn't care why she married him, as long as she did.

"I think I shall marry you for the gloves you will buy me," Emily said, raising her head and looking in his eyes. "Will you deny me gloves?" She took one ink-tipped finger and pressed it against his mouth. There were tears on her cheeks.

Lucien pulled out the two pins that held her cap. "Where is Mr. Ewing?" He tossed the scrap of lace onto the floor.

"There was no Mr. Ewing," she admitted at last. "I was afraid when we came to London. I thought we would be safer if I appeared to be a widow. So. I am accepting your offer of marriage. Will you play the reprobate and withdraw your offer?"

It seemed to be out of his hands. Lucien bent his head and Emily kissed him first.

She had made the most foolish, most irrational decision of her life, and happiness was singing in her heart. She had agreed to marry a man whom she had known a scant few months. She knew nothing about him—nothing.

Nothing and everything.

"Perhaps you are right," she said teasingly. "Perhaps I should weigh your offer against Mr. Hislop's. Of course, I am not entirely certain that his offer is for *marriage*, precisely."

Lucien pulled her tightly against him.

"I'll run him through if he touches you," he said, surprising himself with his vehemence.

"Then I shall marry you to save Mr. Hislop." Emily laughed. "And to support my favorite glover."

"You will marry me because you love me," Lucien said. There was only a tremor of a question in his voice.

Emily's lips trembled under his. "Because I love you," she whispered. "And . . . because you love me, Lucien."

He held her so tightly that she could feel the imprint of his buttons through her gown and chemise. "I do," he said finally. "God help me, Emily, but I do love you."

THE RECEPTION FOR Kao Rasi Holkar, heir to the Holkar throne, was held at East India House in Leadenhall Street. Lord Breksby was at his most genial as his carriage turned into Leadenhall.

Gabby sat next to Quill in silence, wondering whether it would be horribly gauche to slip her hand into his. She was nervous about the evening ahead of them. Then, when they were almost there, his large hand enclosed hers, and a warm glow lit her heart.

The East India Company had spared no expense for the reception. The small stone courtyard was lined with riflemen wearing gaudy uniforms and strange flat caps. As the party entered, they all snapped to attention, holding their rifles very straight. Gabby shivered and hurried past.

The walls of the entrance hall were lined with glass cabinets. Gabby drifted over to one as a footman took her pelisse. Inside was a collection of jeweled birds, studded with rubies and garnets.

A voice sounded at her ear. "These are some exhibits from the East India Company Museum, my lady. The museum is also housed in Leadenhall, if you would like to visit it at your leisure."

Gabby drew back. An imposing butler stood before her. She asked, "Are these the plunder from the capture of Seringapatam?"

The butler bowed affirmatively. "They are. They were sent as a gift for the queen and are here by special permission of Her Majesty."

Quill slipped his hand under Gabby's elbow. "What are you looking at, love?"

Her eyes were shining with anger. "I recognized that bird," she said, indicating a large ruby-encrusted statue of a cock. "It was taken during the capture of Seringapatam. I played with it as a child." She turned away suddenly and walked toward the far end of the hallway, ignoring the rest of the cabinets.

They entered the reception hall to find that the receiving line had just dissolved. There was a moment's confusion, and then a man with long, drawn cheeks and a small amount of wavy hair tied back at his neck rushed toward them.

"My *dear* Lord Breksby!" he cried with apparent delight. "I scarcely dared hope that you would be able to join us today, that you would take note of our small endeavors!"

Breksby bowed. "Mr. Grant, the pleasure is all mine, naturally. May I present my guests? I have been so bold as to bring a few acquaintances to your gathering."

Mr. Grant's face was a trifle bleak as he cast a quick look over the group, even though his words were welcoming enough. "Could it be? Could you have done us the inexpressible honor of bringing the daughter of my esteemed friend, Richard Jerningham, to my little gathering?" He bowed in Gabby's direction. She curtsied in reply.

Quill noticed that there was a little smile playing around the corner of Breksby's mouth.

"Indeed," Breksby replied, "I have brought Gabrielle Jerningham to your party, Charles, although she is now the Viscountess Dewland, as I am persuaded you must be aware. I was quite, quite convinced that you would wish her to greet your rediscovered prince. And this is Viscount Dewland."

Quill thought that Grant's face was looking a trifle longer than it was when the party entered. But he bowed politely enough.

Breksby's voice was practically shimmering with naughty pleasure. "Now, we would hate to waste a moment before allowing the viscountess to meet her dear, dear childhood companion—"

But he was interrupted by a booming voice. "What a true pleasure it is to see you here, my lady, and looking so blooming." It was Colonel Hastings, who bowed low before Gabby. "This is a happy day for the East India Company," he said, addressing Quill. "A *happy* day! The governor-general is most pleased, most pleased indeed. We have located the prince, Kasi Rao, and he will be restored to his rightful place on the Holkar throne imminently, yes, imminently!"

Quill noticed with some interest that Mr. Charles Grant appeared to be grinding his teeth.

But Colonel Hastings was oblivious. "Mr. Grant, you *must* allow me to do the honors. I shall introduce the lovely viscountess to her childhood companion, our honored guest, the Indian prince!"

Gabby gave Quill a helpless look, but Colonel Hastings was towing her into the throng of people. Quill had turned to follow when he felt a hand on his sleeve.

It was Charles Grant. "I didn't expect to see you here, Dewland. I was rather under the impression that you had decided to eschew all contact with India men." His tone was dry.

"I did," Quill replied. "However, I could hardly miss such an emotional moment as this is bound to be," he added gently. "My wife is about to be reunited with her childhood companion, a boy who was raised as a brother to her."

Grant seemed to have nothing to say to that.

"A boy about whom my wife has told me so much," Quill added thoughtfully. "Why, I am alight with anticipation myself."

He cast a glance at Grant's hand, which still held his sleeve. The hand dropped away.

Quill bowed, very slightly. "Your servant." He turned and walked into the crowd, searching for Gabby.

Since he was taller than many of those at the reception, he spotted Gabby and Colonel Hastings almost immediately. They were standing before a slender lad, presumably Kasi Rao, who had his back to Quill. Gabby was in the midst of a low curtsy and he couldn't see her face. Then Kasi bowed as well, deftly tucking the ceremonial sword slung at his side out of the way. A beautiful smile broke over Gabby's face—and a puzzled frown over Quill's.

He stopped for a moment, watching his wife chatter in Hindi to the prince. Colonel Hastings was looking dewy-eyed, clearly moved by the emotional reunion of two childhood companions.

Quill made his way around little clusters of people until he stood at Gabby's side. Gabby looked up at him, eyes glowing. "Why, dearest," she cooed. "Just imagine! Here is Kasi Rao, all grown up. Why, I would hardly recognize him. Of course, it had been *so* long since I'd seen him."

Mr. Grant popped up at Quill's elbow, his face wreathed in smiles. "I see that our long-lost prince has met with your approval, my lady." Surely it wasn't just Quill who caught heartfelt relief in Charles Grant's voice.

"Well, how could he not?" Gabby's eyes were liquid innocence. "I have not seen Kasi since he was a mere child, and I am remarkably impressed by his"—she waved her hand—"his elegance, his demeanor, his princely bearing."

The supposed Kasi Rao smiled at her. Quill had to admit that the lad was the best impostor he'd ever seen. He looked exactly as one might expect an Indian prince to look, with large brown eyes and an innate sense of majesty. Where on earth had they found him? Not in a gutter in Jaipur, that was for certain.

Quill shook his head and slipped away. Unless he missed his bet, his wily wife had more to do with the appearance of the "lost" prince than he had known. In fact, he wouldn't be surprised if she had manipulated Grant into finding the lad in the first place. So much for Grant thinking that he was the next thing to the English government. Lady Gabrielle Dewland was running circles around him.

Briefly thereafter, the Indian prince was formally presented with a jewel-studded crown, courtesy of the East India Company. Colonel Hastings read aloud a letter written by the governor-general himself, Richard Colley Wellesley, for the occasion.

The restoration of Kasi Rao Holkar to his hereditary rights by the aid of the British power was, in Wellesley's hyperbolic prose, *highly creditable to the justice and honor of the British.*

Gabby stood just to the side of Kasi Rao Holkar, her face alight with approval and pride. She curtsied gracefully to each and every member of the Board of Directors, reiterating her pleasure in the fact that they had managed to locate the lost prince and were restoring him to his rightful place.

Quill said nothing and merely threw Gabby an ironic look when she chattered breathlessly in the coach about how lovely it was to meet her childhood friend again.

But Breksby was no fool. He kept looking at Gabby with an assessing air, until he finally turned to Quill and said, "Do you know who the man is?"

Gabby stopped mid-chatter.

Quill shrugged. "No. But he seems to be a decent candidate for the throne."

Breksby turned back to Gabby with a charming smile. "You see, my lady, soon after you arrived from India, we became aware of your visits to the house of Mrs. Malabright. Naturally, we never shared that information with the East India Company directors. However, it appears that you have stolen a march on us, have you not?"

"I don't know what you mean," Gabby said with some dignity.

"Mr. Kasi Rao Holkar, heir to the Holkar throne, was happily living with Mrs. Malabright in Sackville Street, and has since moved to Devon," Breksby replied. "We in the Foreign Office were quite content to leave things as such. We decided that you were correct to fear that the East India Company would make the boy into a figurehead. But I admit that I was expecting you to expose Charles Grant's prince as a fake, my lady."

Gabby scooted closer to Quill and took his hand. "The East India Company almost found Kasi. I had to do something."

"But how on earth did you manage to produce another Kasi for them to discover?"

Gabby looked embarrassed. "He will be an excellent ruler."

"I do not question that. But I am curious who he is."

"His name is Jawsant Rao Holkar," Gabby said. "He is one of Tukoji Holkar's illegitimate sons."

"Tukoji has two such sons, doesn't he? How did you decide which son to place on the throne, Lady Dewland?" Breksby's voice was dry, but not disrespectful.

"There really wasn't much of a choice. You see, Jawsant's younger brother is docile and would never be able to ward off the company's possession of the Holkars. Jawsant is rather militant, *and* he is a very good actor. You could see how well he did tonight. He is quite adept at appearing malleable, although he already led a successful battle, last year, when he was fourteen."

Breksby smiled ruefully. "I can see that your information is much more thorough than ours, Lady Dewland."

"It wasn't as organized as it sounds," Gabby admitted. "I had an idea, and so I wrote to a number of people, including Jawsant's mother, Tulasi Bai. Tulasi Bai has been running the region for over two years. Undoubtedly she will continue to rule the court, and Jawsant will control the army."

Gabby paused delicately. "There is, of course, the possibility that Jawsant will attempt to penetrate the company's territory. I believe he is particularly interested in Bundelkhand."

Quill grinned down at his wife. "Not that you, as a mere female, could speculate on such a complicated subject."

But she was biting her lip and paying him no attention. "Lord Breksby, do you think that perhaps the English government might simply leave Jawsant as ruler? Because I assure you that Kasi Rao could not take over the Holkar throne!" Now her voice had all the strained passion that Quill would have expected the previous day.

"No one could have anything but admiration for you, Lady Dewland. But as it happens, I think that perhaps this knowledge would prove overtaxing to other members of the government. And you know, old as I am, my memory is growing quite erratic. I believe I shall forget that we ever had this conversation."

Gabby clutched Quill's hand. "Thank you!" she breathed.

"Lady Dewland, naturally I speak hypothetically, but if you were to receive any letters from the Holkar court in the future—oh, say from Tulasi Bai—would you be willing to share information with the British government?"

"Perhaps," Gabby said. "I will always be glad to help in any way that I deem suitable, my lord."

Lord Breksby's sigh indicated that he knew precisely how much information the Foreign Office could expect to garner from the viscountess's correspondence. "This has been a most interesting evening, Lady Dewland," he said. "Did you know that I am retiring from my post in the very near future?"

"I believe that my husband informed me of that happy event," she said, giving the retiring minister a sweet smile.

"And I'm pleased to be doing so," Breksby said with a

chuckle. "I would be worried that you'd turn me into a figurehead and run the Foreign Office yourself."

Gabby's enchanting, husky giggle escaped. "Fie, sir! All I did was protect my sweet Kasi, as you well know. I have no ambitions to interfere with British foreign policy."

There was a moment's unconvinced silence in the carriage.

Gabby leaned her head against her husband's shoulder. They might not believe her, but she was being absolutely truthful. Her next project was Quill.

Chapter 22

SUDHAKAR STEPPED OFF the *Fortitude* onto English soil with a sense of profound relief. The journey had been exhausting. He found Calcutta to be conspicuously unpleasant, a great mass of people running this way and that. Each private gentleman was attended by twenty servants at least, if you counted the footmen who ran before his palanquin and the *bahareas* who carried it. Shouting and screaming echoed in the streets. One couldn't take a stroll without being nearly burned by torchbearers or pushed aside by *nakeeves* clearing the way for their masters. He found the number of elephants plodding down the streets particularly irksome, given their propensity to void while in motion.

And he had to admit that he missed his village. At home there was only one such elevated personage—Richard Jerningham. And Jerningham employed only one *nakeeve* to clear his way and one page to carry an umbrella to shade him from the sun. Sudhakar had always thought that Jerningham was a pompous bore. Now he realized that he hadn't even guessed the pomposity of which Jerningham might have been capable.

In contrast, life on the *Fortitude* had been a familiar experience. The four passengers appeared to be trapped in a small floating village, ensnared by their anxieties, prejudices, and sentiments. At first, the English gentlemen ignored Sudhakar, viewing him with supercilious disdain, as such types surveyed all those they believed to be in a humbler walk of life. To Sudhakar, this was familiar, since Jerningham had affected the same sneering contempt—until he realized that Sudhakar was the only English-speaking chess player in the village.

After a few weeks the tides of boredom caused the three Englishmen to drift toward the elderly Indian gentleman. They were young and returning to England after serving, Sudhakar suspected, a less-than-stellar period in the East India army. Soon the four of them took to playing cards every night.

At least one of the men, Mr. Michael Edwardes, privately admitted to being quite impressed by the native—quite impressed. Sudhakar was neatly dressed, with respectable manners and an intelligent mien. Perhaps more than an intelligent mien. The man would get a discomforting gleam in his eye whenever Michael found himself in a bit of a fib. But really, one couldn't tell the truth about the army. It wasn't done. One had to make up some stories of daring attacks; otherwise military life would sound as disappointing and mundane as it had been in fact.

Once the boat docked, all three young men, including Michael, trotted eagerly into the twilight, completely forgetting their promises to guide Sudhakar through London's twisty streets. Michael only remembered late that night, while he was telling his sister Ginny about the Battle of Tajpur (adding a slight gloss to what would otherwise have been a very tedious account). Something made him think of Sudhakar and he struck his knee and swore.

"What is it?" Ginny asked. She was a bright woman who was having trouble reconciling her memories of her timid little brother with his heroic exploits on the battlefield.

"I forgot all about an old Indian gaffer on the vessel," Michael said. "I promised I'd get him safely to—where the devil was he going? St. James's Square, I think."

"Oh, that's off the park," Ginny said. "A really *fine* address, Michael."

Her brother shrugged. "Perhaps he was an uncle to the butler or something. Now, let me tell you what happened the day after I took the Raja prisoner."

SUDHAKAR HAD NOT REALLY EXPECTED aid from the Englishmen. They were young and foolish. Nor did he need such help. A constable directed him to the row of waiting hackneys.

London, Sudhakar quickly realized, was forty times worse than Calcutta. Carriages, horses, and passersby jostled for space. The noise was more piercing than that in Calcutta's streets. Where were all these horses going so quickly and so dangerously? His vehicle was nearly struck by a speeding carriage, and as he looked back, he distinctly saw one of the footmen clinging to its back almost lose his balance. The man would certainly have fallen to his death. In retrospect, slow and smelly elephants seemed marvelously safe.

Thirty minutes later he was facing a very superior type of servant who looked as starched as Richard Jerningham himself. Sudhakar bowed politely and salaamed for good measure. "The viscountess is expecting my arrival."

Codswallop was far more intelligent than Mr. Michael Edwardes, and he had spent his entire life judging degrees of nobility. It was clear to him at a glance that Mr. Sudhakar was the equivalent of a nobleman, over there in India. Something about the way he held his head.

Codswallop bowed in return and then turned to a footman. "John! Take the gentleman's bag to the East Chamber."

Sudhakar gently held up his hand. "I prefer to keep it by my side, thank you."

"Unfortunately the master and mistress are not at home. May I offer you some light refreshment?"

Sudhakar ate a small repast in the dining room and then placidly retired to the East Chamber, telling Codswallop that he would await the viscountess's bidding in the morning.

"Yes, the very best manners," Codswallop muttered to himself that evening. It was mind-opening, that's what. He, Codswallop, tended to put Indians and Irish in the same group—don't hire 'em, as his dad would say. But there are always exceptions in life.

QUILL SAID NOTHING to Codswallop's announcement of their unexpected visitor. He noted that Gabby's face took on a happy glow and that Mr. Sudhakar had been placed in the best spare chamber. Their guest must be formidable indeed to have impressed Codswallop. He waited until the door to Gabby's chamber closed behind them.

"So who *is* Mr. Sudhakar?" he asked, casually stopping Gabby as she reached out to the bellpull to summon Margaret.

"But I told you all about him!" Gabby exclaimed, sitting down before her dressing table. "He is quite my dearest friend in India—the doctor who specializes in poisons, do you remember now? I cannot wait to see him again. It might sound odd"—she cast a slightly ashamed glance at

Quill as she started taking down her hair—"but I miss him far more than I miss my father."

"He sounds like an extremely worthy person," Quill replied. "But why is Mr. Sudhakar in England?" He waited, his face impassive, eyes on Gabby. Surely her cheeks were looking a bit rosy?

"Oh, well," Gabby said, "Sudhakar was very helpful to me with the whole scheme to save Kasi Rao. That is, I wrote him and requested that he aid Tulasi Bai in making arrangements for her son to travel to England, and he did, and then——"

"Why is Mr. Sudhakar arriving after your newly appointed Holkar heir?"

"This was the earliest that he could pay us a visit," Gabby said firmly. "Naturally I asked him to visit us whenever he was able. And you don't need to say 'Mr. Sudhakar,' Quill. Very few Indian people have two names."

Quill strolled over so that he could stand behind his wife as she sat at the delicate little dressing table. He ran his fingers down her hair. "I'm afraid that I am still not quite following, my dear. I understood that Sudhakar is an elderly gentleman. It must have been quite an arduous voyage for him. Why is he paying us this visit?"

"Oh, he's doing it for me. Because I asked him to," Gabby answered promptly.

"And why did you ask him to visit?" Quill's long, clever fingers stroked through his wife's golden-brown hairs as if they were strands of silk to be separated before weaving.

She hesitated.

"Could it be that Sudhakar is bringing his own little miracle concoction with him?"

Gabby bit her lip. "You needn't put it like that."

"And how else shall I refer to his medicine?"

"I . . . I don't know what it's called," she admitted.

"What we do know is that it is in the same genus as those medicines I discarded. I believed that we had a firm understanding, Gabby. *No more.* I will never take another potion—not from an English apothecary, nor from an Indian miracle healer. Regardless of Sudhakar's skill or his friendship with you, I will not take his medicine. Under any circumstances."

"But this is different," Gabby said unhappily. She met her husband's eyes in the dressing-table mirror. "Sudhakar is not a fraud, like those apothecaries I visited. There's no hemp in his medicine."

"Given that Mr. Moore boasted of using *Indian* hemp, the ingredient may well appear in Sudhakar's potion as well."

Gabby twitched her shoulders under Quill's fingers and then forced herself to sit quietly.

"The real point is that you promised not to buy any more medicines."

Her heart was pounding. "I wrote to Sudhakar long before I made that promise."

Quill's voice was steely, implacable. "You said—and I quote, Gabby—'I promise not to buy any more concoctions.'"

"I didn't have to *buy* his medicine," she muttered. Her face was burning.

"That is beside the point." Quill turned abruptly and walked away, stopping with his back to the window. "What I find truly objectionable is the fact that you lied to me, Gabby."

"I didn't really—"

"You lied with foreknowledge. We can distinguish that from lies such as those you told me about Kasi Rao."

"I didn't tell you any lies about Kasi!"

"Lies of omission," Quill said. "Yesterday when Lord

Breksby announced that Kasi Rao had been found by the East India Company, you said naught to me of Jawsant Rao Holkar and your kingmaking activities." His voice had a bitter twinge, and his shoulders were squared as he looked into the black garden. "I gather you didn't trust me not to contact Breksby."

Gabby took a shuddering breath. "That wasn't it at all! I didn't lie to you—"

"Don't!" His voice was like the crack of a whip in the room. "*Don't* tell me any further lies. Can't you just admit, for once, that you were wrong? You broke your word to me." He swung around and faced her.

Gabby could hear her heart pounding in her ears. Blistering tears pressed at her eyes. "But I didn't mean—"

"That excuse is overused," Quill remarked. "Good motives do not excuse lies. Ever since you entered this house, you have flung about untruths as if they were nothing important. I am not saying"—and his voice softened—"that you tell lies for mean or shabby purposes."

She swallowed a sob. "I don't!" she cried.

"I know that."

"The only lie I told was for your own good. I didn't tell you about Sudhakar because I knew you wouldn't allow him to travel to England—and I thought he was already on the way, so what did it matter? He might be able to cure your migraines, don't you see? His note said that there is a medicine that has provided remedy—"

"What I see is that I cannot trust my wife's word." The words fell like stones into a deep well. "I must constantly be doubting you, trying to decide whether you are telling me the truth or whether you have decided to deceive me, *for my own good*." Quill's tone was savage.

More tears were falling, but Gabby refused to give in to

sobs. "I—I . . ." What could she say? She *had* lied to him, at least by omission, as he put it.

"I meant to tell you about Jawsant Holkar," she said, steadying her voice with an effort. "But it was only a matter of a few letters, and I was . . . I was enjoying making the arrangements by myself. I thought it would be a surprise. I didn't think of it as lying."

"That's just it. You don't think of lying as something to be avoided, do you, Gabby?"

She blinked away more tears. "I never tell *bad* lies." Embarrassingly, her voice squeaked. "I just got in the habit because of my father—" She had to gulp back a wrenching sob.

"Your father undoubtedly deserved to be deceived," Quill said. He walked over and stood in front of her, drawing her gently to her feet. "But I do not, Gabby. I am not a tyrant. I would never have betrayed your plans to the government. I can see that your father drove you into acting surreptitiously. But our marriage will be nothing more than a shambles if we are untruthful with each other."

He kissed her hair and then her salty cheek. Words emerged from his chest as if torn. "And God knows, Gabby, I want our marriage to be a success more than anything I've ever wanted in the world."

Gabby burst into a storm of weeping, falling into his arms. "I do as well," she sobbed. "I didn't mean to lie to you! I do trust you, I do, I do! You know how much I love you, Quill!"

There was a queer twist in his chest. "I love you too, Gabby."

"I know you do," she sobbed on, "and that was why—I mean, if I didn't know you loved me, I wouldn't—I just wanted it to be a surprise! Because you love me and you think I'm bright—you *said* so—and I wanted to show you that I was capable of doing something intelligent!"

"I see," Quill said slowly, backing toward the bed. Once there, he pulled her into his lap. "You didn't tell me about your plans for the Holkar throne because I—"

She interrupted him again. "You said that women should be directors of the East India Company!"

Quill settled her more closely against his shoulder and dropped a kiss onto her satiny hair. "I gather that it was my fault." His voice was wryly amused. "I'll never express admiration for your intelligence again."

She raised her head and looked up at him. "Oh, Quill, you're so—" Her voice hiccuped on a sob. "It's no wonder I'm so horribly in love with you."

Quill swallowed. Cripples were not lovable, unless a person was as overly romantic as his wife, of course. "You need a handkerchief," he said brusquely, thrusting one into her hand.

She leaned back against his shoulder again, a last sob escaping from her chest. "I will tell Sudhakar tomorrow morning that you have refused his treatment."

"Why don't you tell him that the problem resolved itself after you wrote?" Quill suggested. "I would not want your friend to think that he made a voyage that could have been prevented. And I must say that I am quite pleased with the unexpected resolution of my . . . problems." His hands tightened around the fragrant bundle in his lap. "Especially given that my problems were solved by my oh-so-intelligent wife."

But Gabby's stomach was clenching with anxiety. "If I promise not to tell you any more lies, do you think our marriage might still be a success?"

Quill tenderly wiped the last tears from her cheeks. "Our marriage is already so much better than I expected that it terrifies me," he whispered, kissing his way down to her mouth. "I—" He faltered, and then continued. "I didn't know it was possible to feel this way about someone."

"Oh, Quill, I'm sorry I lied to you. I really am. I would never be unfaithful or—"

"I know that." He whispered into her hair. "I know you fibbed to me only with the best of motives."

They sat for a moment, an occasional sob still rising in Gabby's throat. Finally she took a long shuddering sigh. "Do you know what Lady Sylvia would say now?"

"I can't say it jumps to mind," Quill said dryly.

" 'Time for some tea. Emotions are so tedious without sustenance,' " Gabby said, in a fairly good imitation of Lady Sylvia's bark. "I should ring for Margaret." She tucked her face against his chest. "My nose must be as red as a cherry."

"It doesn't appear to be red," Quill said, running a finger down the side of his wife's little patrician nose. "And I don't want any tea. It's far too late in the evening for tea. I want *you*, Gabby. I need a draught of my wife."

All he could see of her face were long brown eyelashes, tipped in gold, and the beginnings of a very small smile. Then she raised her arms and clasped them around his neck. Her lips hovered an inch from his.

"I don't know. I really would like a cup of tea."

"Gabby." His tone was dangerously even.

"I expect my eyes are swollen. I should ring for a compress."

"Gabby!" he growled. He bent forward and eased a kiss on those reddened eyes. Delicate fingers played a concerto on his neck. And then . . . her lips opened into the sweetness of a slow kiss.

They were a better sustenance than tea, those kisses.

They repaired and soothed and knit together the weave of married life.

It was quite a while before infinite sweetness changed into something different, something more eager and more wild. Gabby gasped and protested, found herself naked and then grew accustomed to the indecency, finally became too hoarsely incoherent for protest and too openly passionate to care. Quill had decided to teach his wife that there was more to their continuing experiment than she had dreamed.

And he succeeded magnificently. Perhaps too well. By the time Quill drew Gabby down on top of his body, he was blazing with a maddening fire. Gabby's uneven cadence was torment rather than pleasure. He endured. And endured.

But there are limits to every man's patience.

Suddenly Gabby found herself flipped over on her back, Quill's delicious weight pinning her down, pleasure flaring into her stomach as he drove into her.

"No," she said on a wailing note, but then she was caught up in his pounding rhythm and nothing escaped her mouth but cries of pleasure, spiraling higher and higher, joined at the apex by his rough groan. And a second later she heard a hoarse mutter against her neck: "That was worth anything, Gabby. Anything."

She didn't reply.

Her husband slept, his body warm next to hers, but Gabby's eyes didn't close.

She lay awake in the grip of frantic anxiety. If Quill had another attack . . . she'd have to leave him. Or never make love to him. Except that she would die if she never saw his somber eyes laughing at her again. Her thoughts tangled over each other, careening from heart-thumping despair to firm resolution to wild guilt.

As dawn slowly crept through the drapes, Gabby watched Quill's face like a hawk. Was his skin paler than it had been?

When he moaned in his sleep, she froze. When he turned over and then choked, she had the chamber pot ready. She put a wet cloth on his head, rinsed out the pot, ran back to the bed with it. Wrung out the cloth again, cursed herself silently, and rinsed the pot twice more.

When she finally left the room at ten in the morning, Gabby carried with her the image of a chalk-white face, touched by dark shadows. Quill had flinched each time she touched him; his face had twisted in pain as his stomach fought to empty itself again and again. She had watched him fight to maintain dignity before her and had seen the pain defeat him.

He opened his eyes once, only to say, "Don't blame yourself, love." Gabby jumped, thinking that he was reading her mind. She blamed herself, oh, yes, she did. She blamed herself with a vicious twist of her stomach every time she thought of it. They had made love, and that made her party to the migraine. If it weren't for her, Quill would be happily working in his study, instead of lying half dead in the dark.

Blame had the salutary effect of clearing Gabby's mind of all hesitation. They could not continue like this. She could leave Quill forever—or she could talk to Sudhakar. And between the two possibilities, there was no real decision to be made.

"I THINK IT IS an extremely poor idea." Gabby had rarely seen Sudhakar so incensed. "No person should be given medicine without his explicit knowledge and consent."

"Quill will not take the medicine otherwise," Gabby said flatly. "And I can't bear his suffering. You haven't seen it. You don't know."

"It is his choice."

"But he doesn't understand," she pleaded. "He is English, and he's never lived outside this country. It is difficult for him to believe that medicine from India will cure his condition."

"*May* cure his condition," Sudhakar corrected her. "And in fact the primary ingredient is not Indian. The medicine will cure his headaches only if the bodily damage is of a certain type."

"But if I understand you, it won't injure him either way," Gabby insisted. "So there's no harm in trying."

"Given correctly, the medicine will not cause any further damage," Sudhakar agreed. "I agree that there is little physical risk. But I insist that patients have the right to choose their own medicine. I do not treat people without their consent. This medicine is made from a deadly poison, Gabrielle. In the wrong hands, it has killed people. Under those circumstances, it is doubly important that the patient have the right to decide whether he wishes the risk."

"It's for his own good," Gabby protested wildly. She was on the edge of hysteria. Sleeplessness, worry, and guilt were beating an unhappy rhythm in her brain.

"We"—Sudhakar corrected himself—"*I* do not force people to bend to my will. You sound dangerously like your father this morning, Gabrielle."

"My father! My father doesn't give a hang about anyone else!" Gabby cried. It was a relief to say it out loud. "I've been thinking about it ever since I got on the boat to London. He doesn't care about me, and he never has!"

"The question of love is not relevant. Your father believes that he knows what is best for each person in the village," Sudhakar pointed out. "And he makes certain that his way is implemented, whether the person in question agrees or not."

There was a pounding moment of silence.

"I cannot believe that you would compare me to my father." Gabby's eyes were dry and her head high.

"I speak the truth as I see it," came the reply, uncompromising and yet gentle. "If your husband wants nothing to do with my medicine, then he should not be given it behind his back. It is his choice."

"My father allows people to make choices," Gabby protested, grasping at a tangent. "He simply makes them leave the village if they don't agree with him. I don't see any similarity. I love Quill. I love him too much to spend my entire life watching him suffer. I will . . . I will have to leave him."

"In that case," Sudhakar said, "leaving the marriage will be *your* choice. I have seen patients flee from their dying spouses, and I sympathized. There is nothing harder than watching a loved one in pain."

Gabby's lip trembled. "I'm sorry, Sudhakar. I didn't mean to remind you."

"My son died a long time ago." He sounded tired. "Time passes."

"Still," Gabby insisted, "when Johore was dying, you tried every possible medicine. Remember when I came down from the big house and you gave Johore the medicine I had brought? He didn't know that you were giving him the medicine, and what's more, he would likely have refused it! You know Johore hated my father."

"Johore . . . Johore was dying," Sudhakar said. "He could no longer make choices for himself."

"I don't see the difference," Gabby said passionately.

But Sudhakar's face was unmoved. "The difference is that giving someone medicine secretly—someone who is certainly *not* dying—is the kind of action your father would delight in. You were raised in a household in which one man thought he knew best and implemented his rules, his

Christianity, his morals, how and wherever he pleased. I would be disappointed to see you adopt his methods."

"Oh, Sudhakar, what happens between Quill and me is completely different; I *love* him!" Gabby cried.

"I don't see a marked difference." He looked around the library. "It has been most pleasant to see you again, little Gabrielle. And I am pleased to see you in your house, as a married woman. But I shall return to my village on the morrow."

"No," she said obstinately. "You must not leave until you talk to my husband."

"It will not change his mind, Gabrielle. I have found Englishmen to be remarkably unwilling to try unfamiliar cures, especially medicines that come from the 'East,' as they call it." The old man peered at her, a look of great sympathy on his face. "You must grow inured to his pain, I am afraid."

He was right, Gabby thought, given Quill's unrelenting opposition to so-called quack cures. He would never take another medicine, not because Sudhakar brought it from India, but because Quill was infinitely stubborn. Having declared he would take no more medicines, he would never change his mind.

Gabby straightened her shoulders and held out her right hand. "I would like that medicine, please, Sudhakar." Even she could hear the echoes of her father's demanding voice in her ears.

He shook his head. "No, little one," he said, sounding tired.

Gabby's chest was burning, but she pushed on. "I brought your son medicine," she said. "I brought it to Johore because I loved him. And I would like you to give me your medicine. I love my husband and I will not injure him. You said the medicine would not hurt him."

"This is not worthy of you. You are making a terrible mistake, Gabrielle."

"I could have caught cholera myself, entering your home. I could have died bringing Johore the medicine." Her voice was stony.

She waited, hand outstretched.

The old man's eyes dropped. He reached into the small red bag and took out a bottle.

"It will be *my* choice," Gabby said. "Quill will almost certainly leave me when he learns what I have done. But I will know that I tried everything I could to save him from pain. At any rate, I will have to leave him if there is no cure. We cannot continue like this."

"It seems you are your father's child after all," Sudhakar said sadly. "Did you know that your father married his first wife in order to save her soul? He had had no success converting the villagers to Christianity, so he married poor little Bala, knowing he could command her religion as her husband."

"I did know that," Gabby said. "But——"

"It didn't work." Sudhakar's voice was meditative. "When Bala's child, your half-brother, died, she killed herself rather than live without him. That was when your father turned to exporting goods rather than saving souls."

The words pierced Gabby's heart, but she kept her voice steady. "The story casts a poor light on my father's judgment. But I am as much your child as my father's, Sudhakar. If I know how to love Quill, it is because you and Johore loved me. When Johore was suffering, you tried every possible remedy, regardless of his opinion. I am acting in your shadow, Sudhakar. You are doing me an injustice."

A heavy silence fell over the room.

"Perhaps you are right," Sudhakar admitted. "It is true that your motives are always charitable. Ever since you were a child, you have loved too deeply and too quickly for comfort." He handed her the bottle. "This bottle contains two doses calibrated for a grown man. You must measure exactly half the bottle. The medicine has no ill effects at the right dose, but at an incorrect dose, it may well kill the patient. Try the second dose forty-eight hours after the first, only if it is absolutely clear that the medicine did not work."

"I give the second dose only if the first doesn't work," Gabby repeated. "How will I know when the dose has worn off?"

"In general, a patient will become extremely lethargic shortly after taking this medicine and remain so for twelve to twenty-four hours. There is no danger as long as the patient does not fall asleep in the first two to three hours. I have tried this cure only twice, Gabrielle. On one occasion it was effective, and on the other it was not. The patient must engage in the activity that leads to headaches while under the drug's influence." He looked her straight in the eyes. "Do you understand, Gabrielle?"

She nodded, looking at the small bottle. "What is in it?"

Sudhakar shrugged. "As I said, it is a poison. This particular poison is created by a tree frog, who puts his victims into a deep sleep. For some reason, in a very small dose it seems to put injured parts of a human brain to sleep, and certain movements become tolerable once again. I gave it to a young man who had fallen from a tree. After the injury, he could not bend his head lower than his waist without bringing on a severe headache. In that case, the medicine worked."

Gabby swallowed, trying not to imagine how Quill would view the possibility of having parts of his brain put to sleep. At least that settled the question of whether she should ask him again to take the medicine. He would never touch it.

"Please, Sudhakar, will you remain in London for at least a week? My husband has a migraine; he will be ill for the next few days, but I would like you to know the man I have married."

"I will gladly make a short visit, if you promise me that you will reconsider this decision, Gabrielle."

She bowed her head. "I am grateful, Sudhakar, for your forbearance. And I am truly sorry that you think I am acting like my father."

Sudhakar noted that she had avoided his request, and sighed. "I would be proud to call you my daughter," he said. "You are the *dhtu* of my heart. What stems from evil in your father stems from love in you. Now, let me have some rest, Gabrielle. My old legs still think I'm at sea."

Gabby kissed him on the forehead and slipped from the room, the tiny bottle clutched in her hand.

Chapter 23

Quill was having a gloriously sensual dream. He was lying on the bed, and Gabby was undressing him. She was bathed in a rosy light. But the light wasn't coming from behind her; it radiated from her skin, as if she were glowing.

And then he noticed that she wasn't wearing any clothing. He watched her breasts as she unbuttoned his shirt. He considered touching them, but it was enjoyable to simply lie and watch her.

"Mmmm, Gabby," he murmured. His voice rolled out of his mouth like thick molasses.

"Yes?" She was wrestling with his wristbands.

"Why are you so rosy?"

"What did you say?" His dream wife seemed a little irritated. Her breasts bobbed as she tugged at his sleeve.

"You look like a medieval saint," he said, and then giggled. A more rational part of his mind noted that he hadn't giggled since he was a boy. "I'm married to a saint—a medieval saint. I rather like that idea." His voice trailed off. "Of course, medieval saints wore clothing, at least in the pictures I've seen."

A warm hand cupped his cheek and Gabby's face swam into view. "Quill, are you feeling all right? You're not making a good deal of sense." Her beautiful eyes looked concerned.

"Course I am," he said. "I'm having one of the best dreams of my life. Are you going to keep doing that, Gabby love? Or should I call you Gabby o' Dreams? Or Dream Gabby?" He giggled again.

Gabby's face disappeared and he heard a pop. She had managed to loosen his sleeve. She startled wrestling with his other cuff, just as he was thinking that he really had to touch her luscious breasts. Slowly he dragged his free arm up and placed it at the curve of one breast.

This is one of those slower-than-molasses dreams, he thought. One could only hope that he would stay asleep long enough to experience whatever Dream Gabby was planning. He let his hand slide down her smooth side, enchanted by the way rosy light peeked through his fingers.

She had managed to get his other sleeve undone. Quill let her wrestle him out of the shirt.

"Oh, dream maiden," he called.

"What?" Her face swung back into his range of view.

"This being a dream," he confessed, "I don't seem to be able to move very well."

She looked taken aback. "Why don't I unbutton your trousers, and we'll see how you feel then?" she suggested.

"Excellent suggestion," Quill murmured. At least part of him seemed to be functioning properly. Thank goodness. This was his dream, after all, and it would be a nightmare if his whole body had turned as lazy as his arms.

A few minutes later he was completely naked. And Dream Gabby was naked as well. "This is most enjoyable," he muttered.

She wasn't as relaxed as he was, he could tell that. She

stared into his eyes and then said, "Quill, I'm going to kiss you now."

"All right," he agreed.

And she did. He enjoyed it too. He even managed to get a hand up on her shoulder and stroke down over the curve of her back and her exquisite bottom.

"Since this is my dream," he said languidly, "I wish I had a bit more ginger in me. A bit more momentum."

"I can't do anything about that," Dream Gabby said, her eyes anxious again. "Do you think that if you were on top of me, you might feel more energetic?"

Quill thought about that. "I like the way you think," he said generously. "If I wasn't so much in love with the real Gabby, I might take you up seriously."

At that she giggled. "I'm very glad to hear you're in love." Her eyes were a warm golden color, just the color of the real Gabby's. And she kissed him. . . . She was an excellent kisser. It was enough to make a man feel a twinge of guilt about his real wife.

"I wasn't in love with her at first," he said.

Her eyes grew round and startled. "You weren't?"

"Oh, no." Quill shook his head, but for some reason the motion made him feel a bit dizzy. "Would you mind rubbing your breasts against me again?"

She was frowning at him. "Tell me more about not being in love," she ordered.

"Not unless you do as I ask. This is my dream, after all."

Dream Gabby seemed a bit huffy, but she plopped down on top of him.

"Not like that," Quill protested. "Oh . . . well, that feels good. Did you know that your eyes go all brandy-colored when you're excited? It's funny. You look as annoyed as my real wife. But you don't act like her. If I stopped in the middle of an argument, for example . . ." he said dreamily, letting his fingers wander down between her legs. For a moment he lost track of what he was saying. "If I stopped in the middle of an argument with the real Gabby, and I asked her to rub her breasts against my chest, do you think she would do it?" He shook his head again. "Oh, no. She'd likely throw the chamber pot at me."

Her eyes were hazy. At least she responded exactly as his wife did to certain touches. "I'd like to hear about not being in love," she said, with a little shiver and a gasp.

"Oh, that." Quill could feel strength returning to his legs as he continued to caress his wife, his dream wife, that is. "I had to marry her, you see," he said offhandedly, experimenting with a slightly rougher movement.

Dream Gabby cried out and clutched his shoulders. There was a moment of silence. But then his comment seemed to sink in.

"What do you mean, you *had* to marry her?"

There was a bite to her tone. Quill raised his head and peered, getting her face into focus. She had little golden streaks in her rosy halo now. "You know, medieval saints don't have halos that go around their whole bodies," he said genially. "You have the biggest, best halo I've ever seen. Maybe you are an angel. Have I died?"

"No, I'm not an angel." Her tone was quite fierce. "And you're not dead, Quill."

"Well, any self-respecting angel would be jealous of that halo," he assured her. Then he remembered what he'd been doing. He was definitely gaining some strength. He even managed to get his other hand on her hip.

"Quill," said his angel in a rather stern voice, "I want to hear about your marriage."

"Of course," he said. Every time he stroked her, little

golden sparks flew off her halo. They were practically blinding. He closed his eyes. "Well, we were married by my father's deathbed. Not very romantic, that."

"Oh, that's what you meant about having to get married!" Her tone was definitely relieved. But Quill felt he really should be completely honest. If you started lying to your dream wife, well, that was akin to lying to oneself.

"No, that wasn't what I meant," he said. His hands wandered over to clasp her bottom. He made a little experimental thrust upward. Yes, his legs seemed to be regaining strength. "I had to marry her because Peter wouldn't do it. Peter is my brother. Do you think that I could try having you underneath me now?" he added.

Dream Gabby didn't protest, so he rolled her over in slow motion. It took so much effort that he just lay on top of her for a moment. Luckily he didn't have to worry about whether he was squashing all the air out of her, because she was just a dream. It felt uncommonly good.

Except that she was still asking pesky questions.

"Peter thought she was fat and clumsy," he explained. "I told him he should do it anyway, because my wife is an heiress, you know. I don't need money, but Peter does." He had his face tucked into her neck, so he couldn't see her expression. But she started to wiggle under him in a way that told him that dream women reacted similarly to real women when called plump and clumsy.

"I didn't agree with him." He raised his head with a great effort. "I thought she had a luscious body, right from the start." He didn't want his dream wife to leave in a huff. Not when things were going so well.

She seemed a little more relaxed and even opened her lips to his. They kissed until Dream Gabby's halo had more gold in it than red. Quill closed his eyes again and let his head fall onto her shoulder. "I can't do everything at once," he said in a cheerfully complaining way. "I'm awfully tired. But this is quite the best dream I've ever had. I wouldn't want you to think that I'm being unreasonable."

"What did you mean by saying that you weren't in love?"

Only one part of Quill's body was fully awake. "I'd like to be inside you now, Gabby my girl. Do you think you could take care of it?"

Dream Gabby seemed as unprepared in these matters as his real wife. She fumbled about with her little hands until she finally guided him to the spot. Quill gathered all his strength and plunged in. Sweat broke out on his back.

"Damn," he muttered. "Dream or no dream, you feel better than any woman I've ever been with—except the real Gabby, of course. You feel the same as her," he said thoughtfully, "and she's the very best."

Dream Gabby looked a little happier. "Quill, would you like me to move?" she asked. Then she looked as if she remembered something. "Actually, dream women can't do the moving," she said silkily. She walked her fingers down his spine.

"Let's just lie here for a moment," he suggested. He let his eyelids close again. The most active part of his body was sending all kinds of angry signals his way. He managed to thrust forward a few times, just enough to turn his dream wife's halo practically gold. Then he slumped again.

Now she was running her fingers all over his back and kissing his shoulder. "I would really like to know what you meant about not being in love," she coaxed, running a hand between their bodies.

"When you do that, I can deny you nothing," Quill said grandly. What she was doing sent a surge of energy through his body, and he found himself on his knees, actually making love in a seminormal fashion. With each stroke, Dream

Gabby's halo grew more and more golden. Quill watched in fascination. She had her head arched back, eyes closed, and little guttural moans broke from her mouth each time he thrust into her.

He was still caught in the slow web of his dream, so he had far more rational control than he would have had in normal life, with real Gabby. By now he would have been completely lost. But since it was a dream, part of his mind was just lazily observing what was happening. He slipped his hands under Gabby's hips and pulled her up a few inches. She started shrieking, and sparks flew off her body in all directions. He thrust into her again and again, feeling the delicious tightening deep inside her and the way her fingers were clutching his shoulders. And then she literally turned into a blaze of light.

"Damn," Quill said quietly. "I'm making love to an angel. This is quite a dream. Or else I *am* in heaven."

Dream Gabby's hair was damp, and curls were stuck to her forehead. But she opened her eyes, her beautiful eyes, and looked at him. "I'm not an angel," she whispered.

"Next thing to it," Quill remarked. "After all, you're the one with the halo." He was still deep inside her. He decided to try another experiment, now that he had regained a fair amount of strength. Not to mention self-control.

Deftly, he turned her over on her knees and sank deep inside again. Her protests had a hysterical edge that reminded him of the real Gabby's. "This is *my* dream," he had to remind her. "Many women love this position. You will too. That is, if I dream about you again." A little twinge of guilt colored his statement. He didn't want the dream to be too good. It wouldn't be loyal to Gabby.

He was definitely having more trouble with his self-control. But Gabby's halo was still rosy and just starting to streak a little gold. And he wanted her with him. "I wasn't in love with Gabby in the beginning," he said, panting but trying to keep his mind clear. "Though I told her I loved her, of course."

"You lied to her? Why did you do that?"

"Had to," he said. "Gabby is a romantic. I knew she'd fall for it if I told her that I fell in love at first sight. You know, sweetheart, I'm not sure I can keep this up much longer. In many senses of the word." He was appalled to hear himself giggle again. "Perhaps I got drunk before going to bed," he murmured. "Maybe I died while drunk. Too much champagne . . ."

Dream Gabby's shoulders were tense, and her halo looked more blazing red than dreamy gold. "I think we should talk a little more about the lies you told me," she said accusingly.

"I'd rather not," Quill said with great patience. "And this is my dream." He shrugged to himself. After all, she was only a creation of his imagination. He slipped his hands under her body and caressed her breasts. She panted, little ladylike pants.

"You're rather wonderful, Gabby o' my Dreams," Quill murmured. He was having trouble talking. But he wanted to hold on to the moment—to the dream. His dream wife was inexpertly moving against him. "Although you're just as clumsy as my wife," he told her.

"Be still," he growled, and he grabbed her hips so hard that his fingers left white marks. He thrust forward hard. He let himself get swept away. She gave a faint scream, and little gold flames jumped from her body.

He closed his eyes at the end, afraid that she would blind him, his angel wife.

Chapter 24

QUILL WOKE UP with a raging thirst and a most unpleasant taste in his mouth. He swung his legs over the side of the bed, walked to the table, and poured a glass of water. In mid-gulp, the details of his dream flooded back into his mind. He paused for a second and then grinned in silent appreciation of his own imagination. No wonder he was so thirsty. He poured another glass of water and savored it like fine wine.

Just as he finished drinking, he heard a rustle in the bed and turned around. Gabby was sitting up, her hair tumbling around her shoulders. "Good morning," Quill said, with a faint pulse of guilt. It would be a rare day when he could give his wife as much pleasure as he had given his dream Gabby.

"You don't have a migraine!"

He raised one eyebrow as he poured some more water. "And why should I? I think I drank a bit too much port last night, but migraines do not spring from an excess of liquor. Would you like a glass of water, my dear? It tastes unaccountably good."

"It does?" She sounded dubious.

Quill put down his glass with a click and walked over to the bed. He bent over and kissed her lightly. But one touch wasn't enough, so he sat down and ran his hands through her hair. "Let's start over," he whispered. "Good morning, my wife."

Gabby's cheeks turned rosy. "Quill, do you remember last—how do you . . ." She trailed off.

"Do I remember?"

"Last night, you and I—"

"Oh, Lord," Quill said, chuckling. "I dreamt about you all night, Gabby. Did I caress you in my sleep?"

"Actually—"

He pulled her forward and Gabby lost hold of the coverlet she was holding to her neck. "I say!" he said, truly startled. "My beautiful wife is sleeping without her night rail!"

"Well, you—"

Quill groaned. "Oh, sweetheart, you must have felt as if I were attacking you. I truly apologize. I'm a beast. What happened?"

His wife was looking down at her hands. He pushed her curls back over creamy shoulders. "I like you without clothes. Perhaps I will pretend to be dreaming every night and disrobe you in the middle of the night."

"Quill!" But the reprimand didn't have its usual force.

"What's the matter?" he asked, suddenly chilled. "Did I frighten you, Gabby? I'm so sorry; I can't remember. But I assure you that this has never happened before and won't happen again."

"I know that," Gabby said, almost inaudibly.

"What?"

"I said, I know it won't happen again," she replied.

Quill was lost. "What won't happen?" He wasn't terribly interested. "Perhaps I should make recompense for my impoliteness during the night." His hand rounded the curve of her breast and he shifted her onto his lap. Gabby barely managed to clutch the sheet to her waist.

She swallowed. She had promised herself that she would deceive Quill only once, by giving him the medicine, and that afterward she would confess. And leave the house without protest if he sent her away.

"I don't know why it is," Quill was saying, his voice growing slightly hoarse. "I can't seem to think about anything but you, Gabby." He pushed her backward and she was laid out before him, beautiful, generous curves. "Why don't we talk later, hmmm?"

"Quill—"

But his head was bent over her breast and she gasped into silence, her protest dying in her throat. Passion rose instantly, turned her legs to water. But guilt beat an opposing rhythm in her heart. Should they make love? Then he would realize that Sudhakar's medicine had worked— perhaps he would think his injuries healed on their own.

No. The deceit would lie between them for their whole life. She would never be able to make love to him without thinking of it.

"I have to speak to you," she said, pushing his dark head away from her.

"So serious," Quill said, wicked lights dancing in his eyes. "Wouldn't you rather—" And he smiled his devil's smile.

"Yes—no!" Gabby scooted backward on the bed. "We made love last night," she said bluntly.

He gaped at her, dumbfounded. "No." But his tone was not certain.

"We did."

"But," Quill said slowly, "I don't have a headache. I thought—it wasn't a dream?"

"No."

"That doesn't make sense."

Gabby's heart ached as she watched his brows knit together. She loved that scowl and his certainty that every puzzle had a logical explanation. She saw the moment that the truth dawned on him, the way his face grew rigid as he realized his wife's betrayal.

She pulled farther back on the bed, just a fraction of an inch. Then she steadied herself. She had been *right*. Not right in her methods, but right in the outcome. They made love over and over during the night, and he was pain-free.

Quill's eyes had turned the color of an icy ocean wave. "You drugged me," he said flatly. With a sudden lunge he leaned forward and pulled the sheet from her hands and flung it away. As Gabby gasped in protest, he pushed her roughly on her side. There on her hip was a bluish bruise, the shadow of Quill's passionate hold from the night before.

He pulled back without a word. Had she thought his eyes were green? They were black. Gabby's heart was bursting in her chest. This must be what it feels like to be dying, she thought numbly.

"Sudhakar's medicine is potent," Quill remarked. He had himself firmly under control now, she could see that.

Gabby nodded.

"What are the ingredients?"

"I didn't—I don't know."

"You don't know." There was a chilly pause.

"Sudhakar gave it to a young man who injured himself falling from a tree," Gabby whispered. "Whenever the man bent over, he suffered from a headache. The medicine cured him."

"When did you give that medicine to me?"

"After dinner, in your port."

Quill stood up. He realized for the first time that he was naked as well. "That was quite a performance you put on last night."

Gabby willed herself not to cry. He had the right to be angry. "You had to engage in the movement that causes migraines." Her voice came out in a wisp.

Quill's eyes narrowed again. "That seems very odd. Why?"

"I believe that the medicine soothes the injured part of the brain," Gabby said awkwardly. That sounded better than Sudhakar's talk of putting one's brain to sleep.

He was slowly working it through. "The patient takes the medicine and then performs the activity that brings on migraines. So the medicine has healed my concussion?"

"The medicine soothes that part of the brain——" She faltered, unable to make sense of the connections between injured limbs and injured brains.

"And if this medicine had not agreed with me, Gabby. Would I be lying in that bed, unable to move at all?"

"Oh, no," she said eagerly, meeting his eyes. "There are no ill consequences when it doesn't work."

"What else did Sudhakar say about it?"

Gabby bit her lip.

"What else did Sudhakar say about the medicine?" Quill's words were evenly spaced, although she felt as if he had shouted them.

"In some situations, it is a dangerous poison," she mumbled. She looked imploringly at Quill. "But he promised that there would be no ill consequences, even if the medicine didn't work. And it did work."

But he was turning away, pulling on a robe. "So you gave me a dangerous poison," he said. His voice sounded almost disinterested. "You must have been desperate, Gabby. Was it worth it, last night?"

She didn't pretend not to understand him. Tears were falling hotly on her hands. "I couldn't stand to see you in pain."

"But you felt no guilt when you lied to me, Gabby? When you gave me a medicine that may well have killed me?" He turned around, and she shivered at the look in his face. "When my mother bought such a drug, at least she graced me with the decision whether to take it."

Gabby's voice was strangled. "You would have refused!"

"That is correct. I would not have taken it."

"I had to," she whispered. "I couldn't see you suffer."

"Somehow you seem to have missed the fact that I abhor deceit, Gabby." His tone was almost genial. "So I ask you again: do you think last night was worth it?"

In his face she could read the ruins of her marriage, as clear as day.

But he continued, relentless. "As I recall, I believed you were an angel. Quite a joke under the circumstances. Did you laugh? I don't remember you laughing." His voice was as sharp as the prow of a ship cutting through fog.

"I love you," Gabby managed to say.

"I forgave my mother because she bought the potion out of love," he said. He had no need to continue.

"You destroyed our marriage because our relations weren't enough for you? Or was it because you wanted me to be more . . . more manly?" For all his control, he was practically speaking through clenched teeth.

"That wasn't it!" Gabby cried. "I couldn't see you in pain. I couldn't bear it!"

"We had previously made love without my incurring a migraine, if you remember," Quill pointed out. "Therefore I can only believe that you found the experience inadequate."

Gabby couldn't answer.

"I won't be furnishing you with any further experience," he said gently. "You know that, don't you? I will never be able to trust you again, and no marriage could be successful in those circumstances."

Gabby pulled herself together. She had to make herself clear, and then she would leave. "I will not try to change your mind, but I want you to understand. Sudhakar assured me that the medicine would not injure you. Given that, I decided that lying to you was justified."

"Justified!" Quill spat. "God, you are such a smug little thing. Justified lies! To your husband! Were you lying when you said you worshiped me, after we consummated our marriage?"

But she was battling tears again and couldn't answer.

"Of course, that was before you realized just how much my injury was going to affect your daily life," Quill remarked.

"No! That isn't it. I won't have you saying such cruel things!" Gabby had suddenly found her voice. "I never lied to you about important things."

"Only when *justified*." His voice had a savage ring to it.

"I never told you a lie as awful as the one you told me," she retorted.

Quill folded his arms and regarded her. "And what lies have I ever told you, Gabby? I should warn you that I pride myself on my truthfulness."

She raised her chin. "In that case, you should not have lied to me about the reasons you wished to marry me. You said that you loved me."

Quill suddenly remembered a few details from his so-called dream of the previous night.

"I apologize," he said finally. "I did lie to you."

But Gabby was gratefully allowing anger to dull her

grief. "You lied to me at one of the most sacred moments in life," she spat. "You forced me to give up a man whom I loved, whom I wished to marry, and to marry you instead."

"I forced you—"

"You and your brother schemed behind my back," she said. Her eyes met his, and there were no tears in them now. "You were correct, last night. I *am* a romantic. I thought you loved me. I foolishly believed your lies, and so I jilted my fiancé. Of course, he was lying, too, since I gather he found me too fat to marry. Fool that I am, I even believed you when you said that I was beautiful."

Quill opened his mouth, but couldn't think of anything to say.

"At least I lied to you for your own good," Gabby said. "I would never have tricked you into a loveless marriage. I wouldn't have been able to stand the shame."

"It is not a loveless marriage!"

She shrugged. "It is no longer a marriage at all, according to you."

Too late, Quill understood that he had never really meant his earlier threats.

Gabby climbed out of bed and picked up her night rail from the floor. In the heat of anger, she had lost all self-consciousness.

"You *are* beautiful, Gabby." His voice was hoarse.

She looked at him composedly. Then she pulled the night rail over her head. "I will never be able to trust you again, and no marriage could be successful in those circumstances." There was a bitter edge in the way she repeated his words.

"They—your lie was different," Quill said, rather desperately. "You might have killed me with that potion of yours."

"And you might have broken my heart," Gabby answered

politely. "After all, I thought myself in love with Peter. But you didn't give a damn about *me,* did you? I was just an awkward, plump heiress whom your father dredged up somewhere. I gather I should count myself grateful that I wasn't simply jilted and sent back to India. After all, unlike Peter, you didn't need my money."

Quill searched for an answer. "I don't see that you showed much concern for me when you gave me a deadly potion."

"The potion is not harmful in small doses," Gabby repeated. "Would you like to see for yourself?" As he watched, she opened a drawer and pulled out a tiny brown bottle. "I gave you precisely half of this small bottle. There is not enough poison here to harm anyone."

"I doubt that," Quill said, his guilt sharpening his tone. "How many times has Sudhakar administered this medicine? Hundreds?"

"No."

"How many times?"

"Twice," Gabby admitted.

"So based on the fact that two people were not injured by Sudhakar's dose of poison, you decided I was an appropriate candidate for the third experiment?"

Gabby could feel hysteria rising in her throat. "Oh, what right have you to be so angry?" she cried. "You are cured! We made love and you didn't have a migraine afterward. Now you can make love to those concubines you talked of—go ahead! I cured you!"

"I am angry because my wife showed a reckless disregard for my well-being. You know, I received a letter from your father warning me that you had so-called 'nefarious plans for my life.' "

Her stomach clenched into an instant knot. "You have been corresponding with my father?"

"He wrote me a few letters."

She tried to match his careless tone. "Oh? What did he say? And why didn't you mention the letters to me?"

"I thought he was out of his mind. The way he described you—"

"I'm certain I can fill in the adjectives," Gabby said coolly. "I had no idea you were sharing confidences with my father."

"Perhaps I should have paid more attention to his warnings," Quill said, his voice dangerously quiet.

Gabby finally lost her temper entirely. "Yes, you should have! Because you and my father are two of a kind. You are childish, whining, stupid *men*!" she shouted at the top of her lungs. "You made an absurd vow not to take medicines, which you adhered to out of pure stubbornness. And now—and now that you've been cured, you stand around and complain, rather than saying thank you!"

Quill's eyes flared. "Stupid, am I? At least I haven't tried to kill anyone in the recent past!"

"I didn't try to kill you!" Gabby shrieked. "This medicine is harmless! Harmless!"

"Yes?" Quill said, his voice low but razor-sharp. "I don't see you volunteering to take poison! It's easy enough to sneak a so-called harmless poison to someone else."

Gabby met his eyes, and then with a lightning-quick movement she twisted off the top and poured the medicine into her mouth, just as Quill lunged forward and knocked the bottle to the floor.

"Too late," Gabby said defiantly, her chin jutting forward. "I am not afraid to try the medicine, and I did *not* try to kill you."

Quill had gone dead-white. "My God, Gabby, what have you done?" he whispered. "Where is Sudhakar?"

She shrugged. She walked past him and sat on the side of the bed. She was feeling a bit embarrassed by her own dramatics. "On his way back to India."

"That medicine was measured for a grown man, wasn't it, Gabby?"

"I'm as big as a grown man, almost," she said.

"Hardly," Quill said.

"I don't mind feeling drowsy for a day or so," Gabby said, "as long as you don't keep saying I tried to kill you. Because I didn't." But her tone wasn't very defiant anymore. She had a terrible feeling that her temper had gotten the better of her once again.

"Do you know what vessel Sudhakar was planning to take, Gabby?"

"No," she replied vaguely. "But he's likely well out to sea by now. Don't worry. He said the dose wears off in twenty-four to forty-eight hours." She felt as if her eyes were crossing. She could see two or three Quills. He was clutching her hands so tightly that it hurt.

Suddenly he threw open the bedroom door, shouting for Codswallop. She could hear him as if from a long way off, instructing the butler to find Sudhakar if he was still in London. She curled her fingers into the edge of the coverlet. She was starting to feel dizzy.

It felt like hours before Quill suddenly reappeared before her. She gasped as his face swung close to hers.

"The drug affects your eyesight," Quill said. "Remember? I thought you had a halo last night."

"This was quite idiotic of me," Gabby said, her voice a reedy thread. "Wasn't it, Quill?" She clutched the counterpane tighter. She felt as if she were on the deck of a ship as it listed in a storm. "I'm sorry I behaved so badly."

He had her hands in his again and was looking down at them. "We were both idiots," he said heavily. "I goaded you. I know you didn't try to kill me, Gabby. I was angry.

"And you were right." He was massaging her hands

now. "I was stupid, stupid, *stupid* to argue with you. I should have just thanked you."

"Not as stupid as I am," Gabby admitted. "I'm glad Sudhakar has left. He has always scolded me for being impulsive. He didn't want to give you the medicine," she added.

"What did he tell you about the medicine? Can you remember anything?"

"No," Gabby said vaguely. "He said it wasn't dangerous in small doses."

"Nothing else?"

"No." She giggled.

"What is it?"

"I think your ears are growing, Quill! You look like a bunny!" Her eyes grew round. "Look at your nose!" She giggled again.

Quill sighed. When Quill had taken the medicine, it had transformed him into a cheerful, if incoherent, drunk. He could only hope its effect on Gabby was as mild. It was going to be a long night.

But it wasn't bad. After a few hours during which Gabby alternately giggled and yawned, she fell into a deep sleep.

Quill sat by the bed, utterly discouraged. How could they have come to this pass? What kind of marriage did they have, when his stubbornness had led her to deceive him, and then their quarrel had such terrible consequences?

Why was he such an utter idiot about the matter? Why hadn't he thrown his arms around Gabby and made love to her all day to celebrate his cure?

He kept looking at his wife. She hardly stirred, but lay like a statue on the bed. Surely she would be all right. He looked at the clock yet again. Only four hours had passed since Gabby took the medicine, and she had said twenty-four would pass before the effects wore off.

He was still sitting there when an elderly Indian man pushed open the bedchamber door.

"Lord Dewland," he said quietly.

Quill started and then stood up, not letting go of Gabby's hand. "Sir—" He stopped. It was impossible to explain the foolish argument that had led to this situation.

But Sudhakar seemed to expect no details. He walked over to the bed and took Gabby's wrist in his hand. Quill's heart sank when he saw how limp her little hand looked.

"How long has she been sleeping?"

"For around four—almost five hours," Quill said.

Sudhakar said nothing, but it seemed to Quill that his jaw tightened.

"Is that a bad sign?"

Their eyes met.

"No!" Quill almost shouted it.

Sudhakar bent his head. "I doubt she will survive. This medicine is a potent poison. I told her so. She has taken too much for a person of her size and then fallen asleep too soon."

"I don't understand," Quill said numbly. "Why would that matter?"

"The medicine is made from the poison of a tree frog," Sudhakar explained. "The frog puts its prey into a deep sleep before eating them. That deep sleep is invariably fatal for humans."

"Wake her up!" Quill brushed Sudhakar aside and took Gabby's shoulders. Ignoring Sudhakar's protest, he shook her—but she shook like a wet rag, and her head listed awkwardly to one side.

"Give her something," he commanded. "A remedy."

"There is no remedy for this poison," Sudhakar said. "You must live with the consequences. As must I."

"Then why did you let her have it?" Quill said savagely. "You knew she was impulsive. You should have guessed she might take it herself!"

Sudhakar looked at him. "Now, why would that occur to me? I saw a young woman consumed with anxiety for her husband, prepared to ruin her marriage in order to save him further suffering. I saw nothing self-destructive about her."

"She thought it was harmless," Quill whispered harshly. "She had no idea. You shouldn't have given it to her."

"Do you think she is a child? She is a grown woman. Her rash actions are her own."

It was only when Quill fixed him with a brutal gaze that he realized that Sudhakar was also suffering. "We *must* do something," he said desperately.

Sudhakar turned away. "It is beyond my skill." The words were wrung from deep in his chest. "I have loved two children in my life. And now Gabrielle will join Johore in death. I failed each of them."

Quill looked up at him. "She told me you were an expert with poisons."

"But this is not an Indian poison," Sudhakar said. "If there is a cure, I do not know it. I am a stupid old man, unable to cure my loved ones."

Quill barely stopped himself from leaping at the old man's throat. "Think," he insisted. "Why do the patients die? Gabby looks as if she is merely sleeping."

"I am not certain," Sudhakar admitted. "They live for a few days, sleeping all the while, and they do not wake up. I have never seen it myself. But the man who gave me the poison warned of its consequences. Stimulants are not effective in waking the patient."

"There's nothing wrong with sleeping," Quill said uncertainly. "A person could sleep for a week without harm, could he not?"

Sudhakar frowned. "If he had water—" He stopped. "Perhaps the patients die not because of the poison but because they lack water."

"Fine," Quill said. "We'll give Gabby water." He took a glass by the bed and held up her head, but the water poured back out of her mouth.

"It's no good," Sudhakar moaned. "She cannot swallow. No, I am doomed to watch both of my children die. My Johore died in pain. At least little Gabrielle will go in peace."

Quill ignored him. He was trying to think. Finally he rang the bell and demanded a spoon from Codswallop. When he had the spoon, he held Gabby's head up and spooned water into her mouth. It ran out the side. He tried again, and again, and again, until her night rail was drenched.

Then he felt a hand on his shoulder. Tired eyes met his. "It's no use," Sudhakar said gently. "She cannot swallow."

"No!" Quill bellowed.

"I felt the same way when Johore worsened, just before he died," Sudhakar said. "We were isolated—no one in the village would even come to the door because of the cholera. But Gabrielle came. She came down from the big house, and she brought me English medicine. She cared more for Johore than for her own safety."

Quill looked at his drenched wife. He put a hand on her cheek. "She would do that," he said.

"Oh, yes," Sudhakar agreed. "She will do anything for the people she loves. And she loves you, Viscount Dewland. You are a lucky man. She loved you too much to see you in pain. And I believe that she would not begrudge what has happened."

"You don't know," Quill said hoarsely. "The things I said—"

The hand on his shoulder tightened. "I imagine you quarreled and Gabrielle took the medicine when she was in a temper. She always had a temper to match her heart, that one. But she loved you, and she would be happy to know that your headaches are cured. For you are cured, aren't you?"

Quill couldn't even look up; his vision was blurred by tears. "What does it matter?" he said hoarsely. "Without Gabby . . ."

The hand on his shoulder disappeared. "I will not stay to see her die. I have served my time by the bedside of a dying child. I am afraid that it is your *karma* this time, my lord."

Quill stood up. His throat was tight, but he forced the words. "Are you certain, absolutely certain, that there is nothing you can do?"

"I am certain. My only suggestion would be that you continue to try to give her water," Sudhakar said. "Perhaps a drop will enter her throat. Perhaps that drop will save her. But it is more likely that nothing can save her."

Quill gritted his teeth. There was nothing to be earned by slaying an elderly Indian gentleman, after all.

He bowed. "I will write to you when Gabby wakes up," Quill said.

Sudhakar bowed as well, and his voice was kind. "I will await your missive."

By a short time later, Quill had established a routine. Every hour, on the dot, he wrapped a towel around Gabby's neck and spooned water into her open mouth. He had discovered that if he held her head just so, some of the water didn't pour back out. At least he thought that was the case.

He was exhausted by midnight and turned the task over to Margaret. He threw himself on his bed and slept fitfully. Two hours later he woke with a start and peered toward the adjoining door to Gabby's chamber. It was the coldest, darkest part of the night. Had he heard something? Perhaps Gabby was awake?

But one glance through the adjoining door showed him that nothing had changed. Margaret had Gabby propped on her arm, and his wife's head was lolling to the side. The maid turned to him, face white with fatigue.

"My lord," she said hopelessly.

"Go to bed," Quill said. "And ask Codswallop to attend me at dawn." He tucked a towel under Gabby's neck again.

Early in the morning he sent a footman out to fetch the best doctor in London, one among the many Quill had consulted regarding his migraines.

Dr. Winn was a thin and angular man, with a sloping jaw and bright blue eyes. "Interesting," he said, looking at the small bottle. "A very interesting case, my lord. Tree-frog poison, did you say?" He took Gabby's pulse and listened to her heart. "She appears to be in a deep sleep. Have you tried to give her any coffee? I have had some success at waking patients with coffee or a very strong tea."

Quill spent the next two hours watching ugly brown coffee spill out of his wife's lax mouth and stain the white towel. There was no change.

Dr. Winn sighed and ran a hand through his hair. "These Eastern poisons are the very devil," he said frankly. "I know little about them. I am afraid that there is nothing I can do that wouldn't smack of the experimental, my lord." Dr. Winn's caution was precisely the reason that Quill had approved of him years ago. Winn had not handed him concoctions of mashed wasp or Indian hemp. He had advised him to live with the headaches.

But now Quill felt quite different. "Then do your experiment," he said shortly.

Dr. Winn hesitated. "If we give her a stronger stimulant than coffee—you realize that we are in effect fighting a poison with a poison?"

Quill clenched his teeth. "She *must* wake up. I do not know how much water has made it down her throat."

"You are quite right," Winn said. "She may die of dehydration."

Quill picked up the spoon, but his hand shook and the water didn't even reach Gabby's mouth. "Do something," he said.

Winn sat down and steepled his fingers. "I need your full attention, my lord. We are presented with two options."

Quill took Gabby's limp hand in his.

"A stimulant is the most obvious solution," Winn noted. "But I must say that given your wife's utter lack of response to coffee, I am not convinced that stronger stimulants will be efficacious."

"The danger?"

"Her heart may fail," Winn said bluntly.

Quill clutched Gabby's hand.

"The second option is far more experimental, but I believe it would be my choice. I would suggest that we give her a small dose of laudanum. Laudanum is an interesting drug," he said meditatively, "soporific in small doses and poisonous in large doses. And highly addictive, of course," he added.

"What would be the good of administering a soporific? She's already asleep."

"A soporific sometimes counters a sleep-inducing poison. We do not understand the mechanism behind it."

"And the danger?"

"No danger, really," Winn said. "But if it doesn't work, the stimulants certainly will not. She will fall into a deeper sleep, if possible. And a sleep so deep . . . I will leave you to make a choice, my lord."

"No," Quill said, his voice harsh. "I've made my choice. Give her the laudanum."

"You do understand that the chances of the medicine being effective are very small?"

Quill simply nodded, and Winn opened up his small bag. Quill watched silently as the doctor gave his wife a dose of laudanum.

"When will we know?"

"Quite soon," Winn said placidly. "May I suggest that you give your wife some more water, my lord?"

Quill spooned the water into Gabby's mouth, suspecting that the doctor was merely keeping him occupied.

An hour passed. Quill sat by the bedside watching Gabby's face for any change in color, for any sign that she was waking up. A heavy sense of doom was sinking into his heart.

Slowly it dawned on him that *she* wasn't entirely there. Her body had become a shell, discarded by the beautiful self that was Gabby.

"My wife is dead," he said hoarsely, after two hours.

Winn shook his head. He was standing at the foot of the bed. "She is not dead, my lord."

But Quill hardly heard him. "I should like you to leave now," he said numbly. "The laudanum has been ineffective. I would like to . . . to be alone with her for the little time we have left together."

Winn opened his mouth and then thought better of it. "I shall wait downstairs," he said. "Please call me if you require any assistance."

Quill sat numbly, in total silence, for a long time . . . how long he had no idea. He stopped watching Gabby, except when he spooned water into her mouth. It was too painful to see the vacancy in her face. Instead, he thought about Gabby with her halo, Gabby with golden light around her body. It should be a comforting thought, he told himself. She had slipped through his fingers like the rosy light that had surrounded her—except . . . except . . .

A harsh sound burst from his throat. "Don't, don't! Don't become an angel, Gabby. I need you here."

Silence answered him. And shame came with it. Could a servant have heard his outburst?

He looked back at Gabby, and he didn't care if the entire household was listening outside the door. She was gone—she was gone. She had left him. So quickly, in the breath between a quarrel and a laugh, she had left him.

"No!" He screamed it now. Quill had never shown pain, but he had never encountered a pain that could not be silenced. "You must not leave, Gabby. You must come back. Please, please, don't leave. Life"—the words caught in his throat, twisted, came forth unintelligibly from the heart—"life is nothing without you. I love you."

All pride was gone. "Without you, I have nothing to say to anyone, Gabby. No one ever made me smile the way you do. There is no color—" But his voice failed him. He stretched out next to her on the bed, putting his head on her chest. He could hear a faint, comforting heartbeat.

And finally, in the depths of utter exhaustion and despair, he slept, ear pressed to that distant heartbeat, to the bit of Gabby left in this world.

IT MIGHT HAVE BEEN HOURS LATER, or it might have been minutes. Dream Gabby's voice called to him. "I knew you'd come to me," he mumbled. "I knew I would see you again, once again."

He couldn't hear her response. He tried to open his eyes, but he was so tired, so very tired, that he couldn't do it.

"My wife is dead," he told her. "The real Gabby has left

me, and now there's no one but you, an angel, I suppose."
His voice caught and then steadied. "You have to go away,
Dream Gabby. If I can't have my wife, I don't want you. *My*
Gabby is the only one I love."

Dream Gabby sounded a bit irritated.

In his dream Quill shook his head. "I don't want you,"
he repeated. "Go away."

"Hmmph," said his dream wife. But she sounded rather
amused.

Quill supposed that he had better make an effort. He
opened his eyes. For a moment he stared, puzzled, at the
hand before him. It was a familiar hand, with slender, intelligent fingers.

Without daring to breathe, he looked up.

"Good morning, husband," said a voice. That was his
wife's voice. And those were Gabby's warm eyes laughing
at him.

"Oh, God," Quill said. It was a prayer and a thank-you.

His wife raised an eyebrow. "What happened to 'Good
morning, Gabby. Did you sleep well?' Have you forgotten
all the instructions I've given you?"

"Are you all right?" he asked hoarsely.

"No," she said, dropping her teasing tone. "I've been a
fool, Quill, and I need to make an apology. I've been thinking about it ever since I woke up. I should never have lied
to you. And I should never have let my temper govern my
actions like that. Why, Sudhakar's medicine could have had
serious consequences!"

Quill stared at her. "It did, Gabby."

"The medicine?"

"Sudhakar said you were going to die. That we couldn't
save you."

"You found him before he sailed?"

"Yes. He said—"

Gabby shrugged. "He's ever the naysayer, Sudhakar. I'm just fine, Quill. Or at least I would be if you would move off the coverlet so that I can rise out of bed."

Her husband stared at her, not moving an inch. "I may never let you out of bed," he said tenderly. "Oh Gabby, I love you so much." He cupped her face in his hands. "I can't live without you, do you know that?"

She smiled at him. "So you're in love with me now, are you?"

"I should never have lied to you about it. But I'm glad I did, because I maneuvered you into marrying me," he said, kissing her.

"You didn't lie to me," she said gently.

Quill stopped, his mouth just a breath from hers.

"You *were* in love with me. You just didn't know it. Remember?" She whispered, "I burn, I pine, I perish."

And Quill remembered his burning wish to marry his brother's fiancée, the way in which he breached every code of gentlemanly behavior in order to do so. He groaned. "I suppose you are right, oh, uncomfortably intelligent wife. But"—and his lips grazed hers, very gently—"how I loved you from the first moment I saw you on the dock has no resemblance to how many fathoms deep I am in love with you now."

"Oh, Quill," Gabby said, before he stole her breath and sank into a kiss. But she pulled away after a few moments. "Now I have to rise from this bed," she said with renewed vigor.

But Quill had other plans. "You cured me," he said. "My beloved wife cured me, and now I am going to make love to her all day, and all night, and all tomorrow as well."

Gabby stilled. Her eyes shone. "I'm in love with you as

well, do you know that? I think only someone I loved as much as you could make me behave like such an idiot."

He grinned. "Of course, I'm removing all poisons from the house. I think all heavy objects will have to go, too. My wife has a fierce temper. And"—he whispered against her lips—"I'm terrified that our children might inherit it." He shifted his weight, bearing her backward against the pillows.

"Quill! Let me go! I have to get out of bed."

"I want you to stay here with me." His voice had a devilishly sensuous lilt.

"I can't," Gabby said.

"I don't think I'll ever let you out of my sight again. We're going to live in bed."

"Quill!"

"Why not?" He wrestled her flat on her back and lavished kisses on her nose and eyelids as she twisted under him, trying to get free. Dimly, he could hear her protesting, but he was too joyfully intoxicated to listen.

It took a howl to get through to him. "Quill, you *must* let me go! I'm having a very peculiar reaction to Sudhakar's medicine—I feel as if I swallowed a large lake, and I must get to the water closet!"

Quill started hopelessly chuckling into his wife's neck.

It was only when her struggling limbs endangered his future children's lives that he rolled to the side and let her go.

But it didn't change his plans for the day—nay, for the week. He was a well man with a beautiful wife and a passel of children to create. Pleasant work, indeed.

And they had the whole of life ahead of them in which to do it.

Chapter 25

KAMATH THE FRUIT SELLER noticed with some amusement the two lovers lying on the banks of the Ganges River. Likely they thought they couldn't be seen. He paused in his hard climb up the mountain. The woman had the pearly white skin of an Englishwoman. He'd heard that hail fell as large as mango fruit over in England. Struck people on the head, which explained why Englishmen were so foolish. His eyes widened. The hail didn't seem to injure their other faculties.

With a sigh of appreciation and remembrance, the old man continued up the tiny, winding path leading to his house. Good thing the crazed old Englishman Jerningham died a few months ago, he thought. He was miffy about things like that. Tried to exile Kamath's own daughter, Sarita, from the village. Kamath snorted to himself. Of course, Sarita and her husband had returned just a few weeks later, calling themselves a different name. He was as blind as a toad, old Jerningham. Couldn't see farther than the tip of his nose.

DOWN ON THE BANKS of the Ganges River, the Englishman, whose skin was not nearly as pearly white as that of his wife, had rolled over on his back and was looking up at the clouds far above them.

"What do you see?" his wife asked, tucking her head into his shoulder.

"Mmmm," Quill said, running his hand down Gabby's back. He found to his annoyance that she had pulled a length of silk over herself. "I'm looking for my dream wife," he said. "She's up there somewhere, waiting for me, with her rosy halo. *She* would lie here naked in the sunshine without a thought for propriety."

"Lucky her," Gabby said. "Let me know when you find her. I want to warn her about the sunburns in her future."

"There's nothing in her future but me," Quill said lazily. He rolled over, half on top of his wife, and murmured, "*An hundred years should go to praise thine eyes, and on thy forehead gaze; Two hundred to adore each breast, but thirty thousand to the rest.* That's a rather lazy poem by Andrew Marvell. With world enough and time, I intend to keep my Dream Gabby busy—just the two of us, through all eternity."

"Well," said his wife, with a mischievous twinkle in her eye, "then eternity is where the oh-so-lauded Dream Gabby and I part company."

"What are you talking about?"

"Your future on earth," she said.

"What about it?"

"It won't be so solitary by this time next year," she whispered. "Not just you and me anymore."

There was a moment's silence. A frog plopped into the deep green depths of the Ganges. Reeds hushed themselves in a faint wind.

Quill cleared his throat. "Are you saying . . . ?"

"Mmmm," said his wife, her eyes smiling at him.

"Are you certain?"

"Absolutely."

The Englishman rolled away and stood up, showing his naked self to the whole world, had the world shown any interest. "We're going home," he said briskly, reaching for his trousers and pulling them on.

His wife propped herself on her elbows and laughed. "Home to Jaipur or home to England?"

"Home to England."

"I thought you needed a few more months to consolidate your trade routes to England. And Jawsant has truly appreciated your help with the royal treasury."

Quill knelt on the grass next to his mischievous wife. "Home to England, Baggage." He touched her nose with one finger.

Gabby sighed. "I suppose this is your way of telling me that you are outrageously happy?"

Quill nodded. "Of course."

"Living with you is an act of interpretation, do you know that?"

"Living with you is . . . bliss. Did you know that?"

Gabby's eyes filled with tears. A drift of white jasmine that bent over the Ganges succumbed to the breeze and scattered flowers. And Quill's mouth came to hers as sweetly as the jasmine floated on the water.

A Note *about Migraines,*
Ecuadorian Frogs, and Indian Princes

My Indian prince, Kasi Rao, was indeed the only legitimate heir to the Holkar region of central India, a region
that Richard Colley Wellesley, when he was governor-
general of India, dearly wished to acquire. Wellesley was
determined to dispose of Jawsant Holkar and replace him
with his addled but legitimate half-brother, Kasi Rao.
Given these basic facts, I have juggled events to suit my
plot. It was not Kasi Rao's father who imbibed too much
cherry brandy and ended up under restraints, being fed on
milk. It was instead his brother Jawsant, and at least one
historian has suggested that Jawsant's addiction resulted
from his terrifying remorse after ordering the execution of
Kasi Rao. I took an author's privilege by granting my Kasi
Rao an altogether longer and happier life with Mrs.
Malabright.

The battle against migraines, megrims, or, as first mentioned in medieval English, *the mygrame and other euyll pas-
sions of the head,* has been documented for at least two
thousand years. The cures that Quill had undergone prior to
this novel (his encounters with camphor, sneezing powders,
leeches, Indian hemp, and opium) were doled out to unhappy
migraine patients in the 1800s. For anyone interested in the
viability of Quill's personal—and, I am certain, unusual—
source of migraines, there are documented cases in which
migraines follow sexual intercourse. I am indebted in these

details to a wonderful book written by Dr. Oliver W. Sacks entitled *Migraine: The Evolution of a Common Disorder*. I hasten to add that Sudhakar's dose of tree-frog poison is purely fictional. In 1998, *The New Yorker* reported that the future of pain management may lie in poison secreted by an Ecuadorian frog, the *Epibpedobates tricolor,* whose venom is proving to be seventy times more potent than morphine. It is my earnest hope that all migraine sufferers will receive a miraculous cure akin to Quill's, whether due to an Ecuadorian frog or to less-exotic drug treatment.

Want more from Eloisa James's Pleasures Trilogy?
Read on for a sneak peek . . .

POTENT
PLEASURES

Nothing is more seductive than temptation.

Reckless desire sends Charlotte Daicheston into the garden
with a dashing masked stranger. He's powerful, unforgettable,
a devastatingly handsome footman who lures her – not
against her will – into a grand indiscretion at a masquerade
ball. Then he vanishes.

Several years later, after Charlotte has made her dazzling
debut in London society, they meet again. But the rogue is
no footman. He's rich, titled, and he doesn't remember
Charlotte. Worse, he's the subject of some scandalous gossip:
rumour has it the earl's virility is in question.

Charlotte, who knows all too intimately the power of his
passion, is stunned by the gossip that has set society ablaze.
At last, there can be a storybook ending . . . unless, of
course, Charlotte's one mad indiscretion had not been with
him at all . . .

MIDNIGHT PLEASURES

To her legions of adoring suitors, it comes as quite a shock when Lady Sophie York rejects an offer of marriage from the dashing, rakish Patrick Foakes in favour of amiable but dull Braddon Chatwin. He may be an earl, but it is Patrick's stolen kisses that sear her lips.

When Patrick, in disguise, scales a ladder to retrieve his friend's fiancée, he never expects the elopement to be his own. Neither does Sophie, Braddon, or the rest of the tattling ton. One hasty wedding later, the passionate innocent and the sophisticated rogue play out their own intricate dance as Sophie masters what it takes to keep a man where he belongs. And Patrick learns the ultimate lesson in love.

Do you love historical fiction?

Want the chance to hear news about your favourite authors (and the chance to win free books)?

Mary Balogh
Charlotte Betts
Jessica Blair
Frances Brody
Gaelen Foley
Elizabeth Hoyt
Eloisa James
Lisa Kleypas
Stephanie Laurens
Claire Lorrimer
Amanda Quick
Julia Quinn

Then visit the Piatkus website and blog
www.piatkus.co.uk | www.piatkusbooks.net

And follow us on Facebook and Twitter
www.facebook.com/piatkusfiction | www.twitter.com/piatkusbooks

piatkus